# SIGNIFICANCE

*For Mark with love*

# SIGNIFICANCE

by

Jo Mazelis

**SEREN**

Seren is the book imprint of
Poetry Wales Press Ltd
57 Nolton Street, Bridgend, Wales, CF31 3AE
www.serenbooks.com
Facebook: facebook.com/SerenBooks
Twitter: @SerenBooks

ISBN 978−1−78172−187−2 print
ISBN 978−1−78172−189−6 kindle
ISBN 978−1−78172−188−9 ebook

Cover image: © Jo Mazelis
Typesetting by Elaine Sharples
Printed by CPI Group (UK) Ltd, Croydon

The publisher works with the financial assistance of
The Welsh Books Council

# Part One

# NIGHT

*What draws the reader to the novel is the hope of warming his shivering life with a death he reads about.*

Walter Benjamin

*Man is an animal suspended in webs of significance that he himself has spun.*

Clifford Geertz

# Runaway

## Summer 2007

Then she is driving. The road a sleek raven's wing beneath her wheels. Driving faster than ever before, and marvelling, as she presses her foot on the accelerator, at the reasons for her previous caution. Yes, it is night and it's raining heavily, but there is nothing to be afraid of. Nothing in the world.

She is watching the road, her senses sharply attuned to any danger. She pulls into the fast lane to pass an articulated lorry. Guides the car back into the middle lane. Easy. A warning sign inside a red triangle. The vaulting deer. Lucy senses fear in the black painted silhouette. Imagines the sudden clatter of hooves on tarmac. And the jarring screams of the brakes. The dull impact of a car's fender catching the animal's flank.

She shakes her head as if disagreeing with an invisible interrogator. Imagine it all away. The motorways and dual carriageways, the airline coaches, the horse transporters, the Freelanders and Discoveries, the Picasso; the van parked in a field overlooking the road with an advert for laptops on its side.

Lucy wants all of it gone. But instead there is rain, and more rain, pushed to one side of the windscreen by the wipers, then pushed back again by the wind. Rivulets of clear water.

A man in a black Citroen catches her eye and passes her on the inside lane. His expression is leering, greedy, smug. She thinks of accelerating and swerving suddenly so that her car clips his. Her hands tighten on the wheel with intent – at these speeds, with this traffic and the punishing, relentless rain, everything could be altered in an instant.

But no, not now, not that. She is escaping: a runaway again. Just like she was when she was twelve, then fifteen. Not to forget the time she did it when she was eighteen. Now she is far too old to be called a runaway and smiles to herself at the thought. She relaxes her fingers on the wheel, sees in the rear window of the black Citroen a yellow sign announcing there is a baby on board. She slows.

The wind drops suddenly and the deluge eases, then stops. The night she is driving into is suddenly as dry as an old bone. And just as if the storm had been a source of energy for her, now it's abated she's suddenly tired. When she sees a sign for KATHS' KARAVAN KAFE! TEAS, COFFEES, BURGERS, CHIPS she pulls into a lay-by. But the catering van is shut up for the night and there is only one other car: a battered white Mercedes that takes off the moment Lucy draws up. She stays behind the wheel, lets her hands fall limply into her lap, breathes deeply and closes her eyes.

She is not ill like they say she is; she is fine. More than fine. Has never felt better.


Dover. The sea is what you notice as the car crests a hill. The rain has stopped and the day has a rinsed feeling to it – a good day to begin things.

Dover. White cliffs. No bluebirds. Blue sky. Gulls soaring. The air is still and fresh; on deck Lucy gazes at the sea. It's a busy shipping channel, vessel after vessel ploughing the grey-blue glittering water.

Staring down, feeling the throb of the ferry's engine, its surging pulse, Lucy finds herself remembering another ferry crossing years ago. She'd been on the way back from a school trip to Europe. It had been night and she, with a few friends, had been standing on deck watching the molten sea under the blanket of night. One of them, Dougie, a sweet boy who was neither remarkably good-looking nor clever, had bought a Panama hat in Italy that he'd worn every moment of the holiday. They'd all been laughing and joking, when Dougie suddenly asked her if he should throw his hat into the sea. She barely stopped to think about it, but it had seemed right at the time, the gesture of letting go, not only of the holiday, but also of those different selves each of them had been in that unfamiliar place.

So she'd said yes. Yes. The word itself sibilant, dancing from her lips with a smile. Perhaps he had needed permission, the encouragement of a handful of laughing girls.

They all watched as he threw it over the rail like a Frisbee. It flew up, pale against the night sky. Then fell on the churning waves where it briefly swirled and danced before it was swept away into darkness.

'My hat!' he said surprised. Then, more sadly, he repeated the words. 'My hat. Why did I do that?'

She could not answer. She had not expected regret.

She pushed aside the memory. *That* Lucy was so far away it almost hurt to remember her. And there had been, or so it seemed, other Lucys too, all of them fatally flawed, all of them vulnerable to defeat and pain and humiliation. Or capable, as with Dougie and his hat, of hurting others. Better to be alone. To remake oneself.

# France

At La Coquille Bleue, Lucy orders *Pastis*, milky and aniseed flavoured. Then steak, which comes with *pommes frites*. In the corner, tied with a long hefty rope, there's a young dog, wolfish, with guarded blue eyes. After she has eaten, Madame Gallo, the hotel's owner, allows her to smoke at the table despite the signs prohibiting it. There are framed portraits of Joan of Arc everywhere. The girl soldier the English burnt at the stake. Now they would give Joan anti-psychotic drugs; Clozaril, Zyprexa, Seroquel. In the 1950s her shorn hair and cross-dressing would have earned her electroconvulsive therapy; the voice of God would grow mute, scorched out of existence by science. Madame Gallo smiles conspiratorially at Lucy as she sits there smoking.

Lucy orders a bottle of *vin rouge*. Madame Gallo watches her from behind the bar, she is middle-aged, but her face is still pretty, her hair dark and glossy. She dresses well. Looks exactly right for the part. As does Lucy, who is a runaway in the disguise of a confident young woman with money and credit cards and expensive new clothes.

It is dark when she leaves the hotel. A boy is standing on the edge of the pavement across the road. Lucy has the curious sensation that she passed him earlier – hours earlier, when it was still light, although the shadows had been lengthening. He is standing very still, the tips of his shoes over the paving slab's lip as if he were balanced on a high diving board. As she draws closer she sees that he is not as young as she had first thought. His frame is slight, his complexion pale and his posture is awkward, like that of a teenager who has grown too tall too fast. As she draws closer she expects him to look at her. But this boy-man, poised and seemingly ready to dive into the stream of traffic, does not show the merest sign of attention even though she is passing almost within reach.

His eyes, she sees, are very pale blue. So pale and unfocussed she wonders if he is sightless. That might explain everything.

Yes, she thinks, the boy is blind and perhaps a little strange too.

The next night she goes back to La Coquille Bleue but only remembers the strange young man as she nears the place where he was standing. He is not there. Of course, he is not there.

Lucy enters the restaurant and is given a table in the glassed-in area at the front. From here she cannot see the dog with its mournfully sad, sea-blue eyes.

None of the staff seem to remember her from the previous night and there is a large family group from the Netherlands at a nearby table who talk loudly amongst themselves. They laugh and pass maps and guidebooks between them, debating the next item on their itinerary. For the first time since she left England Lucy feels lonely.

She orders *Moules Marinière* but eats without pleasure. She has a single glass of white wine and even that seems devoid of taste, though she drinks it all the same. She asks for the bill, leaves a ten-euro note on the table and goes out into the fading twilight.

And there he is again. The boy-man. This time on a different part of the pavement. He rests one hand on the pole of a road sign. His feet are once again over the lip of the kerb. She walks towards him. He does not look at her; his gaze is fixed in some mid-air spot that hovers above the road.

Swifts dart about at rooftop level making high-pitched squeaks. Little arrows with white bellies that flash by. Little arrows that might pierce her heart, if her heart were not made of stone.

When she is two, perhaps three yards away, she stops walking and stands still, watching him.

He does not see her, nor even sense her presence so close by. He is not only blind, but also lacks the radar that most people possess. The sun is behind her, low in the sky and her shadow falls against his legs, his waist. He should sense the coolness of that shadow, but he does not move, just stares.

She feels emboldened by curiosity, by the fact she is a stranger here. She takes a cigarette from the packet in her bag, positions it between two fingers, steps even closer to him.

'Excuse me? Do you have a light?'

She could have struggled to ask the question in French, but she wants to be certain he knows that she is English.

Her words, like her shadow, do not register. He blinks, but maybe this has nothing to do with any of her assaults on his senses – he does not see, or hear, or feel, or smell her. Touch is all that is left. But touch is so intimate, so risky if he is mad. If he is a mad, crazed boy held in some dark soundless prison, then a sudden touch, a gentle hand on his forearm might scare him into pulling a knife from his waistband and plunging it blindly into her heart.

'He won't answer you.'

A man is standing next to her. She turns quickly; tries to conceal how startled she feels, how guilty. He is tall and thin, with blue eyes not dissimilar to the staring boy-man. He speaks English, but with an accent, American perhaps.

'He's my brother,' the man says. 'He's not…' He hesitates here as if searching for a word, but gives up, doesn't finish the sentence.

'Oh,' she says. 'I'm sorry.'

'What are you sorry for?' he asks, bluntly. It is as if he is accusing her of something. 'Here,' he says and reaches into his trouser pocket, pulls out a book of matches, tosses them at her.

She catches it, opens it, finds none of the matches yet used.

'Oh,' she says, retrieving the packet of Lucky Strikes. 'Do you want a…'

He pulls a face to show his distaste. She wonders why he has matches in his pocket if he doesn't smoke. Something in her would rather not smoke now in front of him, it feels as dirty as rolling up her sleeve, finding a vein and inserting a thrice-used needle. But too late, she's committed. She lights the cigarette, turns her head to blow the smoke away from his face.

'Why does he stand there like that?' she asks.

'Because he can.'

His answers are annoying, aggressive. They are brothers though, so maybe something runs in the family. Maybe this one, the older one, just seems more normal, but underneath is just as disturbed and strange as the other.

'Where are you from?' she asks, and he jerks his head to indicate a house behind him with lemon-yellow shutters.

'No,' she says. 'Your accent...'

'Canada.'

'Ah.'

He looks at his watch, then at his brother. Avoids her gaze.

'I'm from the UK,' she says, though he hasn't asked.

There is a silence then. The sort of silence that hovers between strangers. Human strangers in particular perhaps. If they were apes she might have crept forward and begun to companionably pick parasites out of his hair. Or maybe he'd have screamed, pulled back his lips to reveal sharp teeth, then charged at her with wild eyes and flared nostrils.

She does not know why she is thinking this. Nor why she is lingering there at all.

'Why are you angry?' he asks her suddenly.

'What?'

'You look angry. Is it my brother? Does he offend you?'

'No, no. Of course not. Why should he? I just...'

'Okay, fine,' he says. The words are clean and clipped, as if he is snapping sounds out of the air and leaving mysterious and meaningful shapes behind. Like the chalk marks describing where the victim of sudden death had fallen.

He turns to his brother. 'Aaron! OK. It's time to come in now!' He is unnecessarily gruff, she thinks. She expected more pleading, a gentle coaxing, not these sharp orders. And he asked why *she* was angry! 'Aaron,' he barks.

His brother turns his head slowly at the sound, then blinks at the speaker. She reads sorrow in his expression, the cowed look of a dog that's been beaten once too often.

'Don't talk to him like that,' she says, knowing she shouldn't. Something in her wants to provoke him.

'Now!' the man says, ignoring her.

Aaron seems at last to come to life, he lifts his hand from the road sign as if he were ungluing it. His eyes move vaguely over the two people looking at him; the female stranger and his brother. *His brother.* You could see the recognition suddenly register in the sharpening of his eyes.

He began to move forward, trudging his feet not so much reluctantly as wearily, as if they were heavy, as if gravity was increasing its hold just in the places where his shoes met the earth's surface.

Lucy saw now that she had been wrong to speak out. That it was none of her business.

'I'm sorry,' she said.

'For what?'

'For you. For your brother. It must be hard…'

The younger man had drawn level with them. His face was slack, the eyes dull, and yet you couldn't fail to notice how perfect his bone structure was, how achingly attractive he would be if he were wholly alive. She was surprised to find herself mourning the loss of what should have been a potentially vivid and fully functional human being.

'I'm sorry for you too,' he said.

His words had their intended effect. She could not answer.

She watched them go. The two brothers, the younger one shuffling like an old man, the other stiff – almost bristling with anger. She wanted to know more. Wanted to understand the barely suppressed rage that was directed towards her. To know also where she had gone so wrong.

# Domestic Interior with Three Figures

Marilyn's brother-in-law was standing facing the closed door. 'Brother-in-law' was not a term that suited him. When she thought about a brother-in-law what came to mind was a man very like her husband: self-assured, intelligent, good looking and passionate about life.

Instead there was Aaron.

Poor Aaron.

Standing there staring at the blank face of the door, stepping slowly from one foot to the other and, judging from the insistent movement of his jutting-out elbows, doing something strange with his hands.

Scott was sitting near the window reading a book, oblivious.

'What's he doing?' Marilyn said.

Scott glanced quickly at his brother, then shrugged and shook his head as if to say did she really think he would have any better idea of what went on in Aaron's head?

'I think he's got something.'

Scott lifted his head to study the figure by the door more carefully.

They always had to look out for stuff like this; Aaron had a habit of picking up small objects and worrying away at them until they broke. Or if the object didn't break then after a time he lost interest and dropped the thing wherever he happened to be, so that jewellery, coins, keys and so on had to be closely watched or kept locked up. Four years ago Marilyn had left her engagement ring on the shelf above the bathroom sink in Scott and Aaron's parents' house and, after searching all over, they'd finally found it in the toilet bowl in the outhouse. At the time she thought that

Aaron had done it deliberately. That he was sending her a clear message about what he thought of her.

'You're being ridiculous,' Scott had said. 'I wish my brother was capable of such clarity, such clear signs of possessiveness and emotion. It's not personal, believe me. Forget it. You're wasting your tears.'

She found that last phrase troubling. 'Wasting your tears' indeed – as if tears were precious and had to be carefully guarded, saved for the rarest of occasions. Scott was one of those men who was profoundly discomforted by tears, especially women's tears. And Marilyn had always cried easily and helplessly from both sorrow and joy.

She watched Scott as he put the dog-eared and yellowing copy of *The Handmaid's Tale* on the chair and crept towards his brother. When he drew close enough he peered over Aaron's shoulder and said gently, 'Hey, whatcha got there, buddy? You wanna show me?'

Aaron did not want to show him. He began to groan softly in protest and to rock from one foot to the other with more emphasis.

'You gonna show me, huh? Come on, show me,' Scott grabbed Aaron's wrists and the groaning noise went up in pitch and volume.

'Don't hurt him,' Marilyn said.

'I'm not hurting him. Now come on, give it to me. Let go! Let go, damn you!'

The noise coming out of Aaron's mouth was awful – like that of a tortured animal.

'You're hurting him!'

'I'm not hurting him. For Christ's sake, Marilyn, shut up. Come here.'

She moved across the room so that she was next to them. She could see that although Scott had a firm grip on both of Aaron's wrists he was being measured and careful about the level of force he used.

'Open his fingers,' Scott said.

Marilyn hesitated, then reluctantly did as she was told, discovering, as she pried Aaron's fingers up, that he gave only the barest resistance. His left hand in particular opened as easily as a flower and there in the centre of his palm, resting in the crease of his heart line, was a round white button, smaller than a pea.

'What is it?' Scott asked.

'A button.'

Aaron wailed.

'It's mine,' she said. She had recognised it straightaway as belonging to one of the few dresses she possessed that still fitted comfortably; a flowery print frock she'd bought in a vintage store in Ottawa eight years ago. It had struck her then as a very romantic dress with its row of tiny pearl buttons down the front. She had felt feminine and beautiful in it, like a woman from another age. Scott called it her Emily Dickinson frock, and she was never entirely sure if that was meant as a compliment or not.

Exasperated, Scott sighed loudly, 'Okay. Okay. Here have this.' He let go of Aaron's wrists and reached into his pocket, pulled out his sunglasses' case and removed the glasses. Aaron didn't move his hands once they were released, but stood posed with upraised hands as if he were a saint displaying his stigmata. Scott put the empty case in one of Aaron's open hands, but the fingers didn't close around it and it fell to the floor.

'Do you want milk? Nice milk and cookies?' Scott coaxed.

Aaron was quiet for a moment, then he turned and began trudging in the direction of the kitchen. Scott watched him go, then turned to Marilyn and slowly shook his head.

'What?' Marilyn said.

'How could you say that?'

'What?'

'That I was hurting him.'

'I'm sorry. I didn't think. I know you'd never hurt him deliberately, I just…' The look on Scott's face silenced her.

'You didn't think? Yeah. No one else does either.'

'I'm sorry.'

'Okay, forget it.'

Scott followed Aaron into the kitchen and got the cookie tin from the cupboard.

'Okay, buddy. Nice milk and cookies? Yeah, you like that, eh? Yeah?'

Aaron drank deeply from the glass, then lowered it to reveal a white moustache of milk on his upper lip. He blinked and crammed a whole ginger biscuit into his mouth. His eyes were glazed over with concentration and his left knee bounced up and down in rhythm with his jaw. Scott stood to one side with the cookie jar resting in the crook of his arm, waiting for Aaron to finish the biscuit he was eating before allowing him another.

Marilyn stood watching them. Her hand moved to her belly and rested there for a moment, then remembering herself, she hastily took it away again. She did not want Scott to see her in that clichéd pose, to recognise the gesture for what it was; that of an expectant mother gracing her swelling womb with an exploratory and protective hand.

Busying herself, she got the dress that had lost the button from the laundry basket where it was waiting to be ironed, sat down on a rustic milking stool in the corner of the living room and, like a penitent in a reformatory, stitched the tiny button back on.

# Creatures of Habit

For the third night in a row Lucy is drawn to La Coquille Bleue. There she is, smiling at her old friend Madame Gallo as she seats herself at a table near the bar. And while she looks at the menu, she's sipping milky-white *Pastis* and remembering the bullet-hard aniseed balls she sometimes ate as a kid.

Tonight she orders steak with salad, refuses potatoes when asked. Nods thoughtlessly when the waitress asks if she wants the steak *bleu*. Nods vigorously when she asked if she wants *vin rouge*.

Saying 'yes' she finds, has a sort of sweet madness about it. Yes, yes, yes. *Oui, oui, oui*. She likes the sound of the words – in either language the effect is soft and welcoming.

The steak when it comes, when she stabs it with her knife, bleeds. Red wine and red blood.

She finishes her meal and lights a cigarette, then gets the new silver compact from her bag and applies a slick, bright coat of the red lipstick she bought five days ago. She smiles and nods at Madame Gallo and wonders what it is precisely that makes the woman look so utterly French. She imagines her into black and white photos by Lartigue, Brassai and Cartier-Bresson.

It's the sculptural quality of the woman's black hair, Lucy decides, and the fact that French women don't opt to go frizzy blonde as they age, instead remaining as they were when young. She will try to do the same she thinks. I'll stay here, never go back, never say a word to anyone – not Thom nor anyone at the college nor Mum and Dad. She feels mildly guilty when she considers her parents' reactions to such a mysterious disappearance, remembering as if through a fog their reactions to her younger escapades, but pushes it aside to concentrate instead on this delicious dream of transformation. She'd be known as 'the English woman'. Her accent, mild as it now was, would not reveal her Celtic roots, not here where the only thing to notice was her – so far – very poor French.

She picks up her glass and downs the last mouthful of wine, stubs out her cigarette.

Pays at the bar, leaving a generous tip. '*Merci! Merci. Bon nuit, Madame Gallo.*'

She leaves the restaurant waving gaily and calling, '*Au revoir!*' and wondering if all the damn foreign tourists sitting in the glass-fronted atrium think she is a native.

It's earlier now than on the previous two nights. The sky is a darkening violet watercolour streaked with scarlet. There's no sign of the young man or his brother. She scans the street, looking up and down. She studies the house opposite, the one with acid-yellow shutters. Most of the upstairs windows are flung open; some, where they catch the light from the setting sky, glow rosy pink.

She crosses the street diagonally towards a pay phone. Once there she lifts the handset and holds it to her ear. Pretends to dial, pretends to feed coins into the slot, pretends to speak, to listen and nod, all the time gazing over at the house with yellow shutters.

During this charade, she thinks about where she's come from; the small rented flat in Hammersmith that has been her home for nearly two years. During her first months in London the light was, or seemed to be, grey – grey and thin and unforgiving. The western coast where she'd grown up was hardly known for its sunshine and achingly blue skies, but London had somehow registered its presence on her consciousness during that first rainy October, and now that image of London was fixed in her mind.

She was meant to be back at her job as a part-time lecturer just over a week from now and she was also meant to have finished the final draft of her PhD dissertation. There were other things she was meant to be doing too. Her life was full of loose ends; it was frayed, unravelling, irredeemable. Her sense of dread about work was beginning to seep into where she was now. Freedom and happiness, the trip itself had been dying as soon as it had begun.

Even here in France, she had taken up another routine, as if coming to La Coquille Bleue night after night might give her a sense of security and permanence.

She continued to nod occasionally as she held the telephone to her ear. She imagined she was listening to some distant speaker who spoke such wisdom and sense that she could only absorb it in silence.

She should perhaps not play these games – what begins as a perfectly normal flight of fancy could harden into madness. She'd had a breakdown at the age of eighteen when she was at the Glasgow School of Art. Charles Rennie Mackintosh's ladder-backed chairs still gave her the horrors. She'd been trying to write an essay about form and function in design. There was something about those chairs, their Presbyterian starkness and the unnecessary height of the back rest had made her flip. That and the way she was living: the starvation diet, the drink, the vampiric men and the unwise experiments with drugs. Poor Charles Rennie would have had a fit if he'd known that somehow his chairs reminded her of swastikas and horror films and that she'd had to tear their pictures from the library book and burn them.

Maybe it was happening again. Now. Here in Northern France. A Somme madness, where there was too much spilled blood in the soil.

A light came on in the downstairs room of the house with yellow shutters. A warm orange light that seemed to both welcome and repel her.

She saw a human shape move like a shadow across the window.

A man who moved with a confident stride. Not the younger brother then, whose gait was hesitant, weighed down by a tangle inside his head, the permanent physical knot of brain damage.

She found herself thinking about the rabbits she'd watched in the fields behind her parents' bungalow last time she'd been home, the way they'd take short runs then suddenly freeze. The busy activity of foraging, then what? Sudden fear and the compulsion to be still. The dream of invisibility?

The front door of the house opened. It was painted yellow like the shutters; it caught the last of the light as it swung open and flashed briefly before it was closed again. A tall figure hesitated by the door. She could not see his face. He was pulling on a light-coloured jacket, buttoning it, checking the pockets. Then he moved down to the front gate and into the pooled light of a streetlamp.

She nodded at her imaginary friend on the other end of the phone, mouthed meaningless words.

The man, and indeed it was the older brother, walked towards the telephone box. His pace was neither hurried nor was it quite an aimless amble. She was certain he had not seen or recognised her. He passed within a yard of the phone booth.

She replaced the receiver, left the booth and, after a moment's hesitation, began to follow him.

She followed him without quite knowing why. Perhaps because she wanted to talk to someone in English. Maybe, she thought, this is a Babel trait – a sudden inexplicable need for someone whose language you speak, whose tribe you belong to.

Or is it the desire for adventure? Or curiosity which, as she knows, killed the cat.

He walks down a wide road, crosses another, then cuts down a narrow cobblestoned alley into a broad tree-lined street of residential houses. Lucy is momentarily distracted when an old man steps from one of the houses as she passes. He is bent double with age and his gaunt face is distinguished by extravagant wild black eyebrows that give him a surprised, even electrified expression. At the end of his outstretched arm is a domed pewter-coloured birdcage. Inside the cage is a gleaming blue-black creature with a vivid orange beak. The sight is so improbable that Lucy feels more than ever that she inhabits a surreal dream. Her step slows, then she recovers herself. She catches sight of her prey near the end of the street and picks up her pace.

He turns into a wide boulevard where there are a number of bars. People are sitting outside at tables, eating and drinking. A perfect evening. Couples and families promenade. A pretty girl wheels her bike along and when she stops to chat with a group of young men three of them rise and exchange kisses with her. They talk animatedly for a minute or so, then the girl moves on, steering her bike confidently amongst the meandering crowds until she crosses the road and goes out of sight.

Up ahead the man is still walking along at an unhurried pace. Sometimes Lucy loses sight of him when he is absorbed by small crowds or her view is obscured by slight turns in the road. She decides to follow him just to the end of this street. Her game is beginning to lose its edge and there was no purpose to it in the beginning, only the mischievous idea of acting on impulse.

She slows, decides to walk a little further and then perhaps to stop at one of the little cafés for a coffee and a cigarette. She begins to pay more attention to the tables and chairs on the terraces outside the bars. All of them seem to be occupied and she doesn't want to share a table, wants to be entirely alone. Unmistakably alone. The English woman, mysterious, self-reliant and confident. Needing no one.

Further back, the cafés had been emptier and there were plenty of places to sit. She changes her plan. Walk another thirty yards or so, then turn around. She marks out the spot where she plans to give up; there, where a plane tree's branches and leaves have embraced a lamppost, so that its ornately shaded light seems to sprout from it like a glowing amber flower.

She is so busy thinking about this, projecting the future of her next half-hour, that she fails to see that the man she has been following for the last twenty minutes has disappeared into the very café where she plans to abandon her game.

As she nears the tree, she realises that she has finally lost him. She stops walking and scans her surroundings. Trains her eye further down the road, then looks at the other side of the street – nothing. She searches the faces at the tables outside the cafés. He isn't there, or anywhere to be seen. It is as if he has evaporated.

She is still a few yards from the tree. A question remains. Should she continue as planned or give up now? She hesitates, suddenly aware of how strange and lost she must look. How crazy.

This, she has always thought, must be the borderline between utter madness and a milder form of disturbance. Self awareness. Embarrassment at the thought of being perceived as crazy.

As if to prove she isn't insane, to show she has somewhere to go, something important to do, she looks at her watch. Looks without actually registering the time. She walks on, then stops under the tree. She gets her guidebook from her bag, pretends to study it as she leans a shoulder on the tree, assuming artificial casualness.

She looks about her, then again at her watch. She gives a moue of disappointment, closes the book and returns it to her bag. Looking up she sees that there is now a small table free and decides that this is fate – that this is where she was meant to come, and that now *something* will happen.

A waiter offers Lucy the menu, which she waves away, asking instead for a black coffee.

It is a pleasant night, there is a slight breeze, but it's balmy and she enjoys the sensation of the warm air on her bare legs, the soft movement of it over her face and hair. She could happily sit here for an hour or two.

The coffee comes promptly, an espresso, thick and oily in a very small cup. She adds four cubes of sugar. She'll be awake all night after drinking that. Maybe it's a mistake. She's agitated enough already, without sending a poisoned chalice of caffeine and processed white demon carbs careering through her system. She should have something else; something that soothes her and will knock her out enough to sleep when she gets back to the hotel. Insomnia has stalked her all her life, lying dormant for months and even years at a time, only to return again and again, as it had a month ago – nudging her awake at ten to four in the morning with her mind in the grave.

The outside seating area is arranged in an apron of tables bordered on two sides by low wooden troughs filled with glossy-leaved plants. Her table at the furthest edge of the terrace is next to one of these planters. She tips the coffee into the planter, amazed by how it soaks in quickly, leaving only a dark stain on the surface of the earth. Coffee probably isn't very good for it. She hopes no one saw her. But even if they did, what does it matter? She'll never see them again. They'll never see her. And maybe the explanation will be, Oh, she's English? Well, that explains it.

She replaces the empty cup in the saucer, catches the waiter's eye. 'More coffee?' he asks.

'No,' she says and orders a half litre of the house red.

'Anything else, bread, olives, cheese?' he offers, smiling.

'No, just the wine. *Merci beaucoup.*'

He smiles, though his eyes remain cold. He doesn't like me, she thinks.

He retreats to the interior of the building. Inside she can see a small semi-circular bar where a number of men are gathered on high stools. A slot machine blinks gaudily in the background showing a cascade of playing cards that are illuminated one by one to give the effect of movement.

He does not like me, she thinks again, and gets her mirror and lipstick from her bag. Studies her face, applies more lipstick. She sees nothing to dislike in her reflection, only the slightly surprised, slightly disappointed look of a lonely young woman who nobody loves, not really. Not even Thom – who just pretends.

The waiter returns and puts the carafe and a glass on the table. She thanks him without catching his eye, without smiling. She drinks the first glass of wine quickly, then pours another. Wellbeing seems to flow through her and she smiles wryly at the thought of her own silliness. She is amused by her little spy game and forgives herself the absurdity of it. She is even at the stage of composing this escapade into a story to tell friends. 'Oh hey, and one night I got so bored I followed this guy – this uptight Canadian. What was I planning? God knows! Maybe I'd just have said "hi." Maybe – oh well – it didn't happen.'

Her friends would laugh and gaze at her wide-eyed. They wouldn't choose to holiday alone, not unless they had to for some reason. Maybe she'd add a few adventures – sexual liaisons, romantic interludes, complications with jealous wives, intrigue. Why not? It would keep them on their toes. Keep them in awe of her. No one would dare challenge her or call her a liar.

But then it might get back to Thom and he might not see the funny side. Might object to looking like a cuckold, even if he knew it wasn't true. But then again, she and Thom were finished. Over. And no, he didn't love her. Never had.

She'd picked up her glass and raised it to her lips ready to drink, when a shadow fell over her.

'Did you follow me here?'

He was standing with the light behind him so at first all she saw was a dark silhouette, his blond hair haloed in the light.

'Pardon?'

'You heard me.' He shifted his weight onto one foot, cocked

his head to one side so that now he was illuminated by the light instead of obscured by it.

'Oh, hello,' she said, and smiled at him.

'Did you follow me?'

She stared at him, feeling caught out, but also to no small degree, entirely innocent. She hadn't known he was here *precisely*. She'd followed him, but given up when she lost sight of him. The finer point of the matter was debatable and she resented his accusation and particularly the unfortunate loudness of his voice. Her smile fell away.

'Quite honestly…' she began to say, then stopped and shook her head. She shrugged her shoulders as if shaking him off. She would not deign to even speak to him, leave alone utter a denial. She sipped her wine and without looking at him took a cigarette from her bag and lit it, using the matches he'd given her the day before.

Silence is a useful tool, she had often found, no one could ever accuse her of protesting too much.

Roughly, he pulled out the chair opposite, scraping it noisily over the concrete slabs. He sat.

'Do sit down,' she said, meaning to convey sarcasm, but somehow failing. He leant back in the chair, put his elbows on the armrests and laced his fingers together, then stared at her.

'Look,' she said at last. 'I'm sorry about your brother. I'm sorry if I upset him in some way…'

'He's not upset…'

'Well, then I'm sorry if you think…' She stopped herself as she was about to say, *I'm sorry if you think that I look down on him, on you because he's…* She didn't want to vocalise that. Somehow mentioning any form of social judgement seemed to expose the truth of her feelings.

He waited, then turned his head, signalled the waiter and ordered a beer.

'Why did you say I was angry?' she asked.

'Because you were.'

'I wasn't. Why would I be angry?'

'Everyone is.'

'That's not true.'

He made a quick snort of contempt.

'Maybe you're the one who is angry and so you view the world that way. You imagine everyone thinks like you,' she said.

'I know what I see.'

'That's ridiculous.'

'Why did you follow me?'

'I didn't. I've already told you I didn't.'

'I saw you. You were in the phone box near our house spying on us. Do you think I'm stupid?'

'I didn't know you were here,' she said and with this small truth, found that she was able to meet his eye.

They gazed at each other for almost a minute, then he unlaced his fingers, reached for his beer and took three big gulps. She didn't know why men drank in that way, pouring liquid – it could be water or milk as much as beer – down their throats while their Adam's apples worked up and down like slow pistons. Maybe it was a form of sexual display. Or alternatively it was a show of power – drawing attention to a vulnerable part of the body – the throat – and saying in some oblique way – you dare!

Or he was just thirsty. Then again, displaying his needs, his wilfulness in satisfying these needs, was a way of signalling to her that he might, if he chose, consume her.

There was, despite his accusations and insults and anger, an indisputable sexual charge in the air between them – had been since the start. She was emboldened by this idea, it galvanised her into playing the role of the minx. 'So what if I did follow you?' she said. 'I mean, why would I do that, do you suppose?'

He raised one eyebrow; an enviable trick

She had finished the last of her wine. Had drunk enough to

be feeling wired up and full of energy. Time to go dancing, time to laugh with just a soupçon of too much gaiety. The devil-may-care adrenaline pulsing in her temples, invading her brain with elaborate dreams and schemes.

Why, if she offended him so much, had he chosen (however gruffly) to sit with her? He was as much drawn to her as she was to him.

But she kept her head.

'Do you want another drink?' he asked her.

The waiter was hovering by the table. Here was a debatable situation – was he merely alerting her to the waiter's presence or was he asking if he could buy her a drink? The money – who paid for what – had nothing to do with it really – it was more a question of whether they would continue with this – whatever *this* was exactly.

'I should have a coffee I suppose,' she said, addressing him rather than the waiter.

'Another of those,' he said, nodding at the empty carafe. 'And a beer for me.'

The waiter turned on his heel and was gone.

'I said I'd have a coffee.'

'No, you didn't. You said you *ought* to have coffee, which suggests that you really wanted wine.'

'God! – What are you – a psychologist?'

'How did you guess?'

'Very funny,' she said, though it occurred to her that he wasn't joking and was indeed a psychologist. The last thing she needed.

A second carafe of wine was placed before her. She half-filled her glass, determined to take it easy. She should have had coffee, but he was right, she wanted wine.

'What's your name?' she asked, twisting the stem of her wine glass slowly, watching how the dense ruby-coloured liquid moved and caught the light.

'Scott.'

He didn't reciprocate by asking her name, which made her momentarily angry at the oversight, but then she took to the idea of being without a name, the mystery of it.

'So, Scott,' she said, unable to resist trying out his name on her tongue. 'What do you do for fun around here?'

'I let strange women follow me, then I fuck them.'

Before she had a chance to really absorb this remark, let alone respond, he stood up and crossed quickly to a nearby table where he picked up a discarded newspaper.

He'd left his last remark hanging in the air. Had abandoned it like a lost balloon, 'I let strange women follow me, then I fuck them...'

He came back, sat down and carefully opened, then refolded the newspaper so that the front page was uppermost. It was a copy of *The Guardian*, a day or so old, with a brown ring marking the word 'Guantanamo' in the headlines.

She frowned, watching disbelievingly as he fussily smoothed the newspaper's cover page with the flat of his hand. She could not now say 'Pardon?' or give him some coquettish riposte, but neither could she forget what he'd said. Nor what it implied.

He was, she supposed, a not very nice human being.

Why did that come to mind? The phrase 'not very nice'? It was the sort of thing her mother would say, had said about Lucy's best friend, Tracy. 'That girl's not very nice. I don't like her.' Whereas for Lucy that was the very essence of her friend's appeal. Tracy smoked and drank and read the NME and did things with boys that she described to Lucy in graphic terms afterwards. So when Lucy's mother said that Tracy wasn't very nice, it almost acted as a recommendation, a character reference. Who wanted nice when *not nice* was so exciting and dangerous?

'So why did you come here?' he asked, shaking Lucy out of a reverie in which she was thirteen again and wearing Converse baseball boots and ripped jeans, with an old plaid flannel shirt tied permanently around her waist as she cried extravagantly over a newspaper photograph of Kurt Cobain.

'I just wanted a drink.'

'No,' he said. 'I meant why did you come to France?'

She shrugged.

He shrugged back, then turned to gaze down the street as if she bored him.

Why had she not just answered him? He was perhaps only making conversation, attempting to be friendly, to undo the aggression that had marked the start of this acquaintance.

'I'm sorry,' she said – why was she apologising – she hated saying sorry. 'I didn't understand what you meant.'

He turned slowly to face her, his gaze seemed to track her features, moving between her eyes and mouth, only once dropping down to glance at her breasts. A beat of time passed, then he spoke.

'I meant what I said. The question was clear enough, surely?'

'Yes, but the answer is so simple. Why does anyone come to France? Or go anywhere for that matter? Dull as it may seem I'm here for a holiday. To get away. To relax. To have some fun.'

'Ah, *fun*,' he said and he might as well have made that clichéd hand sign which marks two inverted commas in the air around the word. She felt belittled – which must have been his intention.

'Well, you asked the question,' she said.

What had made her say that damn cliché about fun? Momentarily she pictured herself throwing her glass of wine in his face.

But her glass (she had automatically, as if she were really about to pick it up and throw it, looked at it) was empty. Empty and she couldn't remember drinking it – a worrying sign.

'Who are you here with?' he asked then.

'No one.'

'Ah.' He raised that one eyebrow again as if to show that some assumption he'd had about her had been confirmed.

'I prefer it that way.'

'Do you?'

'Yes.'

'You don't like people?'

'No, that's not it.' Why was he making her feel so defensive, so exposed?

'You just like your own company?'

'Sometimes.'

'Hmm.' He absorbed this. Maybe he was, as he had claimed, a psychologist.

She emptied the carafe into her glass, filling it to the brim. To hell in a handcart, she thought, then not caring how it looked, she bent her head to her glass and drank a quarter of an inch of the liquid without lifting it from the table.

He stood up.

'Are you off, then?' she said.

'Yeah.' He stretched himself, sighed, shrugged. A rapid succession of signs which were contradictory and unreadable. Except that leaving was in and of itself the most uncomplicated sign of all.

He disappeared inside the bar. She watched as he stood there chatting for a few minutes with the man behind the counter. He looked more relaxed, threw his head back and laughed at something the other man had said. Then the man on the stool next to Scott leaned towards him — evidently in order to say something private — and as he spoke he flicked his eyes in her direction. Scott turned and glanced at her. She looked away quickly. She heard laughter again, but had no way of knowing if it was about her.

She gazed up at the large plane tree on the pavement outside the café, noticed for the first time that curling up its trunk and hung about its branches were unlit fairy lights. It would look so pretty if they were switched on, she thought. She took it personally that no one had made the effort – it was as if the world had conspired to always deal her the third-rate experience, the uninspired. The unadorned.

She glanced once more into the bar. Scott was now half-sitting on a bar stool, one foot on the rung, his knee sharply bent, the other leg straight, foot planted firmly on the floor with the toe pointed towards the exit. A waitress was standing next to him smoking a cigarette.

Lucy looked at the wine in her glass and realising that she had already drunk too much, she picked it up and added it to the coffee in the planter. It was swallowed up quickly; the plant was as thirsty, as empty as she was.

# The House with the Yellow Shutters

A phrase had popped into Marilyn's head as she stood at the sink peeling potatoes. She watched her hands as they denuded each mud-caked potato with a string-handled peeler. She tried saying the phrase aloud in a whispered chant, 'like quicksand's kiss, that draws me in...' She knew that she should stop what she was doing and jot the words down, but somehow, an element of self-consciousness or duty stopped her and she continued to peel potatoes.

The water was lukewarm as she had added a little from the hot tap. She remembered peeling potatoes for her mother back home in Canada, her hands bright red in the icy water. Never questioning why they had to be peeled in that way in particular and what was wrong with a little warm water, a bit of comfort?

Not 'quicksand's kiss' then, but more like muddy water. Maybe it was the grit she sensed on the pads of her fingers that had made her think of sand, that and the fact that they had spent that day at the beach. And she was weary; her mind could not entirely focus on any one thing.

'Do you need any help here?' Scott was standing in the doorway of the kitchen; despite his words he looked as if he didn't really want to help, though she was certain that if asked, he would.

'No, it's fine. Won't be long now, thirty-five minutes at most.'

'Okay, I'll get Aaron to have a wash.'

She smiled. The smile acknowledged the difficulty of his task. It was far easier, she knew, to deal with supper – the mashed potatoes, meatloaf, carrots and gravy – than to get Aaron to do even the simplest thing like washing his face and hands.

For the last four years they had been coming here with Aaron.

Two weeks every year dealing with Aaron was completely exhausting. How his aging parents coped for the other fifty weeks of the year she didn't know. Maybe back home in more familiar surroundings he was easier to cope with. And, crucially, his parents loved him, he was their child after all. That had to make a difference. Except that when she imagined having a child like Aaron, she could not picture love at all, only a devastating disappointment, a terrible burden of pain and guilt and regret. And she felt bad for even allowing this thought to enter her head. It didn't matter that there was honesty in recognising it, she should not, she was certain, even think it. Especially now that she herself was pregnant.

She hadn't told anyone yet. She calculated the pregnancy to be eleven weeks, and she'd taken two pregnancy tests, one the week before they left for France, and one after they'd arrived, which she'd done in the ladies loo at the airport after they'd landed. She'd been nervous about flying, had some strange notion that the air pressure in the cabin or the altitude or stress would make her lose the baby.

Losing the baby that early on in the pregnancy wasn't always referred to as a miscarriage, sometimes it was described as a spontaneous abortion – a term which made her shudder.

She planned to do a third test when they got back to Canada. Only then would she tell Scott. Only then could she begin to believe it herself, which at this moment she didn't entirely.

So she stood at the sink peeling potatoes, dreamily letting her mind range freely, while in the hallway she heard Scott chiding and chivying Aaron towards the downstairs bathroom. Threatening no supper, no 'nice meatloaf', no 'buttery mash' if he didn't wash his face and hands, then switching tactics and promising ice cream tomorrow if he was good tonight.

And in opposition to the sounds of Scott's voice, there was Aaron's wall of words 'No, no, no, no, no' which altered in pitch and tempo, rising and falling and sounding to the uninformed outsider like the cries of someone being tortured. And maybe to Aaron it was torture. Did it really matter if he washed his face and hands or not? Sometimes it didn't seem worth the effort, but then as Scott said, you start letting one thing go and the next thing you know you've got him tied to a leash in a dirty basement, and you hose him down once a month and only then because the smell is floating up the stairs.

The phone started to ring.

'Marilyn! Mar! Sorry, can you get that? We've got a situation here...'

She dropped the potato and the peeler into the tepid brown water, grabbed a clean tea-towel and hurried into the sitting room wiping her hands dry. It was seven-fifteen. She knew who was calling, Momma and Poppa Clement, to say 'night-night' to their best boy, Aaron. Though so far he'd never been persuaded to come to the phone. Telephones with their disembodied voices, even the familiar voices of his parents, seemed to scare Aaron. But every evening Scott and Aaron's parents rang up and asked to talk to him.

In the hallway she saw that Aaron was holding onto the newel post at the foot of the stairs with two hands. His body was rigid and his head was bent low at the neck, a sure sign that he was in a defiant mood. Scott was standing next to him with a lavender-coloured bath towel in his hands.

She didn't really need to hurry to get to the phone, her in-laws would let the phone ring for minute after minute after minute until someone finally picked up, and in the event that no one picked up the first time, they would ring every half hour after. They were persistent and vigilant, would seemingly never give up anything once they had started, which might explain their untiring devotion to Aaron.

'Hello?'

'Is that you, Marilyn?' It was, as she'd expected, Scott and Aaron's mother. Her voice was full of warm enthusiasm, like that of a kindergarten teacher talking to a five year old, yet it always made Marilyn think of disappointment.

'Yes, it's me.'

'How's our boy?'

'Oh, he's fine,' Marilyn said out of habit, aware as she said it that Aaron's voice, the angry 'No, no, no, no, no' must be carried, along with her own voice, over the wires, up to the satellite, to be beamed down into Audrey Clement's ears as she stood in the overheated kitchen of their scrupulously clean Ontario home.

'Has he had his supper?'

'No, not yet, I'm just in the middle of it.'

'Oh, what are you having?'

'Meatloaf, mash, veg.'

'Oh, he loves his meatloaf! She says they're having meatloaf, Dave.'

Dave was Marilyn's father-in-law, a man who was tall and stooped, with a white beard and a full head of white hair that made him look like an underfed Santa Claus, especially in the red sweater Audrey had knitted him last fall.

'Will Baby come to the phone?' Audrey said in a needy voice. Baby was the affectionate nickname Audrey and Dave had for Aaron.

'No, Audrey, I don't think so, but I'll just ask. Hold on.' Dutifully, knowing it was a charade, she went to the doorway and said in a loud clear voice, 'Scott, your mom's on the phone, does Aaron want to say hello?'

And Scott, in an equally loud voice said, 'Aaron? You wanna talk to Momma? Momma's on the phone.'

Unsurprisingly, Aaron's answer was no. Though whether it was a particular no pertaining to the specific question or a generalised no to everything except clinging to the newel post was hard to discern.

'No. Scott's just getting him washed. Did you want to talk to Scott?'

'Oh no, not if it's inconvenient.'

'How are you, Audrey?' Marilyn remembered to ask, 'and how's Dave?'

'Oh, fine, fine. It's very quiet here. We went to the mall this morning. I got Aaron some new sports shoes and a winter fleece.'

'Lovely.'

Audrey was forever buying new clothes for Aaron. She paid a lot of attention to what she saw boys and young men wearing and sought the advice of sales assistants in fashionable downtown shops. 'My son's about your age,' she'd say. 'Now which of these jeans are in fashion, which would he like?' So Aaron wore designer label sports shirts, Timberland boots, even his underwear and socks were JM or Sean John or Calvin Klein.

'Well, we'll leave you to it then, Marilyn. Love to all. See you soon.'

'Yes, see you soon.'

Marilyn replaced the receiver and stood for a moment gazing out of the window. The house they stayed in each year was owned by relatives of the Clements, a distant part of the family that hadn't left France for the New World. It was at the edge of the small town opposite a restaurant called La Coquille Bleue, which she and Scott hadn't yet had a chance to visit. Aaron's fussiness about food and his other fears and phobias severely limited what they did, hence the good old Canadian meatloaf, the familiar mash and carrots. Scott had suggested she go out alone some evenings, as he himself did, but it seemed a pointless exercise and one she was happy to forego, preferring, once Aaron had taken his medication and was asleep, to read or, if she wasn't too tired, to write.

They let Aaron go out for a little time most evenings. Scott referred to this as 'going out to play' and while it only consisted

39

of Aaron standing outside holding onto a lamppost while one or the other of them kept an eye on him from the house, it did seem to give Aaron some kind of pleasure or satisfaction and calmed him before supper and bedtime.

Scott went out for a drink or two every second or third night – once they were sure Aaron was asleep – Marilyn would have liked to go with him, but that was impossible, besides which they had all the time in the world to be alone together once they got back to Canada. Time for just the two of them. Except that soon they'd be three.

The phone call had momentarily thrown Marilyn off her train of thought. Partly it was jetlag, partly Aaron; the annoyance at making meatloaf of all things. So she stood there for a moment by the small side table looking at the narrow turquoise glass vase which held a single white artificial rose, trying to remember the words that had danced through her mind just minutes before.

She sighed, then looked at the restaurant opposite. As Marilyn watched a young woman crossed the road towards it. The woman seemed to illustrate the very freedom Marilyn was yearning for at that moment – it was almost as if she had sprung from Marilyn's mind purely for this purpose and was thus dressed for the part. She was wearing a sleeveless summer dress with a full skirt that stopped just above the knee.

A green hatchback travelling at speed appeared out of nowhere as the young woman neared the pavement. For a moment Marilyn was convinced that she was about to witness a terrible accident, such as that she had seen one summer in England when she was fifteen. Then the victims had been a man and a child whom she assumed was his son. They had been in the middle of one of those zebra crossings that lacked traffic lights and relied on the drivers travelling in both directions to notice pedestrians. It had just started raining heavily and the man was pulling the boy along at a jog. Marilyn had been walking towards the oncoming traffic. She was less than twelve paces from the crossing when she saw a yellow cement mixer pull up for the man and boy. The driver was jolly and red-faced with an almost comical bushy black moustache. He gesticulated to the pedestrians by sweeping one hand elegantly through the air, inviting their safe passage. Perhaps because of this, because of the truck driver's smile and the reassuring size of the vehicle, because of the resolute hiss of the air brakes and the torrential rain, the father, his head craned upward as he nodded thanks at the driver, stepped onto the part of the crossing that spanned the opposite lane without really looking to see if it was safe. One minute the man was there, the next he was gone – replaced by the wildly sashaying rear end of the car that had hit him. By some miracle (Marilyn had always been convinced it wasn't by design) the man had loosened his grip on the boy's hand and the child was left standing in the shadow of the truck's huge black wheels, his hand still raised to meet his father's.

This memory had embedded itself deeply in Marilyn's mind – morbidly, Scott said – and now in those seconds as she watched the young woman crossing the road and saw the car approaching at speed she held her breath and felt her stomach grow hollow as she steeled herself for the worst. But the young woman, seeing the vehicle, lengthened her stride and skipped gracefully onto the pavement.

Marilyn breathed out through pursed lips and felt her body deflate. Now she studied the young woman even more closely than before – with her platinum blonde bobbed hair and slender limbs she looked like a character from a 1950s or 60s French film – *Jules et Jim* or one of those Eric Rohmer movies or even (if the girl was to come to a bad end) a Claude Chabrol. She carried a small stylish bag that looked like a basket and she'd draped a white scarf or cardigan over it. She had an air of self-consciousness about her – which was manifested as a kind of awkwardness in the seeming naturalness of her movements that somehow made one want to stare at her.

Obviously she was French, but from one of the larger cities, Paris probably. And she was perhaps a film or fashion student, or so Marilyn imagined, and she was on her way to meet her lover, who was a much older man. No one would think anything of that in France – not if the man was good-looking, rich and powerful, and if the girl was beautiful and over the age of consent.

Marilyn watched the young woman pause at the entrance to the restaurant and stare directly at their house. Marilyn automatically ducked behind the curtain, afraid of being caught staring. When she looked again the girl had gone.

Marilyn sighed. She heard Scott say crossly, 'Hey, no meatloaf for people who can't behave,' and remembered immediately what it was she had been doing before the phone call.

Aaron and Scott were near the door to the downstairs bathroom now. Aaron's hair looked wet and it stuck up at odd angles, Scott had a big wet patch on the front of his olive green shirt and smaller dark patches on his sleeves. He was angry.

Sometimes this happened. Invariably it wore them all out, Aaron most of all, so that on this night he was in his bed and sound asleep by eight thirty-five.

Scott said he had to get out of the house. He was sorry. Did she mind? He'd go mad if he stayed in. He was sorry, sorry, *sorry*. She gave him her blessing, kissed him.

She scraped Aaron's barely touched plate of food into the bin, then did the same with hers and Scott's. None of them had eaten much of the meal. Prison food, Scott called it, but she knew it wasn't that bad. It was more to do with Scott's complex emotions about himself and his family, how he felt caged in by the fact that his younger brother was so damaged, that all his life he'd had to make sacrifices for the sake of his helpless sibling.

Some people might have called this evening a disaster, but

Marilyn knew better. Disasters happened to people who didn't expect them, who were shocked by the disruption to the simple routine of an evening at home. With Aaron to look after she found it was the evenings that went to plan which were the surprise. She understood Scott's need for escape, understood too, that it was nothing to do with her, and that Aaron, his issues and problems and tantrums, somehow weighed less heavily on her. She was not a blood relative – she could, if she wished, just walk away.

# L'écriture Feminine

Michael and Hilda Eszterhas were celebrating ten years of marriage. They had known one another for nearly fifty years, but for most of those years they had each been in relationships with other people.

'Do you know, I always sensed that there was something between us,' Hilda said to Michael as they relaxed in the small boulevard café under the shadow of a plane tree. 'Then when Bill died, I thought… Well, you remember…'

Michael nodded gravely. He was a pragmatist and resisted Hilda's attempts to dwell on romantic notions of fate and lost opportunities. They were together now. That was all that mattered.

Hilda's family life had been fixed and stultifying, middle class and middle England, C of E, tweed and lace, malice over the dinner table, spite in the rose garden, loathing in the bedroom (or so Hilda assumed about this last). Michael was part Spanish, part Jewish, part Irish. They'd first met in a dingy little pub in Cambridge after attending a talk given by E.P. Thompson.

Hilda's hair, though now almost completely white, was still waist length. She rarely wore it loose and tonight she'd woven it into a long plait. Michael was also grey, but these days his hair, or what was left of it, was cropped to a quarter of an inch, and in good weather was usually covered by a jaunty straw hat. In winter he favoured a black bargeman's cap.

They paid little attention to the young blonde woman sitting at the table next to theirs. Though Hilda had happened to glance over just as the blonde (rather ridiculously) tipped a perfectly good cup of espresso into the wooden planter by her side. Hilda had meant to mention it to Michael, but he was busy reminiscing about Paris in May 1968.

They were both still passionate about politics, but had long ago ceased to speak of revolution. The word 'revolution' seemed to have become an obscure pop lyric. Both Hilda and Michael had police records. Not that anyone looking at them would guess that. And, as much as a criminal record might paint a picture of amoral lying, scheming, selfish ne'er-do-wells, both Hilda and Michael Eszterhas believed they were ethical, moral, selfless, honest people. That their criminal activities were righteous and legitimate, and the law itself was unjust.

'I sometimes wonder how things would have been if we'd got together sooner,' Hilda had said, after the waitress had taken their order for a bottle of the local cider.

'The way I see it…' Michael began, and he paused, as he often did when he was about to say something important. In the silence that followed, a fragment of someone else's conversation invaded their ears. Ugly words spoken in English.

Both Hilda and Michael heard it very clearly. Hilda had been gazing at Michael, listening to him, waiting for him to continue. As she heard the other voice, she saw Michael frown at the crudeness of the stranger's words. Hilda's eyes widened and her mouth gaped. Then she shook her head slowly from side to side.

She and Michael understood one another, would not let other people's vileness – their ignorance, lust and cruelty – spoil their evening. Hilda had glanced over at the girl the words had been directed towards. She wore an expression that suggested she was embarrassed, but didn't want to show it. Michael described the same look as a smirk, a smile with indications of cruelty and coldness.

Each of them was absolutely certain of the words the man had spoken. Michael said he had heard the man say, 'I follow strange women and I fuck them.'

Hilda disagreed; she was infuriated with Michael because she knew he was wrong. What Hilda heard was, 'I let strange women follow me, then I fuck them.'

'I remembered you see, because it struck me how unusual it was. I've been reading the French theorists – Lacan, Hélène Cixous, Julia Kristeva – so I was immediately struck by the seeming passivity of the man's words. Or rather by the contradictory nature of the sentence: "I let strange women follow me" is a passive statement and therefore feminine. "Then I fuck them" is active and thus masculine. The young woman did indeed smile, but it was a conflicted smile, defensive, and when the man got up and left the table she looked very confused, and deflated.'

'But,' Michael said, 'when the young woman came to the café she was alone. The man joined her sometime after. So he must have followed her, mustn't he?'

'That may be,' said Hilda, 'but I am certain of what I heard.'

'And so am I,' Michael said, and neither of them would stand down, or be shaken from their respective positions. Each of them was used to being disbelieved by others due to their long involvement with politics – they had warned of the threat of pollution, of the dangers of pesticides and other scientific adjustments to nature, they had spoken of a future with government cameras on every street corner, and bugs (that was how they had described it in the seventies) which monitored every member of the population, seeing what it read or bought, what it watched on TV. They had made grim statements about the blind hedonism of the western world and the effects of its endless consumerism and bullying in the Third World. They had lectured and written pamphlets, and marched and joined organisations. And they had been laughed at. There was not much consolation in finally being proved right.

This overheard fragment of conversation on a French café terrace was one of the few things they disagreed on.

The police inspector, a man by the name of Vivier, believed (just as Hilda might have predicted) Michael. The plain-clothes female officer (Hilda wasn't sure of her rank) whose name was Sabine, seemed to believe Hilda.

On the whole however, the police didn't see that there was any great difference; a man had been overheard saying the words 'follow', 'strange women' and 'fuck them'. And the woman he had said them to was dead. The finer points of syntax, the groundbreaking work of French literary theorists such as Cixous and Irigaray, ideas based around *l'écriture féminine* and Hilda's absolute certainty were as chaff in a hurricane; irrelevances, superficialities and distractions that should not be attended to lest they sway the investigation and the course of justice.

# Miroir Noir

With her empty wine glass on the table in front of her, Lucy considered her options. Scott was still inside the café chatting amiably with the staff and customers. She felt envious of him because he seemed to have formed bonds here in this small town. It was something she would have liked for herself.

She lit a cigarette – the last from her pack – and smoked it reflectively. That was what she liked about smoking, it provided an interval of time in which one could stop and consider the next move. She was also consciously using the cigarette to make decisions. If he doesn't come out before I've finished this cigarette, she thought, I'll stub this out, pick up my lighter, my bag, my cardigan and be on my way. No backward glances, no attempts to catch his eye or wave. I will just become what I was a few days ago, a woman alone, quietly going about my own business.

She looked about her. Only three other tables were occupied. A bodybuilder in a Real Madrid football shirt was hunched over the table by the exit with his back to her. His neck, she noticed, was almost as thick as his head. The shirt was very tight on him, giving the impression that he had been inflated inside it. She supposed some women would find such a build attractive, but it did nothing for her. At the table nearest the entrance to the café were four young people, three girls and a boy who seemed to be playing some sort of game, each of them taking turns to speak while the others paid careful attention. Perhaps it was one of those memory word games where you had to remember and add to alphabetically arranged but otherwise unconnected items bought at a supermarket. She was too far away to hear the words, and when they occasionally raised their voices she didn't recognise the language.

Nearest to her, two tables away, was a middle-aged couple. The woman had a striking plait of long silver hair that reached halfway down her back. You seldom saw older women with hair that long, or certainly not hair which was long and had been left to go grey naturally. She was plump but shapely, with large breasts, large hips and by comparison, a smallish waist. She wore a navy linen dress with a deep V at the neck. The skin on her chest looked red and almost bruised with sunburn, though her face wasn't affected. The man she was with had closely cropped salt and pepper hair. He wore a brightly patterned shirt in splashes of orange and turquoise that jarred and jumped, a mushroom-coloured seersucker suit and a straw hat. He looked like a character from a John Grisham novel, a New Orleans lawyer with some kind of secret weakness that would be his downfall. Lucy's eye happened to drop towards his feet. Socks and sandals. Mottled grey and green socks, a little thin at the heel, and brown leather sandals. Not a Grisham character at all then – he had to be British – the proverbial Englishman abroad.

Lucy had been half aware of voices speaking English close by, but had somehow tuned them out or rather taken them for granted, forgetting for a little time, while she had talked to Scott that she was in France. Now as she measured time with each slow puff on her cigarette, she tuned her ears towards the older couple's conversation.

'Is this the world we created?' the man said. 'Are we culpable? My God, it's worse now than I could ever have imagined.'

In a different frame of mind Lucy might have been fascinated to overhear such a conversation, but at this moment, in this angry state of mind, she felt only a raw resentment and felt that this old man, this straw man was lecturing the woman he was with, lecturing Lucy too.

The woman reached for the man's hand. 'We tried,' she said. 'We shouldn't forget that.'

Lucy stubbed out her cigarette, and slowly gathered her belongings. It was still warm so she didn't put her cardigan on, but draped it over her bag. She stood, resisting the urge to look in the direction of the café. Hesitated. A coffee and two half litres of house wine, plus a tip would cost less than twenty Euros. She took a twenty Euro note from her purse and placed them under the empty carafe, a ring of burgundy liquid seeped onto the note.

She picked her way between the tables and out onto the pavement, and at a stroll began to head back in the direction she'd come.

Her hotel was a good twenty-five minutes walk away, and she needed to navigate her journey by returning via La Coquille Bleue, then doubling back to the hotel. But there were many side streets which could provide a faster route. She did not wish to pass the house with the yellow shutters again tonight, and planned to avoid it for the next few days. She had a fairly good sense of direction and it was only a small town. (Hell, if she could find her way around Glasgow, London and New York, she was sure she wouldn't get lost for long here.) And she enjoyed walking.

But first, some cigarettes. She would stick to the main drag, then stop at one of the last cafés, one of those with the friendly red and white signs that read Tabac.

When she had walked for five minutes, she turned to glance behind her. Scott, she thought, might be hurrying to catch up with her. To apologise. But there was no one, just the few straggling tourists and locals going about their business, none of them paying any attention to her. Which was just as it should be, except that right now she would really welcome some company.

Lucy thought about ringing Thom. It would be good to hear his voice. She imagined him saying, 'Oh Lucy. God, I've missed you. Where are you? When can I see you?' to which she would say, 'I'm sorry. I'm in France. I'll come back tomorrow.' Or 'Well, why don't you come here?'

But he wouldn't say any of that. Would not drop everything and come haring over the Channel to be with her. Instead he would be angry. So she would not phone him. She would not make the first move towards reconciliation. Would not say sorry.

It was stupid to even think of it. Thom could go to hell. He was probably screwing some other woman right now. One of his students maybe, he had never had any qualms about political correctness, nor about college rules. Though actually now she came to really think about it, it would be just like him to come after her students.

She remembered how keen he had been to help her out that night she gave her third-year seminar group a party. She'd had the idea to invite the third years around to her place for a sort of pep talk at the beginning of their spring term when they were about to launch themselves into their dissertations and final exhibition. The party was a sort of acknowledgement that they were almost there, were changing from mere undergraduates to fully-fledged artists. Equals who could be trusted in her home, who could stand about with glasses of wine and have intelligent conversations, instead of drinking too much and throwing up in the punch bowl.

She'd invested a lot in the party, cooking an array of different foods from scratch – fried prawns in batter, anchovy toast, miniature goat's cheese tarts, Thai fish cakes, quail's eggs, the best olives, the best cheeses.

And Thom, when she'd told him about her plan, had not, as she thought he might, told her she was wasting her time or showing off. He got it straight away and insisted on coming around earlier in the day to help. Then it was only natural that he'd stay for the party.

Thirteen of her sixteen students had shown up, including Laura Smith and Rebecca White, a pair of young women who were like supermodels or goddesses and would strike fear into any woman's heart. Especially a woman of twenty-nine who was slightly doubtful about her current partner's ongoing interest in her.

Having Laura and Rebecca there was a bit like having a couple of exotic birds strutting about the room, everyone had to keep looking at them from the corner of their eyes, as if they couldn't quite believe they were real.

But Thom avoided Laura and Rebecca; he barely gave them a second glance. Instead he spent quite some time talking to a number of the male students about big subjects, politics, philosophy and history.

Then after a quiet moment with Lucy in the kitchen – he was washing the limited supply of side plates so that Lucy could sort out the desserts she'd made – he mentioned Imogen Carter. Imogen was a quiet girl who, while she was not unattractive, wore her disquiet and social unease like a second skin that acted to repel anyone who tried to get close to her – man, woman or child. Imogen had spent most of the evening sitting at the far end of the room with her plate on her knees and a glass in her hand, saying nothing and trying, somewhat unsuccessfully, to look relaxed.

With Lucy's blessing, Thom had promised to try to make Imogen feel a bit more at ease.

For the rest of the evening every time Lucy looked in the direction of Imogen's chair she saw that Thom was next to her, at first standing casually in Imogen's vicinity, then sitting on the armchair at right angles from her, then finally sitting on the floor at her feet. And Lucy saw that it was working, Imogen was no longer sitting bolt upright on the edge of the seat, she'd tucked her legs up under her and was leaning with one elbow on the armrest and talking.

Lucy had felt so proud of Thom then, and proud of herself for having succeeded in acquiring such a wonderful, mature and generous man.

'You are so good,' she'd said to him later, after everyone had gone home.

'Who, me?' he'd said, pointing at his chest and wearing an expression of mock surprise.

'Yeah, you. I'm just so amazed that you saw that Imogen had problems, and you just stuck with it. I don't think I've ever seen her laugh before. No, seriously, I think you might have made an impact on that girl, made her feel for the first time that she matters.'

'Really? Well, I didn't do much.'

'What did you talk about?'

'Oh, families mostly. She's had one hell of a life you know. Did you know about her mother?'

'What about her mother?'

'God, you don't know? It was a huge story in the papers, what, ten years ago? And you know Imogen looks a lot like her mother. I had a feeling I'd seen that face before...'

'What story? What happened?'

'So you honestly don't know? Weird. I thought it might have been in her personal records. But then I guess they'd keep the lid on it, you know, give her a clean slate.'

'Oh, I feel terrible for not knowing. I mean, I sensed she had problems, but nothing big. So what was it?'

This conversation had taken place as Lucy and Thom lay together on the big couch, under the window. Ten minutes before they'd been making love, and twenty minutes before that they'd been waving as the last of the students headed off for a taxi.

Around the room was the debris of the party, the smeared plates and empty glasses, the discarded paper napkins, wine bottles and ashtrays. The Nick Drake CD had just finished playing. The silence was palpable. Thom ran his fingers over Lucy's bare shoulder.

'You know what,' he said.

'What?'

'I don't think I should tell you what Imogen told me. I mean ethically it wouldn't be right. She's chosen to keep it to herself and I don't think it's my place to share it with you. It's a question of trust, isn't it? So Lucy, I'm not going to break that trust. I'm sorry if that seems strange – what with her being your student – but that's my decision.'

'But…'

'Really. I've said enough. If you must know then I suggest you do some research. The surname's the same – Carter isn't it – and it's in the public domain. So.'

'But you're contradicting what you just said. If it's in the public domain, then you may as well just tell me.'

'The point though, is not the information itself. The point is me, my ethics, my morals, the trust she has placed in me. I can't tell you because of how that would make me feel. You see.'

'Yes, I see. Okay.'

They lay together a few minutes longer. Lucy's mind was racing. If he hadn't been there she'd have switched on the computer straight away, Googled the name Carter, searched online copies of the *Guardian* and the *Independent* for some horror story regarding a woman with a nine or ten-year-old daughter, and satisfied the hornets' nest of curiosity he'd stirred up in her. Not that she would admit to curiosity; the urge to vicariously delve into the terrors of another's tragedy, she would only allow that she was motivated by a professional interest in the girl and a deepening sense of shame for not trying harder, for accepting the young woman at face value, as a rather dull girl with no social skills, who seemed to want to remain private and got what she wished for.

The next morning Lucy brought up the subject of Imogen again. She had woken with this feeling of guilt, but it was unnamed and its source was unclear. She was also overtaken by this new vision of Thom. Thom as an upright, all-knowing, moral being. Someone better than her. It was like suddenly realising she'd been dating a saint for the last three years and hadn't even known it until now. Someone wiser and purer than her.

'What we talked about last night...' she began.

'We talked about a lot of stuff.'

'You know what I mean – Imogen Carter.'

'Oh, that. Look, I haven't changed my mind. I don't think it would be right.'

'I realise that. I wasn't going to ask, but tell me, do you think I should try to find out? I mean, as you said, it was a big news story and so I probably could find out what it is easily enough. But would that be the correct thing to do? Would I be able to help her more if I knew?'

'Well, you couldn't tell her, could you? You couldn't bring it up without her thinking that I'd told you.'

'I guess not, but what if I knew and didn't mention it directly? I'm supervising her dissertation and she's doing it on fairly emotionally charged subjects – performance art, the body and self-mutilation – and so maybe I need to know.'

Thom thought about this for a little time before speaking, then he said, 'I'm sorry I told you as much as I did. The more I think about it the more I regret it. Don't go digging around. Forget I ever said anything. I think that's the only way to go. And just so you know, I gave her my number – told her to ring if she wanted to talk, and I have a feeling she will call, so let me see what I can do. Maybe it's easier for me as I'm at a remove – you know, I'm not going to be marking her essays or judging her work in any way – there's no power relationship here – no judgement, no pity.'

'Okay. I see what you mean. I won't pry, but if something happens, if she's – oh, I don't know – suicidal or something – you'll let me know.'

'Promise.'

'Alright. Well, I won't mention her again. I won't try to find out. Maybe sometime you'll feel it's okay to tell me.'

'Maybe.'

Why was Lucy remembering all of this now, why did she imagine poor Imogen of all people, having an affair with Thom? Maybe it was because Lucy understood Freud's theories about how people fell in love with their therapists and why the therapist was a saviour, a love object. She still cringed remembering her own feelings about Doctor Skinner, of how she'd confessed her love to him. How he was kind and patient when he quite correctly informed her that she was mistaken about her feelings, and allowed her to read a few pages in one of his books which outlined the nature of such confused emotions clearly. At first it had felt as if she were a star-struck kid being told that she had a crush, that what she experienced as unique and special was actually just a common phase that all girls went through.

So she could imagine Imogen falling for Thom quite easily – but Thom himself? The man had feet of clay. She did not feel she had ever really known him.

And Imogen's secret? Lucy, as she'd promised, never tried to find out, and the girl was doing okay and was, Lucy supposed, busy getting on with life, and as happy as she might ever be. But some day, some day quite soon, Lucy planned to find out once and for all. But it would only be to satisfy her curiosity, to satisfy it and put some ghosts to rest.

And now all she needed was a cigarette. A cigarette and maybe a night cap, something short and sweet and warming. Not coffee though, not now.

# The Golden Boy

Scott was relieved when glancing in the mirror behind the bar he saw the young woman finally get up from her chair. She seemed reluctant at first, hesitating as she fussed with her bag and the empty carafe on the table, but then, with her head held high, her pretty little nose aimed up in the direction of the stars, she'd walked away.

He had sensed in her a rather disturbing edge. The day before when he happened to look through the bedroom window and saw her talking to Aaron on the street, he'd taken her for some sort of mental health professional or social worker. Their family had had plenty of dealings with those folk in Canada. Lately they had suggested that Aaron could not continue to live with his ageing parents; they'd said that the house was too isolated, that it was dangerous on account of the wood-burning stove and its accompanying block and axe in the backyard. One of the assistant social workers, a Mrs Patel, had been frightened by the sight of Aaron after he'd come around to the front of the house with the axe in his hand when she'd rung the doorbell. They'd cited Aaron's father's health – he'd had thyroid and liver problems since he was relatively young. And his mother's – mainly as she'd told them she was getting forgetful lately. But Aaron enjoyed chopping wood; it was one of the few things that seemed to give him a sense of purpose. And their father had always had sallow skin, though it sure looked worse when he wore those god-awful bright emerald and orange and red sweaters that his mother knitted. And as for his mother's forgetfulness? Well, she always prided herself on her good memory and would worry about memory loss if she couldn't remember the names of every single teacher she'd had in grade school and the lines of poetry and prose she'd learnt by rote aged nine. It was absurd, the whole thing.

The social worker had put forward three choices to Scott; one, that Aaron be moved to a residential home eighty miles away, two, that Aaron should within the next year move in with Scott and his partner or three, that Scott should move back home to live with his parents in order to help with Aaron.

Scott had not told either of his parents or Marilyn about this. He did not see the point of spreading worry and misery amongst his family with the problem and was certain he could disabuse the social workers of these ideas by proving to them that Aaron was happy and cared for, and that his parents, despite appearances, would be able to cope for another good ten to twenty years at least.

He did not know how he could prove that Aaron and his parents were fine, but he had talked to a friend about it. The friend was a criminal defender, so while it wasn't exactly his field, he did have some interesting things to say about human rights, liberty and state intervention, and promised he would do some research on similar cases, and also speak to colleagues who were more directly involved in that field. He did say however that the axe incident as interpreted by the social worker, Mrs Patel, was the most worrying aspect, as public safety would always be put before private liberty.

All of this was weighing heavily on Scott's mind when they had set off for their annual trip to France. Perhaps a less caring man would just have let the social services get on with it. Such a man would have made it clear that he and Marilyn could not be expected to take over the care of his brother, nor could Scott (with or without his wife) be expected to give up his very well-paid job, move from the city and take up residence in his parents' home as a sort of unpaid babysitter and mental health nurse. If the consequence of this was that Aaron went into residential care then so be it, it wasn't his problem, he had his own life to lead.

Essentially Scott thought that the health workers and Mrs Patel in particular were blowing the whole thing up out of all proportion. His parents looked after Aaron with the minimum of financial support from the government, and they did this not only out of a sense of duty, but also because, despite his terrible problems, they deeply loved their youngest son. It did not make sense for those in control of social services, who were already overloaded with clients and underfunded, to tear a young man away from the bosom of his family, place him in an institution and wreak havoc amongst all those concerned at enormous cost to the public purse.

The whole situation reinvigorated all the suspicion, paranoia and unease which Scott had suffered through his school years when he had been stigmatised, not only by his peer group, but also those who were older and should have known better. Many of his friends and later girlfriends found it unpleasant and disquieting to come to his house because of Aaron, and their parents had on occasion forbidden it. He used to take Aaron out to play with him – back then when he was seven or eight and Aaron was only a preternaturally quiet and drooling toddler he had been more manageable, but as they got older and Aaron grew stronger and louder and more wilful, and as Scott's peer group began to understand that there was something seriously wrong with Scott's baby brother, it became increasingly difficult. And Scott felt contaminated by association. He was ashamed of having this damaged kid for a brother. And he hated the interviews with social workers, the way his parents always insisted he be there with them, the way he was paraded before these strangers as the good brother, the little helper, the damn golden boy who was somehow the final proof that everything in the Clement family was just hunky dory.

At the beginning of the trip this year, on the first night when Aaron had pointed at the door and begun his endless chant of 'play, play, play!' Scott suggested they shouldn't let him out as they had for the previous two years. Marilyn had argued the point.

'You know he'll be fine. He just stands there. We'll take it in turns to watch him. If anything happens – and it won't – we'll be out there in two seconds flat. And you know we won't get any peace unless we let him…'

Marilyn was so good. So understanding. Few women would sacrifice two weeks of precious holiday to spend them cooking meatloaf and pot roast for a human being who demanded so much and gave no sign of even the minimum of affection or appreciation in return.

So understandably when Scott noticed this young woman attempting to talk to Aaron it set off alarm signals, and raised his defences even before he'd spoken to her. And then when he'd confronted her he'd been disarmed by her beauty. She was so pretty and so seemingly innocent that it had made him bristle with emotion. Men, he knew, often felt rage towards women who stirred up unwanted desire in them, and that's what she'd done.

He'd been surprised too, to discover that she spoke English. He hadn't expected it, and that too threw him off course. For a second (though it was only a second) he imagined she was a spy sent by the Canadian health department to further their case for hospitalising Aaron.

It reminded him, he supposed, that Aaron's condition was a sort of door left ajar; a gaping entrance through which countless bureaucrats and experts poured to invade the Clement family home and inspect their kitchen drawers, their private lives and health and hearts at any time night or day, and all in the pretext of doing good and helping them.

Scott often had guilty and troubling thoughts about Aaron. He often tried to remember the time before Aaron was born, those precious years of his life when there was only Scott and his mother and father in the little house out on the edge of the woods. He tried but could not remember anything, there was no sense of how peaceful that might have been, how glorious to be the focus of his parents' affection and labour.

Worryingly he did remember something from a time just after Aaron was born, but it was so unnerving that by now – through that process of remembering and remembering – he often dismissed it as a bad dream or perhaps a nasty childish fantasy. And when he recalled it, it came to him like a picture on a flash card, or one of those scenes in a film which are barely on the screen long enough for you to properly absorb them. It was horrible and whenever it came to his mind (usually at moments of stress or anger) he had to fight to escape it, to distract himself any way he could.

And here's what it was. A crib in a darkened room. His parents' bedroom, but strangely they aren't there. He has no idea where his parents are. In the crib he sees Aaron, snivelling in his sleep and beginning to whimper. And there is this bad smell. A really bad smell of shit, pungent and stale and slightly cheesy. And in Scott's hands is a pillow – the pillow from his own bed which has repeat motifs of the Lone Ranger astride his rearing-stallion. These specific details are the worst part of it because they make him think that it's real, that it actually happened and is no dream at all. Scott lifts the pillow in two hands and carefully, deliberately he pushes it down onto Aaron's sleeping face.

And that's all he remembers. Just that. He doesn't remember how long he held the pillow in place, nor thankfully can he recall the tiny body of his brother squirming, fighting, gasping for air.

What happens to babies deprived of oxygen? Scott knows the answer. Was Aaron born damaged? Or did something happen to him? The different doctors Scott and Aaron's parents consulted said it was a chromosome thing, a genetic problem, or possibly something caused during the course of the pregnancy – a virus, a particular sort of food poisoning. But Scott's mother always says that unlike Scott who was difficult and colicky, Aaron was a perfect, blissful, good baby.

Of course, their mother wants to believe that Aaron was once fine, because that suggests he'll be fine again; he'll just wake up one morning and start talking about college and girls and football.

Maybe it wasn't such a terrible thing for his mother to believe that. It gave her hope, and hope can wake one up in the morning, it can set the coffee percolating, put a smile on one's face, it can send one scurrying off to the mall, make one joyfully sign the credit card receipt for hundreds of dollars. Hope could sit beside you on the bus as you made your way home; it listened and looked on admiringly as you displayed the Nike trainers you just bought for your youngest son, the orange Puffa jacket with the embroidered logo on the chest – the one that marks it out as the genuine article, not some cheap rip-off copy. Hope can even make you believe that your older son has only ever felt love for his younger more helpless brother.

Who would take that away from her?

# The Golden Girl

Peroxide burns. Lucy had a sudden and visceral awareness of the chemical actuality of the process. She should have known. Cursed herself as she sat in the kitchen with the evil-smelling stuff on her head. It itched and stung and turned her (now she thought about it) beautiful dark brown hair a yellowy orange colour.

And according to the instructions on the packet she was not meant to do anything else to this neon tangerine mess until at least twenty-four hours had passed. Not only that but when she inspected her hair with the help of two mirrors, she saw that the colour was patchy. She rang the college and cited gastric flu as the reason for her absence. Then rang a hairdresser to confess her sin and book an appointment for the next day.

'Oh dear,' was what the hairdresser said, after Lucy took the head scarf off her ridiculous hair.

But after a great deal of work on the hairdresser's part, and a great deal of money and patience on Lucy's, she was transformed into an ash blonde.

The hair colour, the trip to France and the new clothes she had bought were all part of a plan for a transformed identity. She had, it seemed to her, spent far too many years in her mid-twenties trying to look older and thus more serious and intelligent.

Thom seemed to take her for granted. People had begun to assume that she was older than she was, they read her age not so much from her as yet unlined and youthful face, but from other signifiers – for example her partner's age, Thom was twelve years older than her and his black hair was silvery at the temples. She wore her own brown hair in a middle parting and generally tied back in a pony tail. She wore dark earth colours enlivened with the occasional raspberry or emerald sweater.

She had tired of it and like many people nearing the age of thirty she suddenly yearned for youth again.

She had deliberately timed the image change to coincide with the holiday. Thom would not see her new hairstyle for at least two weeks. Her family would have to wait until Christmas. And indeed none of them might see it at all. She may, having tried the new colour out in France, decide to dye it brown again on her return.

She had already noticed that men paid her more attention, but was ambiguous about how that made her feel. Maybe this blonde hair, these girlish frocks gave off signals of sexual availability. That the cliché was true was surprising to her.

Perhaps she had been too effective in stripping away not only the melanin in her hair, but also her old defences. For the first time in her life she felt too visible. The plus side was a sense of a power, the minus side was vulnerability.

The night she followed Scott, she had been driven in part by an excess of energy. The same energy that had inspired her to dye her hair. She felt almost breathless, hollowed out, hungry and lonely. She should have recognised the symptoms. But the last time she'd felt like this had been when she was a first-year art student in Glasgow.

Cigarette. What she needed was a couple more smokes and maybe a brandy. Then back at the hotel she'd order some hot chocolate. Go to bed, read one of the books she'd brought with her. One of those books that was too large to put in the silly little bag she'd bought to go with her daisy print frock.

A book is a fine defence against so much.

Tomorrow she'd rethink it all. Redefine her tactics. Try not to think about the Canadian guy. Try also not to focus so much negative attention on Thom. It was a waste of emotional energy.

A man veered in closer as they passed each other on the pavement. He came at her in drunken loping crab-like steps. He was tall, dark and handsome with a long soulful face, black piercing eyes. When he was almost near enough to touch her, he lunged closer and made a wet sucking kiss noise. She felt his breath, hot, moist and heavily laced with alcohol on her cheek, the side of her neck, and ducked out of his grasp. It happened very quickly. His friends were just behind him; they laughed as they saw her frightened response. He was never going to actually touch her. It was all just fun.

Oh yeah, fun.

Which blondes have more of.

Fun, which Scott had sneered at in their conversation earlier.

Cigarette.

Embarrassed and self-conscious suddenly, she walked on a little way, then at the first sight of the word *tabac* she turned purposefully into the entrance under that sign. Hardly noticing that it was the smallest and most basic café on the street. Outside there were no low planters to separate the clientele from the street, instead there were just two rickety aluminium tables with five mismatched plastic chairs, and the inside was little more than a narrow room with a bar along one side and a row of booths with ripped vinyl benches on the other.

That sense of purpose – buy cigarettes, have a drink – and of escape – get off the street, gather herself together, regroup, calm down, then whisk off again – was shattered as soon as she found herself in the heart of the shabby café.

Her heels clicking sharply, bravely on the wooden floor announced her. All eyes turned in her direction.

Out of the frying pan into the fire.

The eyes, all twelve pairs of them, were male. At the bar nearest her were three working men, paint and cement splashed, bristly and gristly, unshaved in navy nylon track suits, tired denim, raggedy sweatshirts, sweat-stained, flesh bulging, hairy and raw, as they hunched over the counter. To her left, in one of the booths, the younger contingent from the same crew, equally paint and cement splashed, bodies leaner, flesh tight against muscle and bone, hair dusty with plaster and dirt. Five of them, leering and grinning, clucking tongues.

Beyond the three older men towards the back of the cafe, a young man with blue-black skin, cleaner and leaner, more reticent, more shy than all the other men. She noticed a gleam of perfect white teeth as he smiled warmly.

One guy on his own near the front – she must have breezed straight past him – the ashen-skinned loner in a crumpled suit, his tie pulled askew, his collar curling.

At the back of the bar, his body bent over the slot machine, stone-washed denims, jacket and jeans, another man, young and dark haired, but with a bald spot on the crown of his head.

Then last, the patron, slick and shiny, and full of overtures of control, the only one, really, with the right to address her. He lifts up the flap in the bar, growls rapid words at the men, particularly the younger ones, and gestures for her to sit in the empty booth.

She had planned a quick departure, to buy cigarettes then exit stage left not pursued by a bear, but perhaps with dogs, snakes and rats watching the switch of her tail as she went.

But the bartender is partly blocking her way, and his gesture is so theatrical, so kind, and he has swiftly put the other men in order. One by one they look away, go back to their conversations. He makes her feel safe, but also childlike.

She sits. The patron wipes the table in front of her, replaces the dirty ashtray, clears away the empty beer glasses. He has black hair, very straight and very fine, she can make out his scalp just below the lank hair. His hands are very large, meaty and pale, they remind her of wax.

He calls her Mademoiselle. He is respectful without being

obsequious as he takes her order. He brings her a brandy, an espresso and a packet of Marlboro, which he unwraps and offers to her, so she is forced to take a cigarette and smoke it at once. He returns to his station behind the bar and keeps a proprietorial eye on her. Perhaps he has a daughter her age. Or rather a daughter the age he assumes Lucy to be, perhaps twenty or twenty-one.

Lucy takes a sip of the brandy, holds the liquid in her mouth where it tingles and stings. On swallowing she shudders slightly.

She feels oddly peaceful – as if she were a princess surrounded by the men of her kingdom, knights and serfs and peasants, none of whom dare harm her.

The man in the crumpled suit gets up from his table and heads for the exit. His shoes are grey plastic loafers. She knows they are plastic as they have a split on one side which reveals a line of white sock. No one acknowledges his departure. She senses his loneliness; it hangs over him like a shabby miasma, presses his thin shoulders down, hunching his neck.

Behind her in the next booth, the young men are playing cards. She can hear, but not see, the way the cards are slapped down on the table top and the accompanying shouts.

The young black man walks toward her then stands just beyond her table. He looks nervously at the other men, but only the patron is paying any attention.

'*Anglais?*' the young man asks.

'*Oui,*' she says.

The bartender lifts his chin and turns the corners of his mouth down as if to ask her if she wants to be saved. She ignores his signal and smiles brightly at the young man with his gleaming black skin.

'You are English?' he says. His smile is wide; his teeth are even and very white. His track suit is bright red with crisp white stripes. Very new, she thinks.

Lucy nods.

'I am Joseph. I am learning to speak English,' he says proudly.

'Really,' she says, uncertain what else to say.

'You are here on vacation?' he asks. His pronunciation is good, the accent slightly American.

'Yes.'

'I am visiting here with my aunt's son,' he says. 'He is a paediatric surgeon. He has an emergeny now.'

'Ah,' she says.

'My other cousin is at the Royal Holloway Hospital. She is a gynaecologist and lives in Camden Town. Her father, my uncle, is a doctor in Paris.'

He does not make any move to sit at the table with her. Lucy can't think of anything to say but smiles in a slightly glazed way. She is aware that they are being watched and this makes her feel awkward, as if she were in a play and hasn't learned her lines.

'I am going to London to study medicine soon, I hope,' he says. Then abruptly, he adds, 'Goodbye. So long,' and returns to a booth near the back of the bar.

Perhaps she should have invited him to sit, or made a better attempt at conversation. She hopes he doesn't feel rebuffed. Hopes particularly that he doesn't feel rebuffed because he is black.

She swallows the espresso in three sips. It's thick and sweet. Takes another sip of brandy, doesn't shudder this time. Lights a cigarette. Thinks about the walk back to the hotel. Looks at her watch. It's almost midnight. She is surprised; she had thought it would only be ten or perhaps eleven. She should go.

She drinks the last of the brandy, finishes her cigarette, stubbing it out in the Cinzano ashtray. Then just as she uncrosses her legs in readiness to rise from the table, another brandy is placed before her by the patron. She frowns at him in confusion and he gestures towards the three older men at the bar. One of them has turned towards her; he lifts his glass as in a toast.

'Oh,' she says, embarrassed, but lifts the drink, nods and murmurs. '*Merci.*'

Behind her the younger men suddenly roar at the result of their card game. One swears, then laughs and gets up and walks past her. His pockets jangle with loose change. His body is long, but his legs are short and slightly bandy. As he nears her she can smell earth and putty.

One more brandy will not kill her, but she must refuse if another is offered.

She feels safe here amongst these working men. Feels a little ashamed of that frisson of fear she'd felt as she first entered. One should never make assumptions, or jump to conclusions. She should remember that.

Lights another cigarette. Looks at her watch again. Twelve-twenty.

# Underwater

When Marilyn was four years old she'd almost died.

She thought she could remember it, but wasn't certain if she had embroidered the memory – if part of it was what her mother had told her and the rest was a sort of flotsam and jetsam garnered from other sources: films and books. She seemed to remember moving or running awkwardly with her arms outstretched and there was a something she was determinedly heading for. This 'something' was a phenomenon she didn't understand, but wanted to explore. She moved closer. Water. That's what it was. Or more particularly water whose surface was covered with a carpet of green. Green like a floating carpet of grass that you could walk on.

Marilyn had tried at least ten times in her life to write a poem about this, but she always found the resultant verse to be mawkish and naïve. Too reminiscent of certain poems by Sylvia Plath. Or just plain clumsy. She did not fully understand why she kept returning to this subject.

But there again why had she so readily adopted her mother's interpretation of the event? For her mother it was always the day Marilyn nearly died. But she had only been in the water for a second or two at most, before her father, who had been right behind her all the way, plunged his hand into the pond, caught the back of her dungarees and plucked her out in an explosive spray of stagnant weeds and stinking water. It should only have been the day Marilyn fell in the pond.

Maybe that was why the poem would never work. Its premise was dishonest and she knew it.

And yet here she was sitting in the bedroom of their borrowed house in France, attempting the same subject again. This time however, partly because she was pregnant and partly because a few months before she'd seen that Nicholas Roeg film *Don't Look Now* for the first time, she was trying to write it from the point of view of her mother. To make it a poem about her mother's fear and hyperbole.

Occasionally she got up from her desk and went down the hall to check that she could still hear Aaron's heavy adenoidal breathing.

At other moments she went to the window and gazed out at the garden behind the house where there were apple, cherry and pear trees. And beyond them a greenhouse with tomatoes, peppers, cucumbers, herbs and other plants which were not in fruit and which she couldn't identify. Part of the deal with the house was that they would keep everything watered and tended. They had been told to help themselves to any of the fruit or vegetables they wanted, but Scott restricted them to a few string beans, an overripe tomato and the odd pinch of parsley or basil.

She wandered back to the table, picked up the small notebook with its scribbled out and overwritten words, and in a whisper, moving rhythmically around the room, she read the poem aloud.

My mother said, and said again,
that almost dead, my father, oh Polonius,
saved me from the stagnant pool.
Hyperbole, hangs heavy in the drowning
air around the Formica table.
You make a legend of me, Mother.
Amongst the Tupperware and easy mix,
the ennui of a winter evening...

She stopped mid-sentence. Displeased. Closed the notebook and placed it on the table. She went to the window again, rested her forehead on the cool surface of the glass, cupped her hands around her eyes in order to see into the darkness. Sighed.

Perhaps she was too tired to write tonight. Slightly jet-lagged still. She drifted away from the window, out of the room and, after a moment listening again to Aaron's breathing, went downstairs and switched on the TV. In the kitchen she poured herself a glass of milk and put three chocolate chip cookies on a plate, then carried both through to the living room where she curled up comfortably on the couch.

Using the remote, Marilyn flicked through the channels on the TV. French rap music over visuals of skateboarders on one channel, a news debate, a group of seven earnest intellectuals drinking and smoking in a gloomily lit studio on another, a black and white film – a French costume drama featuring foppish eighteenth-century men in lipstick that stained their mouths black. An advert for a car. A soap opera, a woman in high-waisted jeans and big backcombed hair crying, then running from a room, slamming the door so hard that the wall shuddered. Then, at last, a Woody Allen film dubbed into French. Perfect.

Marilyn breaks the first biscuit into four pieces. Licks her forefinger and uses it to capture a stray crumb of chocolate, lets it melt on her tongue. Takes four long glugs of the cool creamy milk, feels something close to rapture as it fills her mouth, slips down her throat. And the film, *Annie Hall*, she sees, has only just begun.

Life is actually rather perfect. Just as long as Aaron doesn't wake up and if Scott doesn't come home and insist on watching the news.

Halfway through the film, Marilyn took the empty glass and the plate out to the kitchen. Back in the living room she switched off the main overhead light and put on the small table lamp. She arranged the pillows on the sofa so that she could prop herself up comfortably on them while she watched the rest of the film. After ten minutes she pulled the grey mohair throw from the back of the sofa and draped it over herself.

She had no plan to fall asleep. She must have been half-dazed with sleep to even think this. Woody Allen and Dianne Keaton were attempting to cook lobsters. Marilyn shifted her body on the couch so that her head was now on the cushion. She closed one eye and continued to watch, then during the commercial break decided to close the other eye just until the film started again.

# Innocence

Why had he said that to her?

Those crude cruel words to that strange girl. Or not girl, but woman.

Not that it seemed to faze her.

Thinking about it, Scott pictured Marilyn finding out what he had said. Overhearing his words, 'I let strange women follow me, then I fuck them...'

'I was being ironic, Marilyn,' he finds himself thinking in his defence.

He imagined her eyes upon him, judging him.

'Hey, you think it's only women who have to deal with predators? How do you think men feel when women throw themselves at them? Offer it on a plate? Say no and you're some weak sexless pussy who can't get a hard on. Say yes and then she's got you – you're snared.'

'But, Scott,' the Marilyn in his imagination said, 'you were the one who brought up the subject of sex, not her. Why didn't you just ignore her?'

'Because...' Even in this imagined conversation he does not want to admit to Marilyn that the young woman had aroused him. She wouldn't understand.

There had been a moment as he sat with the English girl when Scott thought it possible that she might invite him back to her hotel. That he might accept and once there they would have wild abandoned sex with no recriminations, no emotional ties. They would be two strangers pounding it out for the pure pleasure of it. Wasn't that why she'd followed him?

He kept picturing it in his head as he sat with her; this pretty little blonde in bed with her head thrown back, her legs wrapped around his back, moaning and grunting in rhythm with his thrusts. Her mouth tasting of cigarettes.

She sat there coolly pouring wine into her glass, catching his eye, then quickly looking away again. A part of his mind – the id according to Freud – continued to play out various pornographic scenarios even as he carefully smoothed out the three-day-old newspaper.

His words to her, about her following him and about fucking had been a challenge – to himself as much as to her. But he knew he wasn't really that kind of guy and that was why he stood up so abruptly to filch the paper. He was avoiding her response.

Then he'd sat it out, his imagination running riot, until he couldn't take it any longer and he'd walked away from her – a man still faithful to his wife – as long as one discounted thought.

'Who's the girl?' Florian had asked Scott.

'Oh, a friend of Marilyn's. Well, not a friend exactly. Acquaintance.'

Florian had craned his neck to get a better look at her. She was still there, tilting her head back to drain her glass, then tracing her thumb over the corner of her mouth, her lower lip.

'Not bad,' Florian said. 'She married? Got a boyfriend?'

Scott shrugged.

'You gonna introduce me?' Florian half slid off his stool and stood holding his beer, ready to go out, to be set up, though Scott wasn't sure if he was teasing him. 'What's her name?' Florian was resting one hand on Scott's shoulder, staring at him expectantly and grinning. That was when Scott saw her walk away.

'Too late, my friend,' he said and he felt relieved.

Florian misunderstood. 'You dog,' he said with a mixture of envy and pride at Scott's conquest. He took 'too late' to mean that Scott had already marked that particular territory.

Scott did not disabuse him of the notion, except to say, 'It's not like that.'

Suzette, who had been standing next to him during this exchange, understood Scott's final words on the subject to mean that it wasn't just lust, but that he had deeper feelings towards the young blonde woman, that he loved her, whoever she was. Which was in Suzette's opinion beautiful and tragic, as she knew that Scott was married and was, no doubt, an essentially good and loyal man.

As Suzette herself had, not so long ago, had a love affair with a married man, she thought she understood the complexities of the situation. Its inherent sadness and impossibilities.

Florian downed the last of his beer, banged his glass on the counter and called for more drinks. He turned to look at the blonde woman again, but she had gone, her chair was standing empty, pushed back at an angle from the table.

'Drink?' Florian said to Scott when the barman came to take his order.

'Yeah,' said Scott, 'why not?'

Drowning his sorrows, Suzette thought, maybe the girl had ended the affair. Or given him an ultimatum – it's me or her? Choose. I can't go on like this. How can you say that you love two people? It isn't possible.

Suzette had rehearsed these words many times, but never found the courage to speak them. Her last lover, Bertrand Severin, had been a married policeman with three children. His wife's family was very well off. How can you make demands of such a man? You cannot, so you bite your lip and take such pleasure as you find.

The affair had ended seven months ago. He had been promoted and gone to live in a small town in the south. She did not even possess a photograph of him. In time she would forget his face, as he, no doubt, had already forgotten hers.

Florian offered Suzette a drink.

She accepted, and took off the long white apron she had been wearing, rolled it up into a ball and stuffed it into her bag.

Suzette had worked part-time at the bar for eight years and it was here that she'd first met Bertrand.

She turned to Scott, 'Will it be snowing in Canada now?' she asked. A stupid question, but that was always how she pictured Canada, as a country of endless snow like Greenland.

Scott laughed. 'Good God, I hope not, not at this time of the year. You know, last winter we had some of the worst blizzards for years,' and he involuntarily pictured himself as a teenager trapped inside his childhood home, his mother fretting about Aaron's medicine, the phone lines down. His father muttering darkly about the weight of snow on the roof. He'd been thirteen and he thought he'd go crazy if he couldn't get out and blow off some steam. He hadn't always had such a short fuse when he felt bored or trapped. Cabin fever was accurately named – that raging, restless, burning madness. No one else in the family seemed to suffer from it. As long as there was food – his mother's store cupboard could withstand many months before anyone starved. As long as the roof held out. As long as Aaron had his medicine.

'At least we've got each other,' his mother used to be fond of saying. Then when the electricity failed, she'd get the storm lanterns and the board games out of the cupboard. His father would throw another log on the fire and suggest they toast marshmallows. Aaron would stand rocking from side to side staring at the wallpaper over by the door. Nothing changed for Aaron.

Why was it that at the age of six, at nine, at twelve even, Scott had actually enjoyed being snowed in with his family, but as soon as he hit thirteen it became some sort of exquisite and personal hell?

'It's a big enough country, isn't it?' Suzette said. She wanted Scott to tell her stories about Canada, about snowstorms and bears and narrow escapes from wolves. About vast iced-over lakes and soaring mountains. Or at least to keep talking.

'Yeah, it's big,' he said. 'Big and empty.'

He took a thoughtful sip of beer. Did not turn to look at Suzette, but gazed once more into the mirror behind the bar and the blue-black sky and yellow street lights that were reflected in it.

Suzette had no more questions about Canada, or none that she wished to say aloud.

Florian looked at Suzette; three weeks ago she had invited him back to her flat. They had drunk tequila together, biting into oranges between shots instead of limes. He had not expected her to suddenly kiss him, but she did. And had wordlessly taken his hand and drawn him into her bedroom. But in the morning he'd had to get up early and was slightly hung-over. She hadn't given him her number. He hadn't asked, nor given her his. It was his mother's birthday so he'd gone to dinner with her and his two aunts that evening, though he'd really wanted to see Suzette again. The night after that he'd gone to the bar to see her, but it was her day off. Then, for some reason or another, he couldn't get to the bar for another three days, and the next time he tried she was again not working. More than a week had passed before he finally saw her at the bar, but it was unusually busy and Jacques was in a foul temper. When Florian caught her eye Suzette barely looked at him. He took the hint and left after just one drink.

Then someone told him that Suzette was having an affair with a cop. Their information was slightly out of date, so they used the present tense. Florian had crossed paths with the law too many times to risk upsetting one of their number.

Suzette had expected to see Florian at the bar the night after they'd slept together but he didn't show. No one told her that he'd asked for her on two subsequent nights. Oh well, she thought, he really isn't interested. We were drunk. It was just a bit of fun for him, nothing more.

She felt hurt, but was determined not to show it.

Florian also felt hurt – he'd thought she'd really liked him, and now here was Suzette, the policeman's mistress, hanging around long after her shift had finished making a play for the Canadian guy.

He misunderstood her smiles and playful glances, could not understand why she kept catching his eye instead of Scott's. It was as though she was trying to wind him up or something.

For Suzette, Scott was only an excuse to stay and talk to Florian. She did not understand why Florian kept slapping Scott on the back, calling him a dog and winking. Even though, when talking about the blonde girl, Scott had said clearly 'it's not like that', Florian was determined it was; that men were dogs and women were presumably bitches and there was no such thing as love.

And yet, she could not forget how tender Florian had been that warm night almost a month ago, the way he had kissed her, touched her, smiled and said her name.

They hadn't been that drunk. No, she remembered it all very well.

Scott got up and went to the toilets at the back of the bar.

'Florian?' Suzette said. She had plucked up her courage, was about to ask him why he had avoided her, hadn't their night together meant anything to him? But as he turned to face her, the two last customers who'd been sitting outside came in. Jacques was at the other end of the bar polishing glasses with a cloth. The customers hovered at her side; the man with his worn and florid face, and Panama hat, the woman with her long white hair and overlarge bosom, her silver and turquoise jewellery, her sensible sandals.

'Can we settle the bill?' the man said to Suzette, even though she had taken off her apron and was obviously off duty. They were holding hands, she noticed, and this touched her heart.

'One moment,' she said, as she slipped from her stool and went around to the other side of the bar. She found their bill and took their money. The tip they left was exactly ten per cent. Her heart froze over again.

Scott came back from the toilet, drank the last of his beer and asked what time it was.

Florian looked at his watch and said, 'Twelve-fifteen,' then nodding at Scott's empty glass, added, 'another?'

'Well…' Scott said. He had been about to say that he should be on his way, that his wife was waiting up, but then he realised that it was his round and he should buy Florian a drink. In a curious tone of voice that overlapped reluctance with certainty, he said, 'Yeah, but I'm buying.'

Florian put his hands up in mock defeat. 'Fine by me,' he said. 'I'll have a cognac.'

'And you?' Scott asked Suzette.

'Thanks, I'll have a cognac too.'

'Three cognacs,' Scott said to Jacques, 'and one for yourself?'

The four of them talked amiably, Jacques keeping to his side of the counter, smoking an aromatically scented Turkish cigar. Scott sat very upright on his stool, his back straight, his long legs bent at a sharp angle, his heels hooked over the cross bar of the stool. Suzette propped one elbow on the counter and sat in such a way that her leg touched Florian's. Without meaning to, and not really thinking about it, Florian rested his hand on Suzette's knee and as soon as he did, she put her hand on top of his. He turned his hand over so that their palms met, and their fingers, those on her right hand and those on his left, intertwined with one another and formed a knot.

Occasionally, when Jacques was careless with the direction of his exhaled cigar smoke, Scott drew back his head and waved a hand in front of his face. Suzette and Florian had grown very quiet. Jacques was talking rapidly about the latest corruption scandal to afflict a local politician, none of which meant anything to Scott.

He guessed that it was now almost one o'clock, and despite it being their annual vacation, the next morning at seven, if not before, Aaron would be awake and he would have to be persuaded into the bathroom, nagged into eating, wrestled into dressing, and Scott and Marilyn would at times gaze at each other hollow-eyed and exhausted, each of them wondering what they were doing, whether it was worth the effort and for how many years this would go on?

Scott stood up, stretched and caught another face-full of cigar smoke. Coughed and wafted it away. He paid and wished them all good night. They stayed there; all three of them, lazy, malingering, easy and relaxed with one another. Jacques was refilling their glasses with more cognac as Scott pulled the door shut behind him. He glanced back at the brightly lit café as he walked away and saw for one moment in his mind's eye a poster Marilyn had pinned to the wall of the tiny cold-water flat she'd been living in when he first met her. It was a painting of a night café, empty streets, empty people. The same image had been on the cover of a book about loneliness he'd read at about the same time. The difference as he saw it now was that the people in the painting had been closed off from one another with no hope of reprieve or succour; while here in this café in a small town in France something else was going on. Something else altogether.

# Changes

Lucy feels calm for the first time in many days. Or not just calm, but peaceful, as if the rest of the world had melted away and there was only this small café, with these clusters of men whom she had not trusted at first but now felt an obligation to. The obligation was, of course, only to sit there for a decent amount of time as she finished her brandy.

It seemed a long time since she ate at La Coquille Bleue. And an even longer time since, after an hour at the beach, she stood under the shower in her hotel room feeling the grittiness of sand on the tiled floor.

Earlier that day Lucy had explored a small side street. Or not a side street but a cobbled alleyway with a drainage trench cut down its centre. On one side was the back entrance to a restaurant, the clatter of pots and pans being washed could be clearly heard and someone inside was whistling a pretty but repetitive tune that she recognised but could not name. At the furthest corner of the lane was a little shop with a profusion of old china and lace and porcelain dolls prettily arranged in its small window. Lucy pushed the door open, setting off an old-fashioned brass bell that jangled violently. A woman of around forty years of age looked up from a walnut bureau near the back of the shop. She was sewing something small and delicate, black velvet with jet buttons. She was repairing it, in order to sell it, that much Lucy surmised, and also that the woman was happy, at peace with herself. Content.

'*Bonjour!*' Lucy said.

The woman replied warmly, then her eyes fell to her handiwork again and Lucy understood that she was free to browse at will. She was cautious at first about touching anything, but some objects proved to be irresistible; a beaded purse with subtle chevron patterns, a stylised pink satin elephant, a tiny silver rocking chair that Lucy set moving very gently with a little push.

There were so many shelves to explore and she wanted to see everything. And the more she looked and lingered the more she felt she ought to buy something, wanted to buy something. There was such a delicious rush at the thought of alighting on the perfect object, of possessing it, capturing it, then bringing it back to her hotel room and putting it in a place of honour, where she could admire it.

She had felt a little like this when she had bought all her new clothes, the thrill of spending money recklessly, the sense of the changes she was making. The old cautious self cast off, her new self an adventurer.

She picked up a heavy black canvas collar that was decorated with brightly coloured glass beads, cowry shells and silver coins. It looked African, yet the coins showed an oriental-looking lion on one side, Arabic script on the other.

Then she came to a ceramic bowl that was brightly – even garishly painted in shades of burnt orange, lime green and glorious golden sunflower yellow.

Nothing bore a price tag in the shop so Lucy had hesitated until now to ask how much anything was, but she found herself bearing the bowl aloft in both hands to catch the shopkeeper's attention.

The woman, who must have been keeping a subtle eye on her customer all along, responded by holding up ten fingers.

Leaving the shop with the wrapped bowl cradled in her arms, Lucy felt she must have cheated the woman in some way. Ten Euros for such an exquisite object! In London it would have cost so much more. No doubt it wasn't terribly old or valuable, but so beautiful, so bright and cheerful. She would buy fruit to put in it:

peaches and apricots and pears. And she would return to the shop in another day or so, she would find other treasures in other shops. She would discover where and when the flea markets were held and she would buy pictures, mirrors, old tin toys, vintage clothes.

Back in her room she had unwrapped the bowl and put it on the chest of drawers and filled it with the fruit she'd bought, then she sat on the bed to admire it. She remembered, distantly and a little indistinctly, a postcard a friend had sent her long ago: a painting of a Japanese doll seated on a large round dining table, an ivory-coloured box with a duck-egg blue lining behind the doll and other objects scattered nearby. And the room beyond, with its small window, was painted in tones so muted it almost became a flat plane of mere smudges, as if the room had been invaded by a dense fog. For a long time Lucy had kept that card propped up on a mantelpiece in a room in a shared house in Glasgow. Then, between one thing and another, moving to another house, going home to her parents, her 'breakdown', the postcard had been lost. It was there in the background in a snapshot she'd taken of three friends posing in absurd fancy dress before they'd set out for the street party. They'd all taken magic mushrooms that night and their expressions were exaggerated, crazy, the little picture of the Japanese doll the only sober and steady thing in the room. Then it was lost and she could not remember who had painted it.

She got off the bed and took a peach from the bowl, bit in. Sweet perfumed juice poured over her hand and dripped down her chin.

Sight, smell, touch, taste; all these senses were filled. Only her ears were denied in this orgy of pleasure, the near silence of the room could be, at times, quite maddening.

And so, out.

She has drunk quite a bit; red wine, a glass of *Pastis* with water, more red wine, a brandy, an espresso and now here in front of her on the table another brandy, half of it already in her stomach.

She gazes at the double seat opposite, dirty mustard-coloured leatherette, a mirror image of the one she is sitting on. When she has left the café the two will reflect one another more perfectly without the interruption of her form.

She is thinking too much, too deeply, too drunkenly. She remembers other times when her mind seemed to hone in on a subject, to shine upon it brightly, to seek and find illumination. Then darkness. As when she was working on an essay on the Scottish designer and architect, Charles Rennie Mackintosh.

Form and function were part of it, which she had vaguely been aware of as she began to write her essay. That's the funny thing, her life as she looks at it is bisected by Charles Rennie and his furniture and architecture. He didn't really cause her to have a breakdown, he just happened to be there at the exact centre of it. He was all around her too, anyone studying art in Glasgow was in his thrall as he'd designed the building.

She can remember the sense of being both connected to the world and outside of it. Aware of dazzling beauty while being terrorised by it.

A friend, Noel, had been giving her big white capsules which he filched from his parents' house. He told her they helped you focus your mind, gave you all this energy and allowed you to stay up all night and oh, yes, an extra bonus for chicks (his words) you'd lose weight too. Lose weight and lose your mind.

She did both.

Her life before. Her life after.

Once you have gone mad, had a breakdown, stared into the abyss, you are always afraid it will happen again. But will you know?

And if you decide to go on holiday alone, to dye your hair

blonde and buy a whole new wardrobe of clothes, does this mean you are going mad? No, of course not. It was a form of renewal. Of rebirth. It was healthy. Invigorating.

If Thom walked in here now, Lucy thought, if somehow, by some weird chain of coincidence he happened to come to France, to this town, and this bar, he would not recognise me. He would stare at me. He wouldn't be able to stop himself. And he would desire me. There would be recognition and confusion in his eyes. I'd smile at him, nice white teeth, looking even whiter because of the red lipstick I'm wearing, and he would smile back hesitantly at first, then pow! He'd get it.

'Lucy! Oh my God, Lucy. You look ... You are...'

He'd move closer. All the other men in the bar would pay attention, they'd be witnesses, the enthralled audience seeing this beautiful moment in the love story of Lucy and Thom.

'Lucy. You look beautiful!'

Was that all she wanted really? Just for Thom to notice her again? So that she could feel whole again. Because, the truth be told, for some time she'd been feeling not only taken for granted, but invisible. Invisible in the way that the objects which surround us every day are. We see them and we don't see them. Walls, kettles, pictures, the window and what's beyond it, the bed, the bathroom sink, the tube of toothpaste, the chairs arranged at the dining table, one, two, three, four. A chair is a chair is a chair.

Unless it's concocted by Charles Rennie Mackintosh, in which case its regular, centuries-old, tried and tested dimensions are stretched and distorted out of all proportion.

It is the human body which dictates the particular form a chair takes. It is the human form which governs the scale of architecture. You don't mess with a chair unless there is a reason to – think of scaled-down chairs for children, or the high chairs that umpires at tennis matches sit on, or the ones designed for lifeguards at the beach. Or electric chairs for killing people, with straps and wires and God knows what else attached.

Lucy sipped the last drops of brandy slowly. She savoured it and thought that if someone offered her another she'd take it only if she then struck up a conversation. Maybe.

Or maybe she'd be good and begin her walk back to the hotel.

Or, and this is what she would have done if she was back in London, she'd hail a passing cab. Except that this small town didn't seem to have marked cabs, and certainly not black London cabs, cruising the streets waiting for a fare.

So she'd walk. It wasn't far anyway. If it was cold she'd put her cardigan on. She'd walk briskly, which would warm her up, and as a woman walking alone after midnight, the briskness was essential anyway.

The last mouthful of brandy. Not a mouthful at all. The last dregs which seemed to dissolve on her tongue and disappear rather than be swallowed.

She put the glass down on the table. Took her cardigan from the top of her bag and put it around her shoulders, loosely tying the arms together to keep it in place. She put her cigarettes in her bag, along with the matchbook Scott had given her. She wriggled out of the booth and stood at the end of the counter waiting to pay.

Standing up and walking four yards to the counter had set off renewed waves of interest among the men. Some just looked at her in that interested disinterested way; the way they might take in the sleek lines of a flashy car they happened to see parked in the street. One of the younger men managed to catch her eye and he licked his lips.

The bartender raised both of his hands in the air to show his distress.

'You are leaving us?' he said.

The older man at the bar, the one who had bought her a drink, said something in angry quick-fire French to the man behind the bar.

The bartender nodded, his expression had grown serious.

Lucy was certain that the subject of this debate was her. The two men talked back and forth. She stood nearby with a twenty euro note held aloft in a meaningful way.

A phone rang. A mobile trill. Familiar. The Simpsons' theme tune. Then, near her, movement. The young African, in one gesture, retrieved his phone from his pocket, flicked it open and moved past her towards the door. She heard a voice; a retreating refrain, the language animated, happy, a language that was not French, not English, but the language of home. His home.

Her attention was momentarily torn in several directions. The African, his familiar cartoon ringtone, the bartender ignoring her need to pay, the older guy with splashes of plaster, cement, dirt on his clothes. As she scanned the room, her gaze fell on one of the younger labourers as he leaned back in the booth, shuffling the deck of cards, and his eyes bored into her, eating her, travelling boldly up and down her whole being; eyes, mouth, neck, tits, ass, legs then back to eyes again.

Outside sitting on the window ledge, the back of his red tracksuit flattened out and creased on the glass, lit from within, darkness around and beyond him, the young African.

'Excuse me!' she said, leaning over the bar, waggling her twenty euro note, deliberately ignoring the younger guy's eyes.

'Ah sorry, sorry. Our friend here is concerned for your safety. You have far to go?'

'Oh.' Lucy was embarrassed and at the same time irritated. Their concern was touching, but it also reminded her of her vulnerability. Reminded her that she was prey, was object, not subject. Was little girl lost. 'I'll be fine,' she said, 'but perhaps I could call a cab?'

The bartender looked sympathetic, conveyed what she had said to the big guy as if he could not understood her schoolgirl French. They debated some more.

Lucy suddenly feels self-conscious. Raw. With edges that bleed.

'Hey, listen, I'll be fine,' she says. 'Can I just settle up?'

'You want a cab?'

'No, no, really. My hotel is just a few minutes away.'

The big old guy shifts himself, moves off the stool he's been glued to all night, puts a big paw on her arm. The fingers are as rough as sandpaper. She reacts. She overreacts. Badly. Flinches, steps away. She has insulted him.

'I'll be fine,' she says again, puts the twenty on the counter, turns on her heel, takes a step, then hesitates and turns back to the two men. 'Sorry,' she whispers in English, then shakes her head. 'Thank you. I'll be fine.' Head up, bag over shoulder, heels clicking over the wooden floor. The sound of her coming, the sound of her going.

Then she's out, into the night.

# The Running Man

Joseph felt as if he might burst with happiness. He sat on the ledge of the café wishing there was someone he could share his news with. His mother had rung to tell him that his application for funding had been successful. In just a few months his college education would begin. He had been accepted to read medicine and science at London University. His cousin had promised that he could stay with her in Camden Town. She'd sent him a photo of the house her flat was in. It was white with two fluted columns on either side of a front door which was painted a glossy kingfisher blue colour. The house loomed in his imagination, four storeys high with two large windows on each floor and an azure London sky above. He imagined himself seated by one of the windows, glancing up from a weighty book to watch a passing cloud – himself transformed and transforming – a doctor, a healer, goodness passing from his skilful surgeon's fingers to end suffering.

He set off walking slowly and thoughtfully. He felt as if he was airless, floating. He had not gone very far when behind him he heard the sharp echoing sound of footsteps. He turned and saw the English girl he had spoken to earlier, coming out of the bar. She hadn't been very friendly; she had stared at him blankly when he attempted to strike up a conversation. Which was a pity, as now more than ever he needed to practise his English.

She was walking rapidly in the opposite direction. He wondered why a young woman like that would be alone. It didn't make sense to him.

He was about to turn and resume walking when he saw a white object fall softly from the girl's shoulders. He fully expected her to notice this, but she didn't. She adjusted the bag on her shoulder and continued her brisk walk. The white garment lay in a ghost-like heap on the pavement as she hurried off.

Without thinking Joseph ran after her. He was a good runner, had won several medals for his sprinting. He passed the bar and some way beyond it retrieved the fallen white object. It was soft and light and still slightly warm from her skin. He found himself bringing it up to his face, burying his nose in it, breathing in its sweet floral scent.

The sound of her heels clicking over the pavement was rapidly retreating. He looked up and could no longer see her. He sprinted in the direction she had gone. His footsteps, even when running at speed, were almost completely silent, and his breathing was easy and not even slightly ragged or laboured.

He shouted, 'Hey!' and picked up his pace. He crossed two minor roads, quickly glancing up each narrow avenue as he went to see if he could spot her. When he came to a third, he stopped running. He gazed about him in all directions. He strained to hear her footsteps, but there was only the electrical fizz of the streetlight, the occasional sound of a car, then the furious buzz of a motorbike zipping past at high speed as the driver's powder-blue cotton blouson jacket puffed up with air.

Joseph gave up. He was uncertain as to what he should do with the cardigan. He turned it over in his hands, inspecting it, wondering if perhaps there was a pocket and inside it some clue to the owner's identity or where she had gone. But there was no pocket, only a label that read 'Monsoon' which made him think of thunderous rain, the beauty and boundless energy of it, its transforming power.

He resumed his slow walk, uncertainly holding the cardigan loosely bunched in one hand. When he thought he'd reached the approximate place where the young woman had lost the cardigan, he spread it out carefully over a low hedge of red-flowered shrubs, so it could be easily seen.

He forgot about the girl and her lost cardigan almost immediately, let his mind fill with visions of his future life again, wished he could speed up time until he arrived at October and everything that that promised.

# Liberty, Fraternity, Equality

In the bar Jean Laurens continued the argument with his old friend and customer Louis, about the young English woman who had just left. Louis was of the opinion that she should not have been allowed to leave at that hour unaccompanied. Jean reminded him that he was only a bar owner and had no authority over any of his customers, except the authority to refuse them service or throw them out. He cited the principle of liberty to defend his actions. Louis countered by reminding him of fraternity which he said must for any true Frenchman also include the protection of his sisters. Then darkly, Louis mentioned the prostitute who had been found murdered just three weeks ago. Her body was discovered near some industrial bins at the back of the manufacturing works on the Rue de Touvier.

Jean does not want to think about that. He is angry with Louis. He understands that Louis has five daughters, that the eldest is now fourteen and becoming a beautiful young woman. He understands his fears, but that dead woman was a prostitute. Yes, her life is no less valuable, but that was the risk she took, wasn't it? It went with the territory.

Thinking about this and unwilling to look at Louis, whose eyes seem to accuse him of some failure of courage or will, Jean turned his gaze towards the window at the front of the bar. The glass seemed even more fragile somehow, unable to quite hold at bay the blackness of the night. As he looked a figure ran past at speed, moving from right to left. A flash of scarlet from head to toe, white stripes marking out the pumping arms and legs, like diagrams designed to illustrate the workings of human locomotion.

It was the polite young African man who'd been in the bar a few days that week. The one who smiled so readily and so happily that you'd swear he'd never known a moment of pain or suffering his whole life. Jean did not have a clue as to why the young man was racing along the street outside his bar. He was dressed to go running, that was for sure, in his expensive track suit and flashy white and silver trainers. But Jean knew there were thousands, or more likely millions, of young people the world over who dressed like this, only to slouch on street corners and trudge to the employment exchange to draw their state benefit. At least one of them was getting some use out of the ergonomically built shoes, the carefully designed cloth which absorbed sweat and let your skin breathe and protected you from dangerous levels of ultra violet light.

But there again, Jean thought, who runs at night? And he remembered the fascist tendencies of a small minority of the town's disenfranchised kids and the dripping silver swastika spray-painted on the railway bridge near the school. A swastika after what France had suffered during the war!

He kept his eyes on the window, imagining a mob of skinheads appearing, streaking across the night from right to left, a pack of filthy hounds in pursuit, hungry for any blood they deemed less pure than their own.

Jean kept a revolver hidden under the bar, loaded and ready. He imagined himself grabbing it, running out into the night. One warning shot should stop them, and if not? Well then he'd give the scum just what they deserved.

He frowned and tensed his muscles. He was no coward. But no one else ran past the window. A minute passed, then strolling peacefully by, with not a care in the world, went one of the waitresses from the café up the road. A skinny slightly bow-legged guy who was not much taller than her walked by her side with his hand around her waist measuring the dip and swell of her body. They stopped right in front of his window and began to kiss one another. Jean looked away.

'I am sorry,' Louis said. 'You do not see the world as I see it. With a father's eyes.'

Jean grunted and merely nodded. No point getting tangled up in the argument again. No point reminding Louis that he too was a father.

He looked out of the window again. The waitress and her lover had gone.

He felt tired suddenly, and wished with all his heart that he was young again.

'Another beer?' he asked Louis.

'On the house?'

'Yeah, on the house,' Jean replied, and shrugged as if to show he didn't care either way.

# Finders Keepers

Suzette and Florian could hardly keep their hands off one another. They walked towards Suzette's apartment in stops and starts. They were eager to get there, but somehow had to stop every few yards to kiss.

Florian's kisses were every bit as good and tender as she remembered. And his eyes when he looked at her showed, she was certain, not only lust but something more, or at least the beginning of something more.

Suzette had wasted too many good years on that no good cop, Bertrand. She should have known he'd never leave his wife. All those lies about not even sleeping with her anymore, and the last Suzette had heard of him, his wife was pregnant again with their fourth child.

She had thought she was satisfied with the slow and secretive crumbs of happiness she'd got when she was with Bertrand. But they were nothing; as insubstantial as a communion wafer that melts on your tongue. It was either a morsel of rice paper or the body of Christ depending on your belief. When she had believed Bertrand's words about love, about the new start they would make, about his divorce and his stories of the endless cold nights he spent sleeping on the sofa, she had seen their few brief moments together as a taste of what was to come. Now she saw things differently and thought ruefully of how she had been lied to. Fooled and used, distracted from what should have been the proper course of her life, namely to fall in love with a man nearer her own age, to get married and start a family of her own.

And now here was Florian – a man from the wrong side of the tracks, who had (or so she'd heard) a shady past – gazing at her with such honesty, who could kiss her in the middle of the street or openly hold her hand or squeeze her waist without looking over his shoulder, without an ounce of fear or guilt or regret.

They walked at a fast pace, their strides matching one another's, their arms entangled. Stopped. Kissed. Walked. Stopped again.

It reminded Suzette of when she was thirteen or fourteen and had first discovered boys and along with boys her own first feelings of desire. How it felt in the pit of her stomach, flip-flopping. So much of the kissing and groping was conducted outdoors. In alleyways, under bridges, in graveyards, sitting on benches near the tennis courts, lying in fields near her house. The endless, endless kissing. The cool hands snaking clumsily over her back, over her ribs, her belly. Herself allowing just so much. Never going so far as taking any clothes off, but things got disarrayed, unclipped, tugged, unzipped, twisted. Poor boys, she thought, remembering how satisfying it had been to feel the hard press of them against her and how she would never ever touch them no matter how they begged and cajoled.

Kissing Florian on the street was like that. It was even better than that first night they'd got together.

They walked again. Stopped and kissed. Breathless.

'Let's go up there,' she said and pointed to a narrow alleyway between a restaurant and a general store. The ground there was cobbled; a narrow drain ran down its centre like a vein. But as the two of them looked and were tempted, a rotund man in chef's whites came out and threw a bucket of foamy greyish water onto the ground sending up a cloud of steam.

Suzette giggled. 'Oop-la. Not such a good idea eh?'

'You crazy girl,' Florian said, and kissed her again.

They were only a few streets away from Suzette's place. It normally only took her ten or fifteen minutes at most, but this walk had taken much longer, not that she was complaining.

As they passed the Café de Trois, Suzette noticed something

draped over the geranium tubs outside. It was a white cardigan with small shell buttons. Very pretty. Someone had placed it on the plant as if it were a gift for whoever happened to be passing.

'How strange,' Suzette said, picking it up. It felt good in her hands, soft and natural. She, who had spent most of her young life in nasty squeaky, staticky acrylic sweaters, thought she knew fine wool when she saw it, knew for certain when she touched it.

The cardigan wasn't damp or dirty and when she sniffed at it suspiciously, she only detected a lingering scent of something like Yves St Laurent's Babydoll perfume. One of her favourite scents, but she could never afford it.

'For me,' she said and held it against herself so that Florian could see how pretty she would look in it.

'For you,' he said, confirming not only what she'd said, but also his perfectly matched moral system. Neither had any qualms about taking the cardigan. The orbit of a star had made a happy alignment that night, bringing Florian and Suzette together, and giving Suzette this beautiful gift. If he could find a general store open this late, Florian would buy a scratch card, his luck was obviously in.

# Storytelling

As he walked back to the house, Scott was still preoccupied by thoughts of Aaron; of the future and (much as he tried to bat it away) the past.

He hadn't told Marilyn what the social services had said about the choices concerning Aaron; the threat of a residential home, or the suggestion that either Aaron come to live with them, or that he and Marilyn move in with his parents and brother.

Marilyn worked as a part-time sub-editor for a tiny and increasingly embattled independent publishing company. The work at times frustrated her as she would have liked to be more involved with some of the decision making, but she was loyal and ambitious and determined to stick it out and make her mark.

'I'll give it another six months, then I'll tell him that I want a promotion. I won't insist on a pay rise, that's not the point, but I just don't think he is getting the best from me. He's overlooking the fact that I have ideas and talent and, oh, just so much more to give.'

Scott had responded soothingly, although for himself he could not understand why anyone would ask for more responsibility without the reward of higher wages. Especially when her sub-editor's salary was not much more than that of a hat-check girl or waitress. Less if you figured in tips.

But then Marilyn was different. She wrote poetry and strange little stories, some of which had been published here and there in what to him were obscure magazines that you never saw on sale anywhere. Except at those quirky independent bookshops she loved so much. Ramshackle places on beaten-down streets that usually sold dream-catchers and elaborate handcrafted jewellery and pottery alongside the books, and which had bulletin boards advertising book groups and classes in creative writing and shamanism, and had an in-house tarot reader.

Every time one of these independents went under Marilyn was as upset as if a beloved and eccentric aunt had died.

He did not understand that part of her life, but loved her for it all the same, and listened thoughtfully when she read one of her new poems to him and always tried to latch onto some particular phrase or description in order to make a positive comment about it.

She could trace almost every part of her life through her writing. It was all there, her childhood; memories of kindergarten, breaking her arm when she was seven and fell off her bike, falling in love the first time with a boy named Simon, her underage drinking, the way a black squirrel looked when she watched it fly and scamper through a leafless tree and how that had frightened her. The fright, she explained when he asked about it, was existentialist, she compared it to Munch's painting of 'The Scream'. The analogy didn't help him much and some people might have found it inflated, pretentious, but he loved her so he put his cynicism aside. And he and his love for her and hers for him, their words, their lovemaking, all of it entered the pantheon of her life and experiences, was memorialised and fixed, and given a permanence in her writing that he sometimes found unnerving.

Perhaps, were it not for this confessional habit of hers, he might have confessed to her that strange dream or memory that persistently haunted him. The one that would not leave him, and found him forever standing malevolently and guiltily over his younger brother's cot, his boyhood pillow in his hands, the Lone Ranger on his prancing horse about to gallop off to right wrongs and undo evil. What kind of story or poem would Marilyn have created out of that?

It was just as well he'd never told her. Just as he would not mention his bitter exchange with the strange young English woman.

Sleeping dogs are best left sleeping.

But sooner or later he would have to discuss what had been said about Aaron. About his future, their future.

As he neared the house, he saw that a light was still on in the front room though the hall was in darkness. He entered quietly, closing the front door carefully behind him and calling out in a soft voice, 'Mar? Mar. It's me.'

She did not answer. He could hear the sound of the TV and see a slit of pale yellow light under the door to the living room. He walked softly over and opened it. The TV screen glowed bright green and men raced over it like so many ants. A football match. He knew immediately that she must have fallen asleep on the couch, and sure enough, when he peered over its back, there she was curled up with the woollen throw half covering her body. Her lips were partly opened, and the sound of her breathing barely perceptible. She never snored, though at times she spoke in her sleep, giving vent to strange phrases and anxieties. Once he had heard her say in a dismayed voice 'but the fish won't drink lemonade'. In the morning he'd told her about it and recently, just a few days before they'd left for France, she'd heard that her poem, 'The Fish Won't Drink Lemonade', had been accepted for publication in an anthology of poems for children.

He gazed at her, wondering whether to wake her so that she could get to bed and go to sleep again, or whether to leave her in peace. Gently he rearranged the throw so that it covered her shoulders, then he switched off the TV but even the sudden silence didn't cause her to stir. He was not yet ready for bed himself and so he went through to the kitchen, poured himself a whisky, then sat drinking it at the table while he idly flicked through a collection of leaflets about places of interest in the region that the Clement family had left for them.

And while he did not think that Aaron would tolerate, let alone appreciate the medieval architecture and elaborate stone carvings on the many cathedrals, nor the war cemeteries, nor the interesting history of Joan of Arc and her battles with the English, he none the less read about them and imagined that at some future time he and Marilyn would come here again, unencumbered by duty and able to just be regular tourists. Unnoticed, ordinary, free.

He did not see what time it was and when Marilyn appeared blinking groggily at the doorway to the kitchen, with her hair awry and the throw over her shoulders, neither did she.

'Come on,' he said, and rose from his chair leaving the half-full glass on the table, and with his arms around her, the two of them went upstairs to bed.

# Like Alice

Lucy was feeling angry at her lack of ability to handle even the simplest of situations. No wonder during the first few days of the holiday she had stuck to the safe routine of a day exploring followed by dinner at La Coquille Bleue under the watchful gaze of Madame Gallo and the beautiful blue-eyed dog.

She did not fully understand why she had followed the Canadian man. It had been stupid and embarrassing, but thank God, she would never, with luck, see him again.

And the old guy in the bar? Why had she flinched so obviously when he touched her arm? He had only meant to be kind. And the young African who had tried to strike up a conversation? She had a sense that she'd had an unpleasant expression on her face when he addressed her, that she had gaped at him, bug-eyed. But then what was she meant to do with all that information about cousins in Paris and aunts who were doctors in Camden Town. What was she meant to say, I went to Camden Lock market once? I have a doctor?

Her reaction to these men was to some extent due to her years in London. People there do not make contact with strangers so readily. Everyone has their guard up, a cold eye waiting for the fool who tries to chat on the bus. It was not like Glasgow, or the small town where she grew up.

And with her stupid bleached blonde hair and cotton dress, she probably looked more like bloody Alice in Wonderland than Catherine Deneuve or Brigit Bardot.

No more adventures. No more chasing after white rabbits, Canadian or otherwise. And no more diving into drink after drink as if they were the secret gateway to the sodding rabbit hole.

Things went badly wrong for Alice every time she found something labelled 'Eat me' or 'Drink me'. Not that Alice got drunk, but there was certainly a hallucinatory quality to much of Lewis Carroll's famous work. Maybe in the morning everything that happened tonight would seem like a dream.

And Lucy was drunk. Not so drunk as to not even know that she was drunk, but enough to feel disorientated and confused about which way to walk.

She had hurried out of the bar and automatically turned left. She had sensed the men gazing after her, as puzzled by her abrupt departure as they had been by her arrival, and so, because she didn't want to appear lost or confused, she had hurried up the road so that she could no longer be seen from the window.

It was surprisingly dark out on the street, nearly all of the other bars and restaurants had closed for the night, so no light spilled invitingly from their interiors, and where earlier there'd been multi-coloured fairy lights strung up and lit on the awnings these were now switched off. And the pavements were not thronged with people ambling pleasantly about, and none of the outside tables at any of the cafés were occupied. No hubbub of voices filled the air, no music poured out from open doors. No one flew by on a bike, there were hardly any cars. And no taxis either.

Lucy stopped walking abruptly and thought about going back to the bar to ask for help. Her bag slipped from her shoulder, it wasn't really the sort of bag you put over your shoulder, but swinging it in one hand seemed to risk having it snatched. And she knew that she was the sort of idiot who, in the event some guy on a motorbike grabbed her bag (she'd heard that this had happened in Rome. Or was it Paris?) would hang on instead of letting go, and would thus be dragged along in the bike's wake and end up battered and torn as well as robbed.

She pulled her bag onto her shoulder and kept one hand on it, then realising that the longer she stood still the more she looked like she was either lost or a hooker, she continued on in the same direction and did not notice when her cardigan slipped from her shoulders. She only noticed that she shivered suddenly. 'Someone walking on your grave' people said if they detected such a shudder. Goosebumps sprang into life on her arms and neck and legs, tingling and unpleasant.

Just walk, she told herself. Nothing is going to happen.

She sensed something behind her. She was suddenly aware of someone running swiftly towards her. She did not so much hear footsteps exactly, but something alerted her, a movement in the air or some sort of sixth sense. It was far off but as it got a little nearer she faintly heard soft, fast footfalls, a swift rhythmic rustle of cloth. She did not turn around to look, but picked up her pace, tightened her grip on her bag and kept her head high, her back straight.

As soon as she reached the next turning she walked briskly up it and once she was certain she was out of sight she took off her shoes and ran before ducking into the shelter of a doorway. She heard a man's voice call out, 'Hey!' and retreated further into the doorway, her heart pounding, her breath shallow and rasping.

After a few minutes she found the courage to creep forward and peek out from her hiding place. Nothing. No one. No sound.

She lingered a little longer in the doorway. It was a deep concrete-lined portico with a steel-shuttered door at the back and a smashed lamp fitting above her head. There was a strong smell of beery urine, and black marker-penned graffiti on the blistered yellow-white gloss paint. The stone floor beneath her bare feet was slightly sticky. Why hadn't she brought her mobile? If she had a phone now, she could ring for a cab. Or the hotel? Or the police? Or her dad? Or Mitra, her friend from college who she confided in and was always wise and non-judgmental but never afraid of the truth? Or Thom?

She almost wept at the thought of Thom, but bit her lip and fought off the impulse to cry.

Oh, God, Thom, what have I done?

She heard a motorbike buzz by, the noise of its engine rising and falling in pitch and bouncing off the narrow streets so that she wasn't sure where it came from. The sound was sinister. For no other reason than her particular circumstances. She knew that. Even through the booze. Yet she could not help considering how easy it would be to hunt down a lone woman on foot if someone had a fast motorbike. The street she was on had some residential properties on it. She glimpsed them in the distance. Nearly all of them had shutters; either old-fashioned and made of wood, or modern metal grills, all firmly closed. But beyond the shutters there must be ordinary spaces, untidy kitchens, comfortable dining rooms, bedrooms with soft carpets and warm beds with good, decent kind people lying on them, blissfully unaware of the dark streets beyond. It seemed to Lucy that the houses themselves had closed their eyes to her and would not open them until morning.

Perhaps if she continued up this road it would lead to her hotel. Or to another hotel? Would they let her check in so late at night? She had credit cards with her, though not her passport. The other route, being made up mostly of commercial businesses of one sort or another, was far safer while all of the shops and bars and cafés were open. Once closed, however, the place became entirely lifeless and only served to highlight her vulnerability. To make matters worse, because she had been following the Canadian man, she had paid less attention to the route she had taken. She had not taken mental note of landmarks or street names. And even Alice, as she fell down the rabbit hole, had noticed all the curious objects in the nooks and crannies around her. Not that Alice ever attempted to go back the way she had come. But then hers was a land of wonder, not terror.

Or at least not terror like this. Cold and banal in a grubby doorway with sticky black piss-grime on the soles of your bare feet and no certainty about the best plan for the next five minutes, no way of knowing the way back to safety.

Dorothy might have said 'there's no place like home' and clicked her heels; Lucy couldn't even put her shoes back on.

Lucy, her bag over her shoulder again – one hand still gripping it, her shoes in her other hand, peeked out of the doorway in the direction of the main road. Immediately she saw a couple standing in a pool of yellow streetlight. They were holding on to one another tightly, both with their arms wrapped around the other's back, their bodies seemingly locked together from head to ankle. They were just about the same height as one another which facilitated the exactness of the embrace. Then as Lucy watched they broke apart or at least unhinged themselves enough to allow for forward movement.

A young couple. In love. A man and a woman, they would help her surely? She ran on the balls of her feet, the contents of her bag jingling and rattling, the wallet crashing into the sunglasses case, sunglasses case bouncing silently off loose paper-wrapped tampons and scrunched-up tissues. Coins pinged and leapt, keys clanked, pens and lipsticks jumped about in the morass like noisy salmon. Faster and faster she ran. She was not impervious to pain; she felt small stones, sharp fragments of gravel underfoot, but ignored them.

Out of breath, and in less than a minute, she reached the place on the main road where she had seen the couple kissing, but they had disappeared. Had evaporated into thin air just as surely as if they'd been beamed aboard the Starship Enterprise. Or as if they had only been the fragile ghosts of a classic French romance, the fading afterimage of a photograph by Robert Doisneau, another of his famous kissing couples frozen in time for eternity.

Suddenly Lucy doubted that she had seen them at all. But, she considered, trying to garner some positive facts about the situation, at least she was now here out in the open instead of in that filthy doorway. And there was no sign of her pursuer.

She decided it was probably wiser to retrace her route from

earlier that evening than to risk getting lost in a labyrinth of residential streets.

Seeing the lovers had been a sign.

Still barefoot and being careful to walk down the centre of the pavement away from bag snatchers on mopeds and dangerous men who lurked in doorways and down dark alleyways, she walked further and further from the bar where the working men had been, and as she walked she promised herself that she would never again be so stupid. If there was one good thing to come out of this awful night it was that she should in future always have a plan and the number of a taxi service. That being blonde wasn't all it was cracked up to be and drink provides false armour.

And night falls swiftly and changes everything.

# Part Two

# MORNING

*When she looked around she saw that the summer was over and autumn very far advanced. She had known nothing of this in the beautiful garden where the sun shone and the flowers grew all the year round.*

Hans Christian Andersen 'The Snow Queen'

*If I were turned out of my realm in my petticoat, I would prosper anywhere in Christendom.*

Queen Elizabeth I

Part Two

# MORNING

# Song to the Siren

Florian was the first to wake. Although the blinds in Suzette's bedroom were shut, pale light leaked into the room and outlined soft grey objects whose actual form or purpose he couldn't make out in the half light. As his eyes adjusted he saw a chair with clothes thrown over it, a chest of drawers, a mantelpiece with a plaster statuette of The Virgin on it, a dressing table with bottles and containers of different sizes arranged on it; body lotions, face creams, deodorants, hair brushes and spiky-looking clips, barrettes and combs.

Despite the unfamiliar room, he immediately knew where he was and how he came to be there, and she was lying next to him. He lay on his back and grinned at the ceiling. Outside on the street he heard the morning begin, the sounds of delivery vans, cars and motorbikes; of chairs and tables being set out and voices calling to one another.

Suzette stirred and turned over. She had been lying curled up with her back towards him, but now half awake, half asleep, she seemed to be seeking him out. He turned to face her and pulled her to him. She sighed happily, and her eyelids flickered. He looked at her face with the closed eyes and the sleepy grin, ran his hand down her back, revelling in her warm soft skin. Her breathing was slow and heavy with sleep. He explored the round fleshiness of her behind, noticing that the surface of her skin felt marginally cooler there.

He drew his hand up and cupped her breast. She murmured and he ducked his head under the covers and licked, then blew on her nipple so that it immediately turned hard and he grazed it gently with his teeth.

Sighing as she began to fully wake up, her hands came down and touched his hair, his neck. She bent her head down towards his, and sensing this he looked at her. They gazed at one another for a second, unblinking, absorbing the details of the other's face at close range. Then they began to kiss.

He gently eased her onto her back, lay above her and entered her. Their bodies moved together, rocking and undulating. Awake and alive.

Like drowning, dancing, clinging to one another. Eyes watching eyes, seeing pleasure, breath coming faster, noisy with sighs, with each other's names.

The light changed from soft diffuse grey as brighter shafts cut across the room in stripes as the sun moved higher in the sky and burned more intensely.

Then peace.

The quiet holding.

Then.

'What time is it?'

Suzette wriggled free, leaned over to pick up the alarm clock from the floor by the bed.

'Nine-thirty.'

Florian groaned.

'Have you got work?' Suzette asked, snuggling in closer.

'Not 'til twelve.'

And then they hear a siren in the distance. It drew nearer. The sound expanded in the room. Passes. Shrinks.

Suzette and Florian barely notice.

'So,' Florian said, grinning, 'am I the consolation prize?'

'Huh?'

Another siren.

Its sound explodes. Stops. Explodes.

An air horn sounds.

'So?' Florian says, his grin broader, teasing.

'What?'

'You and the Canadian guy?'

Suzette grins back, 'What about me and the Canadian guy?'

Florian moves closer, holds her tighter.

'You know.'

'Oh, do I?'

Another siren joins the cacophony. Loud. Insistent. This time they can't ignore it.

But only acknowledge it by meaningful looks. Looks that say something is out there, something is going on. A car crash. Serious. A fire. A crime of some dimension.

The sounding bell which calls people to their doors and windows.

If Florian were not there, with his legs entwined in hers, his arms around her, one under her neck, her head on his chest, she would go to the window.

The sirens die away.

He kisses her forehead affectionately.

'Didn't you promise me coffee?' he said.

'No.'

'Yeah, you did. You said, "Do you want to come to my place for coffee?"'

'Oh. Last night.'

'Yeah, and I didn't get my coffee so…'

'Oh, okay.' Suzette gets up. She is aware of her naked body. Aware of Florian's eyes following her. Suzette loves her body, loves being watched. Idles deliberately in the room before going through to the small adjoining kitchen to make coffee, leaves the door open as she does so.

Remembers last night. The casual suggestion that maybe he'd like coffee. Him answering, 'Yeah, why not?' just as casually. Then the way they'd kissed and kissed and kissed some more on the walk back. Her unlocking the door downstairs while he stood behind her kissing her neck. Then up the narrow stairway clumsily, stopping halfway to kiss again. The timed light going out, leaving them in darkness. Then into her apartment. Undressing one another awkwardly, throwing each other's clothes on the floor, and her falling and him trying to catch her, but both of them winding up on the floor, laughing and kissing. Growing more serious and kissing with fierce concentration. Then making love on the floor when the bed was only a few feet away. Beneath her body at one point, digging into her back, one of Florian's shoes and also the pretty cardigan she'd found.

Then they had gone to bed and lain beside one another talking for a long time. For some reason their conversation had all been about their childhoods; the TV programmes they used to watch, the toys they owned and those they'd always longed to own. Suzette had wanted a space hopper. 'I'll buy you one,' Florian boasted.

'I'm too big for one now.'

'So?'

'Where would I play with it?'

'Wherever you want.'

'People would laugh at me.'

'I wouldn't let them.'

'I'd be embarrassed even if they didn't laugh. I'd look silly. A grown woman on a space hopper.'

'Okay, I'll buy you a big playground with high walls so no one could see you.'

'I think I'd still feel silly.'

'Okay stubborn girl, I'll buy you one now, then just so it doesn't go to waste, we'll have some children and they can play with it.'

'And I'll have to ride it so they can see how it's done. And because I'll be with the children no one will think I'm crazy.'

How was it, Suzette thought, that she and Florian could talk so carelessly about having children together. For him it must be just talk. But for Suzette it opened up the whole vista of a future life. Not real of course, but worth lingering over in her imagination. She had been glad the room was dark, as she didn't want him to see her expression too clearly, to see how much it had been transformed by this idea of not only Suzette and Florian, but Suzette and Florian and a clutch of children.

Then they must have fallen asleep.

She could fall as easily into love, yet she was guarded, wary.

She poured the coffee into mismatched bowls, one with navy stripes, the other patterned with rose and gold fleur-de-lis and wished she had something nice to go with it – fresh bread or croissants, but all she had was four-day-old sliced factory bread, which was beginning to grow blue-green splotches of mould.

She carried the coffee through and set the bowls on the floor by the bed, then snuggled under the covers to find, once again, the delicious skin-warmed sheets and Florian's languid body, which engulfed her as soon as she was within his reach.

'Come here, sexy,' he said, giving her a little squeeze and kissing her shoulder, then he leaned across her and picked up one of the coffee bowls from the floor, blew on it before he began to suck at it noisily. He smacked his lips together to get the taste of it better.

'Great coffee, Suzette, really good,' he slurped some more. 'A guy could get addicted to coffee like that.'

Her back was to him, she leaned out of bed to pick up her bowl; she drank hers quietly, wondering what it was he was really saying to her with his remark about the coffee, but still determined to remain cool.

'Are you working tonight?' he asked, after they had showered and were dressing.

'Yeah,' she had been searching on the floor for her bra and found it underneath the white cardigan.

'So shall I come in to see you?'

'Sure.'

'Okay.'

She held up the white cardigan by the shoulders; it was every bit as pretty as she remembered from the night before, but she felt guilty about keeping it suddenly. It was slightly rumpled looking as if it were shocked to find itself so misused. 'Can you remember where we found this?' she asked.

'Oh yeah,' he said glancing at it. 'Outside the Café de Trois, wasn't it?'

'I feel bad about keeping it,' she said. 'Maybe I should put it back where it was, then whoever lost it might find it.'

He wrapped his arms around her again, trapping her so that the cardigan was pressed between them.

'You're not bad,' he said. 'You're good.' Kissed her again.

They left the apartment together and walked hand in hand back to the Café de Trois. Neither said anything, but when Suzette draped the cardigan over the geraniums outside the café, each had a sense of ceremony about the act. It was as if by doing this they were proving something to one another, that in being good, they were investing in their future together.

'There,' Suzette said and smiled at Florian. He grinned back.

'I'll see you later,' he said, pecked her cheek and took off at a jogging pace. Late for work, but he'd make up the time.

Suzette set off for her flat and glanced back once to see if she could still see Florian, but he'd gone.

The cardigan was still there, a scrap of white against the green and red pattern of the plants. It would have been bad luck to keep it. She hoped whoever it belonged to found it again, and almost wished that its owner could know where it had been and how very good she had been to give it back.

For the next few days, she thought, she would keep her eyes open in search of some tourist wearing it, some pretty rich girl who, while she might own expensive clothes, might never have what Suzette now possessed, namely a good man like Florian.

She walked past the entrance to her apartment, going further along the street to the small supermarket ten minutes walk away. She planned to buy more of that coffee Florian liked, and fresh bread and cheese and fruit and a small bottle of cognac. All of it really for Florian, all of it to make him stay.

When she drew near to the shop's entrance, her eye was drawn to the place where the road widened at the edge of the old town and the small shops and houses petered out and the industrial units and factories began. There was an unfamiliar contusion of vehicles; marked police vans, an ambulance, a number of other cars; sleek BMWs and a Land Rover or two, and many people, milling about or standing together in groups, dressed variously in police uniforms, white overalls or sharp black suits.

She stopped and gazed up the road, straining to see whatever it was that was going on. Remembered all the sirens they'd heard earlier. A car crash, she thought, or perhaps some industrial accident.

A middle-aged woman came out of the shop, a woven basket filled with groceries over her arm, red lipstick too bright for her sagging tired skin, making her look older than she perhaps was. The woman stopped beside Suzette companionably and gazed in the same direction.

'Oh, it's awful isn't it? Oh, I heard the sirens earlier and I said to my Regis, I said someone is suffering now, and sure enough, that's what it was.'

Although Suzette had disliked this woman at first sight and could hear behind the concerned words a sort of thrilled gloating, she could not help asking 'What happened, do you know?'

'Found a body,' the woman said with grim satisfaction. 'Murdered.' Suzette stared at the woman's mouth as she said the words: crooked yellow teeth, the lipstick bleeding into a radiating pattern of fine lines around her lips.

'Oh God,' said Suzette, 'that's awful.'

'And the Lord saw that they were ashamed and cast them out of paradise,' the woman intoned, crossing herself as she rolled her eyes heavenward.

That was enough for Suzette, without another word she dodged past the woman and went into the shop.

# The Scholar

The body lay on a deep verge above a drainage ditch. At first sight it seemed possible that the young woman had accidently fallen there. She was dressed very prettily in a summer dress whose full skirt had snagged on a tree stump, stopping her progress into the murky stew of the water below.

Her head fell forward so that her blonde hair covered her face. One arm was trapped and hidden under her body, the other dangled limply down from the shoulder as if she were trying to trail her fingers in the fetid water below.

Her legs stuck out at awkward angles. From one foot, with its strap caught around her ankle, dangled one of her shoes. Her other foot, the sole black with dirt, was bare.

Inspector Vivier and a number of other senior detectives were gazing down at the body and trying to figure out the best way of examining it and the surrounding area without contaminating the scene or missing any clues.

From where he stood on the concrete bank above the culvert, Vivier could see the young woman's naked hip and the pale swell of her left buttock. It looked as if she wasn't wearing any panties. This raised the alarm for the Inspector and suggested a sexual element in whatever had happened to the young woman. But there again, she might be wearing a thong. It was impossible to tell, besides which, he understood that the latest trend was for some young ladies to wear no undergarments whatsoever. He had been shocked some months back to see the photograph of an American pop star which had been widely distributed in the media – the one of her caught in the act of getting out of a car with her legs slightly parted, her skirt hiked up and that hairless soft-looking slit on show for all the world to see.

Curiously the paparazzo's snapshot of the pop star had reminded him of one of the background figures in the illuminated manuscript of the Duc de Berry's fifteenth century *Book of Hours*. It was a winter scene depicting the month of February which showed a snow-covered hill under a leaden grey-green sky and inside a farm building, warming themselves by the fire, there was a fine lady dressed in celestial blue and a couple of peasants. The peasants, a man and a woman, had both lifted up the skirts of their outer garments in order to warm themselves, and the creator of the manuscript, one of the Limburg brothers, had painstakingly recorded the pink hairless genitals of each.

Paul Vivier, as a child seeking refuge from his father's uncontrollable rages, often haunted his local public library. It was there in the dusty hush among the towering book shelves that he had first seen this reproduction in the *Book of Hours* and it had fascinated him ever since.

February. The bitter cold. A harsh life for the peasants of France. The picture almost made him shiver every time he saw it.

But now it was a beautiful day towards the end of July. At last the unseasonable rain had stopped. The heavy rain and flooding had been caused, or so some meteorologists claimed, by global warming. Depending on who you listened to or read there was no going back – the polar ice was melting, the ozone layer had a hole in it three times the size of the United States and floating somewhere in the Pacific there was a ten-million-square-mile logjam of indestructible plastic trash that threatened not only that ocean's eco-system, but the entire world's. Thinking about this was enervating. Whatever happened to progress?

It reminded Vivier of the medieval period's fears and superstitions about the end of the world. The sighting of a meteor gave rise to preachers foretelling imminent doom and disease was seen as punishment for a sinful people. Thunder was God's voice. Flood, famine and pestilence all signalled the coming of the promised last days. At the zenith of the first millennium in the year 999 a great army of pilgrims travelled to Jerusalem in anticipation that the sky would open to reveal God. Another crowd gathered on the hills of Hampstead on October the 13th, 1736, to see the predicted destruction of London.

Vivier's father, a uniformed *flic* of the old school, who was as likely to use his fists on his wife and sons as on the criminals he caught, was responsible for the man his son had become. While it was true that both men had entered the police force, the son made his way up the ranks through his quiet intelligence and austere temperance. The father let his brusque manners, foul mouth and explosive temper keep him on the lowest levels of the force until the day he retired.

When the nine-year-old Paul Vivier sat slowly turning the glossy pages of the books he found in the library he entered a different world, which despite its deprivations was free from the malevolent hand of his father. In that vivid winter scene from centuries ago, he saw how the regularity of the seasons held more meaning then; spring with its promise of fertility, summer with its blessed life-giving warmth and light, autumn with its harvest, then the closing in of winter, its barren chills, stark skies and murderous cold.

Human beings, as individuals, as societies, hadn't really changed that much. Progress, science, the Renaissance and Enlightenment only served to add to the illusion that the Modern age was an improvement yet fear still filled the world and murderers walked its streets. Vivier had been a policeman long enough to distrust everyone and everything.

And he was, besides being a police inspector, a scholar of history. It was a private passion of his. Few of his colleagues could have guessed at the hundreds of books which lined the walls of his study at home or of his private ruminations and obscure debates. These last often taking place almost anonymously over the internet with faceless others who might have been equally surprised that abelard3000@historel.net was an inspector of police and not a teacher or postgraduate historian.

As pastimes went it was certainly preferable to watching TV, or reading, as Assistant Detective Sabine Pelat always did, in particular novels, about serial killers and other evils.

Montaldo huffed noisily to express his frustration and shake the inspector from his reverie. 'Well, this is going to be a bastard, eh?'

'It does look like a bit of a logistical nightmare. I think what we need is ladders.'

'Ladders, Inspector? We have rope and…'

'No, it's not as simple as clambering down there, the verge is unstable and it would be easy to dislodge evidence into the drain where it would be carried away. With a few long ladders over the culvert we can get access without disturbing the scene too much.'

'You think it's foul play, then, sir?'

'We'll proceed as if it is.'

'Of course.'

'I can't think why a young girl like this would be here. I can't imagine she was taking a stroll and lost her footing.'

'Perhaps she was working,' Montaldo said.

'Perhaps,' Vivier allowed, 'and yet there is something not right about the dress…'

'No knickers,' Montaldo stated grimly.

'Well, that tells us nothing.'

Montaldo nodded slowly as if absorbing great wisdom from his superior, though privately he thought that the absence of underwear told them plenty.

'So let's get this started, contact the fire department, see if they're in a frame of mind to lend us a few ladders.'

As the ladders were organised and paper suits and evidence bags were distributed by the forensic team, Vivier found himself thinking about the Middle Ages again; paintings from Northern Europe which depicted both everyday life in all its banality and conversely, examples of astonishing cruelty and torture. Pictures by Bosch and Breughel.

There was one in particular that showed Christ's journey to Calvary. Except that the landscape was not that of the Holy Land with its deserts and flat-roofed buildings, but was very clearly the Low Countries. In the picture's centre, almost lost amongst the teeming crowds of peasants and soldiers, Christ bore the cross on his back. To the right of the picture and in the distance there were strange precarious structures; a spindly pole topped by a wheel with what look like rags hanging from it and perched atop the wheel a large black bird; a crow or raven. In the distance a similar structure could be seen, as well as what looked like a scaffold built for the purpose of hanging several men, or indeed women, at the same time. What had always struck Vivier about these constructions was that they were the only man-made objects to stand out against the sky in the stark landscape. That just as a cityscape of the same period or later would have shown church steeples reaching towards heaven, so here in the uncultivated countryside the instruments of torture and cruelty were thrust at the sky.

Man's inventiveness was as appalling as it was wondrous. If the wheel was one of the most important developments in the long climb to progress, why misuse it as an instrument of torture? And what perverted genius was inspired to break and thread a human being through its spokes?

He looked down at the body of the young woman; she looked like a discarded doll. Whatever had happened to her, he hoped she didn't suffer too much. But even as he thought this he suspected that his prayer was futile.

Three weeks ago Paul Vivier had found himself gazing down at the body of another woman. She had been older, a prostitute and drug addict well known to the police – Marianne Sigot. Her death had been no surprise, which is not to say it wasn't tragic. She had been hurtling headlong towards it her whole life. Fighting and fucking her way to damnation, clothed in tight lycra pants, high heels and barely decent skimpy tops, all of them brightly coloured and glossy, making herself look like some cheap plastic toy, exposing her grubby, scarred and often bruised flesh.

He'd interviewed Marianne's mother, Madame Sigot, a tiny woman with a halo of grey fuzz around her head, a perm gone wrong no doubt, whose quiet gentility was oblivious. She had made him tea and served it with buttery homemade madeleines, then proceeded to tell him of how she had called her only child Marianne because she thought of her as a wonder, a saviour, a miracle. She had insisted on bringing out tattered old cigar boxes filled with snapshots of the young Marianne. Christ, it had been heart wrenching to sit there and see the beautiful child the dead prostitute had been; rosy-cheeked in her bassinette, flying high on a swing, grinning with both front teeth absent in a school photo, then demure in her white confirmation dress and veil, a small pale book in her slim hands while her big dark eyes seemed about to brim over with tears.

How did this child become that woman?

Most people knew her not as Marianne Sigot, but as Mazzy.

But Mazzy was no more.

Two women dead within the space of a month? It could easily be a coincidence. One, the victim of a pimp, dealer or client. The other, perhaps the victim of an accident, possibly domestic violence. The answers were all around them, on the women's skin, in their hair and clothes, under the fingernails, on the earth, amongst the weeds, on the path that led here and in the murky silt at the bottom of the ditch.

And there might be witnesses too. Even without the benefit of seeing her face (which was turned away and concealed by a curtain of hair) there was something about her slim frame, the dress with its nipped-in waist and wide skirt, her (almost certainly) bleached blonde hair which would make her stand out from other women, whether natives or tourists. And whatever had happened to her, however she had died, identification was going to be vital; the sooner they knew who she was, the sooner each part of the puzzle would fall into place.

# Star Gazer

Michelle Brandieu lived in the top-floor apartment above the Café de Trois. The apartment had at some time in the last seventy or so years been the residence of an artist and either they, or the house's owner, had made alterations by taking out the small gabled windows and putting in floor-to-ceiling glass. However this was not the gigantic single pane of sleek modernist design; it bore less of a resemblance to a Frank Lloyd Wright picture window than to a dilapidated greenhouse, with a rusted lattice of ironwork holding in place a multitude of smaller panes of glass, some of which were cracked, all of which were smeared and mildewed.

But despite this Michelle Brandieu loved her small apartment as it afforded her a wonderful view of the sky and, on clear nights, the multitude of stars, which she viewed with the affection of a proud mother. She had a mild interest in astronomy with a passing knowledge of black holes, nebulae, comets and asteroids, but her real passion was for astrology, the movements of the constellations and their effect on every human being on earth. No science or religion could compete with the power of the stars.

Michelle spent many nights staring out at the sky. Because of the canopies over the cafés beneath her the view of the pavement tables was obstructed. On warm nights when she had the windows open, she heard laughter, music and the odd strand of conversation, but could not see who created it.

She could see the traffic, both pedestrian and automotive, that streamed to and fro on the wide pavement and the narrow road beyond. Such a busy pointless commotion. While up above, sometimes visible, sometimes not, hung the great canopy of stars.

'Stars do not go away, they are always there, still affect us, even when we can't see them.'

Michelle had typed out these words on a small index card twenty, no, nearly thirty years ago. She had blue-tacked the card to her fridge, though the card showed signs of having been displayed by other means – in each of its top two corners were the tiny puncture wounds made by drawing pins, and all four corners had yellow diagonal bands which revealed that it was once taped to another surface. And the card itself was grubby with age, the black typewritten words now grey and pale. Perhaps it was actually more than thirty years since Michelle typed it out. Time has become a little vague for Michelle, but the stars and her passion for them endures.

And because of this Michelle happened to be standing at her window the night before the body of the young woman was found, and as she stood there, dreaming of fate and eternity, something caught her eye down below where the row of potted geraniums marked the café's boundaries. There was an airy movement of something white. Her eyesight was failing and it took her a little time to adjust from the long-distance gaze that took in the night sky with its pinpricks of light. At first the white object seemed to have a life of its own, but then she saw that someone was holding it.

Yes, very clearly she saw a young man standing facing the café. He wore a track suit that she thought might have been red, not bright red, but a greyish red bleached of light, which absorbed the blackness of the night. And his skin was black.

The sight of him had frightened Michelle. A few years ago the café's owner had moved out of the apartment below hers, going instead to live in a house ten minutes' drive away with his wife and three almost grown-up children. He'd had a plan to rent the old flat to holiday-makers, but had somehow never got around to refurbishing it, and so once the café closed for the night, Michelle was the only person in residence.

At first she had relished the quiet, as her landlord's family had been very noisy, always shouting at one another or playing music too loud (the son had an electric guitar) and the daughter was given to histrionics, and the volume on their TV was set too high. She quickly realised that their noise had at least been a comforting sign that she was not alone. These days, while she never suffered from loneliness, she did at times feel terribly vulnerable.

So she had stared at this young black man, certain that he must be about to break into the café. That the white object which, for a few seconds he seemed to deliberately flap through the air, must be some sort of flag, a signal to the rest of his gang that the coast was clear, and very soon they would be picking the locks on the café door and creeping onto the premises, then irrevocably up the stairs to her small flat, her frail defenceless body.

She watched horrified as he fluttered the white cloth, and then, in a way that she would later describe as 'ritualistic', he draped it over the low-growing plants. Once it had been placed there she saw that it was not a simple rectangle of fabric, but had a sort of human shape, a wide central part with two narrower arms beside it. She could not see the far edge of this shape as it fell on the other side of the hedge, but she imagined the continuation of this human form, with the central part being finished by two spectral legs.

Voodoo. The ancient religion of primitive evil. Worse even than burglary.

When the young man had finished his act of ritual he stepped away from the hedge and Michelle was sure that he smiled. Yes, she saw the flash of his white teeth.

Wicked. Terrifying to see the pleasure his evil act had given him. Then he set off again, walking briskly for a few minutes as he scanned the street as if looking for someone, until he eventually broke into a run.

Michelle stood by the window rigid with fear and uncertain

what to do. She was certain that he or his comrades would return. She was equally afraid of the evil magic he had performed.

And remembering a charm to ward off evil a pagan friend had once recommended to her, she fetched salt from the kitchen and sprinkled a line of it along the bottom of her window and another at the door to her flat.

Then she went to bed and lay in the darkness willing herself to sleep and imagining terrible things. After hours of tossing and turning and being petrified by every sound; the old building's creaks, the noise of a motorbike, the scratching of mice beneath the floorboards, she made the rational decision that if something was coming to get her, it would get her no matter what, she was entirely helpless. So she sat up, switched on the small lamp next to her, opened the drawer of her bedside cabinet, pulled out two balls of cotton wool and stuffed them into her ears. Then at last she fell into fitful nightmare-filled sleep.

Thus, muffled against all sound and worn out, she slept through all the early morning commotion of the rattling shutters being lifted, of the chairs being set out in the cafés, of wailing sirens and all the rest of the hullabaloo. She did not wake until almost twelve o'clock. Something she had not done for years which in itself made her suspect enchantment.

It was at the hairdressers, when she turned up for her appointment at three o'clock that afternoon that she heard of the young girl's murder. Everyone was talking about it and making the connection with the previous murder.

Michelle sat quietly in her chair as Julianne painted the bluish-white dye onto the roots of her hair and talked to the other customers and stylists. Michelle tended to be silent amongst large groups of people preferring the intimacy of a one-on-one conversation. She was unable to relax and talk with the same ease as the women around her, but consoled herself with the idea that she learned much more by listening.

Now she discovered that the body of a young girl who had been brutally murdered had been found early that morning. Michelle was also shocked to realise that another murdered woman – a prostitute – had been a regular at this very salon, or at least she had been until perhaps two, maybe three years ago when she started to go rapidly downhill and no longer troubled to groom herself very much.

'Well, I'm not going out after dark on my own,' Julianne said. 'Neither is Sophie.'

'How old is Sophie now?' the woman in the chair next to Michelle said, looking at Julianne in the large mirror that faced them.

'Fifteen and thinks she knows it all.'

'Oh you mustn't let her out of your sight, not until he's caught.'

Julianne expertly inserted the metal tip of the steel comb she was wielding under a strand of Michelle's hair and flicked it over, before proceeding to paint more dye along the new parting.

'Do they think it's the same man? I mean is it a serial killer?' Julianne said.

'Oh, they won't say, will they? That's why we have to protect ourselves,' the other hair stylist said, then as if to show her strength in this regard – her unassailable resolve – she picked up a large silver hairdryer with a long nozzle like a gun and switched it on, making such a noise that it stopped the conversation until she'd dried her customer's hair.

When the hairdryer was switched off and it was quiet again, Michelle suddenly found herself speaking. She watched herself in the mirror as she did so, and it therefore seemed that it was her reflection that had made the decision to talk and had put the words she said in her mouth. 'I think I saw something,' she said.

Because of the sudden silence after the drone of the hairdryer, because it was the strangely timid Michelle Brandieu who had spoken and because of the words themselves, all eyes turned to the older woman and there was a moment of wordless surprise before all of the women began to talk at once.

'What?'

'Oh, my God!'

'What did you see?'

'You must tell the police!'

The babble of voices came at Michelle like so many shooting stars as she sat – a bright sun – at their centre.

'What was it, Madame Brandieu?'

'Do you want to use the phone? I could find the number for the local station.'

Michelle began to feel uncomfortable as the focus of so much attention. Besides which her hair was nowhere near finished and the white roots of her dyed black hair made her self-conscious about her age and dignity.

'I will contact the police as soon as I leave here,' she said, gazing resolutely at her reflection. 'I do not think I should say any more, it may affect the investigation.'

Her formal words, spoken so primly, produced a sour atmosphere in the salon. The other women caught one another's eyes, imparting sharp signals of frustration and annoyance.

As soon as Michelle left the remaining women began to talk about what she had said.

'I wish she had told us what she saw.'

'It was wrong of her not to tell us, we need to know – to protect ourselves, our daughters.'

Julianne pursed her lips and lifted a strand of her own long blonde hair in her left hand, studying it for signs of split ends. 'I've been thinking,' she said, 'when the old sow said she saw something, she might mean, you know, she saw it in the stars or the cards. Or dreamt it. Otherwise wouldn't she go straight to the cops?'

There was a silence as they absorbed this.

Then one woman spoke up, her voice quivering with indignation, 'Well, I still think she could have told us what she saw, whatever it was, however she saw it,' and all of them nodded in agreement.

# Lexicon

Marilyn had woken up with words tumbling around her head as if she had been dreaming poetry. She kept a notebook next to the bed in which she recorded dreams, ideas, or as now, word sequences.

'Late in the evening we cut through the graveyard,
laughing at nothing and stumbling over roots,
bones, branches, columbine.'

Columbine. Columbine, just a flower. Mentioned by Shakespeare. But now no longer simply a flower. Impossible to use the word without the other association obliterating its simple meaning. But nonetheless it was duly recorded.

Scott stirred beside her, so she turned to look at him.

Love, she thought, and wrote that down underneath the other words.

The house was quiet. Aaron must still be asleep. On waking he usually began the day with a sort of howl of protest. Where did that come from, that attention-demanding noise? Was it some terrible knowledge of himself as a creature locked forever in a mind deprived of true human communication? Or was it like the cry of a baby? An instinctual animal response on waking to find himself alone? No one would ever know. Not his mother, father or brother, nor Marilyn herself. All they knew was that the nerve-shattering sound must be attended to, that it wrenched one from sleep and sent one colliding towards the noise, soothing and shushing, until eventually, he shut up.

How different it must be when the cry is that of a baby, when the sleep-broken nights are rewarded with the looks and sounds of love, when the light of recognition begins to burn in the child's eyes, when it smiles and gurgles and finally begins to speak.

Soon, if everything went okay, she would know exactly how it felt to be a mother.

She picked up her wrist watch and put it on before looking at the time. Almost nine o'clock. An alarmingly late hour for Aaron to still be asleep. It passed through her mind fleetingly that he was dead, and this idea inspired hardly any sorrow in her, which in its turn sickened her.

She reminded herself that thoughts are only thoughts; the brain an engine of conscious and unconscious needs, desires and wishes, tempered by a moral code that grew as much from nature as nurture.

She leaned over and kissed Scott, he responded by murmuring and making a vague blind kissing moue at the pillow.

'Scott,' she said in a low voice that was not quite a whisper, 'wake up. It's nine o'clock.'

He grunted then snuggled closer.

'Scott! Aaron's not awake.'

'Good,' he murmured. 'Come here.'

'Scott.' She nudged him. 'Go and check on Aaron!'

Groaning, he sat up and she watched as he lingered on the edge of the bed rubbing his head as if he was brushing leaves from it. Then he stood and pulled on a pair of cream-coloured chinos and trudged out of the bedroom calling 'Aaron? Hey, Aaron? S'morning, Aaron.'

It was soothing to hear his voice as it travelled away from her. She found herself thinking of his voice as an arrow projected towards their shared future, as if he had gone out of the room to find their baby. She laid her palm over her stomach, it was still almost flat, the skin taut, and yet she sensed that under her hand, under the wall of muscle, deep within her, a new life was growing.

In seven more days they'd be packing their belongings into the hire car and setting off for Paris and from there onto the plane that would take them home. Scott and Aaron's parents would be at Ottawa Airport to meet them. They'd part company on the concourse, Aaron going home with his parents, while she and Scott, with sighs of guilty and exhausted relief, would go gratefully to their old car, their old life, their beautiful, unfettered freedom. And maybe, as they'd done before, they'd celebrate their release by going to an expensive French restaurant and ordering all that food they had been unable to have in France, and they'd pretend they were in Paris and Scott would suggest they have champagne and she'd say no and then she'd tell him about the baby.

She heard Scott running heavy-footed down the stairs, the squeak of his hand on the varnished banister and the sound of doors opening and closing downstairs. Then someone, it must have been Scott, criss-crossing the passageway. No more voices, just this frightening flurry of urgent movement.

Marilyn hurried out of bed and was pulling on her dressing gown when the footsteps pounded up the stairs again. Scott was at the bedroom door, wild-eyed and breathless.

'He's not here! I can't find him.'

'He must be here.'

'I can't find him.'

'But he can't get out, unless…'

'I think I might have forgotten to lock the front door.'

'Oh, God.'

Together they searched the house calling Aaron's name over and over. They looked in wardrobes, under beds. Minutes ticked by. They checked the front door; it was unlocked and the key had been left in it. They looked hopefully out of the front windows thinking they might see Aaron standing resolutely at one of his favoured places on the street outside, but there was no sign of him. Then they hurriedly dressed and went in search of him.

Afterwards they considered that they should have headed in different directions, or that one of them should have stayed in the house in case he returned, but they were not quite thinking straight. Not then. It was only later that they came to this opinion, even though it was useless by then to think that if they'd been more analytical they'd have found him sooner.

At first they only walked the streets, turning this way and that, scanning the length of the side roads as they came to them. Without saying as much, both expected to find Aaron fixed to some spot, locked into the strange stillness that overcame him when he went out 'to play'. But they also worried (though again neither of them spoke their fears aloud) that someone had found Aaron and done something to him. Their imaginations separately concocted a similar array of demons; men who might abuse or rape him, or youths who might taunt, torment and beat him. Others who might misunderstand his strange behaviour, who might accuse him of watching children in a playground, or women who thought he was stalking them. The possibilities were endless and awful.

After much fruitless searching they began to stop people in the street and ask if they had seen a tall, blond, young American man. They said American as it seemed to simplify the matter, and without wishing to split hairs, Canada was part of the North American continent. Scott said, 'We've lost my brother, he is ill; he may appear strange or frightened.' But people shook their heads or shrugged.

One suggested they should call the police. Another, a postman, took their cell-phone number and promised to ring if he saw him.

While they were doing this, they began to hear at first one, then two, then three distant sirens.

At first the noise did not register with either Scott or Marilyn. They were merely a part of the soundscape of a small town or big city, as unremarkable as a lorry's air brakes, or car horns, or the rattling of a metal grille, or human noises; a cough, a shout, a sneeze, or music, angry rap spat out in fever-pitch French, blasting from a sleek black car with the windows down. Nothing to do with them, nothing to do with this urgent searching.

Then Scott stopped walking abruptly, caught Marilyn by the wrist and stopped her too. They gazed at one another as the last of the sirens licked at their ears, poured themselves through their ear canals, vibrated at high pitch on their ear drums where, instantly, intricate nerves sent the message of the sounds to their brains, and finally they understood the implications of the noise and what it might mean for Aaron.

'Oh, Christ!' Scott said.

Marilyn shook her head. 'No. Oh God, no. It can't be.'

Both momentarily pictured themselves arriving back at Ottawa, Scott's mother and father standing at the arrivals gate, their faces scrubbed-looking, beaming smiles of welcome, their eyes searching at first cheerfully, then confusedly, then desperately for their baby boy.

And Scott saying, 'Mum, Dad…'

He'd keep a tight hold of Marilyn's hand as he said it. His palm would grow sweaty. He would hold her hand like a slick knot of bone and flesh; hold it so tightly it would hurt. But that wouldn't matter because at least it would arrest his own hand's palsied trembling.

Then Scott, his voice breaking, creaking and ragged would say, 'We lost him. Mum, Dad, I'm so sorry.'

Those were the exact words 'we lost him'. The phrase was precise, correct, having a double meaning and in this instance the two meanings collided. 'We lost him' as in we could not find him, and 'we lost him' as in he died.

Neither Scott nor Marilyn spoke for a moment; they just stared at one another as the siren faded away. Then Scott's cell phone rang.

Later, remembering that moment, Marilyn would recall a line from a poem by Sylvia Plath, 'the dead bell, the dead bell, somebody's done for.' Once it had been church bells that sounded the clamour of celebration and the call to worship. At other times they signalled warning. Now the sounding bells are everywhere; clanging, wailing, shrieking, electronically bleeping, ringing, challenging one another for precedence. Scott's phone was ringing and it took a moment for him to register what the sound was. Fearfully he pulled it from his pocket. Who would be ringing him here and now? His parents? He damn well hoped not.

'Hello?'

A stranger's voice spoke to him.

'Monsieur, it is the postman. We spoke a few minutes ago on the street?'

'Yes, yes. I'm sorry, I'd forgotten.'

'I think I may have found him…'

# Dreamer

Joseph had woken in his hotel room with the phone call from the previous night in his mind in almost complete detail. He had been expecting the call, had been reassured by his teachers that, with his attendance record and exam results he was sure to be accepted at his choice of college and was certain to receive funding.

There had been moments when he'd accepted this possibility, but even more moments when he pushed the idea of such happiness away. 'Hope makes us vulnerable; it weakens us when we must remain strong and resolute.' He had read words to that effect long ago in a story in his own language. Or perhaps it had been something from Greek myth or even an American movie.

Whichever it was it seemed it no longer mattered. No need to caution his imagination any more, no need to picture himself working the land from sunrise to sunset and only then to barely scrape a living. However, as Joseph's father worked at a bank and his mother was a schoolteacher, he asked himself why he imagined he could fall so low. Perhaps this had to do with how high he could dream. That, and a deep sense of his identity and history. African nations, no matter their long histories; the patterns of colonisation, independence and seemingly bright futures, could erupt into turmoil overnight. The same could befall European nations, or any country in the world for that matter, and yet somehow, in Joseph's view, Africa felt more vulnerable.

Not that Joseph was really drawn to politics; instead his chosen profession of medicine demanded that he see neither skin colour, nor borders, nor religion, nor tribe, but only sick and injured people who needed his help.

His plan was three-fold; graduate from Medical School in London, then go (almost certainly) to America to further expand his practice and accumulate a decent amount of money, then lastly return home to Africa and set up his own clinic in the small town where he grew up.

And yes, noble and self-sacrificing as these aims were, he also saw in the swirling snows of the glass globe of his dreams, a beautiful wife who was as intelligent and dedicated to her career as he was to his. He imagined her with a high proud forehead, sculpted cheekbones, gleaming, deep-set eyes and skin the colour of a betel nut. And he saw the children they would have, and his children's children, and himself fifty or sixty years hence, his black hair transformed to a dignified smoky grey, sitting on the porch of their house overlooking the fields he owned, and in whose rich earth he nurtured grain and vegetables, flowers, horses, grandchildren. The orange sun setting, his work done.

While he lay in bed allowing the full tide of his dreams to wash over him, it occurred to him that they still might yet be dreams and so after checking the time and calculating the hour back home, he rang his mother just to be certain.

'Mamma? Was I dreaming?' he asked, and she laughed.

'No, you weren't dreaming, and by tonight half the town will know. Your uncle is writing about it for the newspaper. I gave him your graduation picture.'

'Oh, I'm so happy; I don't know what to do with myself.'

'Read a book.'

'I should, but, oh, I feel like running, dancing, singing.'

'Read a book, Joseph.'

'Ah, Mamma, you're the best. Love you.'

They said their goodbyes and Joseph picked up the anatomy book he'd brought with him.

Learning never ceased. It only stopped when a person made it stop. Joseph would never stop. Never rest. In order to be a doctor his knowledge of the human body must be perfect. The human body was a country to be explored, mapped out, every bone and blood vessel and organ memorised by rote.

For purely arbitrary reasons, Joseph opens the book to those pages devoted to the workings of the throat and mouth. The book is not the kind of in-depth one a young medical student would consult, but one designed for the serious younger reader or lay person. He studies the full-colour diagram – mouthing the words which describe the parts; pharynx, oesophagus, tongue, epiglottis, hyoid bone, glottis, thyroid cartilage, vocal chords, trachea.

He repeats these to himself several times, but he is restless. He needs movement, needs to shake out his legs, charge his muscles, get his blood racing.

In an act of compromise he carefully copies out the names of the major parts of the larynx onto the palm of his left hand in biro, then after a brief look at the diagram again, he sets off for a morning jog.

The sweat (produced by the eccrine gland) would cause these inky words to dissipate except that in this temperature and at close to sea level, Joseph's morning exercise barely raises his pulse. Like a man on the moon he feels almost weightless and his movements are effortless.

The sun has long risen and the sky is a deep blue and there is a faint breeze in the air. He smells flowers, coffee, baking bread, petrol and diesel fumes. His limbs flex and beat out a rhythm which is without sound, but is felt through his spring-loaded feet. Breathing easily, he thinks about the inside of his mouth, about swallowing, breathing, speaking, kissing; about the sounds the mourning women made at funerals in his home town, the ululations carrying far and wide, the wolf's howl, the newborn baby's cry. And singing too. Miraculous, all of it.

Science opened up the path to seeing, to knowledge, but what was found was so mind-bogglingly remarkable one almost imagined a God-like genius behind it all. Chance, for that was what evolution was really all about, seemed irrational. Preposterous.

Joseph paced himself. Long strides, heels kicking up behind him, hands held high like paddles, head erect; larynx, trachea, hyoid bone, glottis, epiglottis. The opening and closing of a flap to shut off the passage to the lungs, the vocal chords vibrating like the reed in a wind instrument.

So much of this delicate machinery could go wrong, and yet for the most part it didn't.

He slowed his pace when he came to a small café, though he wasn't tiring. He would stop and have something to eat and, as he swallowed, he would pay attention to the workings of his body and, when he spoke, he would picture his phonation, the intricate work of tiny muscles constricting and contracting to make his words.

Inside the café it seems as dark as a cave. He blinks as his eyes adjust to the gloom. Behind the counter there is a middle-aged woman. She is very small and very round, with a mole on her chin and another between her eyebrows, which gives the impression that she is frowning. When he was a child he would have been frightened by her – for who but a witch would have such ugly moles?

'*Bonjour, Madame,*' he says and inclines his head in a respectful nod. She appreciates this and smiles in welcome.

'*Monsieur?*'

'A coffee, please, and bread.'

A siren rends the air and Joseph turns towards the door just in time to see the flickering light of the emergency vehicle as it speeds past.

# Fallen Angel

The young woman had no identification on her, which was not a surprise to Paul Vivier; he had guessed it as soon as he set eyes on the crime scene.

They had combed the immediate area and there was no convenient discovery of a handbag which contained a passport, ID card, flight or rail tickets. No diary or mobile phone. No purse containing foreign currency or credit cards. No personal items; an inscribed book, a letter, no receipts that usefully showed where she had recently been or what she had purchased.

She might have fallen from heaven. Not that Vivier believed in heaven, but he was not above imagining a paradise where angels dressed, not in long white diaphanous gowns, but in pretty summer dresses such as this girl was wearing.

*Demoiselles* were creatures such as she; fairies from the forests, spirits from pagan times who always dressed in purest white. Wild flowers were said to spring into life where they stepped. But then with Christianity they had become visions of the Virgin Mary. The peasant girl Bernadette Soubirous had seen a young woman in an elegant white gown in a grotto near Lourdes no less than eighteen times. But the woman lying in the ditch was dead, her presence there symptomatic of evil rather than heavenly grace.

He found himself gazing up momentarily at the sky. Pure blue, the same achingly luminous blue that is seen in the summer scenes in the calendar commissioned by the Duc de Berry in the fifteenth century. The sort of blue that made you believe there had to be something more than empty air above you.

It would have been so much easier to get away with murder in the fifteenth century – throw a body over a cliff then add a basket and a few broken gulls' eggs. Throw enough girls from the same village into ditches and people will think not of serial killers, but of how the females of that region are particularly accident prone, or bewitched. A legend might spring up about a particular dark lake and how at a certain hour during full moon, young maidens are at risk of meeting their deaths there. A creature, a bog sprite perhaps or some other demonic force might be sometimes glimpsed in the distance, bulky and shadowy amongst the trees at the water's edge.

Maybe it was easier to imagine an otherworldly monster, a spectre of evil that rose out of the swirling yellow-green mists which hung over the land at dusk, than to think that somewhere in the community there was a man; a friend, neighbour or brother who, now and again, was filled with the urge to kill.

Science provided other truths, and society, no longer fixed and insular, provided highways and autobahns, railways and airplanes; the movements of people were free and unfettered, and amongst the crowds who wandered the avenues and back streets of this small town there were many strangers. No one stood out as the obvious culprit, and the victim was unidentified.

Most murders are committed by people who know their victims; a husband or wife, a mother or father, a lover or work colleague, and the circumstances of the event are easily spelled out at the scene of crime or in the events of the next few hours. But here, in this foul-smelling ditch was an as yet anonymous woman who'd been killed by another anonymous person. Nothing could bring her back, nothing could undo what had already been done, but the murderer must be found. Especially if, as Vivier surmised, this was the same man who had taken the life of Marianne Sigot.

In the northern suburbs of Paris, ten or perhaps twelve years ago, Paul Vivier had been involved in the hunt for the 'Seine Boat Man' as the press had dubbed that particular killer. Only two of his victims' bodies were found in or near water, but the label had stuck.

Vivier, like others in his position in the USA, UK, Italy, Germany – wherever – found the press' involvement in the early days of detection, and more especially their deeper involvement in ongoing cases, to be deeply troubling if not actually harmful.

Imagination, thought Vivier, is both man's curse and his blessing.

He looked down at the young woman's form again as she hung there over the soupy-looking grey water, illuminated momentarily by the searing white light of the police cameraman's flash.

Imagination was equally woman's curse and blessing. Some thought, some belief, an idea of trust or love may have brought this young woman to this, and physical evidence aside, Vivier knew that part of his role in the detection of this crime would demand that he begin to imagine a series of dramas which led to the moment of her demise.

The first and simplest of these dramas was that she had simply fallen. Not from heaven, but from the bank just a few feet above the ditch. Such a fall however would be unlikely to kill anyone. He pictured her running at speed along the bank, imagined her laughing, a little drunk perhaps, with the recklessly giddy movements of someone stoked with alcohol. Then he struck the laugh from the scene and added a pursuer.

The path that ran alongside the ditch covered a stretch of flat, open scrubland between one industrial unit and another and although it was approximately the length of a football pitch, there was only one light halfway along.

As he trained his gaze and his imagination to the furthest end of the ditch, he turned to find Sabine Pelat was suddenly at his side, proffering a paper cup of coffee.

'Sir?'

He took the cup, aware of his fingers' overzealous grasp as the paper container gave a little under the pressure.

'Not very hot, I'm afraid,' she said, lifting an identical cup to her lips.

'That's fine.'

They stood companionably side by side sipping the lukewarm coffee and watching the busy scene before them.

'I have a bad feeling about this one,' Vivier said, conscious that his words probably made him sound like a detective from one of Sabine Pelat's murder mysteries.

'Me, too,' Sabine said, 'but then…'

'But then?'

'I always do. With women, I mean, as a woman myself.'

Vivier turned to look at Pelat, curious to see the expression on her face.

Sabine Pelat, who always claimed absolute equality with men, who would not be patronised, or talked down to. Whom one dare not even compliment or speak affectionately to. And now here she was quietly saying this; reminding him that she was a woman?

'Because?' he said.

She frowned. Her dark hair was pulled back from her face in two glossy wings that joined in a chignon at the base of her skull; her olive-coloured skin was scrubbed clean and gleamed in places where the light caught it. Her eyebrows were finely shaped, her eyelashes heavy and dark. Such a woman, Vivier thought, can easily scorn the artificiality of make-up and still look a thousand times more beautiful than her less principled and over-painted sisters.

'Because,' she said, and now she turned to meet his gaze, 'because this is what happens to us.'

He knew it was better to absorb her words in silence rather than challenge them. It was not the time to raise polemical issues about gender, about masculinity and how men die in street fights and construction accidents and wars. So instead he blinked slowly and nodded his head. And then, as if to challenge the limitless potential of human imagination, he pictured himself, without really meaning to, kissing her. And Sabine, suddenly abandoning her steely professional reserve, kissing him back.

He hoped his thoughts were not betrayed by his expression. He looked away from Sabine Pelat and stared at the dead girl instead.

# A Thousand Cuts

Aaron, when they found him, had attracted a small audience of onlookers, and no wonder, as his hands and once pristine white t-shirt were smeared with blood. But he was standing quietly enough, as was his way. With his thin shoulders hunched, head tilted to one side he was gazing into space – into that floating other world that existed only for Aaron. His hands were busy, and what they held, what he passed from one hand to another and twirled between his fingers was a razor blade. The old-fashioned kind, very thin and flexible and extremely sharp, and it had efficiently scored and rescored his flesh as it was passed between his hands. The cuts were perhaps superficial, but there were so many and so much blood.

The postman stood nearby, daring to take up a position closer to Aaron than any of the other onlookers, and somehow, because of his uniform, reminiscent at that moment of the circus ringmaster, or the lion tamer, the only one with the courage to approach the wild beast.

Scott nodded gravely at the postman who responded in kind. Marilyn felt there was more to this man's interest and subsequent actions than just kindness. He seemed to have a personal knowledge of what it meant to deal with someone like Aaron. Perhaps he too had a brother or sister or cousin who suffered from something like that which afflicted Aaron. Or worse, and certainly sadder, he might be the father of a child with disabilities.

Scott stepped forward, clearly aware of the audience Aaron had attracted, and although seemingly calm, he must have been raging beneath the surface. Not raging with anger alone, but with the torments of the public gaze, of being exposed as a man incapable of watching over his brother and keeping him from harm.

And then there was fear too. Fear about how badly Aaron might have hurt himself, fear of involvement with the French police and social services, fear of a legal battle which might drag on for weeks and delay their escape and lastly, but by no means least, fear of his parents' reactions when they heard about the incident. His mother would weep. His father, though less demonstrative, would express his disappointment by failing to look Scott in the eye.

All of this ran like a torrential river through Scott's mind, but when he spoke his voice was both authoritative and gentle, firm yet kind.

'Aaron. Aaron!'

Aaron did not look up, but his hands stopped moving and grew limp so that the blade at last fell and landed soundlessly on the blood-splashed pavement.

Scott put a guiding arm around Aaron and began to lead him away from the crowd and towards home.

The postman, again taking up a quasi-official role, addressed the people in rapid French. Marilyn understood only a smattering of his words. Words, which in hindsight, adequately told a story – lost boy, family, medicine, American, no ambulance needed, no, it's over now.

It's over now?

For them perhaps – those gaping strangers who could walk away, for whom this event would become a piece of fascinating gossip to be told and retold. How much would the witnesses relish the image it gave of tourists – of Americans in particular?

But it was not yet over for her and Scott, or for Aaron and his parents.

Scott got his handkerchief, a large white cotton one, and as they walked he attempted to wrap this around both of Aaron's hands. An act which set off a low moan of protest from Aaron.

Marilyn followed a few paces behind and the kindly postman fell into step beside her.

Someone in the crowd called after them and when Marilyn turned to look she saw a smartly dressed middle-aged man heading in their direction. He was waving a mobile phone at them.

'You must wait for the police to come,' he shouted. 'They will want a report. They will want details, an explanation!'

Marilyn hesitated, but the man looked past her, his face twisted in anger.

'Attention! Attention!' he cried, even after the postman had responded by shouting that it was nothing, not to worry, the boy was not badly hurt.

'But I have called the police already!' the man cried, but his voice was fading away in resignation and he did not pursue them any further, returning instead to the place where the crazy young man had been discovered and the evidence of drips and smears of fresh scarlet that he would eagerly point out to the police when they came. Lying amongst the rust speckles and crimson splashes was the blood-smeared razor blade; its edges still lethally sharp despite its morning's work. The man stood over this, carefully guarding it, his mouth turned down sourly at the edges and his chin jutting out resentfully. He folded his arms. He frowned and narrowed his eyes. Impatiently tapped one foot. Waited.

As Marilyn and the others neared the house they heard another siren in the distance. It was far off. The postman shook his head and clucked his tongue against the roof of his mouth.

Scott guided Aaron through the door and into the kitchen.

Marilyn and the postman followed. It seemed right somehow that this good Samaritan should stay with them, and yet there was something strange about it too. He put his mail sack at one end of the table and Marilyn noted that it was still half-full with undelivered mail, and wondered if the man would get into trouble for not completing his round. Scott sat Aaron down at the other end of the table, then filled a large white enamel bowl from the hot tap and added a few drops of disinfectant which clouded the water.

Marilyn switched on the electric kettle and as Scott began to dip a flannel in the water to clean up the worst of the blood, the postman pulled a packet of Gitanes from his pocket, and without asking permission, popped a cigarette in his mouth and lit it with a silver Zippo, shutting the lighter with a sharp and distinct click once the cigarette was burning.

Aaron moaned softly as Scott cleaned and examined his wounds.

A siren seemed to travel from south to north, the Doppler effect distant, but distinct. Or perhaps it was going from west to east. Marilyn looked at the postman, but her worried eyes only produced a shrug and a cloud of cigarette smoke in response.

She was concerned that they might have committed a crime of some sort by leaving with Aaron the way they had. As happens when an automobile accident is not reported. But the nature of that crime had to do with ascertaining responsibility for the accident. Aaron had only hurt himself. He was both the victim and the perpetrator, yet their status as foreign nationals made it all the more difficult to explain the circumstances. There again, perhaps a French law pertaining to the neglect of vulnerable individuals by those responsible for them existed. Just as it would in the case of minors.

'Alright, Aaron, buddy,' Scott said soothingly. 'Alright, kiddo. Got yourself some nasty cuts here. Okay, that's it.'

The kettle boiled and clicked itself off. Marilyn made coffee in the jug, poured three cups and wordlessly placed two on the table within reach of the postman and Scott, but a safe distance from Aaron. One disaster was enough for a single morning. She sat with the three men cradling her cup in both hands trying to absorb everything that had happened.

The water in the white enamel bowl turned from pale milky pink to bright red. Aaron's moans had taken on a drowsy sound. Marilyn looked at his hands, she had been too frightened before; the sight of blood had a visceral effect on her, turning the pit of her stomach sour and hollow, settling on her tongue with a metallic tang. But as she looked she saw that most of the cuts seemed to be closing up; they criss-crossed his hands in red welts and the skin around them was inflamed and sore looking. Only in one or two places did droplets of blood appear to well up and trickle down in slow moving rivulets.

'I'm sorry,' she said suddenly addressing the postman, 'but we don't even know your name.'

The postman stubbed out his cigarette and offered her his hand, dense black hairs on its back, a little rug, and wild tufts on the fingers too. She shook it, sensing its strength.

'Tadeusz.'

'Tadeusz? Is that a French name?'

He smiled a proud, self-contained smile as if caught possessing a secret, but he neither confirmed nor denied the question.

Aaron moaned again, the sound musical as if he was crooning some strange lullaby.

Scott poured the bloody water away, got the First Aid kit and began the slow and delicate process of applying antiseptic cream to Aaron's hands.

'Well, I have work to do,' Tadeusz said, hefting his bag over his shoulder. 'Thanks for the coffee.'

'Thank you, you've been very kind.'

He shrugged. 'It was nothing.'

Marilyn saw him to the door. Another siren sang in the distance.

'I have a question,' Marilyn said. 'Should we inform the police? About what happened, I mean. Tell them that everything's fine?'

The corners of his mouth quirked down.

'No?' Marilyn asked.

'Too much red tape, perhaps,' he said.

'And there won't be a problem?'

Again he shrugged.

'Okay, well thanks.'

At the gate Tadeusz waved at her and grinned. His grin seemed to indicate that he sympathised, but also that she should know that life was absurd. Absurd and fleeting.

She shut the door, and the hallway was plunged into semi-gloom again. She stood there a moment, thinking about Aaron, and Scott, and herself; assigning and assessing blame, countering her imagined accusations with the defence that none of it could have been imagined and therefore the question of guilt was neither here nor there. But she did feel that it was really Scott's fault; he shouldn't have gone out, he should have remembered to lock the door and remove the key when he came in, and ultimately it was he who bore the greater burden of responsibility for Aaron, who was after all his brother.

Intermittently a short burst of siren and air horn sounded, suggesting an emergency services vehicle caught in traffic, and from the kitchen, almost achieving the same Doppler effect, Aaron's moans rose and fell in pitch.

Marilyn laid the palm of her hand on her stomach and closed her eyes. This was the closest to praying she had ever come, and what she prayed for was hardly extraordinary. 'Please let the baby be normal. Just normal, that's all I want, nothing more.'

It wasn't so much to ask really.

But she felt a dark atavistic fear rising inside her, something vague and barely perceptible. It was like a little death; the death of love and the death of hope.

# Duty

Michelle Brandieu, her hair restored to youthful raven-black and fixed in a halo of tight, stickily lacquered curls, hurried home and, after shuffling her tarot pack, laid them out in a simple fifteen-card spread. At their heart was the Princess of Swords – this represented a wise and vengeful woman, fearless. The card to its left was the Empress, representing beauty and love and success, the one to the right was the four of swords which stood for truth. This told Michelle all she needed to know, she barely glanced at the remaining cards.

She changed out of the unflattering but serviceable clothes she had worn to the hairdressers; a lime-green acrylic sweater with a small white cat embroidered over the left bosom, comfy grey slacks with an elasticated waist and white orthopedic shoes with lace ups, and carefully considered her options for a more serious and elegant look.

Over the years (by means of penury and monomaniacal self-deprivation) she had retained the same trim figure she'd possessed in her youth and thus her wardrobe contained clothing she had bought as far back as the late 1960s. After some thought, she chose a navy polka-dot blouse with an oversized teardrop collar, a pleated red polyester skirt and a royal blue jacket in a naval style with gold buttons and epaulettes, white tights and navy patent leather shoes decorated with a jaunty gilt chain.

She applied her make-up: frosted lipstick the colour of raw veal. Greasy black eyebrow pencil applied with a trembling hand which thus affected a rather surprised and surprising look. Then too much rouge which gave the impression she was suffering from high blood pressure, rather than the youthful and healthy glow she had meant to achieve, but with the light coming from behind her and her somewhat muted vision, what Michelle saw in the mirror was herself as she had been thirty years ago. Thirty years ago when, for a brief rare moment in her otherwise unremittingly lonely life, she had been in love.

Gazing lovingly at herself, forgetting for the time being how that love affair had ended, she perceived a new beginning for herself; she saw how she might solve this monstrous crime and would thus be asked to appear in the newspapers and on TV. How she would gain a platform for her astrology, her card readings, her powers as a medium.

The fear she'd felt the night before had entirely evaporated. There was not one drop of doubt diluting her resolve. Michelle knew what she had seen. Knew what it meant, knew what she now must do and knew what it would result in for her. She even, as she left her flat and passed down the three gloomy flights to the street, imagined her lover from all those years before seeing her on TV or in an interview in *Paris Match*. He would fall in love with her all over again, would regret his past infidelities and his hasty marriage to that librarian.

Michelle had never stopped loving him. Astrologically they were an ideal match; she was a Scorpio and he was Pisces – a conspiracy of stars, the precise day and hour of each of their births making their union perfect. Perfect except for the interference of persons and factors beyond their control. Thus it made absolute sense that they should find one another again. Or at least that was what Michelle now told herself.

It was five o'clock before Madame Michelle Brandieu entered the main door of the police station, walked smartly up to the desk where a junior PC was surreptitiously eating curry-flavoured instant noodles from a polystyrene cup, and announced that she knew who the killer was and needed to speak to the official in charge of the case immediately.

The young PC reluctantly lowered the pot of noodles into the metal waste bin under the counter. He was hungry and tired and should have finished work hours ago, but the unexplained death meant a double shift. Jean-Luc might not have minded if he had been assigned to work in the field alongside a man like Paul Vivier, but to be stuck behind a desk?

Jean-Luc was twenty-four years old, had graduated less than a year before from the police academy with high hopes of rapid progression and an exciting job. But paperwork and lost cats and unlicensed cars had depressed and bored him, and he was considering the possibility of resigning. Or was, until the moment Madame Brandieu had declared confidently to him that she knew who the killer was.

Yet that moment of hope passed so quickly. He picked up the internal phone and spoke directly to Inspector Vivier, repeating in a low tone what the woman had claimed to know of the murder.

'Nutter?' Vivier asked in a perfectly reasonable voice.

'Don't think so,' Jean-Luc said, surreptitiously eyeing the woman as she stood waiting at the desk with two hands neatly resting on it, the fingertips partially interlaced and her gaze directed pointedly at him. The inspector's single word question seemed to the young policeman's hypersensitive ego to imply that both the witness and Jean-Luc (if he believed her) were crazy.

Perhaps Jean-Luc should have thrown the woman out and not troubled the inspector at all, but that would have been a dereliction of duty. He sensed that somehow by being the messenger who announced this woman, if it turned out that she was a time-wasting, and in all probability undiagnosed, schizophrenic, he would be endlessly blamed and teased about her.

'I'll send someone through,' Vivier said, before hanging up.

Seconds later Sabine Pelat appeared and ushered the woman away. Jean-Luc watched through the reinforced glass of the office door as the two women moved deeper into the belly of the building. The light in the corridor had a greenish tint and the walls were painted in washable white gloss paint. It was not a cosy workplace, nor was it designed to be. Once the women had disappeared from view, Jean-Luc found himself staring morosely down at his hastily abandoned supper inside the bin. The cup had tipped over, disgorging the pale yellow noodles with their flecks of reconstituted meat and fragments of unidentifiable vegetables onto the other rubbish.

Sighing, he made a note of the time in the diary and reported the arrival of a witness. Too late he realised that he should have taken the woman's name. But even as he recognised his mistake, and worried that it was yet another obstacle to a speedy promotion, he felt himself giving up, letting impatience reconstruct itself into a valid and well-thought-out decision. Police work did not suit him, it was not as he had imagined, he would resign.

Restless and bored, he reached into his trouser pocket and pulled out a playing card he'd found on the street on his way into work. The ace of hearts, like a message to him – not that he was superstitious – but he'd pictured himself passing it to a girl in a bar, his name and phone number on it. Winking. Smiling. Winning. Ace high. Yeah, fat chance while he was stuck here! He flexed it between his thumb and forefingers until of its own accord it jumped into the air and fell somewhere – he neither knew nor cared where.

He yawned, then gazed ruefully down the empty corridor and pictured himself striding importantly along it, out of uniform, (in his imagination he now held Vivier's job) barking orders to his inferiors and on the brink of some vital breakthrough in the case. He'd be the one to find and confront the murderer, there would be a car chase (he loved to drive fast cars) he would rescue a beautiful girl in the nick of time and he would be forced to immobilise and beat the killer with any weapon that came to hand. Jean-Luc would be a bloodied, but triumphant hero.

If only they'd give him a chance.

He'd sleep on his decision to resign, give it another week.

A month at most.

# Lost Property

At the Café de Trois a waiter, while setting out the tables for the day, had noticed a delicate white cardigan draped carefully over the geraniums. Without thinking too much about it, he picked it up, carried it into the café and put it on a shelf in the back room above the washing machine and alongside some of the clean table linen.

People left things behind at the café all the time; umbrellas, hats, sunglasses, keys, mobile phones, half-empty cigarette packs, paperback novels. Rarely anything of value – such as wallets full of cash. Sometimes they returned the same day within minutes or hours, other times after a day or so.

Some years ago, one lady, a certain chic Parisian, had in the course of a conversation with the patron mentioned a silver bracelet that she'd been very fond of. She hadn't see it for a long time and presumed it was lost forever. It was not an expensive item, but it had been the last gift she'd received from her father. She described it in loving detail recalling the unusual motif of cats and mice which chased each other nose to tail around the chain. She last remembered having it during her previous visit to the area which had been three years before.

Hearing this, the patron clucked his tongue and made a sympathetic moue with his mouth, then excused himself, went up the stairs to the flat above the café where he then lived with his wife and children. He went into his daughter's room and opened her jewellery box, releasing the small plastic figure of a turning ballerina and setting off the slow plinking music of a sluggish Swan Lake. Inside the dusty red velvet interior, amongst paste beads and broken gold chains, a tiny bird's skull and a few foreign coins, he found what he was looking for. Namely a silver bracelet which, after several months in exile in the café's lost property box, his wife had given to his daughter. Not that his daughter had ever seemed to like it particularly, which was why he had no qualms about taking it back.

With the bracelet coiled tightly in his left fist, he hurried back to the dining area and bore down on the Parisian lady utterly unable to temper the broad and quite maniacal grin that had plastered itself to his rather oily face. He was so delighted with the miracle he was about to perform that he quite forgot himself, and instead of politely enquiring if this was the lost item and then respectfully returning it to her, he bent slightly and leaning closer with rather, to the Parisian lady's surprise, too much familiarity, said, 'Goodness, what's that behind your ear?'

Panicked, as she imagined a hornet, bee or worse, a spider, the Parisian lady froze and allowed this rather peculiar man to touch the side of her head. His thumb grazed her ear and his fingers seemed to play momentarily with her hair and the naked soft skin at the base of her skull.

'Ah ha!' he said, withdrawing his hand and showing her his closed fist. If it was a spider then she really didn't want to see it, but the fingers were slowly opening and she could not quite avert her gaze.

'What is it?' she demanded, her voice somewhat shriller than she might have liked.

The patron's grin merely broadened.

'Little creatures,' he said.

She imagined a thousand baby spiders erupting from a broken egg sac and flowing from his palm, then spilling onto the table, onto her arms, into her clothes and hair. But then his hand fully opened and there, nestled on his damp palm, she saw the beautiful bracelet her papa had given her on her sixteenth birthday.

'Oh!' she said and her right hand went to her throat – that

instinctive gesture that suggested extreme vulnerability. Yet she hesitated to take the bracelet from his outstretched hand, as if she could not quite believe her eyes and the silver ornament must be some sort of mirage.

'It has been here – what? Three or four years. We never dispose of lost property, Madame; we value our customers too highly.'

It was only a little lie and one that put him in a good light.

'I can't believe it,' she said, the colour rushing to her cheeks as her eyes began to fill with tears.

He opened the tiny catch and held the bracelet out in readiness.

'Here, allow me.'

She offered him her arm and fumbling slightly he managed to wrap the bracelet around her wrist and close the tiny hook.

When he looked at her again she was openly weeping.

This story had been told to the waiter during the first week of his employment. The patron had a habit of embarking on long-winded tales which were illustrative of his ethics and habits in the workplace. As long as the lecture took place when the waiter should have been polishing glasses or sweeping the floor or doing some other onerous and oft-repeated duty, then he didn't mind too much, but the patron, early on, had a habit of launching into these stories just as the waiter was finishing his shift. Listening patiently on the patron's time was one thing, on his own it was quite another.

On first hearing the story of the Parisian lady and her absurd cat and mouse bracelet, the waiter had disbelieved it. He was reminded of those moral tales told him in childhood where good behaviour was rewarded and bad punished, but last year to his surprise, the same woman returned. She was slightly less elegant, less beautiful and at least fifteen years older than the impression he'd got from the patron. She nonetheless wore the bracelet and happily allowed all and sundry: the chef, the pot boy, the waiting staff and a few regular customers, to inspect it and hear the all too familiar story from her perspective.

So. Lost property.

Not that, on idly picking up the cardigan, the waiter imagined his own tale of happy restitution, rather it had become an ingrained habit, like replacing dirty ashtrays, or wiping down tables, and once he had collected the cardigan from the geraniums and placed it on the shelf in the back room, he promptly forgot about it. Forgetting even to inform the patron of his find. Forgetting in part, because of the commotion of the sirens which had begun to fill the air around mid morning, followed by rumours of an unexplained death that filtered through in fits and starts, much of it wildly inaccurate.

One of the older waiters told him, for example, that another woman had been killed. In his mind he conflated 'another woman' with 'another prostitute' and so when others mentioned a dead woman, he tended to ask a question which took the form of a statement, 'She was a prostitute, wasn't she?' And in this way speculation became fact and half the town was convinced that the unnamed dead girl was a known prostitute.

# Lucy Locket Lost her Pocket

Lucy, even while she lay dead; caught precariously on a stout root above the run-off ditch from a factory, nonetheless lived on stubbornly, resolutely and vividly in the minds of all those who knew her. Her lover, Dr Thom McKay, thought he knew by her sudden and wilful silence that he had, in her mind at least, committed some crime and was now being punished. He knew too, that eventually she would answer her phone, that they would meet, the particulars of his crime would at last be revealed and he would have the chance to defend himself; to disabuse her of her notions of his suspected infidelities, his sins of omission, his lack of consideration. A careless word or look of his would be brought under the scrutiny of her judgement, analysed, contextualised, explained. He would be reminded of her sensitivities, her vulnerability, the stories of her past life.

Lucy was, for him, a sort of representation of everything that was light and joyous and exquisitely girlish. He loved her sense of fun, her lithe body, her curiosity, her wonderful lateral thinking. But he did not like the dark turns her mind took, the way her facility for invention could elaborate on a small detail – a phone call not returned, a misplaced word, a forgotten anniversary. Yet she had, over the years, come to recognise that her mind was capable of this trickery, that she had a tendency to succumb to paranoia, but as Lucy herself often said, laughing lightly, gaily at her own folly, 'Even paranoids have enemies.'

It had been ten or twelve days since they last spoke. She had been edgy and brittle on the phone saying she felt like an interloper in her own life. Thom had misunderstood the earnestness of that comment, had made a rather sorry quip, the substance of which he had instantly forgotten, but she had gone silent.

Or not quite completely silent, and he had pictured her face at the other end of the line, tight-lipped and frowning as she stubbornly responded to all his subsequent questions, apologies and statements with the merest and meanest of sighs, grunts and grudging mm-hms. It was as if she was suddenly transformed into her namesake, that mute and naked Lucy whose effigy stood implausibly in the Museum of Natural Science. Australopithecus Afarensis Lucy was named, during an evening of campfire celebration when the song was repeatedly played, after the Beatles' 'Lucy in the Sky with Diamonds'. *That* Lucy was found in an arid gulley in Ethiopia and had breathed her last over three million years ago.

The dead are instantly removed from the living. Time is irrelevant; three millennia or three days do not make an iota of difference, except in the memories of those who knew them, and Thom McKay, who did not yet know that Lucy was dead, was still confidently conjuring conversations with her in his mind. He was making plans for their trip to Goa in the New Year. He was also still trying to ring her. He only got the answer phone when he tried her landline and until six days ago had not left a message, and he had repeatedly tried her mobile, but it was switched off. And he knew what that meant.

He had no sense of fear, no premonition of disaster, no intimation of a sudden loss. He watched a single magpie flit amongst the trees outside his office window and paid it no heed. Why should he? Blackbirds, robins, sparrows, crows, pigeons all appeared at one time or another; it was hardly a rarity to see a single magpie. Or a black cat. Or, with all the renovation work being done around the campus, to find oneself having to walk under ladders.

Yet afterwards, long afterwards, when the truth was revealed, he felt a combination of puzzlement and guilt at his utter lack of premonition or sensation of loss.

'I should have known,' he said ruefully to friends and family for years after. 'I should have known,' but no one, not even Thom McKay really understood quite what it was he should have known, nor why there could be any expectation of prior or concurrent knowledge.

And there was so much that was unexplained about Lucy's disappearance and death: the secret trip to France, the bleached blonde hair, the pastel-coloured summer dresses, all of it completely out of character and overtly, fussily feminine, so much so that Thom was convinced that the French police had somehow confused Lucy's belongings with another woman's. If Lucy had died in the course of her 'real life', Thom often thought, if she had been killed (whether accidentally or at the hands of some lunatic) with her hair still its natural colour, wearing her moss-green tights and the brown woollen dress he'd bought her from Wallis, if she had been on her way home from a lecture, then he might find it easier to accept.

But as it was, stoked by the reports in the papers, it seemed that the Lucy he had known had evaporated in the days before she even left for France, and this other creature, this brassy usurper had taken her place. 'Secret life of University lecturer' one headline in the gutter press had read. Another: 'Sexual misadventures for "Miss"'.

Thom had particularly resented that use of the word 'Miss', conflating her post as a higher education tutor with that of a schoolteacher in order to provide their readership with an even more titillating contrast.

Thom was offered a sabbatical afterwards. Time off from the daily round of lectures and seminars. He'd even been told that his research paper could wait. Time off to do nothing but sit in his flat all day. To traipse from the coffee percolator on the stove to the living room, from the living room to the downstairs loo, from the loo to the kitchen again. To pour another cup of coffee while the first, forgotten and abandoned, sat cooling on the window ledge above the cistern. Time to hear and rehear that stupid phrase pop into his head, 'I should have known', followed by that other one which he shared with no one, but sometimes said aloud.

'Why Lucy, why?'

Unanswerable, of course.

He did not take up the offer of the sabbatical. Did not take up the offer of money from the press for the inside story of Lucy, though her parents, the poor fools, did. Not for the money, they stressed, but in order to show the world *their* Lucy, their happy, carefree, intelligent and talented daughter.

No, they had never met that man she was seeing.

No, they did not know what sort of person he was. They thought it odd that she had never brought him home to Scotland to meet them.

Yes, she had seemed different after she started seeing him. She had become depressed. Overshadowed. Dowdy.

And he was older. Had a past.

'We thought he might be married. Have a few bairns,' Mrs Swan said as she sat beside her husband in the cosy best room of their Motherwell council house. 'She just wasn't our Lucy anymore,' Mr Swan added, putting a supportive arm around his wife of over thirty years. 'It's like all the light has gone out of our lives now.'

Light and shade. According to this picture Thom was the obliterating cloud that shrouded Lucy's incandescence. The symbolism of her peroxide hair, the pale summer dresses, the sun-drenched blue skies and the romance of France did not escape him. Was he more guilty than he knew?

Again it was unanswerable.

166

# Gratitude

This was how they came.

At night. Sometimes just after dusk when the sky was still red-tinged. Or at dawn. Just at the moment when the cocks began to crow, and the guard dogs began to bark. One dog went mad whenever it saw men in uniform. White foam would gather at and spill from the corners of its mouth. Its muzzle wrinkled, all its yellow teeth showing dagger points. The poor widow's mangy half-starved dog. Chained to a post, powerless to act except with this display of noise and fury. The men, soldiers or police, would run past at a silent trot, feet kicking up clouds of orange dust.

Or it might happen like this, on a quiet street, under a blue sky. The car would screech to a halt, its doors flying open even before it had quite stopped, and the men would burst from it. Too fast, too sudden to think much. Fear set the heart going at a crazy speed, blood, adrenalin flowing. The mind maybe only able to mark time with a single word, no, no, no, no. Only that. Then they bundle you, limp and submissive, or taut and fighting, into their car. The doors slam shut again, the engine revs up. The interior of the car smells like onions and cigarette smoke, sweat and beer and Juicy Fruit chewing gum. The windshield is dusty and splattered with insect bodies; little husks and ragged translucent wings. The car is there and then it's gone. Maybe just a few tyre tracks in the road, and in one spot a multitude of footprints, the kicked-over earth signalling a scuffle. You're there and then you're gone. And you might never know why. They may have mistaken you for someone else.

Your list of hopes proceeds thus: one, they let you go, two, they kill you quickly, three, they don't torture you before they kill you.

His father had been taken. They kept him for two days and two nights. He would not say what they did to him, but he was never the same after. And his uncle's business partner vanished one day just after he had opened the print shop. Where were they? Sometimes you just prayed that they were dead.

So when the police car, coming from nowhere it seemed, swerved in front of Joseph, its tyres mounting the pavement, metal scraping on something, the brakes squealing, it was almost as if it had sprung out of an old nightmare. He watched with incredulity as two uniformed cops stared at him from the car.

But this is Europe, Joseph thought, and I am innocent. Who my father is, what tribe my grandmother came from, does not matter here. Nor my uncle's trade and indiscretion.

One cop gets out from the passenger side and comes at him fast, slams him against the car, presses Joseph's face, open-mouthed against the hot car roof. The driver gets out more slowly. As Joseph watches from the other side of the car, the cop's head seems almost disembodied. He puts on dark glasses, removes his hat, wipes a hand over his sleek black hair, replaces the hat, then walks around the back of the car until he's beside Joseph. On cue Joseph is pulled up from the car to face his interrogator.

'Why are you running?'

'I just run.'

'That's not good enough. Why here?'

'Why here?'

'Yeah. What are you running from?'

'From?'

'Yeah. What have you done?'

'Me, sir. Nothing, sir. I just run.' Joseph lifted his palms to show innocence, emptiness.

'What's that on your hand?'

Joseph raised his left hand, surprised somehow to see the

anatomical words still there in biro on his palm. He read it out to them; pharynx, oesophagus, tongue, epiglottis, hyoid bone…

This seemed to anger them – the one with the dark glasses especially.

'What?' he demanded, and Joseph, by way of explanation pointed to his throat.

'I.D.'

'Oh, I'm sorry, sir. My passport is at the hotel. In the safe. I only have my room key … here…' Joseph tried to reach into his pocket.

'Hold it!'

They slammed his body against the car again, wrenched his arms backward, then he felt hard circles of metal go around his wrists. The handcuffs, he noticed, were not cold as he might have expected, but warm as if they had been heated by someone's skin.

'I am innocent,' Joseph said.

The first cop pulled him backwards off the car, he stumbled awkwardly, stepping blindly, then a strong hand was on his neck and shoulder, pressing him down and as he resisted, something, a boot, kicked one of his feet from under him and he half sat, half fell down on the pavement's edge. The cop with the dark glasses looked at the roof of the car where Joseph's face had been pressed seconds before. Looked at it, a scowl on his face showing disgust, then taking a white handkerchief from his pocket he wiped the paintwork as if it were contaminated.

'Sir, please, I have done nothing. I am a tourist.'

The cop ignored him, spoke instead into a phone, then moved away out of earshot and out of view. Came back. Something had changed. The other cop put a hand under Joseph's arm, jerked a fist into his armpit, pulled him up again, then took the cuffs off.

Joseph felt relief, even gratitude.

No more questions, only a request; would he mind coming to the station to help them?

They weren't arresting him, but his assistance was necessary, and there was the matter of checking his I.D. Foreign national. How did they know he was who he said he was?

Joseph nodded. It was a small matter. This was France, and as far as he knew, its landscape wasn't littered with unmarked graves, nor was it a place where a police car speeding through the marketplace at dawn might disgorge a broken body from the back door. He had no history and no future here. He was a tourist.

He nodded again.

They opened the car, gestured politely for him to get in. A sharp smell inside, perfume and something else, something fainter, urine perhaps. Dangling from the driver's mirror, swinging slightly as the two men got in the front and slammed the doors, a small green cardboard shape with sharp triangular edges like a Christmas tree, and yet it was only the beginning of August.

# Mise en Scène

Paul Vivier pulled into the police station car-park, turned off the ignition, then sat for a few minutes with his hands resting on the steering wheel. It was as if he might, at any minute, change his mind about being there and drive away to another life. As if he did not wish to relinquish the control that the steering wheel seemed to offer. That was it exactly – when he was driving he was the master of his destiny; not only that, but as long as he was driving, was between places, going determinedly and purposefully from point A to point B, he did not have to think about very much else (though of course he did) and so now having arrived, he was in some primitive childlike part of his brain regretting it deeply.

He had been at the crime scene for the entire morning, then at the forensic lab. He was emotionally drained. Would anyone believe that about him? Or about the countless others who dealt professionally with murder and tragedy? As a police inspector, as a detective, he had seen versions of himself portrayed in countless movies and TV series. There was Simenon's Maigret, the witless Inspector Clouseau, the Belgian Hercule Poirot, the very English and iconic Sherlock Holmes, Raymond Chandler's Marlowe. These were, of course, old school. Vivier knew from conversations with Sabine Pelat that there was now a profusion, a veritable swarm, a multitude of fictional detectives, some like him who were trained and worked for the police department, others who were private investigators and lastly there were the amateur sleuths who unwittingly stumbled across murder and (while the idiotic police could not see the obvious) managed to unravel mysteries and gain access to people and places they would not logically in the real world get within a mile of.

Absurd.

And what was more, murder as entertainment sickened him. Sudden violent death in real life, on the other hand, saddened him to the core of his being. Wasted lives. Innocence caught in the snare of evil. Evil erupting like so many smallpox lesions on the body of the world – now here, now there. The profiling of serial killers (and it was by no means certain that this was what they were dealing with) did in some instances help, as did the victim's characteristics and the means by which they were dispatched.

Physically, in terms of age and, well, he hesitated to even think it, beauty, these two women, Marianne Sigot and the as yet unidentified victim could not be more different. He found himself remembering the texture of both women's hair. No one would imagine a police detective laying an interrogative and yet surprisingly tender hand on the heads of murdered women. But that was the case, these women, one with her stretch marks and scars, her loose skin, the tell-tale signs of self abuse, the needle tracks, the other with her pale and unblemished skin, had in death lost all self-determination, and belonged in some sense to the state, or at least until such a time as they were released for burial. Vivier's hand – in his mind at least – symbolised a promise to do all in his power to bring their killers to justice.

The interior of the car darkened suddenly, and Paul Vivier glanced up to see a cloud drift across the sun. A single small cumulus humilis moving slowly and brazenly through the otherwise empty blue heaven.

Vivier sighed, then tapped his fingers twice on the steering wheel as if that signalled action. Then he got out of the car and strode at a pace through the back entrance and into the station.

The first person he spied was Sabine Pelat. She was sitting in an alcove near the coffee percolator, her back straight, legs elegantly crossed, with a paperback book held open at eye level.

The cover of the book showed an expanse of twilight blue snow and beyond that a stand of spindly black pine trees.

He stopped and studied her for a moment.

Without taking her eyes from the book, (and after she had seemingly let him watch her for a few beats of time) she said, 'I'm making fresh coffee, Inspector, do you want some?'

He was tempted to ask her how she knew it was him, but that would reveal a certain weakness on his part, it would reveal him as the guileless subject of her watchfulness; the interrogated rather than the interrogator.

Such games they played.

'Yes. Can you bring it through to my office? If it's not too much trouble?' It was perhaps a cheap shot, a means of regaining power.

At last she turned to look at him.

'Certainly, sir.' She smiled briefly. It was a real smile; the eyes alive and fully animated, the white teeth momentarily displayed and yet the speed at which her face became impassive again, suggested something like insubordination, sarcasm.

'We need to talk,' he said, and recognising the phrase as one uttered more usually by people in the midst of a disintegrating love affair, he added, 'about the case. Catch up.'

'Of course. Coffee will be another few minutes.'

Her eyes went back to the book. He had been dismissed.

In his office, he had no sooner sat down than the phone on his desk began to ring.

'Sir?'

It was Montaldo, his voice sounding hollow and strained, as if the speaker were in pain which, given Montaldo's recurrent boils, he probably was.

'I'm on rue d'Troville, with a suspect.'

'A suspect?'

'Yes sir, he was running away from the crime scene.'

'When?'

'Eleven forty-six, sir.'

'Quarter to twelve?' Vivier's voice was dripping with incredulity. 'He must have been running very slowly.'

'No, sir. Sprinting. Very fast. Very fit. Powerful.'

'Yes, yes. But apart from the fact that he was running what else do you have on him?'

'He's a foreigner, sir. African. Black as.'

'And?' Again his voice filled with weary sarcasm.

'There's writing on his hand, on the palm. It's English I think, and when I questioned him about it he kept saying it was Latin for throat or something. The girl was strangled, wasn't she, sir?'

Vivier's interest was piqued. 'Hmm, maybe you'd better bring him in. Don't arrest him as yet; just issue him with an invitation to assist with our enquiries.'

There was silence on the other end of the line, or not quite silence, but wordless and slightly strained, slightly squeaky breathing.

'Montaldo?'

'Sir?'

'You haven't arrested him, have you?'

'No, but… ah… we did cuff him.'

'Then perhaps you'd like to uncuff him?'

'Right, sir.'

'Does he have ID?'

'No, sir. Says his papers are back at the hotel.'

'Well, that's reasonable enough. How's he dressed?'

'Ghetto, sir.'

'Meaning?'

'Tracksuit, trainers, like they all wear.'

'Athletes?'

'No, ah…' Montaldo seemed to stop and consider his choice of words. 'Black youths, sir.'

'Alright, get on with it.'

Vivier replaced the receiver just as Sabine Pelat appeared at his door with a mug of coffee in each hand, and the paperback tucked under one arm. Vivier noticed how the book pressed against one breast making it rise an inch or so higher than its partner.

He directed his gaze more pointedly at the book itself. 'You're not wasting police time, are you, Pelat?'

She put the cups on the desk, took the book from its warm spot and placed it on the far end of the desk.

'Downtime,' she said. 'It helps me think.'

He raised an eyebrow. Sabine Pelat's work record was exemplary. If reading a trashy novel for a few minutes while she waited for coffee to percolate helped her think, then who was he to split hairs?

'That was Montaldo. Thinks he has a suspect.'

'Really?'

'Don't get too excited, seems Montaldo caught some jogger a few streets from the crime scene, hours after the death, but in possession of black skin and curly hair.'

'Oh.' They exchanged looks. Montaldo had been reprimanded more than once for his use of racist language, his reactionary views.

'But, he did say that the man had some weird writing on his hand and that when questioned about it he said it referred to the throat.'

Sabine thought about this, absorbing the information as she sipped her coffee. 'It could be nothing. What did the words say?'

'Don't know, it wasn't in French.'

'Generally,' she said, 'they stick to their own kind.'

'Who?' Vivier was startled, he had an uncomfortable feeling that perhaps even Sabine Pelat was capable of racism.

'Serial killers. If that's what we're dealing with. They select their victims from the same race as themselves. Blacks kill blacks. Whites, whites.'

'With no deviation?'

'Possibly, but as a general rule.'

'I see, and according to profilers they select similar types of victim – have you seen photographs of the women Ted Bundy killed?'

Vivier looked at Sabine Pelat's face as he asked this and waited for her answer. If her hair was loose she would fit Bundy's type; long glossy dark hair in a centre parting, a well-formed heart-shaped face, large doe-like eyes, a wide sensuous mouth. Though Sabine did not smile as readily as those twelve or thirteen American college students Bundy had strangled and bludgeoned to death, and she was a little older.

'I think so, though I may have, possibly – sometime in the past.'

'Well, they all look remarkably like one another and each in their turn also resembled Bundy's first love – a girlfriend who dumped him and whose rejection he clearly had trouble getting over.'

'Christ, he must have been stupid.'

'Bundy? How do you mean?'

'To not see the difference between one woman and another.'

'Well, he was clearly insane…'

'Didn't he go to the electric chair?'

'I believe so.'

The phone rang again. Vivier picked it up and listened to the young sergeant on desk duty.

'Nutter?' he asked, narrowing his eyes at Sabine Pelat, as he said it. In response she raised her eyebrows questioningly.

'Alright. I'll send someone now.' He replaced the receiver and turned his attention to Sabine again. 'Someone's come in off the street claiming they know who the murderer is. It's a woman, so would you mind?'

'No problem, sir.'

Vivier swallowed the coffee in two gulps, closed his eyes as he felt the hot liquid fall down his gullet and pictured a weird internal waterfall. His throat. The girl's throat.

Initial reports from forensic did not suggest obvious manual strangulation – there was some bruising and swelling, but the hyoid bone was unbroken. Pelat hypothesized a carotid takedown; an attack of such simplicity and effectiveness that the victim passed out from a lack of oxygen to the brain in a matter of seconds. Six months before, Vivier might have asked if that was something she'd gleaned from one of her murder mysteries, but he had learned to hold his tongue – Pelat was not stupid, not gullible.

And the victim had been wearing panties; not a thong, but a style that rose high over the buttocks and were a bit like the shorts Kylie Minogue had worn in a recent video and ad campaign. Familiarity with pop music's idols and particularly their bottoms and how they chose to clothe them was not usually at the forefront of Vivier's mind, but a few months ago someone, no one knew who, had stuck up a picture of the aforementioned princess of pop's pert and meagerly clad rear end on the staff notice board in the corridor outside the canteen. The women members of staff had been outraged and it was swiftly removed. It did however spark a debate about exhibitionism, female sexuality, freedom of choice and vulnerability, including mention of the Muslim veil and French policy; the ironies of tolerance and self-determination and faith.

Again, according to reports, the girl had not been sexually assaulted, but this did not mean sex wasn't the motive – sexual satisfaction could be achieved by more indirect means than simple penetration. According to Freud some adults got frozen in the development of their sexuality, were perpetually stuck at the point of looking or displaying, and while they might masturbate to images of the opposite sex, they might actually fear them. Freud also mentioned some men's fear of full congress because of what is known as the vagina dentata – the vagina with teeth.

# La Petite Mort

Aaron in bed. A drugged sleep. Scott had given him a sedative. Bright spots of red turning dirty brown-burgundy on his bandaged hands. Marilyn and Scott had stood over him, watching him. As if they were afraid he would evaporate. Or as if they willed him to evaporate, to go out of focus, to fade, leaving only the warm bed and the tangled bloodstained bandages strewn over it like abandoned ribbons.

Scott and Marilyn standing side by side, inches apart, afraid to touch one another, as if they did not deserve that comfort.

Scott troubled by secrets. The old memory of himself as a child standing as now by the side of his sleeping brother. And last night too, his words to the young woman, his bottled up anger and desire. Then forgetting to remove the keys from the door. Forgetting perhaps to even lock it.

How does one forget? Is there, in truth, no forgetting? Only the work of the subconscious artfully spinning reality into the form it desires. The reptile brain viciously, heartlessly achieving its selfish needs by any means possible.

'I think you should tell them,' Marilyn said. 'They should know. They'll see his hands; the cuts won't have completely healed by then.'

'No, it'll only worry them. Christ, you know what my mother is like; she'll be on the first flight over here with her first aid box.'

'Will they blame us?'

'Yeah, I guess so. Maybe they won't let us bring him again. Won't trust us or him, or France or whatever.'

'Oh.'

Marilyn and Scott each considered the words he'd just spoken.

To be blamed was one thing; that sat heavy in the heart. They had tried, but failed. And yet what a punishment they might be given for this failure. To be no longer trusted with Aaron. To be deprived of this burden. To be free.

And there was Marilyn's secret too. A beautiful, but still troubling secret. The baby. No real outward sign yet. Her breasts a little fuller than before. A thickening of her waist, so that she had begun to leave the top button of her jeans and skirts undone and to favour the loosest dress she had brought. She longed to see a more visible bulge, a great dome ballooning out. She would be a sort of walking miracle. Not really, of course, and yet for her, for Scott too, this new life they had made was magical.

Unless.

Unless whatever was wrong with Aaron was genetic, could skip over individuals and generations like a girl's feet skipping over hopscotch tiles, landing here, missing there; and then?

Marilyn shivered.

'Hey,' Scott said, and at last put his arm around her shoulder, and she gratefully slotted herself in against his body. 'You cold?'

'No. Yes, just a little, I guess.'

He rubbed her arm.

'I'm sorry,' he said.

'For what?'

'For all of this. For dragging you into this. I'm sorry he's the way he is. I'm sorry I'm not a better person. I'm sorry I'm not like you.'

'Like me?'

'Yeah, you.'

He kissed her. A peck on the forehead, then he ducked his head away again even as she tilted her face, her mouth up to meet his.

'But you're a good person,' she said.

'No, I'm not. I'm lousy.'

'Scott!'

This last word was spoken loudly. Aaron whimpered in response, or so it seemed.

They watched the sleeping young man again. Angelic, as all innocents are when asleep.

'Come on. I'm exhausted, let's see if we can get some shuteye too.'

'It's only seven o'clock,' Marilyn said, but allowed herself to be led from Aaron's room and into theirs. Light poured in through the white muslin curtains, light that seemed to fill the whole space illuminating everything equally. As if the room were some glass aquarium and they were creatures who ate, drank and breathed light. Marilyn, uncertain if she actually wanted to sleep right now, uncertain of the wisdom of it, as she might not sleep later, went and stood in front of the small desk under the window, her notebook upon it, a poem half written, her uncapped pen lying across the page.

Should she write or sleep? Forgetting for an instant Scott in the room behind her until a hand, or the tips of his fingers really, gently, almost imperceptibly, drew the hair from her neck in order to kiss the tender skin there.

'Oh. That's nice,' she said, sighing.

His other hand reached around the front of her, his warmth against her back, his mouth warm and wet, opening and closing on her skin, consuming her. Then his hands, one snaking under her blouse, wriggling into her bra, cupping her breast, the other on her belly, its palm with fingers splayed pressing her against his body. Then him taking backward steps, drawing her with him to the bed, then the tumble, the tumult.

'We shouldn't,' she said at one point, but by then they had already gone too far.

# Labyrinths

Michael Eszterhas, atheist, anarchist, agitator, ex-secretary of the International Socialist Students' Association and ex-jailbird was following the path of the labyrinth set into the tiled floor of Chartres cathedral. His wife, Hilda, was stepping uncomfortably behind him. Since breakfast their conversation had been stilted.

This was not how they had pictured the future. An elderly couple, taking holidays in France, visiting cathedrals. Not that either of them had developed a taste for spirituality or organised religion. Nearer to death, but no nearer to God. Maybe that would come in their dotage, but they doubted it.

And yet it seemed that lately the abstract entity which they believed in, which was in some ways very like that other abstract entity, God, had lost its powerful gleam. This entity, this thing, this belief had shone like the most powerful beacon in their youth. It had been out there on the horizon, almost visible, almost palpable. They knew the journey towards it was hard, there would be sacrifice, physical discomfort and pain, bloodshed even, but the light was so strong. Once they had called this thing revolution. The word had tripped off their tongues with absolute certainty.

It was a case of when the revolution comes, not if. But this was before the word became vulgarised, became a Beatles song. Before the name of Cuba's hero, Che Guevara became a chain of shops that sold jeans and t-shirts. Before everything got mixed up with slogans. 'Make love not war' and 'be sure to wear some flowers in your hair' and drugs and hedonism, the whole amnesic mess. Now instead of revolution Hilda and Michael spoke of 'change', a quieter word, but one spoken with dignity.

Hilda followed a few paces behind Michael, her eyes watching her own feet as well as his on the worn coffee-coloured tiles. They had been set into the floor as a tool for meditation. Monks' and pilgrims' feet had walked here before them.

Michael was wearing sandals and khaki-coloured shorts that seemed to suddenly no longer fit him. Hilda looked at his calves. Knotted with twists of bulging varicose veins, but tanned and shapely, though the skin in other parts of his body had grown loose. After years of being slightly overweight, of carrying a modest paunch, he had at last lost weight. Hilda however, no matter how careful she was about her diet, continued to slowly gain weight. Her breasts in particular seemed determined to swell regardless of their non-functionality. She and Michael, once brave and beautiful revolutionaries – not that she had ever thought herself beautiful or even remotely attractive – were turning into Jack Spratt and his wife. Old people, invisible, safe and probably boring as hell. Who would want to hear now of the things they'd done, the people they'd met, what they had seen? All of it now history without even the chance of being written on a gravestone. To be buried was, after all, politically incorrect, though they had of course been to Highgate cemetery on numerous occasions to visit the grave of Karl Marx.

They had seen Ginsberg at the Albert Hall in '65. They'd met (and given donations for the cause to) Daniel Cohn-Bendit at the University of Nanterre in early March of '68. Had been arrested separately, but within minutes of one another in Grosvenor Square later that same month when Michael was charged with assaulting a police officer, Hilda with disturbing the peace. Disturbing the peace? When peace was what they wanted? They had gone to the Bogside in Derry in '69 to show their solidarity with the Catholic civil rights movement. They had marched in Southall in 1979 and witnessed fellow protester Blair Peach being bundled into an ambulance. Later they heard he had died.

Something had indeed died, kept dying or at least mutating.

There in the cool space of the vast cathedral, walking the labyrinth, still together after all these years as friends, comrades and more lately, lovers, they were true believers who had yet to get to heaven.

Hilda, feeling not so much in a state of blissful meditation as one of stupefaction, did not notice (though she had been watching his feet the whole time) that Michael had come to a halt and so she blundered into him, her shoes catching the back of his heel and scraping the skin where it was most vulnerable. He stumbled and she, trying to arrest his fall, but herself off balance, staggered sideways half dragging him with her. Neither fell, but a group of teenagers witnessed their clumsy hop-a-foot; their pained, surprised expressions as they staggered comically about, and sniggered cruelly.

Thus was ended the sojourn in the cathedral; with two old folks limping out, one with a wound that bled copiously and extravagantly (helped, Michael supposed, by movement and gravity), the other with a pulled muscle in either her shoulder or her neck (always a vulnerable place with those unwieldy breasts to heft around), hissing blame at one another.

Afterwards, sitting in bitter recriminating silence on a bench outside in the sunshine again, as Michael fastened a wad of tissues around his ankle with a camera cord, they might never have spoken to one another again, had not Hilda said, 'Well, He did say "vengeance is mine" didn't He?' And Michael, laughing, had taken her hand and pressed it thankfully between both of his.

'Little sods,' he said after a few moments. 'Laughing at us.'

'Oh, it must have looked funny.'

'It wouldn't have been funny if we'd actually fallen.'

'But we didn't.'

Michael gazed off across the broad square.. Hilda noticed how his cheek had begun to look a little sunken, giving him a gaunt aspect. The weight loss; had they been wrong to celebrate it? Was it not the outcome of a healthy diet (last year they had both given up anything containing wheat as well as whisky and other spirits) but the portent of something much more sinister and troubling; the beginning of disease and the slide towards death?

As this thought entered her mind, the sudden vivid reality of it, Hilda could not help but gasp.

'Alright, darling?' Michael said. 'Where does it hurt?'

'All over,' she said, uncertain really as to just what she meant by that, but unable to utter another word as she found herself weeping suddenly and noisily.

'Time to go back, I think,' he said, when at last her tears had subsided (he had never known her to cry in this fashion before, or at least not for many, many years) and he gently tapped her knee.

They arrived back in the town at around five to see a uniformed gendarme trotting easily up the front steps of their hotel. An old fear gripped them both, that money they'd handed over years ago to the student leader, their names on certain lists, their faces circled in photographs of particular demonstrations, Michael with a motorcycle helmet on, Hilda with a Palestinian scarf being ripped from her surprised face, while her hand was raised in a clenched fist, their old passports criss-crossed with the sites of all their earnest involvement in the struggle. Perhaps they were not the only ones who had long memories, who had not forgotten.

Michael took her hand and bravely, together, they followed the gendarme into the dim lobby of the hotel.

# Blood Ties

It was Lamy who told Vivier about the boy who had been seen covered in blood in the rue Félix. Not that any of the police had seen the boy, let alone spoken to him. By the time they arrived on the scene all the reports were secondhand – some were wildly exaggerated, others sympathetic. A wild boy, blood around his mouth and all over his hands, had been cornered by a mob and it was only this that prevented him from killing again.

Killing again?

There was no evidence he'd killed once. But there was a wildfire rumour, something about a small animal being torn apart and eaten; a rabbit, a kitten, a tame bird.

Several people had called the police, but by the time they arrived there was no sign of the wild boy. No sign that is, apart from splashes of dried blood on the pavement, a partial bloody handprint on a wall and a razor blade which was still lethally sharp.

A wild boy, a frightened boy, a boy who had hurt himself, who had hurt others. A foreigner. German. Or Dutch. English. American. Fingernails like claws.

A stranger in a strange land. A mad boy. A boy or young man who had been taken away by an older man and an unusual-looking, red-haired woman. Then there was also something about a postman?

And blood. A lot of detail about blood. Visceral. Dripping. Splashed. Smeared. Blood as evidence of violence done.

And not so far away, a dead woman. There might be a connection. Or not. But one thing was clear – there was no blood on the murdered woman's body or the dress she wore. No obvious wounds. No clear cause of death and they were awaiting the initial reports prior to the autopsy. At the crime scene there had been no bloodletting.

# The Interpretation of Dreams

As Sabine Pelat made her way down the corridor to the front desk she caught her first glimpse of the woman she had been sent to collect. The woman looked odd, her face distorted by the glass in the office door. It was thick glass, reinforced by a grid of criss-crossed wires. Not bullet proof however; it was due to be replaced later in the year along with a few other vital improvements, such as the damp wall in the ladies loo. Money – that was the issue. It was always the issue with government, with people.

As she walked towards her, the woman's head seemed to distort and ripple as if she were underwater.

Nutter? Paul Vivier had been right to ask it.

Blue-black hair obviously dyed and heavy, badly applied make up. The painted face of a woman desperate to wear a mask that represented her younger self.

Sabine opened the door briskly and once through it did not look at the woman directly.

'Jean-Luc?' she said to the young policeman on duty. She said it in an undertone. First names were not strictly to be used by the force when addressing one another in front of the public, but she had known the young policeman since he was a boy and old habits died hard.

'This is the witness who claims to have information,' he said.

The room smelled odd; besides the usual blend of bleach, air freshener and wood polish, she detected a combination of curry spices, hairspray and stale, oversweet perfume.

'I see,' Sabine said. 'Would you come through, Madame.'

Jean-Luc lifted the wooden flap in the counter to allow the woman through.

The woman passed Sabine in the doorway; the combined smells of powdery talc and chemical hairspray and scent was overpowering once you got within a few feet of her. And the mess she had made of her make-up? The line along her jaw where she had applied thick orange foundation when compared with the unadorned pale papery skin of her neck below was almost comical. And the wonky black eyebrows, the sickly lipstick, the daubed rouge? All of it absurd. Beauty as interpreted by a drunken circus clown. Dust on the shoulders of the jacket, tarnished gold buttons, scuffed shoes, white stockings with a run at the back, twisting over her calf and then the sad nylon wrinkles around her bony ankles.

Sabine showed her into the interview room. Invited her to sit, offered her a drink, told her that someone would be in soon to take a statement.

The woman looked pleased with herself. A tiny woman, she perched on the edge of the chair, her handbag on the table before her, both hands clutching the handle as if someone might try to snatch it. Although she was sitting erect, Sabine noticed the beginning of a hump that seemed to make her neck loop forward and it reminded her of a vulture. Osteoporosis. Brittle bones.

Sabine went to fetch Vivier. He raised his eyebrows quizzically.

'Bit of an odd bird. But then you never know. Could be our guy's wife or mother?' she said.

'I doubt a mother would suspect a son of that, and if she did, well blood's thicker than water. Anyway, let's see what she has to say.'

The two detectives were well rehearsed in their respective roles, expert at listening, noticing not only what a witness or suspect might say or give away in their body language, but sensitive too, to what the other was doing. Not quite the oft quoted and clichéd good cop, bad cop, but something like it, except it was more subtle, more carefully modulated and specific to the subject being interviewed.

Vivier immediately took on the role of a charmer, enquiring if Madame was comfortable, offering a drink again. She said no the first time she was asked but now, fluttering her eyelashes, she accepted.

'Ah, but of course, my assistant, Mademoiselle Pelat will get it, a coffee for me too, if you please?'

'Yes, sir.' So Sabine was to play the female drudge then; to exemplify the negative space of the woman in order to magnify his masculine charm and power. It was enough to make you puke. But then a woman like that; she'd eat it up.

Sabine left the door open and heard Vivier say something banal about the weather. She poured three coffees, loaded them onto a tray with a saucer full of sugar cubes and a glass jug of milk, then added a few packets of biscuits the café owner down the road had given them. Out of date, but he'd assured them they would be fine.

Vivier offered the woman milk, sugar, a biscuit?

Took a packet of cigarettes from his trouser pocket and offered her one. She accepted, and holding it to her lips, gazed at his face as he lit it for her.

'We'll tape this interview if you don't mind,' he said, smiling, then as if to show that actually he didn't care about his job, he didn't care about murders, he was a man and she was a woman, he waved a dismissive hand. 'It's merely a formality. Nothing to trouble us, no?'

The woman seemed to lap this up.

Vivier pushed the button on the recorder and glancing at his watch, gave the precise time and date, then the names of the three people in the room.

'Now, we can begin,' he said and made a steeple with his fingers. 'You say that you have information, Madame Brandieu?'

'Yes, yes. That's right.'

She became more animated as she spoke. Sabine suspected that the woman lived alone. Or if not alone, then with a family who habitually ignored or dismissed her. Chances were whatever information she had would be useless.

'And so would you like to begin?'

'Yes, of course. Let me see now. Last night I was at my window. I have an apartment on the top floor of a building above a restaurant. It has a large window. The flat is modest, and the stairs, oh the stairs! But the window you see, it affords such a wonderful view of the sky.'

Vivier smiled encouragement.

'I am a clairvoyant and an astrologer. This has been my lifetime's vocation and the stars, you see, the constellations. So from the window I…'

'The window?'

'Well, some people think me foolish, but there it is. I spend a great deal of time looking at the night sky.'

Vivier's smile was beginning to appear strained, he nodded for her to continue, but his eyes blinked slowly indicating signs of increasingly weary indulgence.

'So, there I was last night. Very late. The restaurant had closed for the evening, and I was about to go to bed, but first, as always, I looked up at the constellations. It was a clear night, the North Star was particularly bright, and it was very quiet, no wind to speak of. Then suddenly, below me on the street, I sensed something. Yes, that is it exactly. I sensed something, I had a moment of intuition and so I looked down. And I was right. A movement, a white object that seemed to float and hover in the darkness…'

The woman paused here as if to add some drama to the story. Vivier slid his gaze towards Sabine; she pursed her lips and narrowed her eyes.

'Go on…' he encouraged.

'Well, of course at first I could not believe my eyes. I thought it was… well, pardon my foolishness, but there are forces beyond our understanding… by which I mean, I thought it was from the other side. You know, a ghost. I was frightened. Or rather I should say, I felt something; a premonition of evil. The sensation of being near to something inexplicable, a darkness, a cold fire!'

'I see.'

'But then I looked again – well, I mean what I saw became clearer. There was a man out there, there on the street by the perimeter of the café. A black man. Of course, I could hardly see his face, him being black and in the darkness…'

The woman nodded to herself as if suddenly seeing some additional relevance in this. She took a sip of her coffee, little finger crooked in the air, as if she supposed that showed good breeding.

Neither Sabine Pelat nor Paul Vivier said anything. It was better not to break the spell at that precise moment. Besides which both of them were now privately considering Montaldo's phone call about the young African a little time ago.

'Well now, he was facing the café, standing very close to the hedge and as I said there was something white moving through the air in front of him. He is signalling to his compatriots, I thought, he plans to break into my building. But as I looked I saw it was not a simple square of cloth as I had thought, like a handkerchief or a flag, but it was like a body; it had a trunk.' Here the woman indicated with two chopping motions of her hands her own upper body. 'And it had arms,' she indicated each of her arms in turn. 'So then of course I knew what it was, what it meant.'

They waited for her to elaborate.

'Well, it was clear, was it not?' she said, looking in appeal at Vivier.

Her question received only blank, waiting faces. She continued talking. 'A black man with a symbolic human figure? A cloth shape representing someone. It does not have to be a doll, you know. No, a voodoo fetish can take many forms. And this, you see, was one. He laid it over the hedge very carefully. Then, before running away, he smiled. I saw his teeth glint then. Oh, he was pleased with himself. And that was it, you see, I'd felt its presence. I'm very sensitive to that, you see. Not everyone is.'

Vivier managed to shake his head 'no' to show that he agreed with her comment that not everyone was as sensitive as she.

'Hmm,' he said at last, 'and you believe this man was the murderer?'

'Of course!'

'Did you see him with the victim?'

'No.'

'Did you see him near the crime scene itself?'

'No.'

'Pardon me, Madame, this is interesting, but what shall we say? Somewhat indirect? Before we proceed I would like to ask you to keep this information to yourself for the time being. There is the danger that if leaked this could affect the investigation, and of course there is a need for sensitivity in regard to certain of our fellow men.'

The woman nodded, looking mildly confused.

'Do you think you could identify the man if you saw him again?'

She assented somewhat vaguely.

'And this voodoo figure or charm or whatever, what became of it?

She shrugged helplessly.

'But he left it on the flower border, then fled?'

She nodded.

'Why didn't you phone the police that night?'

She looked a little ashamed, as if she had been exposed in her poverty and solitude. 'My phone has been disconnected, sir.'

'Ah, then perhaps you could have alerted your neighbours in the building and asked them for assistance?'

'The apartment below mine is empty, and of course after the restaurant closes…'

'I see.'

'And I was terrified to leave the building.'

'Yes, of course.'

'So I laid a trail of salt, then went to bed.'

Both Vivier and Pelat inhaled breath here as if either of them might enquire what salt had to do with anything, but neither asked it aloud.

'And in the morning? Did you look out of your window? Was it still there?'

'It was gone.'

'I see.'

'Which proves it really, doesn't it?' she said with a renewed confidence.

Vivier tilted his head to one side in enquiry as a dog might.

'The object did not have a solid form,' the woman said. 'It only lasted as long as it needed to. Until its work was done. It's gone. I felt it this morning on waking – the darkness had gone.'

'As it does every morning,' Vivier said under his breath.

'I'm sorry, I didn't quite catch that,' the woman said.

'Quite remarkable. That's what I said. And it is, isn't it Mademoiselle Pelat?'

'Yes, sir. Of course, sir.'

'Well, we'll look into this. We may be in touch again and of course you might be required to make a statement in court. Now, my assistant will see you out.'

He was still playing the gallant, except that now his unctuous words were dripping so heavily with charm that Sabine Pelat could sense sarcasm and distaste loaded heavily on to his tongue like thick pink fondant icing.

Once the woman had gone, they sat together in his office.

'So either there is a link between Montaldo's "suspect",' Vivier indicated apostrophes in the air as he said this last word, 'and this witness, or we have an outbreak of knee-jerk racist stereotyping.'

At that point Montaldo appeared at the door.

'Lamy is with the man in room two, sir.'

'Don't let him go to the bathroom unattended.'

'Sir?'

'You say he's got writing on his hand?'

'Yeah.'

'Well, we don't want him washing that off, do we?'

Montaldo lifted a thumb in the direction of room two. 'But he had to go for a piss when we got here; he may have washed his hands then.'

Vivier sighed and rolled his eyes. The day promised to be endless.

# Love Hurts

Suzette put the groceries away. She was thinking about Florian, piecing together the scraps of everything that had happened the night before and with more clarity the morning's events. She thought about his face as he'd gazed at her. As she had gazed at him. How it had felt when they made love, him moving inside her. The memory vivid enough to make her moan again. She felt the almost fatal pull of greed, she wanted more again, now. To relive it. To step back from this moment into that one again. Addiction.

Addiction or love? Pleasure or fear?

The fear was that this was again just a one off. Her and Florian, casual lovers coming together sporadically, just when it suited both of them. Or rather when it suited him. Herself going along with his desires. Her own needs put mostly on hold. She would bend to accommodate him. She would make a pretence of not caring.

All these strategies of defence were well practised. She was not the sort of woman who was capable of making demands, of setting down rules and ultimatums. Had she always been like this? So weak and needy?

She remembered again him lying on top of her, his face, his expression when he came. So different from her last lover, the cop, who managed to wear a look that resembled hatred when he fucked her, and when he was done, he was done and after a shower was out of there. Pressure of time was meant to be the reason, that and the secrecy.

She would play it by ear. Try to remain cool. Force herself to hide her emotions. She would not reveal herself to Florian, nor

Jacques, nor anyone in the bar. Not that it was any of their business, except that, of course, they had seen. And those who hadn't seen would have been told. And they would tease her. Jacques especially. God, the jokes he used to make about her and the cop! About handcuffs and night sticks and the strong hand of the law. Stupid, stupid jokes that embarrassed and wounded her, and even though she begged him to stop, he would not.

So there was that; the sense of everyone around watching them as if she and Florian were characters in a crumby soap opera.

And wouldn't Jacques find it particularly amusing that she'd gone from an affair with a policeman to one with someone who was habitually on the wrong side of the law. Yeah, ha ha.

But again the memory of Florian that morning rose up in her mind, rose up almost tangibly in her body. It was this that made her so foolish and vulnerable. Pleasure derailing her, making her senseless, as much as it increased her physical senses.

Didn't the flat look different today compared to yesterday? The objects in it more brightly coloured, clearer and more alive? Didn't the coffee she'd bought smell fresher, more infused with an essential coffee-ness?

And the bread (she broke off the end and nibbled a piece) wasn't it sweeter smelling, crustier on the outside while on the inside it was both lighter and more substantial, if that were possible? And her body, didn't it feel somehow more alive, less weary, less dulled by routine; as if charged through with some spectral electric current?

She hadn't felt like this after the first time she'd slept with Florian. She'd felt disappointed that he didn't seem to want to see her again, but she'd half expected that and so she remained … well … impartial.

But now, Jesus, now she almost felt beside herself with longing. Was the effect one of accumulation; namely a single night is one thing, but two nights raised the game, multiplied it not just by two, but by two thousand? Or was it that it had come out of the blue? Just when she had resigned herself to nothing happening with Florian again, he'd floored her.

And yes, quite literally last night he floored her. She had the bruise on her ass to prove it. The heel of a stray shoe under her, the room dim, not the moment to stop what they were doing. Oh, no.

And that was her trouble really, wasn't it? She'd trade one kind of pain so long as she got the pleasure, no matter how brief it was, or how transient.

She broke off more bread and ate it in small mouthfuls. Sometime ago, ten years or more, she'd briefly dated a man who had been involved in some eastern religion. She could not remember now if it was Hare Krishna or Buddhism, but anyway, he'd left the sect by the time she knew him. Most of what he'd told her about it she had instantly forgotten, except for something he'd said about mealtimes in the temple. The sect ate together, but in absolute silence, they were taught to be reverent towards food. He explained that the majority of people habitually just stuff food in their mouths, barely tasting anything after the first bite, and therefore one should learn to eat much more slowly, allowing time to elapse between each morsel. To be aware, to feel each precious second of life, to absorb every sight and sound. That, he said, was the purpose of life. And it seemed at last, momentarily at least, she now understood this philosophy, and yet she also realised how she was suddenly reliant on Florian to jolt her into this condition of acute physical consciousness.

Hopeless. Helpless. She felt herself falling.

Falling.

But there were worse things. That murdered woman.

That poor murdered woman. It didn't bear thinking about.

# Long Memories

The policeman was standing by the reception desk; a slim, tall figure removing his cap as leaning forward he spoke to the receptionist. The light coming from behind him, the yellow glow of the lit dining room. And a smell of meat cooking. The word 'enquiries' floated in the air.

One word.

A man aged sixty-eight, a woman one year younger. War babies. Conceived and born while the world raged and ripped itself to pieces.

The world turned upside down. His mother long dead of a weak heart. His father a Chartist, then later a socialist and a member of the International Brigade. A soldier in the battle of moral right. His father (never mention the name Franco) now ga-ga in a Surrey nursing home. Vases of plastic carnations placed at intervals on Formica tables between wipeable leatherette day chairs. Drool wiped from mouths sporadically. A damaged tear duct. The perpetual leak and drip of old age. A sort of bodily revolution. The anarchy of decay. The decay of anarchy.

Her parents, the opposite. Not socialists, agitators for change, but Christians, conformists, the morally righteous. Her father a clerk for the department of health. Her mother a housewife. Both of them driven mad by a life of dull routine, and a pigtailed daughter too clever for her own good. Her parents, now dead, who lived long enough to launch a long regime of objection to everything in her adult life. Guilt left hanging over her like an obliterating cloud.

And now, Hilda and Michael suddenly old. But possessing long memories and the laming evidence of that near fall in Chartres cathedral, the sniggers of their youthful audience still ringing in their ears. The past at their heels.

Looking straight ahead as if drawn by the yellow light, Michael and Hilda Eszterhas walked as quickly as they could past the policeman. They were almost at the end of the hall, when a woman's voice behind them called out.

'Monsieur et Madame Eszterhas. Excuse me, Mr and Mrs Eszterhas.'

They turned back and saw the receptionist beckoning them, her hand illuminated by the desk lamp to her left, and the policeman in profile, his head bent over so that he could read something on the counter before him.

As they drew closer, the woman spoke again.

'Sorry to bother you both, but there has been an incident and this gentleman wishes to talk to all our visitors, so as you are here…'

'Ah, but my husband has hurt his foot,' Hilda said, uncertain as to why or how that might excuse them.

'It won't take a few minutes,' the policeman said. 'Perhaps there is a private room?'

'Yes, yes of course,' the receptionist said.

She led the policeman and the Eszterhas to a small sitting room and offered them coffee. All three shook their heads, no.

'Perhaps later,' the policeman said.

And the receptionist, nodding, withdrew.

He took their names and home addresses, asked how long they were staying in the area.

'May I ask what this is about?' Michael snapped in a tone that asserted his right as a free individual to not be interrogated by the state. Or rather in a tone which he hoped projected that, but his voice had jumped an octave and came out broken and strangled.

The policeman was unfazed. 'Yes, of course. This morning a

woman was found dead. We believe she may be a tourist and wonder if anyone knows who she is, or if they saw her last night, or in the last few days.'

Hilda felt a surge of relief, which was followed by a cold blast of shame. For one's selfish heart to be lifted by such news was a dreadful thing. Inwardly she apologised to humanity for her second of inhumanity. There was no God to plead pardon from.

'The young woman in question was approximately five foot five, slim build, white-blonde hair, she was wearing strappy shoes with high heels and a sleeveless white dress with a lacy pattern,' the policeman said, reading from his notebook.

Hilda gasped. Michael turned sharply to look at his wife, and Hilda saw that he had immediately pictured the young woman from the night before just as she had done. The young woman and the American man and his terrible words.

'You saw her?' the policeman looked surprised.

'I think so. She was very pretty. Oh, how awful.'

'Do you know her name, where she was staying?'

'No, no, no. We were at a café and she was sitting nearby. A striking looking woman of about twenty-two or twenty-three perhaps. And the dress, yes, I noticed the pattern...' Hilda stopped talking, and lifted her hand which had the effect of creating a waiting silence – a staged moment of expectation, her hand raised and trembling slightly. But in the end no more words came to Hilda.

'That man...' said Michael, and he reached over and plucked Hilda's hand out of the air and lowered it slowly until it rested between them, '...she was talking to a man and he said something vile and outrageous to her. Something like, "I follow strange women and I fuck them".'

'No, no, no,' Hilda said, growing more animated. 'That isn't what he said.'

'Yes, it was! It was naked aggression, this fashionable brazen talk, language as excrement.'

'No, Michael, it was peculiar: passive and aggressive at the same time. There was a diametric opposition, the masculine and feminine interplay – now what was it he said, "I let strange women follow me, then I…" well, I needn't repeat it.'

'Would you excuse me one moment,' the policeman said, and stepped out of the room in order to call the station. He spoke in hushed tones, aware of how the old couple continued to bicker and debate exactly what they'd heard.

Michael was tired and unusually irritable. Hilda was hectoring, determined.

The uniformed policeman re-entered the room.

'Madame, Monsieur, I apologise, but I must request that you come to the station with me to make statements. This is difficult, but we may also ask you to identify the girl.' Seeing their horrified faces and pitying them, he added, 'If no one else comes forward that is.'

'But…' Hilda said.

The word was left hanging in the air. Trepidation, defeat, disharmony. It was a word that resisted movement, attempted prevarication, but finally only hovered uselessly between them.

But.

# Fishers of Men

Vivier was staring into space, seemingly doing nothing. Much detective work consisted of painstaking evidence gathering. At times it could feel arbitrary, or even worse not arbitrary enough – as when men like Montaldo jumped to easy conclusions. Vivier likened it to casting a net in the ocean and catching everything in it; cod, dogfish, prawns, bass, but not having a clue as to which of these were good to eat.

So far he had reports of a young African who had been brought in for interview. He'd been spotted 'running away from the crime scene' according to Montaldo. Curiously he had a list of words on his hand, and the words were the medical terms for parts of the mouth and throat. The dead girl had injuries to her neck, but these, according to early reports, were inconsistent with strangulation. Then there was the woman who lived above the Café de Trois and her report of a young black man performing some sort of voodoo ritual with a piece of white cloth of some description. Finally there was the blood-soaked boy, who was white and reportedly American or Dutch but, unless he had attempted suicide or self harm after killing the girl, (which was possible, if not very probable) it seemed unlikely it was him. And now he had just received the news that a couple of English tourists had seen the girl the night before talking to another American man, and that man had, apparently, openly threatened her.

No one had reported the young woman as missing. There was still no clue as to her identity, but she had been speaking English, or at least spoke and understood enough of it for her to have a conversation with an American.

There were photographs (still smelling faintly of the chemicals from the darkroom) pinned to the board in his office; several of them were of the prostitute murdered earlier that year, Marianne Sigot – some were old mug shots in which she scowled angrily at the police photographer or stared empty-eyed; drugged, drunk or defeated. There were also pictures of her in death. These seemed in some ironic way to show her as becalmed by what had happened to her, as if all her fire and anger had been stripped away to leave a more timid and graceful creature. Photos from the morgue could often look like that, as if it were only a place of rest, the metal table beneath the corpse a silver bed worthy of the grimmest fairy tale.

So far the only photos of the latest victim, if that is what she was – Vivier had to consciously remind himself and the others that nothing was certain yet and they might not have a serial killer on their hands – had been taken at the scene. Her expression was not tortured, her face had not been bruised or mutilated and she was pretty; pretty in that English way; fair with green eyes, soft unsculpted cheek bones, an unlined forehead, a small straight nose. Pretty but not classically beautiful. But then so much of what was taken for attractiveness was created by animation; the way a woman spoke and laughed, the mobility of the face, the eyes that in the act of looking also conveyed expression.

Someone had loved this young woman. No doubt, still loved her.

If it wasn't for the other victim, the police would be looking first and foremost, amongst the young woman's nearest and dearest; her husband or boyfriend or lover, her father or brother. And that may yet be the case. Holidays, despite the promise of nothing but easy pleasure and freedom, were often the cause of petty bickering between lovers and amongst families unaccustomed to spending twenty-four hours a day together. Such bickering could turn murderous, the suppressed rage of years

204

exploding in one quick shove off a hotel balcony, one deadly plunge of a carving knife snatched from a kitchen table in the rented gîte.

So it was possible that the man she had been seen with and was overheard talking to was her lover. Until the witnesses arrived, until it was certain that they had seen the victim that night, until statements were taken, little could be done.

Vivier looked at his watch, eight-forty. His stomach growled. Loud liquid gurgles. Too much coffee and not enough food. He stood up, pushing the chair backwards with his legs so that it gave a grating squeak of protest on the tiled floor. He fished in his jacket pocket, found a strip of foil and plastic and popped out two square antacid pills, put them in his mouth and ground them between his teeth. No substitute for a relaxing meal, a drink or two then to bed with a book, but they might at least quiet his stomach, drug it into silence.

His mind, however, seemed blank, as if this investigation were an elaborate mathematical theorem which he had carefully chalked up on a blackboard, only for someone else, a caretaker perhaps, to wipe the board clean.

Two sharp raps on the office door, his voice automatically answering, then Sabine Pelat's face appearing.

'Inspector, the English couple are here now.'

'Which room?'

'Room three.'

'How's their French?'

Sabine lifted one hand, held it out palm downwards, tilted it rudder-like and pursed her lips.

Vivier noticed the elegance of the gesture; it was like the hand movement of an Indonesian dancer. Her fingers long and tapered, her skin pale and sallow.

His stomach growled again, he spoke in order to cover up the sound.

'Alright, I'll be through in five minutes.'

She did not move, but stood there studying his face, frowning slightly.

'Are you okay sir? You look as if you're in pain.'

Speechless, he shook his head. To admit to being human, to having pain (and feeling pleasure) was more than he could do. Her concern undid him.

Still she lingered.

He shook his head again, this time more vehemently, and flapped a hand at her, shooing her away. Finally she turned and disappeared from view. He gazed at the empty doorway full of longing.

# Education

Lamy stood in front of Inspector Vivier studying him closely. He was waiting for the Inspector to speak, to issue orders. What choice did he have but to stare at him, noticing how at the top of his head (Vivier was hunched over his desk) his hair was growing thin, so that in one area, the size and shape of the pullet's egg, the white waxy-looking scalp was clearly visible between sparse hairs. Lamy felt a twinge of competitive smugness. His own hair was a thick thatch of light brown, cropped close to the skull, and both his father and his father's father still had fine heads of hair, so he was confident that, like them, he would have no worries about going prematurely bald. It was a small triumph, a consolation for his round punched-looking face, his thin mean-looking mouth and twisted nose, his inexpressive fair-lashed eyes. A triumph also against class and power, against the Inspector's position on the force, against Vivier's intellectualism, his easy road; two parents, his mother who was a schoolteacher and a father with a vineyard in the south and a career as a pharmacist. Unless you'd been in Lamy's shoes you'd never know how it felt to fight for everything you'd ever achieved.

Vivier without doubt excelled at his chosen profession, but he was aloof, private, mysterious even. And so much of what he did seemed to be achieved in the space of his own head; give him the equation of two plus two plus two and he somehow came up with eleven, and eleven more often than not turned out be the correct answer. So it was hard to learn from him.

Vivier looked up and caught Lamy gazing at him and gave a look of mild surprise.

'Ah, Lamy,' he said and began to riffle through the papers before him, 'there was a report of something left outside the Café de Trois on the night in question, a white scarf or scrap of material?

Something anyway, I want you to go there now and see if anything was found or if anyone saw anything unusual. The report may be unconnected, but it's worth looking into.'

Lamy nodded and waited. Vivier picked up a pen and began scribbling notes rapidly. Somehow Lamy had an idea that these notes had some relevance to this task, that Vivier was about to elaborate on Lamy's duties in this, so he continued to stand there watching Vivier's hand with its manicured nails and the immaculate crisp whiteness of his shirt cuff. Lamy did not move, but stood with his weight evenly balanced on both legs, his hands clasped behind his back, his head lifted slightly at the chin.

For a while Vivier seemed to have forgotten the younger man was standing there, then he suddenly looked up in puzzlement. He frowned. 'That's all.' And immediately Lamy felt like a fool.

'Sir.'

Lamy spun sharply on his heel, angry with himself. Then as he turned the meeting over in his mind, he became angry with Vivier. As he left the station and made his way on foot to the Café de Trois he grew angry with his father for failing to encourage him at school, for having nothing better to do than fill himself up with cheap wine and to fill Lamy's mother and their overcrowded apartment with more and more babies.

But somehow once the café was within sight and Lamy could see two young waiters scurrying here and there in their long white aprons as they carried heavy trays of beer and food and coffee, his mood softened. While the customers lounged and clicked their fingers in the air demanding service, Lamy was able to console himself; to remember the authority his blue uniform bestowed on him. Lowly as his position was on the force, he was still a figure to be respected and feared by the population at large. He was a cop. And proud of it.

He strode up to the nearest waiter, a tall young man with a bored expression and a lazy slouch who was standing by a large table of tourists, pencil poised in mid air, order book in hand as one of the customers, a rat-faced man in a Liverpool football shirt, attempted to communicate his order by speaking very loudly in English.

Ignoring the customers, Lamy ordered the waiter to take him to the proprietor. Without batting an eyelid (and he was probably glad of the opportunity) the young waiter turned his back on the tourist and walked into the main body of the restaurant, beckoning Lamy as he went.

The rat-faced man who was busy jabbing his finger at the menu did not at first notice that the waiter had gone.

'AND... FRENCH... FRIES...' Lamy heard loud and clear.

The proprietor was sitting at a table at the back of the restaurant eating; a tumbler of red wine within easy reach of his meaty fist. The proprietor invited Lamy to sit and offered him wine.

'No, I'm on duty,' Lamy explained.

The proprietor bobbed his head and continued to eat his omelette. He used only a fork, breaking the omelette up, then skewering small pieces.

'We had reports,' Lamy began, wondering if the man was really listening to him, 'that an item was left somewhere here on the premises sometime last night. Have you or any of your staff found anything?'

The man's plate was almost empty; as he chewed, he scraped up the last bit of food, popping that into his mouth before he'd swallowed the last bit. He held his left hand in the air just above the wine glass. Holding back time, as if somehow time and policemen and questions didn't exist until the omelette was finished. He swallowed the last bit, then lifted his wine glass, drank deeply and ducked his head like a gannet forcing a large fish down its gullet. Finally he wiped his mouth on a linen napkin and pushed the plate to one side. All of it took perhaps a minute, maybe two, but it had felt longer to Lamy, who was not so sure of his authority in such a circumstance, and the man had not even asked his permission to finish his meal first, nor begged his pardon.

'Now what is it?' the man at last said.

'We had reports that something was left here last night, out the front. Have you or your staff found anything or seen anything?'

'Like what?'

Lamy consulted his notebook. 'The woman who lives on the top floor of the building reported that a…'

'Oh her? She's crazy, a troublemaker. Fancies she can see into the future, can cast spells.' He twirled a finger wildly in the air near the side of his head to show the level of his tenant's insanity.

'Yes, but we must look into what she claims, so please, sir, can you answer my question?'

'Is this to do with that girl?'

'I can't tell you that. Now please can you tell me if you or your staff found or saw anything?'

The man nodded morosely.

'You did?'

'What did she say? That crazy bitch, did she say I did something? That one of my staff did something?'

'No, sir. Not at all.' Lamy looked at his notes again. 'She reported that a man left an object, a white cloth, on your premises.'

The proprietor raised his eyebrows and picked up the linen napkin to show it to Lamy. 'A white cloth? Like this?'

Lamy saw his point. In a restaurant where the staff wore white aprons, where the napkins and tablecloths were also white, finding a particular white cloth was somewhat futile and given the vagueness of the description, arbitrary.

'It may have been a garment, a scarf or sweater perhaps? It was placed on the low hedge that borders your pavement seating area.'

'I will ask my staff if something was found. We are particular about this, we have a store for lost property.' He took a mouthful of wine and seemed to warm to his topic. 'Some years ago a lady who had visited this region and my establishment on a previous trip, happened to mention that...'

Lamy broke in, 'Sir, if you don't mind.'

'Ah, but of course.'

The proprietor stood up and reluctantly dropped the napkin onto the table. 'One moment.'

Lamy watched the man head out of the front door and make his way to the nearest waiter. They conversed for a moment and then the waiter shook his head and shrugged. The proprietor moved to the left disappearing from view. Lamy gazed about the bar, noting the stack of crisp snowy linen in a press near the toilets and the clean white aprons hanging on a hook to the left of the door which led to the kitchens. A white cloth reportedly left here by a woman who was possibly mad, it was hardly an important mission, but it was not his job to question orders, merely to undertake them to the best of his ability.

He heard footsteps approaching rapidly and looked up to see the proprietor bearing down on him, a look of excited triumph on his face and behind him, confused and somewhat worried, a younger man in a long apron. He was baby-faced with auburn hair tied back in a stub of a ponytail with a gold sleeper in one ear.

'Christoph found something this morning. Not a cloth at all, but a cardigan. A ladies' white cardigan.'

Christoph stood in front of Lamy nervously, fiddling with his earring. 'I forgot about it. I'm sorry. Is it important?' With the hand that wasn't twirling the earring, he indicated the place where he'd left the cardigan. 'Was it the girl's?' He looked both frightened and sad, as if he had suddenly realised that he had touched death itself, but until that moment, he'd failed to recognise it. 'Shall I get it?'

'Yes, yes' the proprietor said. 'Of course.'

Lamy nodded in agreement.

Minutes later Lamy headed back to the station, a soft pale nest of knitted wool in a paper bag in his hand. In his notebook names, dates, times and addresses.

If he had felt somewhat weary earlier, now he was transformed, energised. He picked up his pace, swung his right arm smartly, while his left, with its precious cargo, he kept perfectly still. It was as if this scrap of almost nebulous fabric had some unusual effect on gravity, transforming itself into lead and thus countering the effects of his brisk movements and the instinct to move both arms. A cardigan. A breakthrough. Lamy's find. He'd bagged it.

# Bloodlines

Marilyn woke to darkness. She still had her blouse on, although it was unbuttoned to the waist and one breast had freed itself (or had been freed) from her bra. Her long skirt was twisted; it coiled itself about her like a winding sheet.

Scott, next to her; right next to her with an acre of empty mattress behind him and her precariously on the other edge. Between her legs a sticky wetness. She imagined blood. The blood that spelled the end of what was only just begun. The end of something she had not yet even mentioned to Scott, which she might now never tell him about. How to explain such a secret coming and going? He would not understand the loss; having never known or believed in this thing, this event, this future, it would be entirely without meaning. He could not mourn what had always been (she saw him thinking this) a figment of her imagination.

She wriggled to untwist herself and turned from her side onto her back. Scott, in his sleep, pressed closer.

'Scott, move over. You're pushing me off the bed.' She put the flat of her palm against his shoulder, nudging him away without quite waking him.

He made a noise that signalled a sleep-heavy protest, then rolled away, turning his face from her.

Marilyn lay on her back, her eyes adjusting to the darkness, looking at the soft grey of the long curtains and sent an exploratory hand to the wet place between her legs. Dipped her middle finger into the slick heat of herself then brought that same finger up to her nose. The sharp tang of sex and a faint, almost fungal yeastiness. Not blood then, though she could not quite be sure. Keeping the finger aloft she leaned over and switched on the bedside lamp, saw that what was there was colourless; was hardly even a gleam of moisture. She turned the light off again. Then breathed a sigh of relief and moved towards Scott again, fitting her belly in against his spine, drawing her knees into the back of his knees, tucking her feet into the smooth undersides of his. She threw her right arm around his waist and her fingers tidied themselves away between the soft swell of his belly and the bed beneath.

She lay there a moment enjoying the nearness of him, the simple fact of his body, the rise and fall of his shoulder. I am happy, she thinks. But no sooner has she thought this than she finds it falling to pieces. As if she had shaped the thought from wet river mud. Or the weighty, slightly gritty black soil from the lake at the bottom of her ex-lover, Lawrence's garden. She had played with Lawrence's children there one summer, making mud pies that they set on rocks to dry in the sunshine. But once dry they crumbled and fell apart.

But she didn't quite feel unhappy either.

She felt, despite the proximity of their bodies, alone.

But then she was alone. Alone in the sense that he was there and not there.

And she had made herself more alone with her small dishonesty. Her secret. And it was not her only secret. She had two secrets. One dead, one alive. They were laid out in her mind side by side. Like twin babies in a shared cot. No pillow under their identical heads.

At the beginning, when she first started seeing Scott, she had also been sleeping with Lawrence. That was no sin. She forgave herself that, as this is what happens. Relationships have fuzzy edges. Grey zones of uncertainty. A dinner date with Scott on Tuesday, the theatre on Friday, then on Sunday a walk by the side of the Ottawa River, holding hands. Head tipped just so. Eyes turning coyly to look at the tall man by her side. That night brazenly telling him she wanted him to stay the night with her, because, so far, he'd been too much of a gentleman.

But on Wednesday there was the regular meeting of the poetry workshop group, and the usual drinks in the bar of the Metropolitan after. Which of course she didn't invite Scott to, because he wasn't a poet and because she'd only had one date with him. The one dry peck on the cheek he'd given her just before she'd stepped into the taxi on Tuesday night had left her thinking he didn't particularly desire her, and probably wouldn't ring again. So on Wednesday, with the usual gang in the bar of the Metropolitan, she found herself sitting next to Lawrence. In a booth that's meant to sit four, but accommodates, at a squeeze, six poets with another three on stools at the end of the table. The wine and words flow freely. Marilyn saying something about cocktails, about Anne Sexton and Sylvia Plath; the moths that danced around a flame. Gregory responding sneeringly by saying something belittling to Marilyn, about women poets and their privileged self-indulgent psyches and their strained verse which was littered with dull domestic banalities. Lawrence standing up for her, saying a clever thing that silenced Gregory. Then, under the table, Lawrence's hand curling around her knee. Comforting her. Then, surprisingly, the same hand – as he twists his head around to look at her, after he has asked 'You alright?' and she has nodded – that same hand moves up her leg and kneads her thigh. Lawrence who is married to an actress and has three children. Lawrence whose first book of poetry was snapped up by one of the best publishers in Canada. Lawrence who also writes plays. Lawrence who has gallantly defended her against the awful Gregory, has his hand on her thigh and, as it happens, she is not wearing nylons, but knee-high socks, and her Indian cotton skirt that still smells faintly of patchouli joss sticks and is constructed in such a way that it wraps around her waist and comes to just below her knees, falls open slightly when she sits. Just enough for one bare knee to poke out, which she might have been more careful about were it not for the booth they're sitting in, and the modesty the table affords.

One by one, the gang departs; Yasmin first, then Gregory, then Daphne, who at seventy-two is the eldest and claims to have seen both W.H. Auden and Dylan Thomas read in New York. Then the others drift away, until there is only Lawrence and Marilyn, who has decided that she is not the sort of woman men want to date and marry, so she had better find consolation by being someone's mistress. Lawrence suggests a drive, wants to show her the place where he wrote the title poem of his second collection and she agrees. How could she not?

She agrees to everything he suggests, in fact. Even sex without a condom as he promises to pull out in time. And does. Or at least she thinks he does.

Then on Thursday, Scott rings and says he's been given two tickets to the theatre. A David Mamet play. A long explanation about the friend who bought the tickets and had to fly to Toronto because of a death in the family. Scott actually bought the tickets himself, but disguises this fact. It protects him from rejection.

But the explanation about the tickets is so longwinded she feels he does not really want her in particular; he just wants company to see the play. Because it's a good play by a good playwright and has had good reviews, and is therefore good culture and good for you, like bran for breakfast, like going to the gym or using unleaded gas in your car.

She says yes to the theatre on Friday. This time, after the play and as she is about to get into the taxi, he stands with two hands lightly holding her shoulders, looks into her eyes, and solemnly bends to kiss her, but again it's only a peck on the cheek.

Saturday she goes to a reading at a bookstore and who should be there, but Lawrence, so they go for coffee after. He buys her a

Greek pastry, sweet and sticky with honey, then after she has complained that there are no napkins, he licks her fingers clean. He holds her hand by the wrist while he swallows one finger after another. There in the brightly lit café with the painting of the Acropolis on the back wall under the stucco arch.

He drives her to a bluff overlooking a steep valley, where he leads her into the trees and undresses her in the moonlight. 'I should write a poem about this,' he says, as she shivers. It's understood that they'll forego the condom and in the nick of time he'll withdraw. He asks her for her phone number, does not give her his, because of the wife, the kids.

Later that night Marilyn rings Sarah; a friend from college whom Marilyn knows has been having an affair with a married man for several years. She confesses about Lawrence, but doesn't name him.

'Be prepared to bleed,' Sarah says, mysteriously.

'What do you mean? Be prepared to bleed?'

'Oh, you numbskull. It's a line from 'A Case of You'. Joni Mitchell? I mean that it'll hurt. You'll always come second. Christmas, birthdays, holidays. Sundays are hell! Who am I to talk, eh? But if I was you, I wouldn't go there. Just don't fall for the bastard, eh? Watch your heart, you deserve better.'

Sunday morning Scott rang, suggested a walk.

Maybe he's gay, Marilyn thought, just enjoys female companionship. But then he'd held her hand, the same hand that she was ashamed to remember had been fellated the evening before by Lawrence.

Sarah's words had stuck. She threw herself at Scott. And he caught her.

Unlike Lawrence, he was careful to use a condom.

But the condom, damn it, the condom wasn't so careful. Perhaps her nail snagged it, who knew? But that was beside the point. It broke.

She saw Lawrence one more time. The next Wednesday she went to the poetry workshop again. She half-believed Lawrence would have new poems to read, hoping perhaps, to find some fragment of herself, a finger, a nipple (small and pink, he'd said, unlike his wife's), a lock of hair in one of his poems. Disguised perhaps as Freyja from the Norse myth, or Brigid the Celtic goddess, or Phaedra or Echo. But he declined when invited to read. They all went for drinks after as usual. There'd been two new writers at the workshop that evening – an attractive mother and daughter from Seattle and he danced attention on them all night long. So she only found a sudden clarity about Lawrence. A clear-sighted realisation that she really didn't matter one bit to him. A lucky escape.

Then her period failed to arrive and there she was caught up in her growing romance with Scott.

So quietly, without telling either man, she made her careful arrangements to undo all the old carelessness. Told only Sarah.

Bled like a stuck pig for days afterwards.

How right Sarah had been.

She'd been prepared to bleed.

But not now, thank God, not now.

# Nature Morte

Vivier was contemplating stillness. Aware of his own body, his stomach at last silenced, leaving a faint buzzing in his ears and beyond that far-off voices and distant sounds, a door opening, then closing, footsteps approaching and retreating, the chirrup of small birds.

In his mind's eye an array of images. He possessed, if not a photographic memory, then something close to one. He can summon up the picture of the dead woman's face without looking at the photograph pinned to the notice board. He can visualise the scene that morning, the sandal which dangled from her foot, the fall of pale hair covering her face. Then, unsummoned, he found himself picturing a painting he had seen at the Staatliche Museum in Berlin two years earlier: Portrait of a Young Girl by Petrus Christus – which had been painted in Bruges around the middle of the fifteenth century.

Oblivious to the crowds moving around him, Vivier had spent a long time gazing at this painting, startled and entranced by the egg-like contours of the subject's face, the hint of a defiant pout on her lips, the steady almost disdainful expression in her brown eyes, the oriental slant of her hooded eyelids, the delicate childlike neck and the nearly complete absence of brows which added to the alien quality of the whole. And the picture's surface, seemingly ruined by the deterioration of paint which had broken down, producing an overall effect like that on a crackle-glazed pot. Crazed lines ran everywhere like a fine webbing, showing up most notably on her creamy skin. She was damaged, but still utterly, unforgettably beautiful.

All this Paul Vivier thought about in mere seconds, as when

dreaming. Epic scenes seem to take up hours in the sleep world, but in reality they are only the product of a few minutes of R.E.M. sleep.

Damaged, but utterly, unforgettably beautiful.

Paul Vivier moved slowly towards the door that led out of his office, feeling as if he were floating; as if the part of him that travelled across the room was some spirit self, while his physical body remained near the desk, lost in contemplation.

It was only a sensation borne out of tiredness and stress. He knew that well enough. And he was particularly prone to it. Had first discovered it in himself when he was a boy of no more than perhaps seven years old. It was the age of self-awareness, of wonder and perhaps also terror. The age where one self-consciously discovers the potential to lie and invent. Or as Vivier did, to fake sickness in order to avoid the rough and tumble of school and spend a glorious day in bed with his books, his crayons and sketch pad, while his mother spoilt him, bringing chilled glasses of freshly made lemonade and tempting him to eat by cooking his favourite dishes. Then as he feigned a headache, his beloved mother fretfully laying a deliciously cool hand on his not at all fevered brow.

At the doorway he glanced back at the place he had been standing seconds before, almost expecting to see himself, almost disappointed to find that he did not meet his own surprised eyes looking back at him.

He needed to eat. To sleep. To recharge his batteries. But first, duty.

Meaning to move forward into the corridor, into action, Paul Vivier looked to his left, subtly aware of someone moving down the corridor towards him. And there he was, Lamy, back already from his mission. His step rapid and weightless. Lamy the plodding, the exacting, the wearying, the over-dutiful, over-keen, was fairly bouncing along the narrow corridor. The overhead lighting was green-tinged and harsh, casting heavy shadows under the eyes, making Lamy appear ghoulish despite the obvious energy and earnestness in his step. In his hand a paper evidence bag and in the bag something white and almost weightless.

The ectoplasm of an evil spirit, a voodoo charm or, as it turned out, a cardigan.

# Written on the Body

Hilda and Michael sat in the back of the car that had been sent for them. The car was a courtesy offered in regard to their age and also because they were assisting the police – not resisting them as in their many previous encounters with the forces of the state.

Both of them, without knowing it, were thinking about the young woman they had seen the night before. As they sat on the sun-warmed, burgundy-coloured seat in the back of the car they instinctively linked hands and threaded fingers through fingers. When the car started up, their bodies inclined away from the other as they gazed through their respective windows, his on the left, hers on the right.

It was a short drive and the car was unmarked so no curious bystanders gawked at them, causing them even more uncomfortable degrees of self-awareness. The small town that they had enjoyed so much before suddenly looked different. Harsher and more full of danger.

Each man that Hilda saw looked potentially evil. Not just the obvious suspects; the rangy youths in their baseball caps, with cigarettes held between finger and thumb as the smoke curled up the shielding palm, or the powerfully built workmen pausing amid churned-up road works to scratch their lean bellies while their eyes followed the rolling heft of a passing woman's ample buttocks in tight jeans, or the gruff man with extraordinary eyebrows, the pensioner in braces and beret scowling into a coffee cup. No, it was every man – the hippy tourist with his baby strapped to his back and his t-shirt with the tree-hugging eco message. It was the three sharply dressed bank employees with their briefcases and manila folders heading for their car. It was the man pausing to carefully tuck in the exposed shop label of his girlfriend's singlet – who touched her shoulder tenderly when he was done and planted a quick kiss at the nape of her neck. It was the butcher turning the sign on his shop door from open to closed.

One of the feminist claims Hilda had struggled with most was the belief that all men were potential rapists. The idea that all men were bad, were the source of all evil; beginning with capitalism and war and ending in the control and violence acted upon women's bodies. The argument went that the only defence was to exclude men from as many aspects of your life as it was possible. Certainly from one's bed and from one's body. Maybe also, as Lady Macbeth had threatened to do, to pluck the boy child from one's breast and destroy it or at the least, banish him.

And what of the other lesson of feminism? That the male constructed legal system often blamed the victim. Especially if the crime was of a sexual nature. If the woman dressed in a particular way – if she drank or took drugs, if she danced in a certain way, if she walked in dark deserted places, smiled, laughed, breathed. Or failed to find herself a male protector – father, brother, husband, boyfriend, lover.

Tinker, tailor, soldier, sailor, rich man, poor man, beggar man, thief.

Did young boys have an equivalent device for divining the future in their prune stones?

Gypsy girl, seamstress, typist, librarian, rich woman, poor woman, beggar woman, whore?

It hardly tripped off the tongue, besides which, a man's destiny is seemingly not defined by his choice of life partner.

And what are little boys made of?

Slugs and snails and puppy dog tails.

And girls? Much sweeter, more fragile stuff.

And that particular young woman last night? So feminine in her pretty white frock, her long golden legs, perfect and hairless, her platinum blonde hair that shone and danced as she moved. The funny little (and thoroughly impractical) bag she carried, the white, not very useful cardigan.

Now that Hilda thought about it, she remembered it more clearly. The tall American had left the young woman sitting alone and she had lit a cigarette and smoked it, sometimes tilting her head back and blowing the smoke directly upwards. Then she had stood and picked up the cardigan and draped it over the silly little bag. Hilda had seen this seemingly out of the corner of her eye. Peripheral vision. The edge of their lives; hers and Michael's. They had been talking of Paris, of hope and youth. Love too. She saw the young woman stand up. Then, when Hilda looked again, she had gone and the waiter was clearing the table and Michael was saying something that Hilda felt compelled to disagree with, if only a little.

Michael was also thinking about the young woman and her conversation with the tall man. He should have intervened, told the man that he should be ashamed, that he should apologise. And if he refused? Then what? Would Michael threaten him? Would he strike him?

Defending a woman's honour was hardly the stuff of anti-establishment politics. Feminism had killed chivalry. Or rather it had killed it for men like himself. Good men who, ironically, by paying attention to what women said and thought, had channelled their chivalry into something that carried a different label, but was much the same. Respect.

If Michael hadn't liked overhearing what the American said to the young woman, he was equally sickened by the fact that it didn't seem to bother her. She had seemed thoroughly unshaken by it.

If the man had done something; tried to drag her off perhaps or threatened her more directly then there was the case for direct action. Or if the young woman had looked about her in appeal, wide-eyed and fearful. If she had cried, or stood up and left with the man following (as he had promised to do) then Michael was certain he would have acted.

He pictured himself standing up and bellowing 'leave her alone!' then striding deliberately towards them. Sometimes it was a matter of the authority one put in one's voice, the expression on one's face, which was enough to imply that you had an equivalent degree of physical strength and fighting skills to back up your intent.

He pictured a struggle between the younger, taller man and himself, felt his own weakness, but knew that such an event could have potentially changed the young woman's eventual fate. If only he'd acted.

He also imagined the same scene but with a different denouement, one in which he tried to challenge the American, but was transfigured into a weak, shambolic, humble, rather dusty man. Like Charlie Chaplin's little tramp, a figure of fun, only to be mocked and pitied.

The young woman might have told him to mind his own business; she might have laughed in his face. Laughed, as those young people had done in the cathedral earlier today.

The world was rotten. Maybe it deserved its fate.

The car pulled into a small parking area around the back of a severely functional-looking building and came to a sudden standstill as the driver braked without warning. Michael and Hilda both lurched forward in their seats then fell backwards again and, in that moment, each tightened the hold they had on the other's hand. It was as if one of them had stumbled while walking and the danger was transmitted directly, palm to palm.

Save me, catch me, help me.

Stay with me even if I'm beyond all hope.

Hilda and Michael turned to look at one another. Each read fear in the other's eyes. Fear and also love. They would get through this. Together.

# Sancta Camisia

The cardigan came from a chain of English stores. At the back of the neck was a label with the word Monsoon woven in deep fuchsia on a pale pink background. Sewn below the large tag was a smaller one that gave the size, UK 10. On the inside left seam there was a white satin label with extensive text in English that gave the material's mix, the washing and care instructions, and on the verso the same text appeared in French. Fabrique en Hong Kong.

Sabine Pelat had checked online for information about the company. It had been established in London in the early seventies selling dresses and coats from India and Afghanistan. Sabine vaguely remembered one of her mother's sisters wearing those sorts of clothes, how they smelled of musky perfumes. Also the overpowering whiff of something like wet dog when the richly embroidered shaggy sheepskin coat Aunt Beatrice habitually wore had been out in the rain. She remembered too, a visit to the same aunt's flat in Paris, her boyfriend's long beard and hair, the low table and chairs in the centre of the room. They had sawn off the furniture's legs and painted the resulting squat and slightly wobbly articles an azure colour. Her aunt wore no bra and Sabine had been shocked to notice how her nipples brazenly displayed themselves behind the thin fabric of the gauzy cheesecloth top she was wearing.

But this cardigan bore no relation to the ethnic purity of those early imports. In style it was thoroughly European. Beautifully made and chic enough to be French, but actually English, though there were several branches of Monsoon in France. Which was a pity as it might have helped to identify the young woman who had owned it. The cardigan had been fairly expensive, not couture prices of course – nowhere near, but neither was it as cheap as C&A for example. And the same was true of the dress and sandals the girl wore, and also her underwear. So she had money. But then a prostitute, if she wasn't also an addict or a drunk, would have money. An escort, a kept woman, all might invest in expensive clothing. As would any woman who earned a decent wage.

The cardigan was slightly creased and dusty. Wearing disposable gloves Sabine turned it over, inspecting it in a general way. It would be sent to forensics the following morning and tested for traces of fibre, blood, hair, saliva and semen. There was a cream-coloured stain on the inside back of the cardigan that Sabine thought could possibly be semen, though the position of the discolouration was unusual in terms of normal sex if the woman had been wearing the garment. But vaginal swabs had not revealed any semen. It was not beyond the realm of possibility that the killer had masturbated either into the cardigan or had used it to clean himself up after he had finished.

Semen offered two possibilities for identification; blood typing and DNA profiling. But neither were any good if they didn't have a match on file, unless of course they did DNA sampling on the entire male population of the town and managed to net anyone travelling through the region whether tourist or itinerant – which of course, the law did not allow. On the other hand Sabine Pelat knew that some serial killers stuck to particular areas close to either their homes or workplaces, and that many of them might have minor convictions for sexual assault, for exposing themselves or trespass with intent. So there was a chance that the semen, if indeed it was semen, would score a hit.

Sabine handled the cardigan as delicately as if it were a religious relic. She was wearing disposable gloves, which she absolutely knew were necessary, but she wished she could take them off in order to feel the fabric of the garment under the sensitive skin on the pads of her fingers. To touch was to absorb something of the young woman who had met this terrible fate. It was to imagine the victim standing in a quiet shop, laying this cardigan on the counter in front of the sales assistant, then watching as it was carefully folded in tissue paper before it was handed over in a shop carrier bag. Objects of desire. What complexities of ritual and commerce we make of our lives – the young woman had desired the cardigan for its softness, but also for how it flattered her body and displayed her sense of style. This in its turn transformed or added to the effect of the woman's own desirability. So that, just as the woman had wanted the cardigan, by containing her body within it she herself became a thing to be desired and possessed. The idea was oblique, but there was something both vivid and ironic about it.

Clothes are so much the shells of ourselves, the sloughed-off skins which, after we are gone, become indexical reminders of who we were.

Sabine thought of her father's woollen scarf which she kept in a plastic bag in a closet drawer and which still smelled faintly of him, though he had been dead for almost twenty years. She had his pocket watch too and the letters he had written her, but it was the scarf, with its must of hair oil, tobacco and soap that most heartbreakingly brought him back to life for her.

It was her father who had taken her to see Chartres cathedral and in particular the Sancta Camisia. It was the gown that the blessed Mary had worn while giving birth to the saviour Jesus. The gown which had miraculously survived the fire which destroyed the original cathedral at Chartres in 1194 and which had prompted the rebuilding of the church on such a huge and magnificent scale.

A sacred relic that supposedly bore the traces of a birth long ago, two thousand and seven years to be precise. Had anyone ever suggested DNA testing on such a holy object?

Sabine felt a sudden surge of shock at such a thought, as if a gulf had opened up beneath her feet. The old instinctual fear of God; of His eyes upon her, of His ears miraculously strained to hear the thoughts inside her head. Just as it had been when she was a young girl at the convent school and her mind, of its own accord, strayed in the most imaginative and sinful directions.

The battle between God and the Devil, goodness and evil had once seemed real and vivid to her and indeed it had directed her towards her current career. Her devotion might have led to her becoming a nun, but such passivity would have driven her mad. She had once had much more dynamic dreams of goodness, imagined herself a slayer of dragons. Well, no, not quite, but she had been young and idealistic. It had taken a little over two years for her to realise that evil as a concept, as a tangible force did not exist. Evil deeds were committed in the world, people did terrible things, but none of it was quite as simple as black and white.

Inspector Vivier often teased her about the books she read; all those (to his eyes) trashy novels with their almost pornographic murder and autopsy scenes. To him it was a kind of sickness, but for Sabine it was soothing. Yes, soothing for there was always a resolution of some sort or another, and it helped her to think imaginatively about crime, and to enter, albeit through the author's intervention, the psychopath's mind.

And yes, perhaps there was also a certain guilty pleasure to be had in these books. Similar perhaps to those pleasures obtained by readers of romantic novels, with their enactments of love strived for, then finally won, the heroine thwarted; misunderstood, invisible, unhappy until at last she finds her perfect mate. And then?

Bullshit.

Sabine pulled a face at this thought, tossed her head angrily.

The door opened behind her.

'Sabine?'

Paul Vivier stood at the threshold, his left hand on the door handle, the other at his head with his thumb kneading his right temple.

'Sir?'

'Anything?'

'There's a stain that might be semen, but no blood. Or none that I can see with the naked eye.'

Still frowning and nursing his head, Vivier came towards her. She laid the cardigan down on the paper sheet and with a gloved finger, pointed at the place where the slight discolouration was. An irregular centime-sized blot, which was barely visible.

He leaned over to see it more clearly, but was careful not to touch it as he hadn't put on gloves.

Sabine, who had looked at the cardigan for quite some time, found herself looking at him instead. His skin was pale and slightly greasy looking; deep wrinkles were clearly visible at the corners of his eyes and one wild white hair stood out from his otherwise shapely black brows. A small silvery scar with a row of satellite pinpricks along its edges showed up clearly on his cheekbone. Vivier would never tell how he got the injury, but Sabine guessed it was probably from some innocuous childhood accident, like falling off his bicycle.

'Alright,' he said at last, 'get it off to the lab first thing. Make sure you bring that area to their attention.'

'Of course.'

'Good work, Detective.'

He straightened his back slowly, sighed.

'Long day, sir?'

In response he nodded slowly and brought his hand up to thumb his temple again. He seemed lost in thought.

'What time is it?' he asked.

Sabine looked up at the wall-mounted clock. 'Nine-forty, sir.' She did not question why Vivier himself couldn't have looked.

'This case…' he said, then stopped speaking.

'Sir?'

'There are too many loose ends. The black kid, the report about the young man covered in blood – has he been traced yet?'

'No, sir, but…'

'That crazy woman with her voodoo claims. A cardigan. Nothing fits.

'No, sir.'

'I keep trying to force everything to fit, but force doesn't do it, does it?'

'No, sir.'

'But even if they confirm it was the same girl they saw and that the cardigan belonged to her, that doesn't tell us who she is.'

'No.'

'But if you're right,' he nodded at the white cardigan on the table, 'and if that is semen, then maybe we'll find our man.'

Sabine nodded solemnly. Both of them knew that the chances were slim that anything would be that easy. His words depended more on hope or faith or will, than anything more tangible. Sabine breathed in deeply through her nose, aware of the sound of her breathing in the silence.

'Are you done here?' Vivier asked, after a few moments had passed.

'Just about.'

'I'd like to begin the debriefing … so if you could?'

'Right, sir.'

He drifted away to stand at the entrance again, holding the door open, waiting for her while she carefully repacked the cardigan.

Taking off her disposable gloves and tossing them in the bin, she stole a glance at the inspector; his body seemed to have sagged in the seconds that had passed while she was repacking the evidence. It seemed he was now not so much holding the door ajar as using it to hold himself upright.

'There,' she said sharply as if to snap him to attention, and her word had its effect. He drew himself upright, his back straight, his head erect. As she came near he even managed a faint smile.

He stood aside to let her pass, and as she did so she was surprised to feel his hand lightly touch her shoulder. The sensation was so brief and so tentative that she almost thought she had imagined it.

# Part Three

# AFTERNOON

*Then I considered all that my hands had done and*
*the toil I had spent in doing it, and again, all was*
*vanity and a chasing after wind, and there was*
*nothing to be gained under the sun.*

Ecclesiastes 2:11

*And at the closing of the day*
*She loosed the chain, and down she lay;*
*The broad stream bore her far away*

The Lady of Shalott, Alfred Lord Tennyson

# A-tisket, a-tasket

It was six-thirty in the morning. The baby was making sleepy mewling sounds. Not quite awake, but she would be soon and then the snuffling noises would grow louder and stronger until they turned into ragged howls. But six-thirty wasn't so bad, yesterday it had been much earlier, while it was still dark outside.

In the double bed beside the cot, the baby's mother and father lay at its furthest edges, their limbs escaping from under the covers in attitudes of exhausted abandon. Celia was the first to wake. David slept on. He had promised to share all the work involved in caring for a new baby, including nappy changes and night feeds, but the complication of switching between breast and bottle made it seem absurd. Why use a breast pump, a bottle warmer and sterilizer when all Celia had to do was lift the baby to her breast and give suck? But she loved David for at least being prepared to do it, for offering. And yes, it tended to be her that did the nappy changes too, especially the spectacularly smelly ones, but she so hated to see him suffer – didn't like to see the revulsion he showed the one time he did it. So before the noise her daughter was making got too loud, Celia slipped from the bed, scooped the baby from the cot and went downstairs to feed her.

The gîte they had rented had a beautiful garden behind it. Celia loved gardens. She'd been working as a humble gardener for the parks department in west London when she and David met. Then she'd changed jobs for better money, for their future together. They had seen photos of the cottage on the Internet; the view from the upstairs window of the Bais de Somme, the open plan kitchen-diner, the living room with its wood-burning stove. All of it perfect.

Celia settled herself in the comfy apple-green wicker chair near the sliding glass doors that opened onto the garden. It was still cool, but as the sun rose higher in the sky, it would get hotter. Polly had barely awoken, but now with eyes closed in some ecstasy of gluttony, she was sucking heartily at Celia's breast. Ten or fifteen minutes, then Celia'd change sides.

David had asked her several times what it felt like to breast-feed and had been frustrated when she had been unable to describe it exactly. 'There is a drawing sensation,' she'd said, 'a tingling, but it's also very peaceful.'

He'd also asked about the birth. 'What was the pain like? How did it feel?' Her memory of the pain was already dissolving. 'I remember thinking at one point,' she told him, 'that I had never experienced such an all consuming and terrible pain in my life before, and that I would never, never do this again. But I can't really remember the actual pain.'

'Oh,' he'd said, 'maybe it's like getting a kick in the balls?'

'I wouldn't know, would I?' she'd said.

Celia gazed down at Polly, at her fine brown hair, her tiny amazing fingers with their even tinier, even more amazing nails. Nails that were getting long and would soon need cutting, or rather chewing off, as that was what the baby book recommended. If they weren't trimmed, Celia had read, baby would scratch her little face.

Polly seemed to be drifting back to sleep, her mouth's grip on the nipple was growing weaker, but this was deceptive, if put back in her crib now, she'd be howling again within minutes.

Holding Polly in the crook of her right arm Celia stood up and using her left hand slid the glass door open. Then on the threshold, she turned Polly around. Polly opened her eyes with surprise. Such dark blue eyes, so seemingly knowing. For a beat of time mother and daughter gazed at one another intently. This was the exact distance a baby's focus is fixed at, the distance between the nursing mother's eyes and the infant's. One of nature's perfect little touches. A God-proving quirk.

As Celia watched, feeling an almost spiritual sense of oneness with her child and with the universe, Polly's expression changed, the nose wrinkled and suddenly the lips distorted to become those of the Greek mask that represented tragedy. Celia quickly freed her left breast from her nightdress and guided her nipple to the agonised mouth. Instantly Polly's expression switched to one of blissful satisfaction.

While she nursed the baby, Celia stepped out onto the small patio and absorbed the stillness, the lush greenness and silence of the morning. The garden was long and narrow with a concealed shed at the bottom and high bushes on either side. A path led down one side of it to a gate that in its turn led to a lane overlooking the estuary.

They had arrived on Saturday and had less than three days left. One week was not enough, but with a new baby and big mortgage, it was all they could afford. And in just over a month Celia was meant to be back at work and poor little Polly would be left with a stranger. A stranger who would cost the unbelievable sum of over two hundred pounds a week! It didn't bear thinking about.

Celia humming quietly (the tune was, for some reason, 'Paperback Writer' by the Beatles) and swaying gracefully from the waist up, wandered slowly down to the bottom of the garden.

Why can't we just stay here forever, she was asking herself, isn't this how we are meant to live? Why can't we escape everything that ties us down, all those things which are meant to be good for us, that make us secure – the mortgage, the job with a pension scheme, the two cars, the ISAs, Polly's name on the waiting lists for three different schools, the credit card insurance, the cable TV, phone and broadband package, the Neighbourhood Watch Scheme. Everything geared towards the moment when one could finally relax and reap the benefits. When was that – a few hours in bed with the papers on a Sunday morning or at dinner parties with friends (and those were hardly cheap or relaxing) or did the reward come far down the road with retirement? Youth might be wasted on the young, but retirement was certainly wasted on the old.

Their terraced house in Wimbledon was reportedly now worth nearly half a million. Couldn't they just sell up and move to France or Portugal or somewhere?

At the edge of the lawn, a large bush concealed the garden shed; hippophae rhamnoides with its slender silvery green leaves. I know things, Celia thought, I've learned things I never use. Hippophae rhamnoides, also known as Sea Buckthorn.

She imagined teaching Polly all the proper names for plants, or revealing their many secrets. Together they would plant seeds; flowers and herbs and vegetables, watch them push through the dark loam searching for the sun.

Something caught Celia's eye as she surveyed the flowers that edged the path. It was pale yellow and hump-shaped. Not a plant, but perhaps some uniquely French style of cloche. Distantly, she seemed to remember seeing something a little like it in one of her many gardening books. Because the garden was so neat and perfectly cared for, it didn't even occur to Celia that the object didn't belong amongst the flowers. She stepped closer; Polly was now fast asleep in her arms, her cheeks warm-pink, her mouth a moist and satisfied pout.

Celia adjusted her nightdress and, being careful not to disturb Polly, she crouched down in order to see what the curious object was.

It was woven from strips of ochre willow stems and lay like an upturned ship amongst some straggly rosemary and lavender bushes. Celia reached for the edge and carefully lifted it up.

What had she expected to see? Some rare bog orchid or tender shoots just breaking the earth's surface? Perhaps, but that is not what was there. Instead what spilled from this woven object was a cigarette packet, a red lighter, a plastic hotel room key, some tampons, a Rimmel lipstick, a mirror, Maybelline mascara, a scrunched-up tissue and several coins – Euros as well as the familiar silver and brass of British currency; a couple of pound coins, a fifty pence, fives and tens and two pences.

Celia drew back her hand as if she'd discovered a nest of wasps. She glanced at the gate that led to the path at the back of the house. Remembered all the fuss and sirens and the news about the murdered woman. A prostitute, she'd heard, murdered at the edge of town near some industrial works.

But this bag was nothing to do with that. It had been thrown over the gate as some sort of prank. Celia thought of a boy and a girl at that in-between teasing age where cruelty was sometimes the expression of a desire. The boy would snatch the girl's bag, she'd chase him, fight him, both of them laughing all the while, both enjoying the physical contact that the wrestle offered. 'Don't you dare!' the girl would say, unable to keep the smile from her face. The boy's eyes glinting, he would lift the bag high, out of the reach of her grabbing fingers. 'Think I won't? You gonna stop me then? Huh? Huh?'

Then he would forget himself and fling the bag in a great arc into the air.

Ruin everything in that instant.

Yes, that's how it went. Nothing to be frightened of.

Celia shivered. The sun still hadn't begun to burn off the morning mist. She stood up a little unsteadily, hurried back into the house. Pulled the glass door shut behind her, locked it for the first time since they'd been there.

Then she went up the stairs calling out her husband's name with increasing urgency. 'David, David, David…' He stirred, grunting groggily.

Then, he registers her panic, saying anxiously, 'What is it? Is it Polly? Oh, God…'

On this point, Celia can soothe him. 'No, no, she's fine. It's not that. I found something … in the garden. We may have to tell the police.'

Although the baby is fast asleep, Celia does not put Polly in her cot yet, does not want to leave her alone. Not now.

Together, in their nightclothes, David in blue striped pyjama bottoms, Celia in her white cotton nightdress, the baby in her arms, they walk down the path to where the basket is.

David surveys the spilled contents in silence for a beat of time.

Breaking the silence, Celia says, 'So should we ring the police?'

'Yeah,' he says at last. 'Yeah, better had.'

They walked back to the house. He began to look through the local information pack provided by the gîte's owners for the number of the local police station.

'I'm not going back to work in September. I won't. I don't care about the money,' Celia says suddenly. David frowns at her, but cannot think of anything to say.

'I mean it,' she said, then went through to the kitchen area, filled the kettle and put it on the stove to boil.

She stood there rocking the baby gently, and with her back turned listened to him stumbling through his schoolboy French on the phone.

'Je suis discovered une valise de femme. Dans le jardin. Wee, wee. Je suis une angleterre. Wee, wee.'

Why had she said she wouldn't be going back to work at that moment? Later she would console herself with the notion that her motivation was fear. That finding the dead woman's bag in their garden had, with its awful proximity to violent death, propelled her into, first understanding and then acting on an unrecognised anxiety about Polly's future life and safety. But at the back of her mind, barely acknowledged was the idea that it had been a much more cunning move. A perfect time to make her announcement, to bury one significant bit of news under an event of far greater magnitude.

Whatever her motivation or her timing, Celia was determined. She would not go back to her job; she would never let Polly out of her sight.

When the police came she once again carried her sleeping child when they went into the garden. Held the baby close and stroked her downy cheek as she answered their questions.

# Evidence

Vivier had gone to bed at 3.45 only to wake again at seven. Three hours sleep was not enough for any man. The Central Office had promised more personnel to assist with the investigation but there were delays. Always there were delays, complications, paperwork, politics. He had been due to take a holiday starting the week after next, when he had planned to go to London. He had not yet booked anything. Indeed he had still been pondering whether to drive or fly. Despite this indecision about the means of travel, he'd visualised himself there. He'd studied street maps and marked places of interest on them; the British Museum, the National Portrait Gallery, the National Gallery, the Tower of London, the British Library, the Victoria and Albert Museum. These all now dissolved in his mind. For the time being anyway.

He sat up in bed and swung his legs over the edge and just sat there for a moment gathering his thoughts. Last night he had left the door of his wardrobe open. It was unlike him to do so as he was particular about such things, which showed how tired he must have been.

The central door in the old-fashioned walnut armoire was mirrored and now Paul Vivier saw himself reflected in it. A naked man, thin and sinewy, hunched on the bed, black hair on his legs, arms and chest, his lower face darkened by stubble, his attitude one of defeat. He stared at this image of himself distantly, as if surprised to see that he possessed a physical being, and such a naked ape-like being too. His hair was a mess, one part at the top of his head standing up in a crazy tuft. He looked dangerous, like a man with no conscience. Like a Blakean vision of despair.

The phone rang while he was putting on his last pair of clean boxers and weighing up the chances he would have that day to either do the laundry or get to a shop and buy new ones.

'Sir?'

The voice was Sabine Pelat's and the caller display told him she was already at the station.

'Yes.'

'We've just had a report about the discovery of what might be the girl's handbag. Looks like it was thrown into someone's garden.'

'Any ID in it?'

'From what they said, no, but there's a hotel room key and the description of the bag seems to match the one described by the English couple.'

'Good. Where is it?'

'House overlooking the Bais de Somme. Holiday rental, garden backs onto a lane.'

'Okay, meet me there in twenty minutes and ... Sabine?'

'Coffee, sir?'

'You read my mind.'

'It was hardly challenging, sir.'

If he didn't know better he would have thought such a statement was insubordination, but her tone had been warm and teasing, and his appetite for strong coffee, especially in the morning, was hardly a secret.

He hung up the phone and continued dressing, his mind settling back on the banalities of his underwear situation. How much easier would life be if he had a wife? Not one iota perhaps, as he imagined this wife not only doing the laundry and shopping and preparing meals, but also crowding out the quiet spaces of his life, demanding holidays spent, not in the cool of a London museum, but on the beach in the south or perhaps Spain, or even further afield. This wife of his imagination sprang partly from the sort of ciphers of ordinary women one saw on popular TV soap operas (not that he watched television) and partly from recollections of his own mother who was extremely house-proud and whose overzealous shopping and cleaning routines imposed unnecessary noise and disruption on his father and himself.

Vivier sat on the edge of the bed to put on his shoes, black lace-ups with leather soles. Expensive shoes even for a police inspector, but they were made to last. He already wore his jacket, tie and watch. He put his left shoe on and laced it tight; he'd be on his way in a minute or so. He lifted his right shoe and discovered that on removing it the night before he hadn't properly untied it and that the bow was now a tight and impossible knot. The sort best unpicked by someone with smaller, more nimble fingers and longer nails.

Pressed for time and not really thinking too much about it, Vivier, wearing one shoe and carrying the other, left the flat and took the lift down to the basement car park.

He drove to the address Pelat had given him and pulled up as soon as he saw Lamy. He rolled down his car window.

'Lamy, is Pelat here yet?'

Lamy nodded. His eyes were hooded as if he wasn't quite awake yet.

'Can you ask her to come here immediately?'

Lamy turned into the path that led to the holiday home's open front door and disappeared. Sabine Pelat appeared seconds later looking as fresh and well-groomed as ever.

She leaned over to talk to Vivier at the driver's window.

He jerked his head to the right.

'Get in please.'

She nodded and walked around the front of the car watching his face quizzically through the windscreen. Got in the passenger seat and began to do up the seat belt.

'No need for that, we're not going anywhere.'

Vivier reached for the shoe in the well of the car and handed it to her.

She took it, at first handling it as gingerly as if it were a new and puzzling piece of evidence.

He sighed, realising the absurdity of the moment.

'I'm sorry,' he said. 'I couldn't undo it. Could you?'

She looked at him, then her eye travelled down his legs to his feet; one in the matching shoe, the other in a finely knitted black sock. A smile crept over her face, but she avoided his eye, concentrating instead on undoing the knot in the lace. Her fingers worked at it with precision and delicacy, as her smile grew broader and broader. She sensed him watching her, but could not control her expression.

'Yes, I know,' he said at last, 'it's very amusing.'

She laughed.

Her laugh was lovely; musical and sweet and not unkind.

She composed herself, continuing to work on the knot in silence while she fought back a grin. Finally she untangled the knot.

'There!' she said, but speaking had released her from the composure she had struggled to maintain, and she laughed again.

Handed him his shoe.

'I'm sorry, sir,' she said, laughter bubbling through her words. Her eyes were dancing and glittering with merriment.

Straight-faced, he put his shoe on and tied it up, then he turned away from her and spoke sternly.

'A little respect, if you please.'

She was silent.

A beat of time passed, then he looked at her, she had a hand clamped over her mouth and her eyes looked anguished. Her shoulders were hunched and trembling spasmodically as she fought the urge to laugh.

She looked helpless and almost childlike.

Now he was the one to laugh and released from his solemn spell, she laughed easily and gaily with him.

Lamy came out of the gîte to smoke a cigarette and was surprised to see the Inspector and Pelat sitting side by side in Vivier's car laughing uncontrollably.

And when Pelat noticed Lamy watching them, she laughed even more.

Some joke eh, Lamy thought, look at those two – so pleased with themselves, laughing at his expense. He stared at Sabine Pelat and scowled, screwing his eyes up as he sucked at his cigarette, then angrily tossed it onto the road.

Bitch!

Inside the car Vivier and Pelat began to subside into soberness by degrees. Sabine wiping tears from her eyes and exhaling breathy 'oh's, while Paul Vivier cupped his face in one hand, pressing his fingers into his cheeks to inflict a little pain on his undisciplined mouth.

'I'm sorry, sir,' Sabine managed to say.

'That's alright, but can I ask that you keep this to yourself. At least for the time being.'

'Of course.'

They simultaneously opened their respective doors, and climbed out of the car, slamming them shut within seconds of one another, producing a two beat sound that reverberated in the quiet street.

Lamy had disappeared inside the house again.

They entered and made their way to the back, where they found a woman with strawberry blonde hair tied back in a ponytail sitting in a straight-backed chair, breast-feeding a baby. A man, presumably the child's father, was standing at a kitchen counter putting a filter into a coffee maker. Lamy was standing near the large patio window staring, without an iota of discretion, at the woman's exposed breast.

The man in the kitchen area picked up the glass jug from the machine, filled it at the sink and then put it on the hot plate and flipped the switch.

'No,' Sabine said. 'That's not how you do it.'

He turned to look at her, surprised, then said by way of explanation, 'We don't really drink coffee.'

Sabine crossed the room, switched the machine off, lifted the lid on the reservoir and poured the contents of the jug in.

She had brought the packet of coffee herself that morning, baffling the English couple when she took it from the large aluminum case she carried – the case whose other contents had briefly been glimpsed; white disposable gloves, clear plastic jars and paper bags.

'I hope you don't mind – it's an early start for us and last night was a late one,' she said, casting the beam of a smile around the room to take in the man standing near her and Paul Vivier and the woman with the baby and lastly, Lamy. Lamy's look was hard and unresponding, almost a look of hatred.

Sabine was used to such looks. They came from those lower in rank and those above her in rank too. As if in any matter of dispute, she became not a colleague whose opinion and authority were respected, but a woman who had no business being there or saying the things she did. Not all of her male co-workers were like this, and indeed, she would not have advanced in her career if they had been, but they still existed; those old-school Neanderthals whose egos easily retreated into the cave of gender division.

She stared at Lamy, and her smile fell away in an instant. Her face wore no expression. He blinked and turned away to look out of the window.

They drank their coffee quickly, standing up, while the English couple sat amongst them looking brave, but bewildered. The baby was now asleep and her mother had rebuttoned her shirt.

Vivier drained his mug of coffee, throwing his head back to gulp the last of it.

'We'll make a start then,' he said in English and put his cup down on the counter with a decisive click. 'Now which of you found the bag?'

'Me,' the woman said.

'Then, if you would, can you show me where it is and talk me through how you came to find it.'

'Yes, of course,' she said, but she did not get up from her chair, although everyone else was standing around expectantly. It was as if the baby was fixing her there, its weight like an anchor holding her down.

Her husband, seeing this, stepped nearer, bent and reached for the sleeping child.

'I'll put her down, shall I?' he said, his voice gentle and full of consideration.

'No,' the woman snapped and hugged the baby closer.

'Alright,' he said, 'I was only trying to…'

'Well, don't,' she said. 'She's fine where she is.'

To prove her point the woman quickly stood and after readjusting the position in which she held the child and fussing with the blanket, she stepped towards the patio doors.

She led them down the garden talking in a quiet, but calm voice to Vivier as she went.

'It could have been there before, but I don't think it was, but then yesterday we didn't use the garden as we drove over to the beach at Belle Plage.'

She stopped a few yards away from the place where the bag lay and pointed at it quickly.

'Did you touch it?' Vivier asked.

'Yes, I'm sorry, I didn't realise …'

'That's fine, but we may have to take your prints to exclude you. So is this where it was or did you move it?'

'No, I just lifted the edge, I think it's more or less in the same place.'

A flash bulb went off startling the woman.

Lamy had moved onto the lawn and begun taking photographs of the object in situ.

'And did you see anything else?'

'I saw the stuff that had been inside it, everything that had spilled out and that's when I knew I had to report it.'

'Was that closed?'Vivier nodded at the gate.

'Yes, closed and locked. Or at least, I think it's locked.' She looked at her husband for confirmation of this, but he merely shrugged.

'And have you seen or heard anything else? For instance, the night before last, any unusual noises or voices?'

The woman shook her head 'no' but the headshake turned into a shudder and her eyes seemed to glaze over.

Sabine stepped nearer and cupped the woman's elbow.

'Are you alright? Do you want to sit down?'

The woman's eyes remained fixed and staring.

Vivier spoke, 'Thank you.You've been very helpful. Go in now. You too, sir.'

The couple turned and made their way back to the house. After a few paces the man put his arm around the woman and she leaned heavily against him, stumbling slightly as she did so.

She gave a ragged sob as they neared the door and her husband responded with whispered hushing.Then he drew the glass door shut behind them and there was silence.

'Okay,' Vivier said, snapping on a pair of latex gloves. 'Let's get moving.' And with that all three set about their respective tasks. They worked with few words exchanged amongst them, until the bag and all of the spilled items beneath it had been photographed, stored in clear plastic bags and carefully labelled.

Whenever Sabine Pelat happened to catch Lamy's eye he

avoided her gaze. There were no more hard stares as before, but something was up.

She would be wary of Lamy now. She would be guarded around him and study him at a distance. And if the problem continued she would talk to Inspector Vivier who did not like personal dissent amongst his staff.

'We live or die as a team,' he'd once said, and that was true and yet in other ways, Sabine thought, Vivier was a loner. Then she remembered their earlier laughter, how easy and almost flirtatious it had been. But she had forgotten seeing Lamy staring at them as they laughed together in the car. She had blinked and he was gone.

# Punishment

'What were you doing with that prick, anyway?'

Florian was lying on his back, smoking a cigarette. The bed sheets covered his lower body leaving his chest bare. Suzette lay beside him propped on one elbow as she traced her fingers over his chest and shoulders. At his words her hand stopped moving.

He was staring at the ceiling, attempting unsuccessfully to blow smoke rings.

'Does it bother you?' she asked.

'What do you think?'

'Does it change things?'

'Maybe.'

She thought about this and considered what she could say or do to amend it. Nothing, it seemed. The thought made her feel that she was being condemned twice for the same crime. 'Unfair!' cried a small voice inside her. 'This is just not fair.' She withdrew her hand from Florian's chest, uncertain if this was done to punish him or herself.

Half an hour ago they had been making love. She had watched his face; his closed eyes and the almost anguished expression that had overtaken him as he came. How happy that had made her. Then afterwards that bliss of lying together, bodies still entwined, saying hardly a word.

Then the cigarette and the question that came out of a clear blue sky; the intense blue sky which almost seemed to vibrate against the open window. Florian leaned over the side of the bed and away from her, stubbing out his cigarette in the saucer on the floor beneath the bed. His skin looked like gold against the cerulean sky. She watched his muscles ripple under his skin, the smooth plane of his back, the diminishing slope from his shoulder to his waist, the coffee-coloured moles sparsely scattered like distant stars.

What she felt at that moment must be love, she thought, real love.

Or perhaps it was only desire?

Not that the definition mattered at this point. He would get out of her bed, dress without looking at her. Pick up his keys and loose change from the table where he'd put them last night, then say grimly, 'I'm going now.'

He would say these things, act in this cold way because, ironically, he had experienced the same rapidly developing feelings of affection or desire or love or whatever it was, that she felt for him. And now because she had let herself be used by that filthy lying *flic*, Florian would no longer want her – he would shut out whatever feelings he might have had. And there was no consolation in that. None at all.

She rolled over so that she was lying on her side with her back to him. He would go, but she would not watch him. She felt the bed tip as he sat up, then spring back as he got up off the mattress. Heard the sounds of his bare feet move softly away over the rug, then the change in sound as he walked on the floor boards. A door creaked on its hinges; the one to the bathroom, which she should oil. Then the watery echoing sound of his pissing.

Then he would come back; search the room for his clothes, jeans by the table, one shoe by the front door, the other a few yards away, t-shirt over the back of a chair.

She closed her eyes, faking sleep.

Why had he asked her about the cop if he hadn't wanted to hear anything about it? Why ask when he already knew, as everyone in that damn bar knew, that she was the cop's mistress?

It had seemed right to answer his question, to confess her sins, her stupidity, her weakness.

She stared at the wall and replayed their conversation of

minutes before. She had told him how much she now she regretted it. That she could not even recognise herself as the woman who had allowed herself be treated in that way. How the cop had hurt her when he fucked her and had even seemed to relish the fact. How he had lied to her.

She'd said all that while Florian listened in silence. She'd stopped speaking, waited for him to respond, but instead he'd lit a cigarette, taken two slow puffs, then said with unmistakable disgust, 'What were you doing with that prick anyway?' And now he was leaving. For good.

She heard the toilet flush, then as that sound diminished the gush of the tap, the swish and slap of hands moving in the half-filled sink.

Yes, take a piss, wash yourself, then find your clothes, dress and leave.

Leave in silence.

Look, I'll pretend to sleep. Hear my breathing? Deeper, slower. See my shoulder rising and falling? I'm not even dreaming.

If you could listen to my thoughts, you would hear this over and over in a whisper: I love you, I love you, I love you.

Here come the footsteps again, crossing over the wooden floorboards, the scratchy slaps of naked human feet moving nearer, then the altered sound as once more he gains the carpet.

Then he stops somewhere near the bed.

Hear my breathing? See my closed eyes? I'm making it easy for you. But please don't linger or I will give myself away by crying.

In my imagination I thought we would be happy. That life would begin again with you. That the past was only the past. He is long gone. He no longer even lives in this town. What if he were dead? Would that make it better for you, for me, for us?

I'll wish him dead if you like.

Oh, Florian. Now I'm almost sorry that this ever happened.

Then a miracle, the mattress tips again, and sinks slightly as behind Suzette a warm body stretches itself on the bed. It moves closer and closer until it has tucked itself against her back. Then an arm loops over her shoulder and a hand holds her hand, as a mouth, with slightly cool lips, finds her neck, kisses her.

'Mm,' he says, 'you're warm this morning.'

She twists around quickly until she is facing him.

'Hello!' he says. 'I thought you were sleepy.'

She shakes her head quickly, no. Then gazes at his face as he gazes back at her. Then she dips her head and they begin to kiss once more in earnest.

After a few minutes he stops and pulls back, squinting at her, in order to focus on her face.

'Did he ever tell you anything about his work?'

'Who?'

'That cunt, Severin.'

'No, only that he hated the authorities and his superiors for keeping him back. Because they were jealous of him, afraid he would show them up. That sort of thing. He was an angry man.'

Florian snarled at this, then shook his head.

'What?' Suzette said.

'I always fancied you, you know,' he said. 'But…'

He stopped speaking, stared at her face thoughtfully.

She waited, then spoke when it was clear he wasn't going to elaborate. 'But now you don't. Because of him.' Her tone was reproachful, yet weighed down with resignation.

'What!' Suddenly he turned her onto her back and rolled with her so that he now lay above her. His arms were wrapped tightly under her back and neck, he squeezed her and pressed meaningfully against her with his hips. 'Of course, I still fancy you. Are you nuts?'

'Oh.'

'You're hot. Who wouldn't fancy you?'

She shrugged. This was news to her.

'A couple of years ago I was talking to one of the guys at the bar and I said something about you. You know, I asked who you were, what your name was or something, and he said, point blank, no hesitation, that you were off limits.'

'Off limits?'

'Yeah, like do not trespass if you like your body the way it is, if you don't want it rearranged by a good kicking from a certain member of the local gendarmerie and a few of his carefully selected colleagues. Or better yet, why not get sent down for a few years on account of some serious drugs you didn't even know were in the boot of your car, and so with my record…'

'I'm sorry,' Suzette said.

'Sorry for what? Nothing happened, I backed off sharpish.'

She sighed. 'So did everyone. Maybe that's why I kept seeing him.'

'But you're not seeing him now,' Florian wriggled his lower body so that he was lying between her legs. 'And you're not feeling him now.'

She could feel his penis hardening against her.

He cupped a hand around one breast and then brought his head down and nuzzled her nipple.

'And he's not doing this now.'

'No. Oh, that feels nice.'

Florian grinned and brought his face close to hers, staring at her with frank appraisal.

'You're too fucking good for him.'

Then he kissed her and she kissed him back and it all felt so different from that thing which she and the cop used to call lovemaking, but was nothing of the sort.

How had she been so deceived?

Florian's fingers were now working between her legs. In her mind's eye she pictured humming birds captured in slow motion, beaks delicately dipping into an open flower. Nectar.

'Oh,' she said and opened her eyes as he entered her and found him gazing intently at her.

'Florian,' she said.

'Suzette,' he replied

# Written in the Contract

It had been nearly ten days now. Thom had rung Lucy's flat, her mobile number. The latter went straight to voicemail, so she must have switched it off. He'd left several messages on her home machine and in the last of these he'd pleaded with her to at least talk to him, to tell him whatever it was he had done wrong. Or if it was over, if she had no more feelings for him, to at least have the decency to let him know.

He'd sent her a couple of emails too, but as she only used her email at work and as no one had seen her at the college, he doubted she had got these. In one of the emails he'd written some probably ridiculous and pompous statements about the unspoken rules of a relationship, about mutual respect and honesty and trust.

His emotions changed by the hour, by the minute. Now sad, now angry, now worried, now guilty. He wanted to yell at her and tell her she was acting like a kid. Then he wanted to tell her that he knew he was a selfish arsehole at times, but that didn't mean he didn't love her. Then he imagined her with other men; that young photography lecturer, Damon for example. He was always sniffing around her. Hadn't she said something about modelling for him. She'd said she couldn't decide.

'What do you think, Thom?' she'd asked.

What had his reply been? 'Nothing to do with me, it's up to you.' Then a dismissive shrug.

So maybe that was it, they'd have done the photos and something had started between them.

He'd go to her flat, get there good and early in the morning, at seven or eight o'clock. If Damon whatshisname or whoever was there at that hour, then the meaning was inescapable.

The anger rose up in him again, he imagined with a sort of glittering pleasure how it would feel to punch that effete bastard, Damon, in the face. Damon with his lank black hair, his Ian Ashcroft lope, his cooler than cool demeanor.

The punches Thom imagines do not stop. His hand does not hurt. He pounds his rival's face to a bloody pulp, without grazing a knuckle, without suffering a bruise. A movie pounding. A denouement in which only anger wins.

Cut.

The movie in his mind stops.

He tries another take.

This time the character he plays is aloof. He is in her flat. Don't ask how he got in (he doesn't have a key) but there he is moving through thick silence. Through the hallway, into the empty living room, the kitchen, down the corridor to the bedroom. At the closed door he pauses momentarily. Listens. There is no sound, no indication of anyone in the room. Quietly, he opens the door to find them in bed. He does not discover them in flagrante, but instead finds a moment of perfect stillness and unaccountable beauty.

Lucy, her head fitted into the apex of her lover's arm and body, lies asleep.

No sound, except for the lovers' measured breathing.

He sees.

His hand trembling on the door handle. He sees and retreats. In silence. Then, pulling the door shut quietly, he leaves.

Walk away, in silence.

Leaving the scene as a snapshot of perfection.

He goes to sleep with this image on his mind. Wakes at six-thirty. Cannot remember his dreams, nor very clearly his train of thought last night, but is nonetheless decided. He is going to dress, then go to Lucy's flat first thing to confront her. To confront the demons of his imagination.

Out into the crisp, still-dewy morning, London filtered through a fog of early morning mist. A slight chill in the air. Footsteps echoing sharply as he moves down the flagged path to his car. His body brushes the honeysuckle vine that oozes from his neighbour's garden. The scent briefly entering his consciousness, a vague memory of something familiar; hotter, stronger, more pungent at night.

To the car. He unlocks the door. He could be going to work. It could be an ordinary day. The time on the dashboard is seven. Some idiot has pulled up tight behind him making the job of escaping his parking space next to impossible, but he works the gears, the brakes, shunting forward and twisting the wheel, then shunting back until, by degrees, he is free.

The time on the dashboard is now six minutes past seven.

After that, he's in full punching mode again, ready for a fight. Not that he has been in a fight since he was sixteen or seventeen, and that was only a semi-serious scuffle with his brother. The traffic gets worse near Shepherd's Bush, but it's not far from there to Lucy's flat on Hammersmith Grove. He parks a few doors down from the entrance, fits the lock on the steering wheel, gets out of the car and surveys the street. The mist has lifted now and the air seems heavier. It's going to be a hot one.

A youngish couple are walking towards Lucy's apartment block. The woman is wearing red shoes and a navy linen dress, her hair is sleek and black, the man she is with is sharply dressed in a dark suit that reminds Thom of those smooth Italian looks from the films of the nineteen-sixties; *Blow Up* or some Fellini extravaganza. The couple look unreal, too smart, too young, too rich, too confident, too stylish.

Just before they reach the entrance to Lucy's block, another man, also dressed in a dark suit (though his is more conventional) gets out of a parked car, carrying a leather document case. He calls to them and they stop walking, then stand holding hands as they listen to whatever it is he has to say. Then, when Thom is just a few yards away, all three mount the steps leading to Lucy's building. Thom, sensing an opportunity, speeds up his pace so that when the main entrance door is open, he is able to confidently slip into the building behind them. Predictably Thom caught in their wake the scent of expensive cologne and also the faintest aroma of new shoe leather.

The three proceed up the stairs with Thom following close behind. One, two flights. Then they turn into the hallway where there are doors to four flats, two near the stairway, two further off down a corridor without natural light, but where low energy bulbs burn day and night in frosted mint-green wall sconces.

The three strangers ahead of him pass two doors and head towards the last two. Thom finds himself imagining some weird sexual tryst going on between the three of them. The smartly dressed man and woman are high-class prostitutes or escorts; they are making porn films. Renting the flat next to Lucy's to shoot movies. He wants to discuss this with Lucy, to question her about strange goings on, peculiar noises from the flat next door.

He is confident the threesome will disappear into the flat next to Lucy's and hopes to catch some telling glimpse into that flat's interior; a ruby-red velveteen couch, a large gilt mirror, studio lights and a video camera on a tripod.

But they go to the right-hand door – Lucy's door. They are mistaken and will soon discover their mistake.

As Thom closes in on them, the man with the document case uses a key from a large bunch to unlock the door. To Thom's surprise the door opens.

'Hey,' Thom calls. 'Hold on.'

They seem oblivious to him and troop into Lucy's flat, talking loudly and confidently amongst themselves, not even noticing when Thom follows them in through the front door.

The flat is full of Lucy's things; straight ahead at the end of the hall, framed in blonde wood, is her 'Sensation' poster from the Royal Academy exhibition. The image on it, a slippery pink labia-like tongue descending from the top edge of the picture to meet and mirror the hard cold tip of a domestic iron, had always disturbed Thom, though he did not quite know why. To his right between the Ikea side table and the door he was shocked to see piles of mail – slip-sliding mountains of it, letters and documents from the college, numerous magazines and journals which Lucy subscribed to, invitations to gallery openings and conferences, bank statements, junk mail.

Scarves and hats are hanging on a set of antlers Lucy had bought in a car boot sale in Arbroath, and on the table there's a silver-rimmed, turquoise Moroccan bowl filled with black and grey and white pebbles, and beside it a wooden hairbrush from the Body Shop with pale hair tangled in its plastic spikes. Lucy's hairbrush, but not her rich brown hair. Not that this registered with Thom at the time.

And beyond the hall lay Lucy's living room; her furniture and curtains and rugs and three strangers who look like characters in a film. But no sign of Lucy herself.

The man in the cheap suit is talking.

'The living room is a good size,' he says, 'and benefits from a view onto the Green. Double glazing throughout and the service charge is reasonable for a property of this quality and location…'

'Hey!' Thom says, cutting off the man's well-rehearsed patter. All three turn to look at him with mild surprise.

'What do you think you are doing? This is my…' Thom had been about to say 'my girlfriend's flat' then changed his mind and said, '…my flat.'

'Pardon?' the man with the briefcase says.

'I said, what do you think you're doing?'

The perfect couple gaze at Thom wide-eyed. He is nothing to

them, an irrelevance, about as interesting to them as a tramp or *Big Issue* seller.

The letting agent, looking mildly confused, pulls a document from his case, and squinting, reads it.

'Lucy Swann?' he says, without a hint of sarcasm.

'My partner,' Thom replies. 'This is her flat.'

'And you are?'

'Never mind who I am, who the hell are you?'

The man digs in his pocket, produces a business card, hands it to Thom.

'Josh Maguire, London Living.'

Thom stares at the card. He senses a wave of mild irritation seeping from the young couple. 'And?' Thom says, glaring at the estate agent.

'I'm conducting a viewing.'

'You can't do this.'

'I'm sorry?'

'I said, you can't do this. I know my property law and I suggest you get your arse out of here now!'

Thom turns towards the couple and rather relishes the chance to speak directly to them. 'You too,' he says with nuanced menace.

This has no visible effect on them, but galvanises the agent into twitchy, snivelling authority.

'I would ask that you do not address my clients. I would also like to inform you that our contract with Ms Swann and the terms of the lease which she signed, do give me every right to be here. She was sent a letter informing her of the date and time of the viewing and was quite free to change the date according to her wishes and could have picked a more convenient time. Furthermore, as you are clearly not the tenant mentioned in the legal documents, I would suggest that you leave the premises and let me get on with my work.'

As Thom listened to this it came back to him that Lucy had

been unhappy with her lease as she had to renew it yearly and it was filled with many sub-clauses that stripped her of nearly all her tenant's rights. He'd only half listened to what she'd said about it, as he thought she was hinting that the best thing for her was to move in with him and he hadn't wanted that. Not then.

He pondered the situation. The three of them watched him, waiting. Finally he conceded. 'Alright, carry on. But, as she's not here, I'm going to stay.'

He sat down on the sofa, leaned back with his arms stretched along the back, rested his right ankle on the knee of his other leg. Expansive. At home. His castle.

'Fine,' said the agent, with a tight little smile.

This battle won, Thom now remembered his real purpose for being there. It had been a stroke of luck in a way that he had come at this precise moment, otherwise he'd be down on the street ringing her buzzer. Or inside the building, but locked on the wrong side of Lucy's door, knocking it repeatedly, and peering, then calling through her letterbox. Not knowing if she was inside and stubbornly ignoring him.

The agent was leading the young couple into other rooms.

'The second bedroom is currently used as a study, but the shelving could be easily dismantled and as you see, there's enough room for a double bed here.'

Thom's gaze went to Lucy's answer machine; the red light was blinking indicating that she had new messages. He was tempted to press 'play' so that he could hear them in order to figure out how long she had been gone, but the heap of unopened mail by the door told its own story. She hadn't been here for several days, possibly over a week. Maybe even longer.

The three interlopers emerged from the study and trailed into the bathroom.

'Now although the bathroom lacks a natural light source, it is of course fully ventilated.'

There was a click followed by the noisy rattling buzz of the automatic ventilator that came on every time you pulled the light cord.

'It's very claustrophobic, terribly depressing.' The young woman's voice, a sort of posh drawl with a hint of cockney twang unconvincingly peppered over the surface.

Thom got up from the sofa and went into Lucy's study.

Claustrophobic. A room ten foot by eight. A small window, with a desk under it. All the walls, floor to ceiling, lined with shelves. Every shelf filled with books. Sections on art, fashion, culture. Fiction, mostly novels, mostly published in the last thirty years. Mostly unread. Lucy, a sucker for those book clubs where the dazzling opening offer gives you five books at ninety pence each. SAVING YOU ALMOST EIGHTY FIVE POUNDS!

Lucy who was so hungry for knowledge she could eat the world. Or imagined she could.

He would tease her about this.

Where are you, Lucy?

What the fuck is going on?

Distant voices emerging from the bathroom, retreating down the passage to the bedroom.

Lucy's bedroom. Almost everything in the room was white. Her double bed against the furthest wall away from the cold draught by the window. He imagines it. The candles she had lit the first time she'd invited him in. Vanilla scented. Her leading him by the hand, saying, 'Here, come and see where I sleep.'

Yeah, the guided tour of her flat.

The white room. The candles. The past.

It seemed so long ago now.

Lucy putting a cassette into a player. What did he expect? Chopin? Miles Davies?

Seduction?

266

She had moved across the room, fished through a wobbly pile of cassettes, then found what she was looking for.

Joy Division. 'Love will tear us apart'.

How much attention had he been paying?

This creature. Lucy the seductress with her web lit by the flickering soft flames of candles.

Joy Division? He'd never heard of them.

And the song: 'Love will tear us apart'?

Threat, promise or repressed fear?

Now three strangers were in that same bedroom – he could hear the agent's voice droning on distantly like a badly tuned radio.

No computer on her desk. She had a laptop, but didn't use it much.

Then, feeling as if he were violating her somehow, Thom opened the top right-hand drawer of her desk. Here was a dense sea of pens and pencils, scissors, papers, glue sticks, paint brushes, paper clips, rubber bands, drawing pins, loose change, books of stamps, scalpel blades, marker pens. Nothing else.

He opened the drawer on the other side to find another sea, this one of paper, mostly consisting of shop receipts, bus tickets, business cards, vouchers. Lucy had a habit of letting her purse fill up until the zipper on it would hardly close and the seams were stretched to breaking point, then she would empty everything she didn't need into this drawer.

He picked up a tube ticket from the top of the pile near the front, it was dated twelve days ago. Close to it there was a Waterstone's receipt for a book called *Picturing the Self: Changing Views of the Subject in Visual Culture*. The date on this receipt was from the beginning of July. Another receipt was from the college coffee bar. She'd had soup and fruit. What soup? What fruit?

He picked up another folded slip, opened it and was shocked to see how long it was and how many items were on it. Dress

£45, dress £55, shoes £49.95, dress £45, bag £29.95, accessories £10.99, accessories £20, dress £65, knitwear £55. Total payable £375.89!

He snatched up another receipt – this one was from Next and totalled £128.97.

Suddenly the voices of the agent and the young couple were coming back down the hallway.

'It's a very short walk to the tube station at Hammersmith, and you have the shops on King Street, the Lyric and of course the river is no distance at all…'

'And when might it be available?'

The three interlopers had drawn to a halt near the study and the agent had peered in at Thom, a dubious expression on his pinched face. 'We can discuss availability in a moment,' he said to the couple. Then he turned to Thom. 'Sir, we're done here. Perhaps you could ask Miss Swann to get in touch.'

And with that all three departed leaving Thom alone in Lucy's flat, which seemed an odd thing to do. Except, of course, for the fact that he had followed them in without being noticed – meaning that the agent must have assumed that Thom was already in the flat and had emerged from another room before confronting them in the living room. Thom felt that he had every right to be there as Lucy's boyfriend, even if Lucy wouldn't see it that way.

As he considered the situation he grew increasingly troubled. No, not troubled – angry. He was angry because it had been so easy to get into her flat, angry with the letting company for beginning the process of finding a new tenant, and angry at the young couple for their elegant insouciance, and furious with Lucy for her stubbornness and stupidity and recklessness and silly childish silence.

Lucy…

Now they were gone, he felt Lucy's absence even more palpably.

He was still holding the receipts. Four new dresses. Over five hundred pounds spent on clothes in one go! It was so unlike Lucy.

Feeling fury tinged with guilt, but desperately trying to justify himself, he made his way to her bedroom where he opened both doors of her wardrobe. Hanging there he saw the clothes he was used to seeing her in – she favoured earth colours; moss-green or cinnamon skirts, tawny linen jackets and trousers, blouses and sweaters in mustard and amber and mulberry. At one end of the rail there was an awful scarlet taffeta ball gown that she'd only ever worn once long before he knew her and which she kept for sentimental reasons. He'd seen a photo of her wearing it when she was seventeen. Her hair was long and full of twirling, twisting glossy curls, her cheeks glowed pink as if she had applied too much rouge or, judging from the champagne bottle she brandished, had drunk a wee bit too much. And she was laughing, her head thrown back, her mouth open and her eyes a little bit glazed and squinty. This was not a person he recognised. But then hadn't she said much the same about a photograph she'd seen of him in his youth? The one of him in cricket whites with grass stains on the groin where he'd rubbed the ball before bowling. He was grinning and frowning squint-eyed into the sun, his arms loose and simian, expressing all the self-consciousness of being photographed like this on the sports field, by his mother who, to make matters worse, had on that day, worn a ridiculous over-sized hat as if she were at Ascot not St Benedict's Grammar. He'd been angry and defensive when on first seeing the photo Lucy had said, 'That's you? You!' She seemed to be mocking him for his gauche middle-class, middle-of-the-road, provincial earnestness.

While he could easily see that he and the awkward-looking young man were one and the same, with Lucy it was different. The drunken laughing girl in the red dress would always be laughing at him. He couldn't possibly be in love with that girl.

Only the taffeta dress in her wardrobe provided the direct link between his Lucy and that Lucy.

He realised he was staring at the press of clothes in a rather meaningless and unfocussed way, and so to counter this he hefted the tight row of hanging clothes as far along the rail to the right as was possible, then began to move each item, one at a time in the other direction, examining them as he went.

There were hardly any dresses at all, and those that were there he recognised from previous occasions. He could not find four brand-new dresses. Then something else struck him and he looked up to the top of the wardrobe where she kept her suitcases. The smaller of the two was there, but the large red one was gone. He closed the wardrobe doors and wandered past the bed to the window.

He did not understand why she had not told him she was going away. It was unkind of her, cowardly even. Especially if she had gone away with some other man. A man who had perhaps footed the bill for these dresses, paid for the trip – some extravagant week-long break in Italy or Iceland. Or for that matter in the UK in some cosy boutique hotel in the Lake District or Cornwall.

He went into the living room and pressed the play button on her answer machine. A mechanical voice announced that she had twenty-six new messages. The first of which was his. He was surprised at the brisk formality of his own voice.

'Thom here, I'll be finished work at six. Give me a ring.'

The second message was also his.

'Lucy? You there? Pick up.' A silence. Then, 'Okay, ring me.'

The third was Lucy's mother. 'Hello, hello? Lucy, darling, Mum here. Just ringing for a wee chat. Daddy sends his love. Bye for now.'

The next was a brief listening silence.

Then Thom again, sounding edgy and ticked off. 'Lucy, I've tried your mobile and the college. Give us a ring, eh?'

Then the letting agency. 'Hi, it's Julie here from London Living. Just a reminder that your lease is due for renewal. The papers are in the post and we need them back by the specified date on the form. Thank you.'

A message from the college. 'Hi Lucy, Mitra here, can we meet up to talk about the screen-printing project? Noel's quite keen now to set things in motion. Bye-ee.'

So it went, all of the messages increasing in urgency or frustration or confusion.

'Hi Lucy, okay, the meeting is tomorrow. I've arranged for me, Noel, Keith from finance and Susan Walters from surface pattern design to be in the print area at one. Bye-ee.'

'Lucy, it's three o'clock now and to be blunt, it didn't look good you not being there; you are after all the project leader. What's up? Is it Thom? Is he giving you a hard time? Again! Anyway, at the meeting I told a little white lie, said you had food poisoning. Okay? Anyway hun, give me a ring. I'm beginning to get worried.'

Mitra had rung Thom at the college the day before yesterday and left a message asking if he knew how she could get in touch with Lucy. Her tone had been bristling with polite contempt. Now he understood why.

The last few messages chilled him.

'Hello, this is a message for Miss Lucy Swann; we haven't received your renewed contract for the flat. This may be an oversight on your part. If so could you drop into the office by close of business today with the paperwork? Thank you.'

'Lucy, Mum here again. Is everything alright my darling? We haven't heard from you for over two weeks now. I know you're busy, but just give us a wee tinkle so we know all's well. Bye for now.' Her voice sounded frail and on the edge of tears.

'Hello Lucy. Daddy calling. Your mother's getting very worried now. Well, you know what a worrier she is with you there in the big bad city. Alright doll. Ring us! Okay?'

'Lucy, it's Mitra again. Look, I had a chat with Noel. I came clean about my fib and he said that he was also worried and how last time he'd seen you, you were a bit spaced out. Kinda not yourself. Sorry. And … oh god … don't hate me for saying this, but I remembered something you told me about what happened before. You know, the breakdown when you were at college. And you know, now I think about it, you were a bit hyper these last few weeks. Look, I don't want to make things worse, I'm just worried. Please get in touch and I'm sorry if I've overstepped the mark here. Love you.'

Thom sat down on the sofa. Stared for a long time at the answer machine. The red light no longer blinking, just glowing faintly as if waiting.

# La Barbe-Bleue

Vivier and Pelat were back at the station by eight-thirty in the morning, while Lamy had been left with another officer to search the rest of the gîte's garden and the area immediately behind it for any other evidence. Pelat had expected Lamy to respond somewhat grudgingly to this order (not that there was any question he could challenge any task she assigned him, but certain facial expressions could give him away) but in this instance, surprisingly, he looked positively delighted with the prospect.

She remembered the steady, somewhat disturbing gaze he had fixed on the mother's breast as she fed her child, but allowed that this might have been an entirely benign sort of stare, not one borne of sexual desire, but rather awe and wonder at this perfectly natural and beautiful act.

Vivier was making coffee while Sabine laid out the plastic bags which contained the newly found evidence on a table.

It was curious how the contents of the bag had landed in a neat sort of pile in the flower bed, it almost gave the impression that it had been carefully positioned there, but on the other hand if it had been swung in an arc, then centrifugal force would keep the contents safe at the bottom of the bag until impact. The basket (she was sure her mother had possessed one very like this, though larger – it had been abandoned in the woodshed and contained a few old wooden pegs, short lengths of string, boxes of matches and some rusty hinges, hooks and shutter fastenings) evoked for Pelat an aura of the nineteen-fifties and sixties, as had the dress the young woman wore.

When the old couple, the Eszterhas came in (if they came in) they might identify the body in the morgue as the young woman

273

they had seen two days ago, and also recognise the cardigan and bag as hers. So that the girl, the bag and the cardigan could then be tied with each other and they could begin to piece together a journey of sorts. Or several journeys rather; the cardigan's to the lost property store at the café, the bag's to the garden overlooking the Bais du Somme and the young woman's to her lonely death on the waste ground near the industrial estate.

Now it seemed they could learn certain intimate things about the murder victim; what brand of mascara she favoured, where she shopped. They knew that she smoked cigarettes and that she was almost certainly staying in a hotel. The key fob was numbered six, but it was unfortunately one of those generic ones that could be bought at most locksmiths, a simple circular black tag with the number in an inset white shape. It could belong to any number of small hotels and guest houses in the town, or for that matter any other town. The woman may have had a car and could have driven into Neuville-Sur-Mer for the day with the intention of returning to her hotel later that night.

Despite the news about an unidentified woman being found dead, no hotelier had come forward to report the disappearance of one of their guests. There again the rumours were rife that the dead woman was a prostitute and so perhaps the connection was not entirely obvious. Equally, in the event that the woman had booked in for a whole week or perhaps two, her comings and goings would not necessarily have been noticed, nor, crucially, her absence.

Sabine pictured the woman's hotel room in her mind's eye, a smallish room, simply furnished. The bed made up in readiness for its occupant, some personal items on the small table next to the bed, a paperback book perhaps, a travel alarm clock, a packet of tissues, a lip salve. On the dresser, a make-up bag and some jars of moisturiser, eye make-up remover, cleanser, perfume. In the en-suite bathroom, shower cream, shampoo, conditioner. In a glass near the sink, a toothbrush and paste. Hanging on the shower rail to dry, underwear that had been hand-washed in the sink.

In the wardrobe, more pretty dresses or light summer skirts and blouses. In the suitcase on the folding stand, an accumulation of souvenirs and gifts, a bottle of cognac. There too, perhaps, the woman's passport, her house keys.

All of it waiting for the occupant's return, the pillows on the bed cool and smooth and somehow achingly lonely – sensing their uselessness without a human head to cradle through the sweet dreaming night.

And the imagined dresses too, which hung uselessly in the wardrobe like lonely and disembodied dancing princesses deprived of their night at the ball. Another image abruptly invaded Sabine's mind, that of the locked room in Charles Perrault's La Barbe-Bleue. It had haunted her dreams for years, the nightmare of that forbidden room where the walls were hung with the corpses of young women and the floor was sticky with their spilled blood.

'Sabine!'

She jumped at the voice and turned to see Inspector Vivier.

'Oh, sorry,' she said, 'you startled me.'

He did not apologise, but merely raised one curious eyebrow.

'The witnesses are here, so I thought we'd show them the bag first, then the body.'

'Of course.'

The English couple looked as if they had aged ten years overnight, but there was something heartening about the way they sat side by side holding one another's hands, giving and gaining strength from each other. Although they looked immeasurably tired, they lifted their faces bravely and sat straight-backed in preparation for whatever horrors lay ahead.

'This is Sabine Pelat whom you may have met yesterday,' Vivier explained, 'and this is an item which we hope you may be able to identify.'

As one, they turned their faces to Sabine, then dropped their eyes to the bag she held. She stepped forward and offered the object to the man who, unthinkingly jerked his head back as if repulsed, but more likely he was trying to keep the object in focus. The woman, however, did not hesitate, but reached past her husband to accept the bag inside its protective plastic covering. She handled it confidently, turning it around in her hands several times, frowning and slowly nodding. Then she offered it to her husband – who accepted it, and seemingly taking the lead from his wife, turned it over in his hands, inspecting it.

'Yes,' he said, at last. 'It rings a bell. There is something familiar about it, but…'

'It is the bag the young woman carried,' the woman said with certainty. The man glanced at his wife. He looked like the sort of man who listened to his wife's opinion, respected what she had to say. She continued confidently, 'Or if it isn't the actual bag, then it is exactly the same style.'

'Thank you,' Vivier said. 'This is a great help to the investigation, but there is a more onerous task ahead which I hope you will undertake?' He stood up pushing the chair back, making a sudden harsh noise that caused the couple to visibly wince.

'Sorry,' he said, then lifted his hand graciously to indicate the door. The couple rose hesitantly and, still holding hands, followed Sabine out of the room. Vivier went through last.

The morgue was located in the basement of the building and as they were halfway down the concrete stairway a strong smell of disinfectant and bleach permeated the air. No one spoke and the sound of their footsteps echoed in the confined space.

Sabine half turned to check that the couple were alright and noticed how the man was walking in an uneven shuffle, putting his weight chiefly on his left leg, while using his right hesitatingly. She had been walking briskly at her normal pace, but now she slowed down a little.

'It won't take very long,' she said in an attempt to soothe them. They murmured in response.

At the door to the morgue itself, they stopped.

'Could I ask that you view the body one at a time and that you do not indicate by any word or facial expression to one another whether this is the girl you saw?'

The man and the woman nodded, then drawing her hand reluctantly from her husband's, Hilda Eszterhas said, 'I'll go first,' and stepping forward she stood side by side with Vivier at the threshold. Vivier grasped the door handle. 'We shouldn't be longer than a few minutes.' He opened the door and with one hand lightly cupping the woman's elbow led her inside.

# Revenant

Scott was having his old nightmare again. He was standing in a dim room holding the all-too-familiar pillow. He could feel it in his hands, warm and slightly damp beneath his palms. He could see the mustard colour of the fabric and the repeated vignettes of the Lone Ranger on his rearing horse, the brightly coloured wigwam, the tomahawk and the tall cactus with two curving branches like upturned arms.

But the room in the dream was this room and not that other room from long ago. There was nothing in the room. No cot, no bed, no sleeping brother. And he was not a child, but a fully grown man. Something was closing in on him, something heavy and black. The darkness itself seemed animate and malevolent; thick and dense, it seemed to pinion his arms and legs, then every part of his body. Yet all his focus was on the object in his hands. Then suddenly – in one of those rapid reversals so peculiar to dreams – his hands were no longer holding the pillow; they were pushing it away, because it was being forced onto his face, suffocating him.

He woke abruptly. He had been sleeping (unusually for him) on his belly, three-quarters of his face pressed into the pillow.

The room was beginning to grow light. He was bathed in sweat. He gave a groan of complaint and lifting his head, saw Marilyn seated at the table under the window. She turned to look at him, frowning sympathetically.

'Bad dream?'

He grunted and flapped the hot damp covers away from his body, then moved over to the other side of the bed where it was cool and dry.

'What time is it?' he asked.

'Don't know. Early. What time's sunrise?' she said, then shrugged and turned back to her work.

He breathed out noisily, shut his eyes and felt his body relax. From across the room he could hear Marilyn's pen scratching over the paper. Short staccato sounds, then silence, then a decisive single noise. A straight line, a crossing out, the sound which was not dissimilar to that of an arrow being dispatched.

She murmured under her breath a few words from whatever it was she was writing. Her voice was musical, incantatory, fragmented.

'My mother said, and said again,' he heard, then the fierce sound of the pen as she scored out some of the words.

'Marilyn?' he said, opening his eyes.

She was hunched over the desk, writing another line, rocking slightly as she did so. She didn't seem to hear him.

He waited, watching. The small movements of her right arm as she wrote, barely perceptible. Then she stopped writing and twisted to face him.

'Sorry,' she said, 'I had to get that down or I'd forget.'

'That's okay.'

'Do you want some coffee?' she asked, brightly.

He considered this. It wasn't what he had interrupted her for, but her question demanded some sort of an answer.

Did he want coffee? Yes, probably, but there was something else too.

He threw back the bed covers and swung his legs over the side.

'I'll make it,' he said. 'You carry on.'

'I looked in on Aaron, he's still asleep.'

'Okay. Coffee?'

'Please.'

'Marilyn?'

'Mm?'

'Let's go home.'

She had turned back to her desk and was once more scratching the pen rapidly over the page. She wasn't listening, not really. He stood behind her, wondering whether to say it again, but even as he did so he was calculating the cost of three more flight tickets, the lies he might tell in order to get their existing return tickets altered, the insurance claim he might be able to swing. If they got Aaron to a doctor here, if they lied, if they could invent some tragedy back home. Or he could pay for the flights with his American Express card. His credit was good and somehow at that moment, paying thousands of dollars back over the next three or four years sounded a small price to pay to get back to Canada now or at least within the next twenty-four hours.

'Coffee then,' he said and pulled a t-shirt over his head.

Distractedly, still scribbling away, she nodded, her head dipping rhythmically in time with whatever was happening between her mind, her hand and the moving pen.

He could not fathom how he had wound up with this strange creature. Poets he had always thought, (not that it was something he thought about a lot) should couple with other poets. Painters with painters. Musicians with musicians. Or even, he thought reproachfully, good people with equally good people.

Or so it seemed.

But he loved her. There was no doubt of that.

Marilyn was trying once again to rewrite the poem about her mother, about the idea of escaping death, about drowning. She could not understand why she kept going back to it, the poem didn't work, its sentiments were inauthentic, her heart wasn't in it. It lacked grace notes and depth, and the word 'hyperbole' was like a great lump of undigested food lodged in the belly of the poem.

She should abandon it. She should write about her pregnancy. But of course she was afraid Scott (though she had rarely known him to) might read something from over her shoulder and discover that she was expecting a child.

With each subsequent attempt at the poem she felt more lost, more useless; incapable of completing it, unable to produce any poems that had worth, and with that thought her past successes also crumbled. All her small triumphs seemed mere trickery, based on luck rather than real intelligence, skill or talent.

'Okay, coffee,' Scott had said.

And she had said, 'Please.'

Then he'd said something else, but she hadn't heard what it was.

She was half aware of him hovering in the room behind her, lingering as if he was waiting for something from her. But her mind was elsewhere. She was summoning the past, trawling her memory for the elusive, physical actuality of her mother; her scent, the sound of her voice, the precision of her movements and expressions, the theatrical widening of her eyes when outraged, the close press of her lips when concentrating, how the flesh on her upper arms wobbled when she was beating cake mixture and the irritating smack of her lips when she licked her finger in order to turn the page of a book. Her greedy boastful possessiveness when Marilyn did something well, her derision when she failed.

Marilyn crossed through one word, tried another, then crossed that out again and replaced the original.

Finally she heard Scott go out of the room and into the hallway. A few footsteps, then a brief moment of stillness and silence. He would be looking in on Aaron, checking that he was okay and still asleep. Then the footsteps started up again and she heard the second tread of the stairway creak as he went downstairs.

The poem, she suddenly realised, was not about her mother nor about almost drowning; it was about herself as a child. It was about her mother's words, the expression of awe and pride on her mother's face as she gazed at this miraculous back-from-the-dead child and how this had made Marilyn feel. It bestowed upon Marilyn a sense of uniqueness that was undeserved. There was a smugness in her child self that Marilyn squirmed to recognise. She had bought into her mother's version of events (how could she not?) and that had gone on to be a constituent part of her personality. And it was based on nothing. Or almost nothing.

There was no miracle.

Marilyn, aged two or three or however old she had been, had no active role in the story. She fell in a pond and was plucked out almost instantly, but at five, at six, at eleven she had heard and reheard her mother tell this story to whoever would listen and Marilyn had felt like a revenant, like one who has died and returned and is thus the bearer of rare knowledge and talent. A walker on water, a seer.

Hyperbole.

Her entire self was built around this and now that she looked more carefully at it she saw that where there was once legend and faith, there was now only a hollow space.

She put her pen down carefully so that in coming to rest it made no noise.

What was it Scott had said? Something about home? Something about wanting to go home? Or had she imagined that? Made him express aloud what she now desired more than anything.

To go home. To begin again.

# Bodies

The man is tall, six foot two or three. Blond. And either American or South African or Australian or British. He is aged somewhere between twenty-five and thirty-five.

Hilda Eszterhas reports him as saying, 'I let strange women follow me then I fuck them.'

Her husband insists that what the man said was, 'I follow strange women then I fuck them.'

Hilda saw the victim in the morgue and said that without doubt it was the same girl, or young woman rather, and that she was convinced she was English with a slight regional accent – possibly Scottish or Irish.

Her husband, Michael, could not identify the woman at all. But agreed that the man was tall and blond and unpleasant – if not sinister, but cannot define in what particular way he was unpleasant, aside from the words he'd spoken.

Then there was the other rather curious report. Another tall, blond man. No, not man, but boy. And this one, on the morning after the murder, is discovered either bleeding profusely from self-inflicted wounds or is spattered with blood from a presumed act of violence; the murder of a young woman. This boy or young man is five foot ten or eleven, very slight, with bad posture. Wide-eyed, dazed, mute, monstrous, craven, evil, ill, dangerous, vulnerable. Possibly Dutch or German. Also possibly American.

There were no less than fifteen witnesses who came forward with reports of this boy. Fifteen versions of a single truth, each of them inadvertently filtered and altered by the individual telling the story, and distorted by news of the murder, by gossip, by the desire to be a part of this thing, this evil visited on a peaceful small town.

Then there is the business about the cardigan, and the reported voodoo. A young black man running. An African who claims he is about to begin his training in medicine – who is running. A white man may run. Dress him in shorts, in a tracksuit, in Adidas or Nikes. A sweat band. What is he doing? He is running for the exercise, for his heart, training for a race, a marathon. But this African, his gleaming blue-black skin hardly even breaking out in a sweat, he must be running from something. He cannot just run. He must be guilty. If he finds a woman's cardigan and places it on a hedge so that its owner can reclaim it, he is not doing a kind and thoughtful deed. No, his act must be misinterpreted as ritualistic, as evil.

Witnesses: their words tumble and fall, spill out elaborations, interpretations. Never meaning to lie, but each is susceptible to the workings of their imagination.

This is now the accepted truth about eye witnesses, their absolute fallibility.

This is why the hard science of forensics is so important.

The phone rings on Vivier's desk, he reaches out for it, snatches it up clumsily, clattering the hand piece as he does so.

'Vivier.'

'Sir.'

It is Sabine Pelat; her usually reserved tones are unmistakably breathy as she continues to speak at a rapid pace. 'The path lab got back to me. It was sperm on the cardigan, and they've done a DNA profile and got a match with a local man.'

'Who is it?'

'Florian Lebrun.'

'Lebrun … doesn't ring any bells. He's got a record?'

'Yeah, mostly petty stuff, drugs, handling stolen goods, shoplifting, car theft and one rape charge.'

'Convicted?'

'Not of the rape.'

'He's done time, though?'

'Yeah. Started young.'

'Violent?'

'Apart from the rape, no.'

'What about physical description? Is he tall, blond, American?'

'Five eight, light brown hair, French citizen.'

'Yeah. I guessed that from the name. Anything else?'

'Unmarried. No kids.'

'Alright, let's get everyone in the briefing room in half an hour.'

Vivier was about to hang up when Sabine said, 'Ah, sir?'

'What?'

'This seems too easy.'

'Yeah.'

'You thought the same?'

'But a DNA match?'

'I guess.'

'Well, if she was a prostitute she may have encountered both men. Others too.'

'Zero trace of semen on the body. The vaginal swab was clean as a whistle.'

'Hmm.' Vivier considered this. 'We'll have to bring Lebrun in. We have no choice in the matter, but in the meantime can you find out what you can about the rape case?'

'Yes, I was thinking that.'

'Thanks, Sabine.'

She hung up and he immediately noticed that he felt curiously troubled. It was not just the case, but something else, a sense of loss. He pondered this and after a few minutes convinced himself that his feelings, if indeed they might be really called feelings or emotions, were to do with some aspect of his appreciation of Pelat's intelligence; her patience, diligence and respect. It could not be, as it had almost seemed, that her voice at the other end of the phone line was somehow seductive, that he had pictured her as he listened and responded, that he was remembering how they had laughed together earlier that morning, and how her eyes had shone.

He recognised that she was a beautiful and desirable woman. A man would be blind not to see that. But to think that she would be remotely interested in him, that was a folly bordering on madness.

Vivier had long ago resigned himself to a bleak, lonely existence. His first wife had said that he was too remote, too intellectual, too cold to really ever love anyone. And because he truly believed that he had loved her, her parting words had sunk deep and made him question his own feelings. Subsequent love affairs seemed to confirm the accusation she'd made.

He steeled himself against the possibility of falling for Sabine Pelat. He would only make a fool of himself. No doubt she found him cold and ugly; as appealing as the carved stone effigies of the centuries-dead lords and knights who lay piously, hawk-nosed and hollow-cheeked on their austere tombs in the cathedrals of Northern France.

He would not make a fool of himself.

His stomach growled. He reached into his pocket, thumbed an indigestion tablet from the foil pack and put it on his tongue. Sat quietly while it melted. His guts carried on with their curiously musical gurgles and groans. An orchestra of comical effects. Without dignity. All too human.

# Reasons to be Cheerful

Jean-Pierre Laniel was late for work. But, as he was always deliberately early, usually arriving in the office at nine instead of the contracted hour of ten, being ten minutes behind his self-inflicted schedule was an issue only to Jean-Pierre himself.

But it was an issue that made him grip the steering wheel of his Renault Clio so hard that his knuckles whitened. A touring caravan had broken down at the junction of the main road causing a tailback of seven cars. Jean-Pierre had pulled up and waited for all of two minutes before, with gritted teeth and a string of loud expletives, he'd turned the car around and headed back up the road he'd just come down. He knew another way. It was less direct and involved one narrow country lane and a detour through the northern part of the town, but at this hour he would have no difficulty.

He was in a bad mood, but as his moods usually ranged between moderately grumpy to bad to very bad to blind raging fury, with few incursions into peacefulness or full-blown happiness, his short temper at this delay was hardly exceptional. And this day, like the others in his 33 years, provided him with an array of excellent reasons to be angry.

During his shower earlier that morning he had noticed that the water was not running off as freely as it should. The drain wasn't blocked, merely a tad sluggish. He had stopped washing himself and crouched (the hot water pulsing down relentlessly on his bony spine) on the shower-room floor to investigate. Caught in the silver spokes of the plughole he could see the offending object: a flotilla of pale stringy strands. Using his thumb and forefinger he was able to grasp this and pull (with some difficulty) a tangle of long wet hairs and soapy glutinous stuff from the drain. He placed this for safe keeping on the edge of the sink, then recommenced showering. When he was done, and had shaved, applied cologne and hair gel, he padded out of the bathroom in his slippers and dressing gown, with the hair from the drain held between his fingertips at arm's length, and made his way to the kitchen where his wife was preparing breakfast.

She was standing at the work counter cutting pears into quarters. She seemed unaware that he had entered the room – blithely innocent – the way she always played it.

He stood there waiting for her to sense his presence.

'Oh!' she said, when on turning to get something from the fridge she finally noticed him. She smiled weakly.

'Here,' he said, advancing on her.

'What?' she asked, but held out her hand anyway.

He dropped the greasy damp tangle into her outstretched palm.

'Yours I believe,' he said.

She apologised and promised to be more careful in the future, though he somehow doubted she was capable of it and said as much.

He did not like issuing these reminders and reprimands day and night. If it wasn't his wife, it was his daughters, his colleagues and other staff. Or occasionally his elderly parents or the home help, Bette, or his neighbours and anyone else who crossed his path; the girls' schoolteachers, shop assistants, the doctor's receptionist, his brother, his fool of a gardener. The list was endless.

It was exhausting always having to think for other people, continually pointing out the flaws in how things were done and explaining how these might be improved. And if he didn't do it, who would? How much better would the world be if only people would learn? If they, like him, paid more attention to the small details? The driver of the stalled camper van for example, who had caused Jean-Pierre and several other motorists so much inconvenience, should have checked his oil and water and fuel before setting out. And furthermore for a tourist to be on the roads at an hour when other citizens were on their way to work was clearly shortsighted and selfish. The van had a foreign sticker on it. 'D' for Deutschland. Arrogance. Typical Kraut.

Following his alternative route, Jean-Pierre figured that he would arrive at his desk at 9.25 – in plenty of time to note, as he always did, who was next to arrive, who left it until 10 o'clock and who drifted lazily to their post at one minute or two or ten past the hour. He pulled up at a traffic light on rue de Bainville, and with the engine ticking over and his hands growing sweaty on the wheel, he glanced to his left just in time to see the front door of a nearby house swing open. A woman with red hair emerged. Her hair was long and unruly, the dress she wore a rather unflattering floral sack. She was dragging an overlarge trolley suitcase of the sort that invariably tripped one up or was rolled over one's toes at airports. She looked vaguely familiar, but then she was one of a type – a henna-haired hippy wench, slovenly and probably loud and opinionated. Following her was a man carrying an even larger bag, an olive green hold-all of monstrous proportions. He was very tall, with broad shoulders and blond hair. He struggled with the bag, his whole upper body swaying as he hefted it out through the doorway.

Lastly, a younger man wandered out of the house. He was also blond and stepped out of the house entirely unburdened by any luggage.

Jean-Pierre was thinking that, strictly speaking, if they must have such a quantity of possessions with them on holiday, then surely five or six smaller cases would be better. That way the load could be more evenly distributed between the three.

But then, just as he was thinking this, he realised that he did indeed recognise all three of these people. The youngest man had been that lunatic he had seen on the street only yesterday. And now Jean-Pierre looked closer he could just make out multiple thin red scars on his hands and wrists.

Yesterday, arriving upon the scene late, Jean-Pierre had been just in time to see the boy being led away by the blond man and another in a postman's uniform. The woman had been with them too, though he hadn't paid much attention to her.

Jean-Pierre had immediately phoned the police on his mobile and attempted to order those involved back to the scene of the incident, but they had not listened to him. He had therefore waited at the place where the boy had been until the police finally arrived.

Or rather one rather young policeman on foot who had arrived after an hour or so.

Later Jean-Pierre had heard about the murdered girl, and although the policeman had taken a brief statement from him about the boy dripping with blood, they had not been in touch again, and now these people were escaping.

The red-haired woman left the case on the path outside the house and crossed the lawn to a drive at the side of the house where a car was parked.

The lights changed then and immediately the driver in the car behind Jean-Pierre sounded his horn. Infuriated, Jean-Pierre crashed his gears and put his foot hard on the accelerator. He crossed the intersection, slowed down, pulled into a driveway (he didn't care who it belonged to) reversed out and returned to the house where the tourists were. The woman was standing by the driver's door on the drive. The younger man was in the back seat of the car, his neck twisted so that his forehead was resting on the side window. The other man was lifting something into the boot of the car.

Without hesitation Jean-Pierre pulled up onto the pavement and parked his car so that it was blocking their exit from the driveway. Then he pulled his keys from the ignition, tossed them under his seat and took out his mobile phone.

They did not notice him at first, as they were busy with the luggage. Then the woman got in behind the wheel and turned to talk to the boy in the back, while the man went back to the house and tugged at the front door making sure it was locked.

Jean-Pierre dialled the number of the local police station direct. It was a number he had memorised as he'd had excellent cause to use it on numerous occasions – good citizen that he was. It rang seven times and he counted, mouthing the number under his breath.

The older of the two men got into the car beside the woman. They talked to one another and then she shook her head and, smiling, she turned around and took the steering wheel in readiness to set off.

Jean-Pierre pushed down the catch on the driver's door locking himself in. He heard the ring tone pulse twice more. Still no answer.

The woman started the engine. He saw her suddenly look at him with an expression of annoyance and surprise. He saw her lips move, though he could not hear what she said, and she lifted both hands from the wheel as if in supplication.

Then the man looked at Jean-Pierre. He frowned and shook his head, then said something angrily to the woman which caused her to sound the horn in two quick bursts.

Jean-Pierre pressed the button to end the call to the local station and dialled the three digit code for the emergency services.

The man and woman seemed to be debating what to do. The woman shook her head and then the man reached in front of her and pressed the horn. Three long beeps filled the air. Jean-Pierre, who had his window three quarters open, now shut it until there was only a slim gap at the top.

The horn sounded again, this time an extended angry blast, impossible to ignore. Pedestrians and people in cars craned their heads to see what was going on.

The switchboard operator at the emergency number answered the phone just as the man was getting out of the car and coming slowly toward Jean-Pierre and gesticulating for him to move the Renault. Jean-Pierre did his best to ignore him. The man tapped on the driver's window, waved his arms indicating the driveway and the waiting car.

Then he began yelling, partly in bad French, partly in English.

'Monsieur, monsieur! Alle oop! Hey! Hey, guy! Hey, move your car! Sir. For Christsake! Monsieur, vite. Je suis's getting mad as goddamn hell.'

There was more banging on the side window, then some sweeping arm movements, which indicated forward movement.

'Police, please,' Jean-Pierre said into his mobile phone.

'One moment,' the woman's voice at the other end said brightly.

Jean-Pierre had been looking straight ahead, determined not to look directly at the man, only seeing what he was doing from the corner of his eye. Suddenly the man bobbed into view, thrusting his face in the direction of Jean-Pierre on the other side of the windscreen, and yelling, 'Are you deaf?' then slamming his hand three times on the bonnet, making a series of resounding bangs and probably denting it.

Then just as suddenly, the man seemed to give up. He moved away from Jean-Pierre's car and crossed the pavement to his own, shrugging at the woman behind the wheel as he did so. He got back in the car beside her, slamming the door behind him. They talked to and fro animatedly for a few moments, throwing the odd hostile glance at Jean-Pierre as they did so.

The boy in the back, Jean-Pierre noticed, was rocking rhythmically from side to side and letting his head repeatedly collide with the window. The couple, bickering now, did not seem to notice. They should stop him from doing that, Jean-Pierre thought, they should tie him up, pinion him, put his head in a brace of some sort. Drug him. Keep him home. In a home. He wasn't safe.

Then the man tilted his body to one side in order to reach into his trouser pocket.

A gun? Jean-Pierre thought with alarm.

An object was brought into view and waggled aggressively in Jean-Pierre's direction. A slim silver-grey object. No gun, but a mobile phone. Somewhat ridiculously Jean-Pierre mimicked the gesture. Two little boys threatening each other with toys. Bang-bang, you're dead.

But this was even more banal, two grown men threatening each other with cell phones. Gonna tell the police. Gonna tell Daddy.

But this is a fight Jean-Pierre will win. He has a head start.

At first it's difficult for him to explain over the phone, what happened yesterday, what happened today. Lines get crossed. The person on the other end of the phone thinks it is Jean-Pierre trapped in his driveway and when he persuades them it is the other way around they sound nonplussed. Why did you do that, sir? Because they were escaping. Escaping what?

So it goes. On and on.

Finally Jean-Pierre remembers the man slamming the flat of his palm on the bonnet. Three times. Hard. Causing untold damage. Deliberate. Reckless.

A patrol is on its way, the telephonist says.

Scott, speaking to another operator, is told the same thing.

Quietly, Scott told Marilyn to take Aaron back into the house. He could handle this. It was nothing to worry about. Nothing at all.

# The Hanged Man

The layout of the police station was such that from Sabine's window she could see into the briefing room, which was in a wing at right angles to the main block. She had been typing up a report when she glanced up to see Paul Vivier standing by one of the stacking chairs near the front of the room. His back was to her and his right hand was resting on the chair, while his left was hanging loose and lifeless. His head was bent forward, so that her first quick impression was that of a hanged man.

The first dead body she had ever seen had been that of a man who'd hung himself. This was long before she'd joined the police, long before anyone should see such a thing – she had been twelve years old. The man, a neighbour, was a bureaucrat of some sort (she never found out exactly what he did to earn his living) and Sabine's mother, noticing that his shutters were still closed at midday, had sent her round to see if there was anything the matter.

'If he's not well, ask him if there's anything he needs. I'll make some of Aunt Bridget's special garlic soup.'

Sabine had gone to the man's front door first, rang the old fashioned bell and waited. The man lived alone, he had no wife or children, and his mother had died three years earlier after a long illness. Sabine's mother took a great interest in him. 'A young man like that…' she'd say, though to Sabine he didn't look young at all. 'Poor thing, he was devoted to his mama. She gave him life, then she took his.' It had taken many years for Sabine to understand what that meant.

She had rung the bell again, rattling the chain and enjoying the loud clamour that seemed to echo in the unusually quiet street. No one answered, but his car – a four by four fitted out with a special ramp so that he could take his mother out and about in her wheelchair – was parked in its usual place in front of the house. Sabine went around to the back of the house and, after rapping her knuckles on the glass panel, she tried the door and found it was unlocked. She crept in, calling loudly, 'Monsieur Thorez! Monsieur?'

He was hanging over the stairs, his head lolling forward and his toes pointing down like a string puppet. He was in his black suit – perhaps he had no less formal clothes – but he'd taken his shoes off – perhaps to prevent damage to the *belle époque* chair he'd stood on.

Vivier moved then, lifting his head and looking around as if he'd suddenly had a new thought. Or as if someone had called his name. He moved to the corner of the room near the window where there was a flip chart. He stood staring at it, as if reading, though the sheet of paper was white and empty.

Sabine Pelat watched him for a few minutes. She remembered how earlier she'd teased him, laughed at him and then, delightfully, laughed with him. All over a stubbornly knotted shoelace. It had been as if a peculiar sort of insanity had overtaken them both. The nature of the work really, which was often so terrible. She knew from one or maybe several of her translated English novels, that one of the slang names for the police in the UK was 'the filth'. Certainly filth was what they dealt in. Nightmarish, visceral, tragic and real. Filth. Not their filth, but when you dealt with it day in and day out it entered you; seeped into your pores, coated your tongue. You breathed it, lived it, dreamt it.

But Paul Vivier, that most remote of men, had laughed. And laughed. And it had been thrilling to see him laugh, to recognise that this was possible. Without recrimination. It could quite easily have gone a different way. He may well have been less than amused. And then?

But he had laughed. His face transformed. So that she could see his strong white teeth, the sharp incisors, with a single nugget of gold glinting towards the back. His eyes gleaming brightly, the creases at the outer edges of his lids, which were not unattractive, as one presumed wrinkles to be, but almost like accent marks which highlighted the act of smiling.

Sabine had been quietly focusing her attention on Paul Vivier for some time. For a year or two, if somewhat distantly. But now, in these three or four minutes, it dawned on her that lately her interest in him had been less formal, less to do with admiration and respect for a superior, with a keenness to watch and learn, and more to do with… She paused and looked away from him in order to gather her thoughts.

Was it lust? No, something deeper and more complex.

Then did she like him a great deal?

'Like' was such a flaccid word, it needed the hard on of a qualifier such as 'very' or 'a lot' or 'loads'.

No, the word she was reaching for presented a leap of perilous risk; the word was (how could it be?) love.

She smiled. She could not help herself.

And then as if to remind her of where she was, of who she was, the phone rang.

She picked it up and gave her name. On the other end of the line there was only silence.

'Who's there? Hello.'

She listened. There was no breathing to be heard, only a sort of hollow quiet rushing noise, like faraway waves in a seashell. Like the sound of an asthmatic twelve-year-old girl's lungs when something has frightened and shocked and saddened her, and stripped away the last illusions of childhood.

She listened and looked up again to where Vivier had been standing seconds before, but he was gone.

'Paul?' she said into the mouthpiece, then realising her mistake, she hung up the phone and went back to the report she'd been typing.

# Road Rage

It was Lamy who was sent to deal with the traffic incident in the end. A waste of a morning as far as he could see. Two motorists squabbling over a parking space, turning nasty, but mostly just the loud venting of rage.

Dawn had been hazy, but now as he drove in the direction of the rising sun, its piercing light seemed to rip right through his eyeballs to drive a dagger of pain into his head. He adjusted the sun visor, but that didn't help, and so with a flick of his hand, he slapped it back to its original position.

He turned onto rue Jules Verne; a tree-lined avenue where the sun, now to his left, benignly sparkled and shone through the trees. Then, turning left, he saw La Coquille Bleue and, on the other side of the road, a blue Renault Clio parked on the pavement, and in the driveway beyond, a silver Saab estate. A tall blond man was sitting hunched on the garden wall a few feet from the car. He wore a blue short-sleeved shirt, faded denims and yacht shoes. In the Renault another man sat defiantly upright. He had a sharp little face, all pointy nose and narrow chin and scrawny neck topped by an unusually bouffant hairstyle like a coxcomb, which gave him a disturbingly bird-like quality.

Lamy pulled his car onto the pavement in front of the Renault, effectively blocking that car's escape and, after first sizing up the situation between the two men, he got out and signalled to the Renault driver that he should get out of his vehicle. In response, the driver in the Renault looked at the blond man who had been sitting on the wall, but was now leaning against it, then back at Lamy. His glance was theatrical, a head-twitching performance of double takes.

297

The blond man, watching this, pushed himself off the wall and made a move to approach Lamy. Lamy, like a cop on traffic duty, showed his palm to the blond man and beckoned to the scrawny man in the Renault. Reluctantly both men did as they were told and stood five feet away on either side of Lamy, shifting and posturing restlessly.

Lamy stepped forward and, applying a little theatrical panache himself, he removed his notebook from his pocket and flipped it open.

'Now,' he said, glancing from one man to the other, 'which one of you gentlemen called the police?'

Both answered in the affirmative.

Lamy considered this, then as one man was illegally parked and a good deal smaller, he asked the Renault owner to get back in his car and approached the blond man.

'So what's the trouble here?'

'I don't know, sir. My wife and I were about to leave. We were in the car, in the drive,' he jerked his head to indicate the parked estate car, 'when this guy,' he nodded in the direction of the other car, 'blocks our exit.'

His French was laboured, but fairly good, Lamy noted, though the accent was slightly off.

'And?' Lamy asked.

'And we tried to get him to move, but he wouldn't. I mean, he just sat there. I don't get it. It was like he had done it on purpose. But why? It doesn't make sense.'

'Is this your house?'

'No, but it's ours while we're here. The house belongs to a distant cousin. We're Canadian. Here on holiday; we come every year.'

'And do you know this man?' Lamy thumbed the air in the direction of the other man.

'No, never seen him before.'

Lamy considered this, and looked from the parked car in the driveway to the Renault on the pavement.

The blond man was growing agitated, shifting his tall frame around impatiently.

'God damn it, this asshole is gonna make us miss our flight.'

'All right, sir. Now let's keep things under control, eh?'

'I mean, is there some stupid French law that says if you want to use your goddamn cell phone you can just pull up wherever?'

The phrase 'stupid French law' was not music to Lamy's ears.

'Seems you are a little angry, sir,' Lamy said.

'Damn right I'm angry,' the man said, through clenched teeth.

Lamy pretended to write something in his notepad, then said, 'Could you go and get in your car now.' As he said it he turned to indicate where he wanted the tall man to go, and happened to glance at the ground floor of the house where he noticed a red-haired woman standing at the window, watching them. One arm was crossed over her chest with the hand tucked into her armpit, while the other was raised to her lips. She was frowning and chewing on a thumb nail. Watching her, he heard a car door open and slam shut. His eyes followed the sound and he saw the blond man sitting in the passenger seat of the vehicle. He watched him for a moment, then indicated that the Renault driver should come forward now.

The smaller man began to speak in rapid and formal French. His tone was pompous and he delivered his words with a jerky emphasis.

Lamy hushed him; he wanted to get to the point.

'So you pull up here,' Lamy said, 'and he asks you to move?'

'Yes, but you see the heart of the issue is...'

'Sir, please just answer my questions.'

'Alright, I apologise. I'll try. Yes, he asked me to move my car.'

'And you didn't move straight away?'

'No, you see what you are failing to appreciate here is the seriousness of...'

'Sir,' Lamy held a silencing palm up.

'Sorry.'

'Just the questions for now. So you didn't move the car quickly enough for his liking and then what, he got angry?'

'Oh, yes. Yes, that's right. Very angry. Swearing, waving his arms about, threatening me.'

'He threatened you?'

'Yes,' the man was getting very animated now. 'He threatened me. I stayed in my car, of course, but that just enraged him more. So then I tried to ring the local station, but I couldn't get through, so then I called the emergency services and he starts banging on my windows.'

'He banged on your car window? With force?'

'Yes, I thought the glass would shatter. Then he started on the bonnet.'

'What do you mean, he started on the bonnet?'

'He hit it, three, four, maybe five times.'

'With a weapon?'

'No. Or at least I didn't see a weapon. Perhaps it was concealed. I don't know … but the noise it made!'

Lamy looked at the Renault's bonnet, tilting his head from side to side to detect a dent or mark of any sort. He drew closer, still moving his head and studying the car.

'Is it damaged?' Lamy asked.

'It must be,' the man replied. He came nearer, then squatted down on his haunches so he was nose level with the tip of the bonnet. He couldn't see any damage, but that, in his mind, meant nothing. His car had been violated.

Lamy leant over and stared carefully at the perfect blue surface. He couldn't see any dents or damaged paintwork and was about to say this when he happened to glance over at the blond man sitting in the other car. Scott happened at that moment to be signalling his frustration to Marilyn who had been watching

300

everything from the front room. Scott had pointed to his wristwatch, then to the two Frenchmen and then he tapped the side of his head to indicate madness.

'I think there is a dent,' Lamy said, noticing how an unusual shadow fell on one part of the bonnet's curved surface.

Lamy took the Renault driver's name, his address, the registration number of the car and ordered him to delay any repairs until the matter was sorted out. Then he sent Jean-Pierre Laniel happily on his way. Once the blue Renault had disappeared down the road, Scott got out of his car. He checked his watch again. There was still just enough time if they could get Aaron into the car quickly, if he floored the accelerator and drove like a lunatic, they might yet make the airport in time.

He gave a thumbs up sign to Marilyn and was about to thank the policeman when he spoke.

'Sir, I must ask that you accompany me to the police station.'

'What?'

'I am charging you with intent to cause criminal damage and threatening behaviour.'

'What? Are you kidding me?'

'No, sir. This is an extremely serious charge and I would ask that you come quietly.'

Lamy, with deliberate calm and grace, gestured towards his police car as if he were the lord of the manor inviting one of the lower orders to ride in his gilded carriage.

Scott hesitated. It was all too strange to take in. It was surreal – everything that had happened since they left the house that morning. As bizarre as a René Magritte painting or a film by Louis Bunuel. Even the dappled light. The figure of his wife beyond the window, her face drained of colour, while her red hair suddenly seemed to glow even redder as if it might crackle and spark with fire.

'Surely…' he began, but suddenly felt defeated.

'Otherwise I will be forced to place you under arrest.'

'My wife,' Scott said hopelessly and flapped his arm towards the house.

'You may inform her. Call her outside.'

Scott put his hands on his hips and letting out a low groan, looked down at his feet. It passed through his mind that one punch aimed squarely at the policeman's jaw could knock him out, then they could get away from this country, never come back.

The absurdness of the fantasy matched the absurdity of the situation. He lifted his head to see Marilyn at the window. She mouthed some words at him which he could not read. With one hand still on his hip, his shoulders hunched in defeat, he gestured for her to come out. She touched her breast bone with the tips of her fingers, as if to say 'me?'

He nodded then watched as she turned away. Her red hair which had been shining in the light near the window, dimmed, then vanished entirely as she moved into the shadows at the back of the room.

# Pleasures Taken

'Are you hungry?' Florian asked.

'Maybe,' Suzette said.

'Yeah? What do you fancy?'

Suzette thought about the food she had in the flat; some bread, some eggs, garlic, a handful of black Muscat grapes, a very little goat's cheese, a short stump of *saucisson* that was probably past its best, apricot jam. In her freezer, wrapped up in a Carrefour carrier bag, a pair of mackerel an American tourist had given Suzette in the bar one day last summer.

'Oh, I don't know.'

'You know what I fancy?'

'What?'

'Steak and mayonnaise.'

'Mmm.'

'Yeah.'

'It would be nice, but I don't have any…'

'I know. But, hey, maybe I can conjure some up. Except…'

They were sitting side by side in bed, backs propped against the pillows. Suzette's shoulder was pressed against his, which felt so much warmer than hers. She would have liked to stay that way all day, then on into the evening until it was night and they would snuggle under the covers to make love and then sleep. The next day it would be the same and the one after that too. Nothing would change, they would not get bored. Just his warm skin against her slightly cooler skin would be enough. Forever. Amen.

He was thinking. He had left his last sentence hanging in midair, the last word he'd spoken 'except…' So she was waiting. Finally, as if to signal that his thoughts and words were still pending, he gave a long drawn out growling, 'Hmm.' Then he spoke. 'You got any money?'

'Pay day's tomorrow, so, no, not much.'

'Alright,' he said, decisively, then he sprang out of bed and pulled on his jeans. She missed the heat of his body immediately, not because it was cold, but because it had been so comforting.

She gathered her dressing gown from the floor and while still in bed put it on.

'Stay in bed,' he said. 'I won't be long.'

'Oh, where are you going?'

He was putting his shoes on, pale sand-coloured desert boots. It made her think of Jean-Paul Belmondo in an old '60s film.

'Never you mind,' he said, and leaned over to kiss her. 'I won't be long, keep the bed warm, eh?'

She grinned. She could not help herself, even though he was going. And he had given her a purpose. A task. To keep the bed warm until his return.

'Okay.'

At the door, he turned and blew her a kiss, then he was gone.

Florian set off walking at a fast pace. He had a mission. He was going home to where his mother would be busy in the kitchen. She was always busy; cleaning or cooking or standing at the ironing board in front of the TV watching soap operas. She was a demon with that iron, and the clothes and linens she smoothed and steamed into perfect submission belonged to strangers. Crisp shirts, tiny baby girls' dresses with intricate ruffles and lace, silk paisley-patterned boxer shorts, cotton undershirts with indelible stains and a sour, stale odour of sweat that resisted even the hottest wash and should have been replaced long ago. Some people had no shame. But as his mother said, so long as they paid, what did she care?

'Oh, Florian,' she'd say, always somehow surprised to see her own son back home, then her next question was always the same. 'Hungry? Let me get you something.'

'No, Ma, don't worry. I'm fine. I just ate.'

'What did you eat?' she'd say, staring hard at him. 'You're too thin.'

'Ma,' he'd say, then go to her, throw an arm around her neck, plant a big kiss, a wet one, on her cheek. 'I'm a big boy now, okay?'

She'd smile greedily; wipe the back of her hand over her face where he'd kissed her. 'All right, son,' she'd say, 'have it your way.'

Then he'd maybe snatch a piece of fruit from the bowl; an apple or peach. Eat it as he climbed the stairs to his room. This room which had been his for as long as he could remember. Same narrow single bed pushed under the window. Same painted pine chest with the missing knobs and the drawer that stuck. Same athletics and swimming certificates in their cheap frames on the wall. Same 'Taxi Driver' poster yellowing at the edges, half sticky-taped, half blu-tacked above his old desk.

He did not quite live here, or anywhere exactly. He mooched, he slept on friends' floors, in women's beds. In cheap hotels in small towns when he had building work. Or other work. Delivering cars. Grape picking. Whatever.

Not by choice. You don't choose to live this way. It chooses you. In the past he'd had rented rooms, flats. Once a house with a duck pond in the garden. But then bad luck caught up with him, sent him to jail, made him drink too much one time too many, made his woman decide she'd had enough. There were countless reasons to find yourself upended, broke, locked up, plans scuppered, bruised, staring at nothing, starting from scratch, back (God bless her and keep her) home with Ma.

And now, here was Suzette.

He broke into a light jog. Ten minutes and he'd be there, snag a fistful of Euros, go to Emile's for the best *filet de boeuf* the butcher had. He could imagine the cool weight of it, bloody in a plastic bag. Eggs, oil, lemons, whipped up by hand.

Did Suzette have a hand whisk?

She'd better have.

And cheese. Because 'A meal without cheese is like a beautiful woman with only one eye.'

A beautiful late morning. Sky a blue ache. Clouds stately.

Suzette. Best steak. It was enough to give him a hard on.

He turned the corner onto the old familiar street. Twenty proud houses, some grown shabby at the edges. The ten on the right hand side seemed to crouch in their own shadows; the others puffed up their chests in a blaze of light. His home with the glass-fronted niche cut into the wall, shrine of the painted plaster-cast Madonna, faded now.

In through the side door. Ma at the ironing board. She is startled by him.

'Oh Florian, love.'

Her left hand fluttered to her chest. Colour high on her cheeks. Steam rising from the iron in a hiss. Limp pale orange Y-fronts vulnerable and exposed on the silver cover of the ironing board.

'Just popping in, don't mind me,' Florian said.

'Are you hungry?' she asked, predictably.

'No, Ma.'

He kisses her. Her cheek is soft and powdery.

'Sorry,' he says. He meant he was sorry he couldn't stay longer, to eat with her, be a better son. And in the word 'sorry' there was also, in his mind, the intention to not only acknowledge his failings on that day and many others, but to change himself, to make more effort, get steady work, make her proud.

She turned sharply to look at him.

'Oh, what have you done now?'

'Nothing!' he said and his voice went up in pitch as it had always done when he was accused of wrongdoing by his mother.

She clucked her tongue on the roof of her mouth, shook her head as if she didn't believe him. Resumed her ironing.

Upstairs in his room he slipped his arm under the mattress and drew out an envelope containing around seven hundred and fifty Euros. He took out five twenties, stuffed them into the pocket of his jeans and replaced the envelope.

At the bottom of the stairs he called goodbye to his mother then left by the front door. He shut it just as he heard his mother say his name.

'Florian?'

But he was gone. Stepping lightly down the path and through the open gate where he once more broke into an easy loping run.

If he had ten Euros for every time he'd run up or down this street he'd be a millionaire. Which he wasn't and never would be, but at that moment it didn't matter; there would be steak, lightly charred on the outside, red in the centre, and the magic of the emulsified eggs and oil, his wrist aching pleasantly after its labour with the whisk, and most of all, there would be Suzette, warm in bed and smiling so happily to see him.

# Consent

'This is interesting,' Sabine Pelat said.

She was standing behind Paul Vivier holding the transcript of the investigation into the alleged rape in 2003 of Genevieve Quinet.

Vivier looked up from the papers he was working on, and craned his neck to see her.

'The suspect asked that DNA samples be taken. Indeed, at every stage during the interview he demanded that DNA be taken,' Sabine said.

'Who is this?'

'Florian Lebrun.'

'Ah.'

Vivier was distracted, only half listening to what she was saying.

'It wasn't a matter of consent. He wanted the DNA test.'

'And?'

'Well, he got his way. DNA was taken and it didn't match. He was innocent.'

'But he has a record.'

'Yes, but nothing sexual, nothing violent. Only this rape charge and he was acquitted.'

'It doesn't matter.'

'No?'

There was a beat of time. The detective inspector and his assistant detective regarded one another warily.

'His semen on the cardigan?'

'Yes.'

'That's pretty cut and dried, isn't it?'

'Seems that way.'

'So?'

'It's a conundrum.'

'By which you mean…?'

'The only reason we have his DNA on file is because he was falsely accused of rape.'

'He has a record as long as your arm, Sabine. He's a chancer. Anything he can get away with.'

'Petty stuff. Shoplifting. Cannabis. Drunk and disorderly. Fraud. Public disorder. Theft from a building site. It's all just stupid, messy stuff. And by the way, the woman who accused him?'

'What about her?'

'Genevieve Quinet. *Quinet*.' She emphasised the girl's last name.

'Quinet?' Vivier repeated, as if the penny had finally dropped.

'She's the sister of François Quinet,' she said, meaningfully.

'She was from that family?'

'Yes.'

'Alright, I see what you're saying, but that doesn't mean…' Vivier hesitated, Sabine had come around the desk and was looking at him intensely. Her eyes were very clear, the whites glossy and bright, making the rich brown iris all the more distinct. Her eyebrows were perfectly shaped and the eyelashes thick, dark and silky with no obvious mascara on them. He reordered his thoughts, '…that doesn't mean that her claim was false.'

'You're saying that even girls from villainous families like the Quinets might be raped?'

'Yes.'

'Well, of course that's true. But it's a shame Mademoiselle Quinet didn't go to the trouble of actually seducing Lebrun before she accused him. Shame no one explained to her about DNA.' Sabine looked angry.

'But the cardigan,' Vivier said wearily.

'I know. I know. But if it's not our guy?'

'Okay, point taken.' Vivier stood up and drew back his cuff to look at his watch. He did not speak, but with a circular motion of his head he indicated the door. They walked towards it together and after he had opened it, he waited for her to pass through first. Once again she felt his hand graze her back. The lightest of touches, a guiding protective warmth – innocent and yet charged with meaning. She would have liked to stop in her tracks and fall back against that hand. For the hand and its partner to encircle her body. For...

She forced herself to snap out of this way of thinking. It was distracting. It made her usually sharp brain feel as if it were enfeebled somehow. Besides which it was never going to happen.

Her and Vivier? Some joke.

# Control

Marilyn said nothing after he told her what had happened with the policeman. She listened with her eyes wide and attentive, nodding occasionally to affirm that she understood. It was what she did at those poetry readings she (and sometimes Scott) attended.

His words were hardly poetry, but they had a calm logic. 'It's just a misunderstanding,' he'd said. 'I'll just go to the station, have a chat, sort things out. Give Aaron a sedative if you need to. I'll be back in an hour or so I guess. Okay?'

She nodded.

She'd come out of the house without any shoes on. He noticed how vulnerable her feet looked, how pale and slim. The skin covering the intricate bones, veins and muscle seemed particularly fine. Her toes were long and elegant and she'd painted the nails a dark opalescent blue so that they reminded him of mussel shells gleaming in a stew. Curious how things like that grab your attention, he thought, something which was completely irrelevant to the moment. Her toes got up like mussel shells and him accused of criminal damage and threatening behaviour. He was certain he hadn't damaged the other man's car. In Canada (he was certain) the police would have arrested the other guy for wasting their time and for illegal parking. It gave him a fleeting sense of self-satisfied pleasure when he thought of that, but it couldn't last. He wasn't in Canada, he was in France.

The policeman who accompanied him to the police station, despite being on the short side (he couldn't have been much more than five feet seven), was powerfully built and he gave off an air of barely suppressed anger. While he was driving, Scott noticed how the police officer clenched his jaw and how an occasional ripple passed through the musculature of his face. Scott got the distinct impression of an almost tangible rage combined with a probable desire to inflict pain. He'd seen this type of character on the ice hockey rinks at high school, time and again – knew to give them a wide berth.

Yet the matter would be easy to resolve. He had done no damage to the man's car, he'd hit it with the flat of his hand and yeah, it made a noise and his palm stung like hell, but that was it. And even if there were the slightest damage he could pay for the repairs; a bit of panel beating and possibly a re-spray wasn't going to cost much.

As long as he kept his cool, explained the matter calmly, told them about the flight they were due to take, the unreasonable way in which the other motorist had behaved, about his sick brother, then they would surely see it from his point of view. It was nothing.

The car followed the twists and turns of back streets heading east, then north, then east again. Finally they came to a halt outside an unprepossessing building that could have served any dull bureaucratic purpose. The policeman got out of the car. Scott tried to open his door, but found it locked. They called these child locks back home and whenever they hired a car to take Aaron anywhere they always specified child locks. Now Scott saw another side to their use and it shocked him to find himself locked in. It made him feel vulnerable and childlike, and conversely, dangerous like some wild and unpredictable animal.

The policeman was standing by the car and saw Scott's attempt to open the door. He wagged a finger at him. Obediently Scott withdrew his hand and sat submissively, his hands cupped limply between his legs as if he wore invisible cuffs while the cop wrote in a small notebook.

Then the door was opened and he followed the policeman across a concrete path and up some steps into the building.

As soon as they were inside the policeman's demeanor changed, his body seemed to relax and he became almost casual. He spoke in rapid French to the younger uniformed man behind the desk, laughing loudly at some comment he'd made, and the young cop smiled weakly.

Scott stood helplessly waiting, hearing only brief phrases and words that he recognised and feeling unusually tall and awkward. It was as if his centre of gravity had shifted somehow, displacing his normal physical confidence and, perversely, his ability to understand French.

The cop's laugh was cut short when, through a door behind the desk, a woman emerged. She was not in uniform, though her clothes were sedate and formal; and she possessed an air of quiet authority. Her gleaming dark hair was parted neatly down the centre of her scalp and pulled back in two wings to hug and define her skull.

Scott took her to be a secretary or someone involved in administration. She looked frowningly from one of the uniformed police to the other, then she looked at Scott. Her face registered ill-concealed surprise. Scott tried unsuccessfully to give her the sort of warm smile which would convey that he was just a regular guy.

She narrowed her eyes, then looked away. Well, who could blame her? His expression must have been more grimace, than smile. She said a few quiet words to the younger of the two men, then disappeared through the door again where she stood a little way off, as if waiting for someone or something. Through the glass Scott noticed how she nervously brought one hand up to her head. She seemed, by touch alone to be checking her hair. The hand brushed the surface of the cunningly swept-up knot of hair at the back, then with light patting gestures checked the rest of the hairdo.

Scott was so taken up with watching her unselfconscious

preening that he did not notice the two cops speaking quietly to one another.

The policeman who had brought him in advanced, and taking him by the elbow, indicated wordlessly that he should sit on a wooden bench off to one side. Scott complied and the man went through a hatch in the counter and through the same door the woman had used.

From his new position on the bench, Scott could no longer see the dark-haired woman or anything beyond the door's glass window but a sliver of greenish light.

He sighed and thought about the flight they would miss – which was probably boarding about now. It had seemed a simple, though expensive, solution to an irrepressible urge. To go home. To get back to normality. To shed the burden of his brother and just be with Marilyn. And, he considered, half the time he wasn't even sure if his parents really wanted to be parted from Aaron at all and seemed to miss him and love him with increasing neediness as the years went by. It was as if they were anticipating losing their youngest son if only by virtue of their advancing old age and dwindling strength.

Was that love?

He sighed again, lost in thought.

The door behind the counter opened and the young woman reemerged. She lifted the hatch, and without quite looking Scott directly in the face she indicated that he should follow her.

It should have been a relief, a sign that things were beginning at last to resolve themselves, but something about her unsettled him. This beautiful but stern woman was no mere secretary, she exuded a quiet power and yet she would not look him in the eye. He had the unsettling but unmistakable feeling that she was judging him.

Or rather – past tense – she had judged him and found him wanting.

# Hunger

Thom sat staring at the red eye of Lucy's answer machine for fifteen minutes. He blinked occasionally, though the machine did not. His blinking was a reflex, as was his breathing and the actions of his heart, his liver, his kidneys. His mind however was another matter, it had raced through this morning's labyrinth of puzzles and mysteries; he had taken on the guise of detective, of thwarted lover, but with the inevitable exhaustion that ensued, his brain had turned into something like the human version of a frozen computer.

As he had no key to Lucy's flat and as he had now gained entry, he did not feel able to leave until he had done as much as he could to solve the riddle of her disappearance. He was searching for something, but he did not know what it was.

Thirty minutes of blank time. His gaze regarding the steady glow of the red light as the sun shifted itself by degrees around the room until it reached the shadowy alcove where her telephone was and seemingly extinguished the tiny light.

Perhaps he had blinked as the sunlight hit the phone. Perhaps he had forgotten why he was staring at it. Forgotten indeed where he was, who he was – who Lucy was. But suddenly he realised that the light had gone out, and thought that someone, Lucy or some other evil tormenting trickster, had crept into the flat without his knowledge and switched off the machine.

He was familiar with the sort of narrative where the main protagonist is deliberately driven mad by tricks such as these.

He stood up with a start and crossed quickly to the phone. He peered closely at it. There was no sign of an electronic light. Then he cupped his hand around the edge of the machine shielding it from the sun and saw with relief that the light still gave off its signalling red glow.

He sighed and shook his head, annoyed at his momentary foolishness and gullibility. He needed to stay calm, to think straight, to above all remain rational.

He wandered unthinkingly into Lucy's kitchen and opened the fridge. Her fridge, but as familiar to him as his own. In the middle of a restless night, while Lucy still slept, he'd creep through to her kitchen in darkness, opening the fridge to find in its welcoming light, juice or beer or cold leftovers. Or on a Sunday morning he might, while Lucy went out to get the papers, rustle up some fried mushrooms or eggs. A cheese omelette with sautéed potatoes.

In the fridge door was a two-litre container of semi-skimmed milk which was half full. He unscrewed the cap and sniffed. A sour cheesy smell invaded his nostrils. He poured it down the sink, ran the cold tap to wash the last of it away, then threw the empty container into the rubbish. On the shelf there was a small and unopened carton of long life milk. Typical of Lucy to prepare for her return (and the possible need for milk) but to fail to throw away what could only perish while she was away. In the salad drawer he was not surprised to find a liquefying cucumber, sad blackening lettuce and furry tomatoes. On the shelves, a cream cheese with an exotic landscape of grey and khaki-coloured mould, as well as out-of-date smoked salmon, cartons of 'fresh' soup, yoghurts and pepperoni sausage.

Thom closed the fridge and opened the small freezer compartment. Lucy tended to use the freezer as a back up for her often disorganised and admittedly busy life, so there were quite a few ready meals always to hand. Chicken kormas from Marks and Sparks, pizzas, reduced-price Naan breads, anything that could be zapped in the microwave or under the grill at a minute's notice.

She rarely, unlike Thom, cooked things from scratch, but when she did, she made enough for a small army, and here at the front of the freezer was a clear plastic bag filled with a reddish brown substance that was bejewelled with burgundy-coloured kidney beans.

He took it out, got a Pyrex dish from the cupboard next to the sink, put the bag inside it, then put it in the microwave and set it to defrost. He filled a saucepan with water and set it to boil on the stove, then washed some rice in a colander.

While he waited for the water to boil, he went back to Lucy's study and scanned the books on the shelves. She swore that, while she was disorganised, she knew roughly where everything was. She arranged things according to some mysterious system which was based on emotional connections rather than any other logical means he could see.

'What you have to understand,' she'd once said to him, laughing, 'is that I am a lateral thinker, which is both a blessing and a curse, but I can't change it, and you, my love, shouldn't try.'

His eye traversed the rows of books picking out the odd title at random: *The Body, Schizophrenia: A Very Short Introduction, White Bicycles, Lizzie Siddal: The Tragedy of a pre-Raphaelite Supermodel, Women, Art and Society, The Bell Jar, The Ongoing Moment.* No clues there.

In the kitchen he tipped the rice into the boiling water. Without thinking he had washed enough for two portions, as if at any moment Lucy would come banging through the front door, calling out, 'Oh, God! I'm knackered. How long's food gonna be?'

He emptied the partially defrosted chilli from the freezer bag into the bowl and broke up the solid mass with a wooden spoon, then returned it to the microwave and set it on medium.

In twenty or so minutes he would eat, but first, in a flash of inspiration, he realised there was something he wanted to do. Needed to do. It was suddenly a desire as acute as his hunger. He got his mobile from his jacket pocket, found Lucy's home number and pressed call. There was a moment of silence before his phone made the ringing tone twice and then Lucy's phone itself took up the cry. It rang seven times, then the machine clicked into action and he heard her voice.

When her message ended and once the bleeps had signalled him to speak, he said in a quiet voice, almost a whisper, 'Lucy, where are you? Don't do this to me, please.'

He hung up, stirred the rice and the chilli, then stood by her kitchen window looking out vacantly.

Her voice, or at least the familiar echo of it from her answer machine, still filled his ears.

He was in her flat surrounded by her belongings. He had looked at her photograph, he had heard her voice, he could smell her, or if not her exactly, then the traces of her that lingered in the flat in the form of her particular perfumes, soaps, shampoos and bath oils. But she was not there and all of these signs and signifiers of her only exaggerated her absence.

The microwave dinged. Mechanically he switched off the gas flame under the rice and tipped it into the strainer over the sink, got the slotted spoon and then two plates from the cupboard which he placed side by side on the counter. He scooped up a portion of rice and looked with surprise at the plates he'd set out. He shook his head at the folly of it, at the madness, and before he put any food on either plate, he quickly put the unwanted one back on its shelf.

At the table he sat in the chair facing the window. It was the chair he habitually sat in. Lucy always sat to his right beside the window. If he had lain down on her bed, he would have chosen the side nearest the door. His side – where the top of the bedside cabinet was a void, except for when he was there and put his loose change and wristwatch on it.

The first night they spent together, joking, she had said, as he stacked paper money and coins from his pocket on the cabinet by the bed, 'It's fifty quid for straight sex, more if you want fifty/fifty. Or anything… you know… kinky.' She had shocked him, and for a nanosecond, he thought she meant it. Then she'd laughed. She undermined him, dizzied him – changing rapidly from seriousness to hilarity and play-acting, to real tears. She confused and unnerved him at first, then she'd begun to change, to mature, to be more controlled.

Moving around her flat he found that there were particular, more highly charged absences within the greater space of her general absence; hotspots that, if measured by such a thing as an emotional Geiger counter, would have set it beeping wildly.

The chilli was good. He had first eaten it with her, three or perhaps four weeks ago. Then there had been a pot of natural yoghurt that she had glooped over the dish. She had unselfconsciously complimented her own cooking, making 'mm' sounds and saying how she loved the cool sharpness of the yoghurt contrasted with the heat of the meat sauce.

He had said nothing. Why had he not told her it was good? Because it had been good, but somehow, perhaps because he suspected her of bragging, he had only nodded in accord with her words.

Maybe he had sensed that her enthusiasm was becoming overblown, that she was heading towards one of those slightly mad, frenzied moods when she tried to do a dozen things at once, talked incessantly; laughed, danced, drank and fucked like all four were due to be banned by government order the next day.

But then that was Lucy. Who wouldn't love a woman with such appetites? Except for those moments when they seemed to reach an apex and then she could become belligerent or sulky or burst into tears.

Had he missed something there? Was there a pathological aspect to her moods?

He spooned the chilli into his mouth. It was spicy and the heat seemed to increase exponentially with each bite he took.

Last time they'd eaten chilli together, Lucy had, again somewhat unselfconsciously and with enthusiasm, blown her nose into a piece of kitchen towel after they had finished eating.

His eyes had been watering.

'Don't cry, laddie,' she'd said in an exaggerated Scottish accent. 'There's nae need ti greet ony mair. Wheesht, wheesht ye auld fule!'

'Yeah, yeah,' he had said, tiring of the silliness, the patched together vernacular which he could make little sense of and which he found faintly embarrassing.

If it was pathological, if she had a bi-polar disorder or manic depression, then which parts of her personality were really her?

He chased the last grains of rice around the plate scooping up smears of sauce as he did so, then he took the empty plate to the sink, ran it under the hot tap and put it in the drainer.

Went back to her study and looked at her bookshelves again. *Women who Run with the Wolves, Morvern Callar, Post Modern Fairy Tales, The Virgin Suicides.*

You could read something into her state of mind in that selection, he thought, but that would be a madness in itself, and it did not tell him where she was, or what was happening.

As he stood, considering this, her phone suddenly erupted into life. The noise startled him and the urgency of the ringing drew him to it.

'It's her,' he said to himself, 'it's got to be her.'

Why he thought this, he could not later explain, perhaps it was because the last voice he had heard speaking from this machine had been hers and thus the next voice and the one after, ad infinitum, must also be hers.

He picked up after the fourth ring.

'Hello?' he said.

There was a listening silence on the other end of the line.

'Lucy?' he asked.

A beat of time passed, then an unfamiliar man with a gruff Scottish accent spoke sternly to him.

'Who're you?'

Lucy's father.

Thom almost put the phone down on him, then stopped himself, breathed deeply and began to talk.

# Voyeur

The suspect, Florian Lebrun, entered the rear of the house occupied by his mother, Madame Eve-Marie Lebrun and exited thirteen minutes later from the front door. He ran from there to the butcher's at St Bernadette's where he was observed purchasing red meat. At the general store nearby he entered and exited four minutes later with a carrier bag.

Montaldo had left his unmarked car and followed the man on foot until he disappeared through the front door of a building on the rue de la Roche. Now Montaldo was sitting on a bench near the building and drinking a can of lemonade. He had reported the suspect's movements and noted them down. Not that he thought this was to any purpose.

Montaldo was acquainted with Lebrun having arrested him four years earlier on a drugs charge. Lebrun had got off with a fine. Lebrun was no one. Small fry. He had, at one time, been linked to the Quinet family, he had attended the same school as the youngest kid, François Quinet, and the two boys had been caught shoplifting together. No doubt Quinet's father had issued his son a far harsher punishment for the crime than the law offered. Not from any moral high point or concern that François was going off the rails, but because the son's misdemeanor represented a crack in the carefully maintained fortress which surrounded the Quinet family's criminal dealings.

Florian Lebrun was a clown in comparison to the Quinets. A drunk and an opportunist thief, a fraudster and fool. But a murderer? No way.

Montaldo drank the last dregs from the can, burped, then

crushed it in his right hand and threw it into a rubbish bin five feet away. It pleased him that his aim was still accurate.

He lit a cigarette and leaned back on the seat keeping watch on the door opposite. Now and then, certain women caught his gaze as they went by. He liked to watch how women moved, the roll of their hips, the sharp attenuated clip of a woman in high heels, the graceful glide of a girl in casual footwear, long slim golden legs in shorts, the dimpled knees of chubby young tourists, the round jiggly breasts of one woman, the pert high bra-less points of another's. It was a pleasure just to consider the endless variety of women, long and lean, taut and muscular, or oozing with plump pinchable flesh. All of them with their secrets, their weaknesses and foibles.

The door Montaldo was watching remained shut. Some woman's apartment, Montaldo surmised, and he pictured a woman lying in bed waiting for that idiot Lebrun to show up.

He pictured her welcoming smile, then suddenly it was not the suspect Lebrun crossing the room to the bed, but Montaldo himself.

'Pleased to see me?' he imagined himself saying, then he sat on the edge of the bed and leaned over to kiss her. His hands slipped under the covers, exploring her body. Her skin, warm and smooth, slid gratifyingly under his hands and she was sighing hungrily. He kept his shirt and trousers on, even in his imagination he couldn't quite get rid of the enflamed boils on his neck and his arse.

What Montaldo didn't imagine was a tiny kitchen, a kitchen not much bigger than a cupboard if the truth be told, and a frying pan on the two-ring stove heating up butter. He did not see a man separating egg yolks, then beating them furiously with a balloon whisk. Who makes mayonnaise when there's a woman waiting for you in bed? Perhaps if Montaldo had been hungry he might have imagined this. Not that Montaldo's imagination really mattered. What mattered was the job, keeping his eyes on the closed door.

Forty minutes had passed. A thought occurred to Montaldo. The suspect had neither used a key, nor had he waited for someone to open the door for him. He had simply, in one easy movement, turned the handle, opened the door and slipped inside.

Montaldo crossed the road. The door was a plain cream-painted wooden one secreted between a hardware store and a shop selling sewing and craft materials. A clear amber blind, which was meant to protect the goods on display, had been pulled down in the window of the craft shop, turning all the goods a sickly piss colour.

Montaldo put his hand on the door handle and pressed down, the unlocked door opened easily. Cautiously he swung it back. Ahead of him was a long narrow passage and halfway along a flight of steep, uncarpeted stairs. There were no signs of life, no sounds. At the far end of the passage, Montaldo could make out the outline of another door. He entered the building, closing the door quietly behind him. The light in the passage was dim, but there was just enough light to see by. He took a few steps towards the foot of the stairs and glanced up, there were three floors and above them, set into the roof, a dirty skylight that showed a smeary blue sky and one ragged cloud. He moved along the passage, which he figured ran the depth of the building. To his left, concealed under the slope of the first flight of stairs were two bicycles and a baby stroller. He tried opening the back door, but it was locked. Montaldo squatted on his haunches so that his face was level with the lock. He peered through the keyhole and glimpsed a breeze block wall in shadow and a few straggly weeds banked against it. His view was limited so he could not tell if the back yard had a gate that could provide an escape route.

Montaldo started up the stairs. He caught a waft of meat frying close by. Someone was here.

On the first floor, he stopped by the single door and studied it for clues as to its occupants. He listened, then hearing nothing, moved away and made his way up the next flight of stairs. Another door was directly above the one below. Montaldo paused to listen again. It was here that the cooking smell was the strongest.

Inside he thought he could hear a fast repetitive noise. Bed springs? An old-fashioned headboard beating against a wall? He leaned in closer so that his ear was almost pressed against the door.

What the hell was that noise?

Then his radio cracked into life.

Montaldo sprang away from the door and, with his hand pressed over his breast pocket, managed to muffle the sound to some degree.

He moved quickly back to the stairs and descended them two at a time. He was surprisingly light on his feet, graceful even.

# Sur la Table

Suzette had put on a vintage black silk slip. She wasn't sure if it was a petticoat or a bed gown, but she wore it as a dress. It had cost her just five francs at a fleamarket years ago. It made her feel like a character in a film; someone played by Isabelle Huppert or Juliette Binoche.

She was sitting at the table and watching Florian in the kitchen through the open door. He was frying steak and making mayonnaise at the same time. He jiggled the pan and prodded the steak with a fork, then he'd drizzled oil into the emulsifying eggs, beating the mixture like crazy, clenching his teeth with the effort.

Suzette watched, her bare legs stretched out straight and crossed at the ankles, her head tilted to the right while she languidly stroked her left shoulder and arm with her fingertips.

A sudden noise startled her. It sounded like a dial tuning into a radio station, then rapidly tuning away again. There was a staticky voice, then a muffled electronic buzz.

'What was that?'

Florian looked up at the sound of her voice, raised his eyebrows and gave a questioning flick of his head.

Suzette could not tell where the sound had come from exactly. It seemed to be in the room itself.

She looked about the room, searching for the source of the noise.

'Huh?' Florian asked. He put the bowl down and was eyeing the steaks in the pan.

'I thought I heard something. A radio maybe.'

Florian nodded and shrugged, then with a flourish he switched off the flame under the meat.

She watched as he got plates, then sliced a beef tomato into slithers which he fanned out on each. He lifted the steaks out of the pan, and finally spooned a big dollop of mayonnaise on the side.

He brought the plates to the table and proudly set one in front of her, before sitting down himself.

Suzette looked from her food to Florian, and before even picking up her knife and fork, she stood up and placed her hand softly on the crown of his head.

'Thank you,' she said, then leaned in close to kiss him quickly on the lips.

He grinned.

Then together, they ate in companionable silence.

Halfway through, Florian remembering the wine he'd brought, went to the kitchen to fetch the bottle and two tumblers. Back at the table, he sloshed it generously into the glasses.

'To life!' he said, tapping the rim of his tumbler against Suzette's. They each took a sip.

'To good food!' Suzette said.

'To good sex!' Florian replied, then smiled broadly and winked.

Suzette blushing, returned her gaze to her food. She did not know what to say to that, it rendered her momentarily speechless, partly as she was remembering, in an acutely physical way, the sex they'd had just a couple of hours ago. And it had been good, so good that she wanted to do it again. Right now and to hell with the food.

Florian watched her and noticed the blush. The way she'd coyly turned her face from him made him worry he'd said the wrong thing. He hadn't meant to be crude, he hadn't used a slang term.

'Hey,' he said, 'Suzette? Sorry, I didn't mean…'

She glanced at him, then looked away again.

At first he could not quite read her expression, but then he saw an irresistible smile dance around the edges of her mouth.

She carefully cut a small piece of the steak and dipped it into the mayonnaise and popped it into her mouth, then slowly nodded.

He watched as she chewed, then swallowed.

'It's good,' she said at last, composing herself enough to meet his eyes. 'It's all good. Really good. The best!' She left it to him to interpret that as he might.

They finished eating the steak, then sat at the table nibbling fruit and cheese, each waiting for what would happen next.

Florian refilled their glasses. Outside it was hot, the sky blue, the estuary and the river glinted in the sun. The little locomotive engine set off on its scenic trip to the even smaller town of Belle Plage on the other side of the bay. The river boat, which did hour-long trips out to sea and back again, filled up with tourists. Inside in this quiet room Florian and Suzette sat on either side of a small table. Within sight was the still rumpled bed. This, then was civilisation. Food, wine, conversation. Unspoken, and unacted desire ran once more like a dangerous and unearthed electric current between them.

How to get there; how to move from sitting and coolly drinking the Bordeaux Supérieur to touching and kissing, to undressing, to Suzette straddling him, to all that delicious and sweet passion. To climax. Then falling from one another, until the next time. The rise and rise and rise and fall of desire.

When something good and pleasurable is experienced, one wants it again. A fairground ride, a lamb chop done in a particular way, a lover's kiss.

Again and again and again until it loses its meaning, its rarity.

The table then, Suzette thought, the table offers some protection. She feared the loss of love even as she felt herself falling, falling.

She could hardly look at him, though she knew his eyes were on her.

God, all this stupid coyness! This fear. When all she wanted to do was rise from her chair and go to him.

Needing courage she drank the last of her wine in two gulps.

He had lifted the bottle to refill her glass, but she was on her feet standing next to him.

She stood there in her slip, her black silk slip with its pretty lace border at the neckline and hem. She took his hand. He did not protest, but put down the bottle without pouring any of the wine. She pulled his hand gently towards her. He stood up and with her free hand she touched his neck, his face. He understood. What was there not to understand? They kissed.

The blinds were still drawn. The sun at its edges burned with sharp white inexhaustible light. The train to Belle Plage sounded its whistle, a thick clot of people made their way onto the jetty that led to the river cruiser. Delicately, Florian slipped the shoulder straps of her slip off her shoulders and pulled the top down so her breasts were freed. He dipped his head and licked, lapped, sucked at her nipples.

She sighed and awkwardly slid her hands under his t shirt then tugged it off over his head.

The moment they had each privately and secretly sought, was upon them stepping crabwise towards the bed. Then. Now. In the moment. Tangled. Outside time for as long as it lasted.

And then.


To feel. To live, and love, and perhaps procreate. To hold onto love until death.

Ultimately that was the end.

So the point was to say, I lived. I felt this. While the sun shone and the locomotive once again chugged along the coast to Belle Plage, I existed.

Suzette held onto Florian. She held on with the pretence of passion. There was passion, but also something else. Eternity. The everlasting. The moment.

Then, a knock at the door.

# Mirrors

Scott was shown into a small windowless room. There was an ugly metal-legged desk with a wooden top and four mismatched chairs. On the table attached by wires to a wall-mounted switch was a microphone on a small stand.

To the left of this table a large mirror filled the entire top half of one wall.

Yeah. *A mirror?* Scott had seen enough films and TV cop shows to know what was hidden by this seemingly innocent glass. He pictured shadowy figures behind it, watching him and analysing his every move and gesture.

And actually, he reasoned, (after he had been instructed to sit on the plastic moulded chair on one side of the table and had watched himself do it in the mirror) even if it was only a perfectly ordinary mirror with a completely solid and ordinary wall behind it, it was still unnerving if only because it forced you to continually regard yourself in the guise of the accused. You became, in short, the bad guy. Or in another fictional version of this dislocated image, you became the guy who is accused, but innocent, you were the character in 'The Fugitive', Dr Richard Kimble, the one who is fated to hide and run endlessly in order to clear his name after being accused of his wife's murder.

It crossed Scott's mind that he should have insisted on contacting his embassy in Paris, or at least tried to find a lawyer. But there again it was only an altercation in the street, a minor matter, and involving the Canadian Embassy or a good English-speaking lawyer would no doubt involve a delay of hours as well as money.

Scott looked at the two people in the room with him, analysing their body language, the tics which betray what they were thinking or feeling; the young man, who was clearly a junior member of the force attempted, even with his young shiny little-boy's face, to give an expression of severity. While the beautiful dark-haired woman somehow managed to emit contempt for Scott without really doing much at all. It unnerved him.

Well, the French were singularly patriotic and while they might tolerate foreigners, even Americans with their 'Le Big Macs', and also their old enemies the Brits, they perhaps had little sympathy (or rather less) sympathy for law breakers who were not citizens.

What, in his encounter with that whack job, the Renault-driving, birdman, had he missed? Was there some byelaw about right of way? Did the man have some important function which allowed him (in an emergency) to park wherever he wished? Was he a doctor for example? Or a law enforcer of some description? Or the Marie?

The Marie of the town wielded far too much power and influence. Or at least this is the impression he'd got from the sporadic conversations he'd had with his French cousin.

With that thought it dawned on him that his cousins were the people he should contact. Not the Marie or the embassy or a lawyer. His cousin. Who lived in this town, in the very house outside which the incident had occurred. They had left a contact number pinned to the notice board in the kitchen. Except that they were in Thailand, the lucky bastards.

When the man in the Renault would not move his car that morning, Scott should, he decided, have gone calmly into the house and rang the Clements. Clearly of all the people in the world, they were the ones who could have shed light on the situation which was unfolding on their doorstep. And who knew, perhaps the idiotic little man was waging some sort of war of attrition with them. There might have been some ongoing dispute between neighbours, something about right of way and access, but then wouldn't they have mentioned it – warned him?

Well, the matter would soon be sorted out. Yes, he had been wrong to hit the man's car, but surely anyone with a reasonable understanding of human nature would see that he had been provoked. They would see too, that he was sorry, and that if there had been damage (though he was certain there was none) he was more than happy to pay for any repairs.

The dark-haired woman asked Scott if he would like a drink, Coca Cola perhaps?

He shook his head, no.

Then coffee? Or tea?

Again he shook his head. As far as he was concerned this thing would only be delayed by the making of and consumption of tea or coffee.

She spoke very quietly to the young policeman and then slipped from the room without explanation.

It struck Scott that the power relationships between the ordinary person and the police hit a sharp gradient as soon as one deviated from the straight and narrow. There was no other situation in which a man was so stripped of his ordinary rights and freedoms. Where another human being did not feel the need to be polite or explain or excuse themselves on leaving the room. And he was afraid to challenge them.

Scott turned his attention to the young policeman. He was perhaps in his early twenties, though he barely looked sixteen. He was standing near the door with his feet planted ten inches or so apart while his hands were clasped loosely in front of his genitals. His hair was light brown, but his skin was the washed-out waxy pink that afflicted red heads. He would burn in the sun, unlike himself and Aaron, who had inherited the blond hair and golden skin of their Scandinavian forebears. Their height and build too, though of course that was due in part to a few generations of good diet and the advantage of not having one's country invaded, its fields destroyed, its livestock stolen and so many of its young men slaughtered in two world wars.

Scott looked the policeman up and down, then rested his gaze on his face. The young man glanced quickly at Scott, then shifting the balance of his weight slightly and setting his jaw, he resumed his disinterested, but nonetheless alert stare across empty space.

A few minutes limped by.

Scott checked his watch. He had been here for at least twenty minutes already, though it felt like a good deal longer.

At least he still had his watch – he thought – then felt horrified to find he was even thinking that.

At college the compulsory course Introduction to Psychology as taught by Professor Mort (the fact his name meant death seemed no coincidence given his lifeless monotone drone) was purgatory. Or it was until it was announced at the beginning of the spring semester that Professor Mort was on sick leave due to a malignant melanoma. Rumour had it that the mole in question looked remarkably like a skull. His replacement, who insisted on being called by his first name, Daniel, and whose long hair and Zappatta moustache clearly marked him out as a rebel, energised his students in his inaugural session by showing a film about the Stanford Prison Experiment as conducted by Zimbardo in 1973. Scott and his entire cohort were electrified and divided – half believing the experiment to have been valid and revealing and thrilling, the other half were horrified, disgusted and morally superior in their outrage.

It was a pity that Scott had lost his hunger for psychology over the years, but his job in human resources for an Ottawa government agency had that effect on most of its staff eventually.

'Excusez-moi?' he said suddenly. His voice was surprisingly loud, and his French sounded rehearsed, like a phrase revised and then repeated for a school oral exam.

When the policeman turned, Scott noticed a faint expression of fear in his eyes, though the cop covered it up quickly by raising his eyebrows and jabbing his chin upward in a gesture of enquiry.

'How long am I expected to wait here?'

The policeman merely shook his head and shrugged.

'What's that supposed to mean?' Scott asked him in English. 'It's a fair enough question.'

He caught sight of himself in the mirror again. He was frowning and his mouth was set in a hard line. He looked, especially with the harsh overhead fluorescent lighting, like a bad guy; like he had evil on his mind. But his face often betrayed him like this; while he wore what he thought was a perfectly placid expression, Marilyn often said, with a note of alarm, 'Oh, what is it? What's wrong? Have I done something to upset you?'

Sometimes in response he would snap angrily at her. 'Christ! There's nothing wrong. I'll say if something's wrong. Okay?'

This would silence her, but did nothing to console her, or to disabuse her of the notion that he was in a bad mood, or that something was bothering him. And something was bothering him – had been for years. His brain had a loop of thought that turned inevitably on that dream (or was it a memory?) where he held the murderous pillow in his hands and looked with hatred upon his sleeping baby brother.

Half the time he probably was angry, though he believed himself to be the master of his anger. But teasing and interrogation from women; his mother, Marilyn, schoolteachers, social workers tended to make him lash out defensively. This was probably why he'd been nasty to that woman the other night. He had despised her smug flirtatiousness, her prurient interest and phony concern for Aaron. And she had followed him. Though God knows why.

Scott, still watching his grim, dark-shadowed face in the mirror, attempted to relax his expression. He blinked slowly and imagined floating in a warm salty sea while the sun beat down on him. This was what a therapist had once advised him to do when he became stressed. Not that he had really attempted it. Until now.

He closed his eyes and imagined his body prone and the weight of his head supported by the water. Marilyn had a thing about deep water, she was always afraid of it, afraid of not being able to feel the bottom of the pool or the sea when she had tried to stand up.

He had told her that such a fear suggested a fear about sexuality, about losing control to pleasure. He'd hit a raw nerve when he'd said that. 'Don't be so idiotic,' she'd said. 'It's not fear of sex, it's a fear of drowning!' but their lovemaking that same night (initiated by her) had been explosive.

Involuntarily he suddenly opened his eyes. The policeman had been staring impassively at him and looked away as soon as Scott caught his gaze.

He wondered what would happen if he just got up and made for the door. He would stand up, look at his watch and say very calmly, 'I'm sorry, I've spared you enough of my time. As I've missed my flight now, should you need to, you can contact me at the address on rue Jules Verne.'

It seemed easy and perfectly reasonable, and yet he knew he couldn't do it.

The door opened and the woman with the sleek black hair entered the room, followed by a dark-haired man who was tall and rather gaunt-looking and whose skin looked like it had never seen the sun.

The young policeman clicked his heels together and pulled himself up to his full height, somehow this made him appear younger and even more earnest.

It also emphasised the gravitas of the older, plain-clothes police; the man and the woman in their sombre black suits looking like sinisterly handsome undertakers.

They shuffled papers and exchanged some of them. Scott could not comprehend the degree of formality his minor infraction had set in motion. Had he, somehow by his actions, caused something terrible and tragic to occur? Had he delayed the man in the Renault, kept him from stopping some terrorist plot, or from the bedside of a dying patient? No. It was absurd. This rigidity, this purse-lipped solemnity must be the French way and he should just go along with it, keep his cool and answer their questions, then pay whatever costs or fines they demanded. Christ, he'd just add it to the credit card bill he'd already sent sky high.

'This interview is conducted by Inspector Paul Vivier and Detective Inspector Sabine Pelat at eleven hundred and sixteen minutes, August 1st 2007. The suspect Scott Andrew Clements has agreed to be interviewed without the presence of a representative. Also present are Jean-Luc Aubry and myself, Sabine Pelat.'

Again, for Scott, this was familiar police procedure learned by rote via TV, film and books. It gave the experience a déjà vu quality. He had been in this room before, but as a spectator, as one of those shadowy figures who hovered behind the mirrored glass. He had never before sat in this chair, had never been the subject of the interview.

Looked at in a detached way it was interesting. He should be grateful for this unique taste of experimental realism in psychology.

Marilyn and her writer friends often had conversations about experience, even or more especially bad experiences, as they were the meat of poetry and prose. Then would come a roll call of famous writers' names: Coleridge, De Quincy, Plath, Sexton, Lowell, Brautigan, Woolf, Carver, Thomas and their honesty, their suffering, their alcoholism, their drug use, their broken hearts and damaged souls and suicides. Cheerful stuff, all of it.

If Marilyn were in his shoes now she'd be comforting herself with thoughts of the poems she'd later write.

She was probably writing at this very minute. As long as Aaron was all right, anyway.

# He Hears a Different Drummer

'Are you arresting me? Are you arresting me, sir? Please, I need to know. I need to...'

The metal door swung shut, silencing Joseph. Noise like a rung bell. Or like a crowbar hitting an oil drum. He sat on the wooden bench and put his head in his hands.

That was a bad game they played once, Abrahim and James had persuaded a smaller boy to climb inside an empty oil drum they'd found. They were both smiling at the kid and so he smiled too. The kid was wary at first, but those smiles must have convinced him that these were friends. Joseph thought they might pick the barrel up and run around with it giving the boy a ride as if he was in a plane or rocket ship. The three of them lifted the barrel and rocked it to and fro. Joseph looked down into the small boy's face to see excitement only faintly tinged with fear.

After a time Abrahim began to push more violently while the other two tried to resist. They battled back and forth for some time, the small boy inside hardly aware of the struggle between good and evil being fought on his behalf. Then Abrahim gave one last half-hearted shove and let go. James and Joseph managed somehow to keep the barrel from falling and resumed their gentle rocking. Abrahim walked a few paces away then spat on the dry earth leaving a gobbet of foamy spit that shone momentarily in the hard sun.

The oil drum wasn't all that heavy, but still with the other child inside it was heavy enough and hurt their hands as they struggled to continue the game. The first excitement had quickly passed. It was dull for them, dull for the boy too. James lowered his side of the barrel and wiped his hands on his shorts; dirt and crumbs of orange rust left multiple finger marks like the outstretched wings of a bird on the white cloth.

The kid struggled to climb out. Joseph watched him for a few seconds, then the boy lifted his arms up, his face full of trusting expectation. Not much older than the kid himself this was new to Joseph. To be looked up to as if he were an adult. To be needed. He was about to reach in and grab the boy's arms when Abrahim came running at them, a short metal pole upraised, a battle cry on his lips.

Automatically Joseph leapt back and barely breaking his stride, Abrahim struck the oil drum a ringing blow. He ran on past then slowed and tossed the pole over a fence. James ran to catch up with him and the two walked off, not looking back once either to beckon Joseph or see what had become of the kid inside the barrel.

Not that banging on the oil drum could hurt the kid. Or could it? Joseph didn't know. No sound had come from inside it since the reverberations had died away. No sound. No movement. No sign of the kid's hands grasping the lip to haul himself out. Joseph couldn't see inside but he didn't take a single step closer. He just stood there wishing it all away. Wishing he had turned around when Abrahim and James fell into step beside him. Wishing he'd stayed in the yard under the shade of the big tree reading a schoolbook. Wishing to unravel the day.

Was the kid okay? What if that was a way of killing a small boy? Putting him in a metal drum then banging on it. Could it stop his heart? Frighten him to death? Make his head explode?

He didn't know. He was only eight. The kid was about five. Why didn't the kid scream or cry?

Abrahim was a very big boy, he was almost eleven. James was nine. When Joseph looked he could still see the figures of the two boys shimmering and receding in the distance. So far away that it seemed astonishing that they had ever been there at all.

The oil barrel was as dumb and lifeless as it had been when they'd found it lying on its side with the weeds half covering it. Joseph circled it at a distance until he reached the path that led back to the town. Once on the path he began to walk as fast as he could. Faster and faster until at last he broke irresistibly into a run.

Never knew what happened to the kid. Always fretted and wondered. Eventually the fear fell away and logic told him that nothing (besides being scared out of his wits and a ringing in his ears) had happened to the younger boy. It was a small town, he'd have heard.

Certain sounds however … certain sounds had always haunted him. Metal striking metal. Long awaited retribution. Innocence was no defence. Not then, not now.

He shivered, uncertain of his fate.

# A Man of Constant Sorrows

Thom put the phone down. He'd come dangerously close to weeping as he spoke to Lucy's father. He'd felt the distantly familiar, hot pricking sensation in his eyes and he'd pinched his nose at its thinnest part just below his brows to stop it. He was not a man given to weeping, nor indeed was Lucy's father, but the angry bafflement, the fraught worry in her father's voice combined with the unmistakable sounds of Lucy's mother sobbing uncontrollably in the background had almost started Thom off.

All his anger about Lucy, all those assumptions about her running off with another man, had entirely flown. Now he was left with only worry and guilt.

How many times had he said over the phone to Lucy's father: 'I don't know where she is. I didn't know about her breakdown. She didn't say.' Or, in a variation on that theme, 'If I'd known, if she'd told me…'

That was precisely what was so unfathomable, that Lucy hadn't (or had she?) told Thom about her previous breakdown. Not the whole truth about it anyway. The odd quips she made about Art College being enough to drive anyone loopy made any suggestion about her mental instability seem safely consigned to the past.

He stared at the red light of the answer machine trying to remember something about 'the eye of the little God'. What was it? A line from a poem by Kipling or a story by Wilkie Collins. Something spewed out of the old prejudice of Empire, the fascination and fear of 'uncivilised' peoples.

This particular little god (or was it a demon) with its one

glowing red eye held him in its thrall for a few minutes more as he sat absorbing the conversation with Lucy's father.

'We must inform the police,' her father had said with certainty, then in an aside to Lucy's mother he'd added, 'Alright hen, don't take on so. The lassie'll be fine, we just need to find her, eh?'

Then he'd ordered Thom to stay in the flat until they arrived.

'But you're in Scotland! You can't surely…'

'Seven or eight hours on the motorway, we'll be there by suppertime, son.'

'But…'

Thom had meant to say he had an appointment at three and essays to mark, but that was irrelevant now. Everything in his life was irrelevant now, or at it least withered into so much banality.

And there he was. In Lucy's flat, somehow consumed by her, absorbed into the body of her life by her absence. Standing in for her, listening to her phone messages, waiting for her parents to arrive, checking her mail, being moved by her mother's tears, eating her food.

'The eye of the little god.'

Maybe it was a line from a film, whatever it was, you were probably not meant to stare at it in case it drove you crazy, hypnotised you.

Thom stood up abruptly and checked the time. He felt trapped in the stillness of the flat. All he had to do was wait in these empty haunted rooms while Lucy's parents hurried down the motorway from Scotland. Was it easier for them to be moving towards some specific destination? Or easier for him? To do nothing but wait.

And (he comforted himself to some degree with this thought) who knew, Lucy might breeze in at any moment, perhaps after her parents had arrived, and say, quite understandably, 'What the hell are you all doing here in my flat?'

And there would be absolutely nothing wrong with her. She'd be good old perfectly sane but slightly scatterbrained Lucy. And

Thom would suddenly look like a lunatic. Breaking into her flat and scaring the bejesus out of her poor old parents. Terrifying them into coming hundreds of miles when her dad was a nervous driver and had lumbago and sciatica, and her mum, scarlet-cheeked with hypertension, did nothing but weep the whole way.

Thom went into Lucy's kitchen and began to search for something to drink; something stronger than black coffee or water, but there was nothing, only three empty bottles of red wine lined up in a row next to her tall chrome rubbish bin from Ikea. Thom picked up each bottle and checked it against the light, but all had been thoroughly drained and nothing was left.

He drifted from room to room, there was nothing particularly strange anywhere, nothing to suggest that the person who lived here had suffered a breakdown or entered some terrible manic phase.

He kept picturing Lucy's parents; for some reason he saw them driving down the M1 in a tiny rattling Morris Minor surrounded on all sides by huge articulated trucks. He also pictured them arriving at the flat, their questions and looks accusatory, their worries about Lucy far more acute than his had been, and the worry would be contagious.

He could not face them alone, he suddenly realised. He could not and would not. He picked up the phone, called the college and asked to speak to Mitra Vali in the fashion department.

Her tone when she finally picked up turned frosty as soon as she understood who it was, but she said she might be able to come after a departmental meeting at two. Yeah, sure – like she'd help him. He heard that loud and clear.

Thom put the phone down and avoided its evil red eye. He walked down the hall to Lucy's bedroom at the far end of the flat. He had a strange sensation that the walls were closing in around him; the light flickering in time with his heart. He closed the blinds then drew the heavy grey wool curtains shut and lay down on his usual side of the bed. He turned so that he was facing Lucy's side and tried to visualise her face on the pillow next to his. But there was nothing there in the half light, nothing but space and darkness.

He closed his eyes and tucked his hands between his thighs. He felt his penis harden against his wrists. He tried to summon Lucy through his memories of how she had always felt next to him in the darkness. They knew each other's bodies, knew how to touch and when and where. They were beyond awkwardness and fumbling, and apart from those times when they had quarrelled or Lucy was in either a grey sulk of depression or a belligerent rage, their lovemaking was both easy and violently passionate, intimate and somehow deliciously dirty too.

It crossed his mind that he could masturbate. What did the massage parlours in the city call it – tension relief? Would it relieve him of this growing burden of fear though? Temporarily maybe, but afterwards he'd be drained and ashamed and nothing would be any different.

He dismissed the thought and willed himself to think about Lucy's parents again; their creased faces, her mother's round belly and snub, almost piggy nose. Her father's wild eyebrows that met in the middle giving him a permanently angry look. He was also round-bellied and wore high-waisted casual slacks that sat just above the swell of his stomach thus emphasising it and reminding Thom of John Tenniel's drawings of Tweedledum and Tweedledee from Alice in Wonderland.

He pictured the motorway again, this time Lucy's parents were in a bone-rattling, pale-blue Volkswagen Beetle. Coaches, lorries and fully loaded car transporters surrounded them on all sides. Fast cars and motor bikes wove in and out. Lucy's father would cruise inexorably down the middle lane at barely forty-five miles an hour, his knuckles white on the wheel, his face, with its bristling monobrow, frozen in a grimace of intent.

They might crash and be killed, but as in some disaster movie, it wouldn't only be them, would it? Thom added a diesel tanker to this nightmare, a busload of happy children.

All because of him.

His erection had gone and despite the visions he'd conjured of tangled metal and sheets of flame he somehow managed to fall asleep.

# Close Quarters

The interview began innocently enough. Full name, date of birth, date of arrival in France, full name of wife, his brother's details. (Scott had duly reported this information about his brother just as if everything about Aaron were normal and Scott almost pictured it through their eyes; the two brothers and one of their wives on holiday, the shared driving duties, the laughs over drinks, the tennis games, the camaraderie, the winks exchanged when Aaron began chatting up some young woman, the guidance and encouragement Scott would give Aaron about his college work – everything in short that he should have had with a brother, but was cheated of.)

'And how long have you rented the house for?'

'Two weeks. The owner is my cousin, Monsieur Louis Clements and his wife, Madame Kristell Clements, they're in Thailand.'

'I see, and you say you were angry because you had a flight home booked and the incident was delaying you?'

'Yes, but I should explain…'

'You had the house for fourteen days…'

'Ahm, fifteen actually, because…'

'But you had been there only six. Why were you suddenly leaving, may I ask?'

'Well,' Scott said. He realised suddenly that if he were to tell the truth, then the incident with Aaron might open up a whole other mess of trouble. On the other hand, the truth was the truth, and it was not as if Aaron had hurt anyone other than himself. But there was the matter of his and Marilyn's failure to take care of a vulnerable adult. He had no idea of French law in this regard.

Why the hell hadn't they researched it? How could they have been so stupid as to bring Aaron to another country without a full understanding of its laws?

He grew aware that he had been sitting there for far too long thinking about his answer and that this in itself was suspect.

'My wife wasn't happy,' he said suddenly, surprising even himself with his lie.

'She wasn't happy?' the woman detective raised a quizzical eyebrow, as if to suggest that mere unhappiness was a sorry reason for abandoning a long holiday in la belle France.

'I'm sorry,' Scott stuttered. 'My er … my French is not so good. Excuse me. I meant she wasn't well.' And now he remembered Marilyn being sick a couple of times, of her complaining of heartburn and refusing any wine.

'So she was ill.'

'Yes. Ah, nothing serious, but…'

'And it was she who was going to drive to the airport?'

'Yes, we take it in turns. She likes to drive.'

'Even when she was so unwell that you felt it necessary to cut short your holiday?'

Scott nodded. His mouth felt tacky and dry. He wished he had said yes to the Coke.

'And did you enjoy your holiday before your wife became ill?'

'Yes. Yes, of course. We love France.'

The policewoman smiled indulgently and nodded, then read some papers in front of her. She picked one page up and indicated a particular paragraph for the attention of the man beside her who had not yet spoken. He nodded.

The woman once more took up the conversation on the pleasant topic of holidaying in France.

'So you managed to get out and about to dine and drink and enjoy all there is in our little town?'

'Well, yes, of course. Except that my wife has, well, because she didn't feel so great, and because she is a writer, she has preferred quiet evenings at home.'

'Oh, your wife is a writer?'

'Yes, a poet really and ah…' Scott ran out of steam here, he had no idea why he'd mentioned that Marilyn wrote – did he think this would mark them out as a family with a particular sort of sensibility, a grace or gravitas that allowed or explained any odd behaviour in the eyes of the law.

Jesus, he should have just stuck to the truth. Who could not be sympathetic to Aaron's plight, to their essential charity and love in bringing him here, even if they had for one unfortunate moment failed him?

'So you all stay in the house? Eat at home? What a pity! You might as well have stayed in…' the woman looked at her notes, '…Ottawa.'

'Well, yes, but, we hadn't planned it this way. We didn't know that my wife would…'

'…be unhappy?'

'Unwell. Though, of course, she was unhappy that she was unwell.'

'So you nursed her?'

'Nursed her? No, she wasn't that unwell.'

'But she was unhappy.'

'Yes, but…'

Suddenly out of this tangle of words, the insistent litany of 'unhappy' and 'unwell', the older man at last spoke. His voice was deep and slightly husky, but there was intelligence and warmth in his delivery. It was the voice of a man you could trust and also respect.

Scott looked at him, noticing for the first time that although his hair was very dark, almost raven black; his eyes were blue-grey, like wet slate in a certain light.

'So, did you stay in last night, for example?'

Scott remembered the nightmare of the day before, losing, then finding Aaron, the blood, the worry, then sedating him – not because he'd particularly seemed to need it – by the time they'd cleaned and bandaged his wounds Aaron was moderately calm, but because they'd needed it. He and Marilyn were exhausted, but not only that, they'd needed some kind of comfort, some reassurance about who they were as a couple and that was why, quite naturally (though it could be viewed otherwise) they had made love. Last night then, Scott knew exactly where he had been.

'Yes, we stayed in.'

The policeman shrugged and made the corners of his mouth quirk downwards in a seemingly typical Gallic dismissal of these foreigners' bizarre choice of lifestyle – non-smoking, non-drinking, non-meat eating, desexualized 'good' living which was no life at all.

'And the night before?'

'I went out,' Scott said, glad to show he wasn't quite the wife-nursing freak he was being painted as. 'Marilyn stayed in with my brother; there was a film on TV. Woody Allen, I think she said.'

'Ah, ha ha ha, Woody Allen, yes – who would not stay in to watch a Woody Allen film?'

Stumped by this remark, Scott merely shook his head and attempted a weak smile as if to show that here, finally, in Woody Allen they had found some common ground.

'So you went out?'

'Yes, just for a couple of beers, just, you know, to enjoy the evening air.'

'And to escape your unhappy wife?'

There it was again, the unhappy, unwell business which he thoroughly regretted bringing up. He shook his head, dismissing the question.

'And where did you go?'

The question was put so pleasantly, in such a tone of innocent enquiry, that for a moment it seemed to Scott that he and the older man had just struck up a conversation in a bar.

'Oh, to a couple of cafés on the waterfront. I've got to know a few people there. We've been coming for so many years.'

'Ah, so you met up with friends – lady friends I suppose?' A wink here from the detective. An unsettling and surely unusual signal from this quiet but hawkish man.

'No. Not in the way you're implying. My friends are both men and women. And besides all that, what has this to do with the car, with what happened this morning?'

'We're just trying to get a picture of the background to this morning,' the woman cooed as if all of it were perfectly natural and reasonable.

'But I don't see…'

'This matter will be cleared up with more haste if you would just allow us to do things our way, sir. A little cooperation is all we ask.'

Scott nodded, defeated.

'So you met your old friends. Did you meet anyone new?'

Scott searched his memory of the night before last. There had been Suzette, the waitress, and that guy Florian. Also Therese, but she'd left early, and the bar owner and some regulars he was only on nodding terms with. But there had also been the English tourist, the bottle blonde.

'Uh, not really. Oh, there was an English girl, we chatted for a while.'

'An English girl? Oh, that must have been nice – to talk in your native tongue?'

'Canada has two languages – English and French.'

'Ah, but earlier you apologised for your difficulty with French. To confuse unhappy for unwell is not easy for someone who is fluent in French, is it?'

'Look, I didn't need to talk to her or whatever it is you're implying. She came on to me. I guess she was lonely or whatever.'

'Or unhappy?' the woman officer said.

'Or unwell?' the man added.

They made quite a double act; the two of them in their funereal black with their quick-fire word games and grim irony all of which they mixed in with moments of beguiling friendliness.

Scott glared at them. He didn't know what their game was, but he'd had enough.

'You seem angry, sir,' the woman said, and tilted her head a little at the neck in a spirit of sympathetic enquiry. 'Would you like a drink, a coffee perhaps?'

Scott took a deep breath, nodded.

The plain-clothed man and woman left the room and he was left with the young policeman again and his shiny pink-faced supercilious silence.

# The Quickening

She had never been left alone with Aaron at this time of day before. Her duties had always been nocturnal, taking over sole guardianship only when her husband's younger brother was safely in the land of Nod, usually assisted by a mild sedative.

Aaron tended to pick up on people's bad moods and other emotionally tense situations. It distressed him, which would in turn distress those who were trying to cope with him and so a vicious and self-perpetuating cycle was formed.

Physically Marilyn could not do anything to control Aaron. Her only way of dealing with any situation was to sedate him.

She had watched unbelieving as the police car drove off with Scott in the back seat. She did not understand why the man in the Renault had blocked their driveway that morning. It had seemed calculated, and then Scott had got so angry. It was almost as if the Renault driver knew Scott. As if their paths had crossed before and there was a score to settle. There was something in the air, she thought, something he was hiding from her. It had been so unlike Scott to forget to lock the door and remove the key the night before last. He must have been distracted. And then to be so desperate to return to Canada immediately, no matter the cost. Almost as if he was running away from something. But what? An affair? With the Renault driver's wife? Or his daughter? Or sister? Or (terrible thought, but it had to be considered) with the man in the Renault himself?

Aaron was standing in the open archway that led into the kitchen, shifting his weight from one foot to the other and rocking from side to side in a stiff movement as if he were a mechanical tin soldier. His head was tilted back at the neck and his eyes were fixed on the white painted cornice.

Looking at him, Marilyn suddenly felt a cold wave of immense and seemingly endless loneliness.

If she had been entirely alone, she might have gone for a walk. She would stroll or even march through the streets. She could explore, daydream, find words in rhythmic patterns that matched each footfall.

But, she reminded herself, Scott would be back soon. It was all a terrible mistake.

Without thinking about it too much she filled a tumbler with water, opened the plastic bottle that contained Aaron's medicine, slid one onto the palm of her hand and went to him.

He snatched the pill greedily and threw it into his mouth. She saw the hard lump of his Adam's apple leap as he swallowed the dry white pill.

'Water,' she said making her tone deliberately firm.

Shaking his head to mean 'no', he nonetheless took the glass and swallowed all of it.

In twenty minutes he would begin to feel tired; she might succeed in getting him upstairs and into bed, but there was no way she could wrestle him into his pyjamas. Not that it mattered.

She checked her watch, just fifteen minutes had passed since Scott had gone and in another forty or so minutes their flight would begin its juddering acceleration along the runway before (and it was always, always a miracle to Marilyn) rising into the air and staying up there as it flew over fields and rivers and houses and seas until it landed in Toronto.

Twelve hours from now she and Scott should have been falling exhausted into their own double bed. Aaron would be back home with his parents. It would be over.

Out of the corner of her eye she noticed that the pace of Aaron's rocking had slowed and its arc had narrowed. Now he was not so much shifting his weight from foot to foot as just swaying his upper body.

Marilyn knew that she was also prone to rocking movements; she had a tendency to do it while she was writing poetry, and Scott had teased her about it numerous times. But she was almost completely unaware of it. As unaware as a sleeper is of their snores. As unaware as a pregnant woman is of the life growing within her. Until there is movement – a quickening – and as yet there had been none.

In the midst of this fearful loneliness, a question came into Marilyn's mind. The question was couched in a tone of wonderful simplicity and rationalisation. Why had she not told Scott that she was pregnant?

Superstition and some weird almost pagan sort of magical thinking. As if somehow by not speaking of it; by essentially sealing the news of it inside her mouth, she kept the baby safe. To speak of the growing foetus was to tempt fate.

She half remembered something she had read of superstitions among a certain African tribe. It was to do with the need to always claim that your child was the ugliest and most unappealing of babies, lest bragging about their beauty attracted the spite of gods and devils.

But why had she not told him?

And why was he so blind to the truth about her changing body?

Only once had he ever mentioned darkly that Aaron's problems might be due to a dysfunctional genetic code. Dormant for generations, then springing into life because Aaron's parents each carried the complementary distorting chromosomes. Scott had been lucky, but that did not mean he didn't carry the gene.

That was all he said, then before she had a chance to ask questions, he had rapidly changed the subject. And as this had happened fairly early on in the relationship she was afraid that talk of Scott's possible reproductive future was not a topic she should raise; talk of babies could scare a man off. And it was not only that; dwelling too much on Aaron's problems might seem insensitive and cruel, and Scott often seemed so weighed down by Aaron, so burdened by a shared responsibility and guilt, that she did not talk about it, but waited for the time when he felt able to unburden himself. That time had not come, so a silence hovered between them, shielding and distorting their wishes, desires and fears.

But there again he had agreed when she said she was going to stop taking the pill. This had been in January, a few days after New Year. They had been lying in bed together early one morning; both of them were feeling particularly affectionate. He had said he was glad he'd found her, that he loved her optimism, her spirit, her seriousness and passion for poetry. He loved her wild red hair, her sexy ass, the way she smiled. She had paid him back in kind, telling him how he made her feel safe; that because he was so tall and she was so small it was as if they were different breeds of human, something like dogs and so she was a King Charles spaniel and he was an Afghan hound.

'Hound?' he'd said. 'No, you're wrong. I'm a wolf and I'm gonna eat you up. But first I'm going to see how ticklish you are…'

And he'd tickled her until tears were pouring down her face and after they grew quiet and lay staring at one another.

Then she'd said that she was going to stop taking the pill.

He nodded and murmured that it was a good idea.

Their conversation had not then gone on to consider other means of contraception, nor the realities and practicalities of being parents. Instead they had begun, for the second time that morning, to make love.

Now, as she remembered this, she realised that deep down she remained uncertain as to what Scott's meaning had been, what his wishes were. There had been stories in the news around that time linking the pill to cancer; perhaps that was what he'd been thinking of. But she had immediately stopped taking the pill, and they had made love as before, without condoms, without a diaphragm, or sponge or spermicide.

And so here was the source of the silence. The beginnings of her secret. Maybe she was delaying telling him not from fear of tempting fate; not because she wanted to protect him from possible disappointment if she lost it, but so that it would be too far advanced to be stopped.

Aaron was now standing perfectly still. Marilyn stepped toward him. 'Time for bed, Aaron.'

Immediately he commenced the energetic pace of his side-to-side rocking. She backed away again.

He had never really frightened her before, but now she found her heart was racing and her knees felt weak and rubbery. She could not cope. It was all too much.

She tipped another of Aaron's pills onto her palm and offered it to him. Once more he snatched it up and threw it into his mouth hardly breaking the rhythm of his sideways swaying to do so.

Marilyn switched the kettle on, then she got her notebook from her purse, sat at the kitchen table and began to write. It was a way of escaping, of retreating from the present. Aaron rocked. He did it diligently, painstakingly, as if he were not swaying from side to side on the spot, but travelling in earnest along a lengthy and unforgiving road. As if at the journey's end he'd get his reward.

# Part Four

# TWILIGHT

*The French call dusk — "Entre chien et loup"*
*(between the dog and the wolf).*

*While I thought that I was learning to live,*
*I have been learning how to die.*

Leonardo da Vinci

# Part Four

# TWILIGHT

# Out of the Corner of your Eye

Two figures lay on the bed under a single limp white sheet. Except for the man's arm flung possessively around the woman's shoulders, their bodies sprawled away from one another while their heads lolled together as if each depended on the other's oxygen in order to breathe. The blinds were drawn but the afternoon light cut through at its edges sending forth bright shafts that illuminated certain objects. A bottle of amber-coloured perfume glowed as if lit from within. Opening her eyes, Suzette gazed at it, surprised by its sudden beauty.

Happiness can happen. It is possible even in this dying world. If happiness comes you should grab it with two hands, wrap your legs around it too, get rope and bind yourself to it.

This happiness which possessed her had a human form; a body and free will and a name – Florian.

It startled her to think that this feeling of happiness was somehow to do with love. It could not be love, it was far too soon. Lust then. Lust or passion which could, with time, develop into love. She began to consider these as algebraic sums; lust plus time equals love, lust plus sex plus talking multiplied by habit minus fear and distrust equals love.

Her sister, five years older than Suzette, had at the age of fourteen begun to waste hours in their shared room, lolling on her bed and filling out quizzes in *Cosmopolitan* magazine. Does he really love you? Are you his type of woman? How sexy are you?

Suzette, at nine, hated the stupid magazine because her sister no longer wanted to play with her, and she still hated it. She preferred *Paris Match*. But maybe this was why her sister had been happily married for the last twelve years (though the man she married had numerous affairs) while Suzette had only experienced three affairs with other women's husbands and quite a few one-night stands and brief relationships, but nothing lasting and nothing that was purely her own.

As a child nearly everything she got was secondhand; her clothes, many of her toys, her books and even comics – all hand-me-downs. There was no element of choice, everything had been selected to her sister's taste, so the clothes were inevitably pastel-coloured and had motifs of cute animals; kittens, puppies, baby elephants, or fussy bows and frills and flowers. And the toys were baby dolls, scaled-down ironing boards, irons and vacuum cleaners and nurses' sets.

Suzette had been told she must be grateful for what she was given and she should be ashamed for complaining because there were girls her age in the orphanages and the slums who had nothing.

Florian had fallen asleep with his arm across her chest, his hand loosely cupping her right shoulder. She was trapped and could not move without disturbing him. Suzette had never before felt herself to be so happily imprisoned.

Making sense of all these feelings was impossible.

Suzette closed her eyes, lay there (Florian's arm was heavy on the bones of her shoulder, sweat moistly gathered where their skin met) dreaming, thinking, feigning sleep for no audience except God (whom she hoped understood and forgave this mortal sin).

She did not hear any footfalls on the stairs, no shuffling of feet in the hallway outside her flat and, if she had, nothing would have changed. Only the neighbours passing by, only the sounds of an innocent day.

The knock at the door was a surprise.

Two knocks, the sort made delicately with fisted knuckles on the door panels. The echoing sound of living bone on dry wood.

One. Two.

Suzette tried to lift Florian's arm with her right hand, but he held her even tighter.

Two knocks sounded at the door again.

Suzette wriggled free by twisting herself down and under his arm.

She wriggled into her black slip, went to the door and opened it a little so that her partially dressed body and the room beyond were hidden behind it. She expected to see Madame Sardou from the flat downstairs, or possibly someone from the bar with a message for her to come into work earlier or later or not at all. It crossed her mind that it could be her mother paying a surprise visit and she would have to pretend that she was ill and not let her mother in. Not that her mother ever paid Suzette surprise visits. Her mother expected certain courtesies when she paid a call: Suzette should be demurely dressed, the flat cleaned and furniture polished, shop flowers arranged in clean vases should be set about the room, the pot-pourri should be fresh and not dusty. Her mother liked English tea served in cups and saucers with cream provided in a matching jug. Such affectations. None of which had existed until Suzette's father had died and her mother briefly dated a retired English stockbroker who had bought a timber framed Normandy farmhouse which he was renovating. He loved everything French, or so he said, which did not stop Suzette's mother from adopting these weird English tics. When he left her mother for a much younger woman the affectations seemed to increase in direct relationship to her self pity – as if she had lost him by not being English enough.

But it was not her mother at the door, or anyone from the bar, nor Madame Sardou. It was a man dressed in jeans, with a green polo shirt tucked in the waistband and dark patches of sweat under his armpits.

'Florian?' he said, trying to peer beyond Suzette and into the room. 'I'm looking for Florian.'

In an automatic gesture, Suzette turned in the direction the man was looking.

'Florian?' she said.

Then suddenly she was brushed aside as the man pushed open the door and strode into the room.

Florian was awake and struggling to sit up.

Two more men followed quickly on the first man's heels.

Then one of them spoke, his voice harsh and threatening, 'Florian Lebrun, I am arresting you on suspicion of murder.'

The voice was like one that comes out of a dream, or from a television set just at the point when, bored, you looked away from the screen, so she was uncertain which of the three had said it.

Florian looked bewildered, frightened, he was now sitting on the edge of the bed with his feet on the floor, the sheet covering his groin.

'No,' Suzette said and the sound of her voice surprised her; such a broken wail.

'Get up!' the man ordered.

'No,' Suzette said in her new strangely dramatic voice and she began to walk in Florian's direction. She took two steps and then one of the other men roughly grabbed her from behind and held her so that her arms were pinned against her body. She was aware of her vulnerability; the slip she was wearing barely covered her. Her mind skittered over the terrible things that might happen. The irreversible things – *Irreversible* like that film with the nine-minute rape scene – that film she wished she'd never seen.

Florian was now standing up; naked, exposed.

'I've done nothing,' he was saying. 'I'm clean!'

The word 'clean' said at that moment seemed to merge with Florian's actual nakedness, as if one proved the truth of the other.

'Get dressed,' the first man ordered. He had picked up Florian's trousers and now he threw them at him. Awkwardly Florian caught them and put them on, then his eyes searched the floor until he spotted his t-shirt. 'My t-shirt,' he said and pointed to it. The policeman nodded and Florian picked it up and pulled it on over his head.

'Florian!' Suzette said, her voice now pleading.

But Florian did not seem to hear her. He had found one of his shoes and pushed his foot into it.

'Right, come on.'

'My shoe,' Florian said, but the first man was behind him pulling his arms back and handcuffing him, then propelling him past Suzette towards the door.

'Ring my mother,' Florian said, twisting around to look at Suzette, his eyes wild and pleading.

Suzette said his name again. The man who had been holding her now released his grip. Florian disappeared through the door, one foot bare. The other men followed and the door was slammed shut. Suzette was trembling, her heart pounding, adrenaline flooded her body; she thought she might throw up. She had to do something; help him, save him.

His shoe. It suddenly seemed important that she find his other shoe – that she should search for it and run after them with it. She scanned the floor, saw her own kicked-off shoes, her clothes from last night tossed here and there. She lifted items up, thinking the shoe might be under them. The flat was such a mess. Why was she such a slob? She searched with more urgency, blaming herself for the lost shoe, for the fact that Florian had been naked and vulnerable, for opening the door, for letting the man push past her, for being so weak. She picked a shirt up and threw it down, only to pick it up again a few seconds later.

Her hands trembled as she ripped the crumpled sheet from the bed. No shoe there, but a discarded tissue flew up in the air, borne on the flying sheet. She hated herself.

She hated herself because the seconds were ticking by and they would be down the stairs and onto the street and she couldn't find his shoe.

She walked around the bed in order to pick up the balled-up tissue, she wanted to get rid of it, to prove that like Florian she was clean. She bent to grab it and as she did, she saw, tucked in snugly next to the mattress, Florian's shoe. She picked it up and stood hugging it close to her chest. It seemed as if it was all she had of him now, all that remained.

She let out a wail of anguish, dropped onto the bed and cried in the fierce, painful way that was entirely unstoppable, and which completely immobilised her while she was in its grip.

Then slowly, in stops and starts, the crying abated and she was able to think more clearly, to replay everything in her head. She must ring his mother. Though she did not know her number or name, or where she lived.

And the other thing was a remembered word. The word dangled on the end of a curiously familiar sentence she'd heard or thought she'd heard. And the word was a terrible one. The worst.

Murder.

They had arrested him for murder?

Her Florian, her beautiful and gentle Florian?

It could not be.

And here was his shoe, damp and splashed with tears. The sobbing possessed her again. Its noise unbearable; someone would hear. She pressed her hand over her mouth, but to no avail.

She was helpless.

# Killing me Softly

Marilyn could detect Aaron at the edge of her vision; a decelerating metronome, a mechanical tin toy. In the beginning she had pitied Aaron, had imagined how it must feel to be him, to be locked away inside himself, to have no real ability to communicate or express love. But that feeling had gradually diminished and this was a matter of shame for Marilyn.

Perhaps at one time she had thought she could make a difference, but her efforts to smile at him, to talk sweetly, to evince signs of anything like affection in Aaron had no effect whatsoever. She had wanted to win his love, to effect a miraculous cure – she'd crooned and gushed at Aaron whenever she and Scott went to visit his family. Had it been arrogance on her part – the idea that she could change him? Or was it done to mask the fear and discomfort he evinced in her? One was as bad as the other in its way. Now, like Scott, she was limited and functional in her communication with Aaron. As now, ignoring him, cold.

Scott had been gone for three hours. Marilyn, trying to distract herself from the worry, had been going through her recent work adding a comma here, a line break there. Then she went back through it and crossed them out again.

Repetition. Maybe she was no better than Aaron, only marking time with this ritualistic process of making symbols in ink on paper. Measuring out her life in coffee spoons as T. S. Eliot had done. She had always hated the banality of that metaphor or rather, had done when she was younger; now she was beginning to see the sad truth of it. Poetry did not transform her existence any more than her smiles changed Aaron's.

She looked up suddenly, sensing a change in the room, an

absence. Aaron was still there, in the same place as before, but he had stopped moving. She watched him, uncertain what to do. He might grow agitated again, or he might at last be tired.

She could see the edge of his face, the same sculpted cheekbones and jaw line as Scott's, and the same blue eyes. He was blinking slowly and repeatedly.

'Time for bed, Aaron. Do you want some warm milk?'

He blinked rapidly for a few moments as if absorbing this information, then turned away from the wall and began to trudge wearily in the direction of the stairs.

Marilyn followed a few paces behind, saying a few words of encouragement and silently praying that he wouldn't want to use the toilet or insist on putting on his pyjamas. The pyjamas were still packed in the big suitcase in the trunk of the rental car.

But as usual, Aaron had no interest in undressing or brushing his teeth and merely slouched on through to his room where, without even lifting the covers, he lay down on the bed and closed his eyes.

'Night-night, Aaron,' she said, then crossed the room and drew the curtains against the late afternoon light. She left the room and on closing the door behind her, she found her eyes drawn to the key in the lock on the outside. She considered turning it, trapping him inside so that she could at least relax without worrying that he might somehow escape again. But no, that would be wrong, something could happen, a fire perhaps. And anyway, Scott had to be back soon. Or he would ring and let her know what was happening.

She went back to the kitchen; the fridge was still packed with the food they'd bought in anticipation of a longer stay, she picked up two eggs and held them in the palm of one hand sensing the slightly gritty, slightly smooth coolness of them. They weren't date stamped and so Marilyn (who had always been cautious about gone-off food and pesticides and listeria and salmonella, and was even more so now she was pregnant) filled a clear Pyrex dish with cold water and gently put the eggs in. Both sank to the bottom, but one lifted its nose slightly upwards as if eager to take a look around. Marilyn removed this one, put it in the bin and fetched a replacement which she added to the water. It lay at the bottom like its twin, incurious and rather tame.

Marilyn poured the water away then broke both eggs into the bowl and after adding a little milk and water she beat them with a fork.

The omelette she made was so thoroughly cooked it was rubbery and disappointing. She pushed it around her plate, eating it all finally only from a sense of duty to her unborn child.

She tried not to think about Scott, because whenever she did her imagination elaborated wildly on the limited information and extemporised, beating out antic threats and distortions; Scott was gay, Scott had been kidnapped, Scott was not gay, but he'd secretly had her life insured and now someone was going to break in and kill her, then make it seem like an accident. It was insane how her thoughts could race away.

It was better to try to continue as normal, to go through her notebooks, to eat a very late lunch, to make sure Aaron was okay, to perhaps watch a little TV or read. But she found her mind would not settle and so she sat at the kitchen table and read for the hundredth time.

My mother said, and said again,
that almost dead, my father, oh Polonius
saved me from the stagnant pool.

She crossed out the 'oh Polonius' as it struck her as too pretentious. It cast her as a precocious Ophelia. Stupid.

Then very quickly from that brief moment of focus and lucidity, she found herself gazing dully out of the window, her sense of purpose entirely gone. For a few seconds (thirty seconds at most) she did not know who she was or where she was. She had experienced this before once or twice and mentioned it to Scott who gave the phenomenon a name; a fugue state or dissociation of the personality. But Scott had gone on to laugh about it when Marilyn had asked somewhat nervously what she should do about it, whether she should see a psychiatrist.

'Just stress,' he'd said. 'It's nothing. You're normal.' And Marilyn had almost been disappointed.

She looked down at her poem again, drew a wriggly line under 'oh Polonius' and scribbled 'stet' in the margin to indicate that the words should stay. Then she recapped her pen and went to the sink and washed her hands under the cold tap, dried them on a paper towel, went into the living room and turned on the TV. For a time she stood a few feet from it, firing the remote control at the screen as one channel rapidly changed to another. She did this until she had exhausted them all and was back on the first one which showed an Indian elephant being dressed and decorated in preparation for a religious festival; its dusty, wrinkled skin transformed by bright powdery colours and elaborately embroidered headgear.

If it weren't for Aaron, she and Scott might have gone to India, to Vietnam, to Thailand. In previous years at least, but not this year, not in her condition. She turned the TV off again and looked out of the window at the hotel opposite. Her gaze wandered to the right, where, its front fender nosing into view, she spied the hire car. For a moment it seemed that the car itself was the cause of all their present worries.

The sun had moved over the house and now the front garden and half of the road beyond it lay in shadow. The windows of the hotel glowed with a rosy hue as if lit from within. It was getting late, and Scott had been gone for far too long.

She lifted the telephone receiver in order to check for the ring tone. Then she went to the front door and tried opening it. It was locked and the key was in its usual hiding place.

Is this how Aaron feels, she wondered; is he perpetually locked in a state of not knowing what was going on, restless, stripped of any powers of concentration, with nothing but a blur of meaningless pictures and noises, of tasteless food and sudden sensory pains or pleasures – the washing of hands, the scrubbing of teeth? She would rather be dead, she thought, then just as quickly, something reasserted it in herself and a small voice (God's?) firmly said 'no – not true'. She hurried back to the notebook on the kitchen table, sat down and uncapped the pen.

'Free will,' she wrote on a new clean page, 'free will is water, its many forms defining nothing. To drink is drowning...' Then she stopped writing. A new thought had occurred to her. She could ring the police. Enquire as to where Scott was, what was happening. She had a right to know and there could be no crime in asking.

# Verso

Scott had sat in the soulless interview room with the seemingly soulless young policeman for a long time. Someone had knocked the door three quarters of an hour ago and delivered an unasked for can of warm coke and a white plastic cup. Scott did not see who brought it and no words were exchanged.

The young policeman had cracked open the tab and poured a quantity of the bubbling hissing liquid into the cup. He placed the cup on the table for Scott, but put the can out of reach. Was he trained to do that, Scott wondered? Were suspects, even suspects in such trivial offenses, not to be trusted with soft drink tins? What could he do with it, rip it apart with his bare hands, then use the sharp ragged edge to cut the younger man's throat? Or his own throat perhaps?

You never really fully appreciate the Kafkaesque nature of the law's processes until you're on the other side of them, Scott mused. There was a certain comfort to be had in intellectualising his current situation. He could sit outside himself, pondering his experience. Not that this case was serious, it was merely a misunderstanding, therefore (notwithstanding the cost of the missed flight and his vague worries about Marilyn coping with Aaron alone and then the inevitable fretfulness of his parents when they learned of the mess he had, one way or another, created) he should relax, pay the sort of attention to his fears, to the windowless room and the absurdity of it all, in the same way that he was sure that Marilyn or one of her writer friends would. One of them, now he thought about it, Marc Kincaid, actually worked with prisoners, teaching them creative writing. Scott remembered scoffing at Marilyn's gushing awe when she talked about the project Marc was involved in at the prison. She had also, in a misguided attempted to sway Scott, shown him a chapbook of poems written by several of the prisoners and while she (as patiently as ever) tried to explain what was so good about one of the poems in particular and why the use of this word followed by that word created some resonance that he couldn't for the life of him see, he had cruelly interrupted her to point out that these men's victims would be thrilled to think that everything that had happened to them had caused (in the end) the production of these delicate little poesies. 'I'm sure it was well worth getting raped or robbed or murdered for,' he remembered saying with a sarcastic grin, until he noticed how wounded she looked, and then he regretted it.

'But Scott...' she had replied, then her voice trailed off and she sunk into gloom. She'd closed the chapbook and put it back in her bag. His words had made her remember something and he guessed what, though he didn't say as much. Sometime before, when they had first started seeing one another, there was that inevitable stream of stories about their past lives and experiences, an exchange of truths and confessions. Sometimes these disclosures were about other people and the point was that these narratives illuminated some aspect of the teller's personality and how it had affected them. Thus Marilyn told him a dark tale about a girl she had roomed with during college. Marilyn had never really warmed to the young woman as she'd seemed standoffish and almost religiously studious. There were three other girls in the house besides Marilyn and this bookish young woman, and somehow, though she still couldn't quite fathom why, four of them instantly bonded and began to do everything together, while the other remained outside the group.

'We must have tried to involve her at the start,' Marilyn said, 'but then we just assumed, for whatever reasons, that she didn't want to join in. Then...'

And here, Scott remembered, Marilyn had paused, obviously searching for how to go on with her story.

'…then one night the girl went out on a blind date. It was some man she'd met through a lonely hearts column in the local newspaper. The four of us came home a bit high, loud, laughing, full of whatever fun we'd been having and I went to the bathroom. The lights were off in there. Indeed there'd been no lights on in any part of the house so naturally we assumed the other girl was still out. I flicked the switch without thinking about it, and straightaway, I saw her there in the tub. The bathroom was all white you know, white tiles, white tub and the light was one of those industrial strength fluorescent ones, clinical almost. And there was Sharon…'

Yes, Scott thought, that was her name, Sharon.

'She was lying on her side. She was a very small girl, very thin and she was curled up in this tight little ball in the bath. Naked. Not a stitch on. Her back was to me and I remember noticing the bones showing white and lumpy along her spine, the wing-like quality of her shoulder blades. The tub was only half full of water and she was shivering. Just kind of trembling and quivering all over. And the skin of her shoulder and her back was very pale and white. Everything was white except that there were smears of blood on the rim of the bath and the water was pink. I screamed. At first I thought she'd done something to herself, you know cut her wrists or something. I couldn't see her face. She turned around when I screamed with a sudden scared jerk of her head. And then I saw that her face was distorted and bruised; her mouth was swollen and cut, one eye barely open.'

'The rest of the girls came running in as soon as they heard me scream and Sharon covered her face with both hands as if she were ashamed and couldn't bear us to see her. We helped her out of the tub and she kept her hands over her face even though she was completely naked. She was bruised all over, cut too, and she was bleeding from between her legs. Heavily, like she was haemorrhaging. She'd been raped. Raped and beaten up. By this guy. This fucking lonely heart!'

It must have been one of the only times that Scott had ever heard Marilyn curse, though it was no wonder.

Marilyn said that she and the other girls blamed themselves, of course, and Marilyn said she'd have liked to have seen the guy who did it tortured in some terrible way. So, of course, when Scott had reminded her of the probable causes for those 'poets'' incarceration, it was natural for her to grow silent and think more deeply about the reality of their crimes.

Scott had been lost in thought for perhaps twenty to thirty minutes when the door opened and the two smartly dressed detectives re-entered the room. The young man in uniform snapped his heels together and stretched his neck raising his chin.

The tape was switched on; the date, time and names of those present were recorded again.

'Scott David Clements, I must hereby inform you that you are to be held for questioning in the matter of the murder of an unidentified young woman who was discovered on the morning of 31st July 2007. You may have a legal representative should you wish.'

Kafkaesque, yes. It was perfect.

Scott laughed. He imagined a hidden camera somewhere. The whole thing must be a spoof for some hilarious French TV show.

'You are allowed one telephone call only.'

'You're kidding me, yeah?' he said in English.

The beautiful young woman grew even more solemn, directing her stony gaze at him, then answered in almost perfect English. 'No, there is no joke. Not for us, at least.'

'I need to phone my wife,' he said at last. 'She...'

He did not finish the sentence, a moment passed while the two detectives sat very still watching him, waiting for more words to spill from his open mouth.

But nothing came. Scott closed his mouth and nodded slowly. 'Now it begins,' he thought.

# Second Thoughts

Marilyn got the local phone directory from the cupboard in the narrow hallway and took it into the kitchen. Her open notebook and pen were placed near the chair she habitually chose at the table, but now she sat in Scott's chair and opened the directory on the table in front of her. She already knew the three-digit number for calling the emergency services, but clearly that should not be used for this enquiry and while her French was okay she might struggle against an inexorable tide of questions which pertained to real emergencies; fires, crimes and accidents or sudden illness.

So she began her search for the number of the local police station, but she did not understand how such things were listed. She turned the pages to and fro, the small type becoming at times a blur. Inwardly she cursed herself for her inadequacy at so simple a task, her complete lack of foresight – how could she have travelled here so guilelessly over and over again without a clear picture of how to deal with a circumstance such as this? Yes, they had been careful to arrange full travel and medical insurance, yes, they were equipped with maps and first-aid kits and sunscreen and after-sun lotion and insect-sting creams and brochures about places of interest they never got to see, but this – this simple piece of information? No, in that they had failed miserably.

Well, perhaps Scott knew. Certainly his French was far better than hers as his father's side of the family were Quebecois who had settled on the other bank of the Ottawa River.

Usually self-reliant and capable, Marilyn was shocked to recognise how much she had relied upon Scott's knowledge and contacts. It was quite natural of course, as the links with France were due to his family, the journey undertaken for his brother's good – though really it was done to relieve their parents. Yet still Marilyn heaped scorn upon herself. She should have known. Especially after Aaron managed to slip from the house and find, of all things, a razor blade. That was the point when they should have discussed what action might be taken in an emergency or a problem with the law. Instead they had merely cleaned up Aaron's wounds, sedated him, then – oh, it was unbelievable to think it really – they had made love.

Marilyn closed the telephone directory and sat thinking.

Perhaps the thing with the police had been cleared up hours ago. Perhaps Scott (and it wouldn't be entirely out of character) had left the police station and on his way back to the house, had stopped for a nerve-calming drink somewhere. Or maybe he had bumped into some of the friends he had made over the years.

Perhaps from his perspective it was nothing. Nothing at all and the journey of her imagination over these last few hours was only that – an entirely fictitious ramble through an increasingly alarming substratum of possibilities.

Hyperbole. A family trait inherited from her mother. Take a small and actually innocuous incident (her toddler self falling into the pond) and remove her father's nearness, his strong hand reaching in to the water and plucking her out the moment she had gone in, and let the child instead splash, and sink.

It was the difference between what might have happened and the reality.

A close shave. A narrow escape. These are perceptions of mortality glimpsed, but avoided.

After the attack on the World Trade Centre Marilyn had been amazed by the number of her acquaintances who wanted to claim some sort of nearness to the event by saying things like, 'We'd planned to go to New York that week but then my mother had a stroke so we changed our plans', or 'My God, we were on the observation platform at nine-thirty in the morning exactly a month before', or 'I was interviewed for an insurance company with offices in the South Tower – they didn't give me the job and I was really knocked back, but I guess that was fate…'

Hyperbole, all of it.

Marilyn stood up, suddenly remembering something. The Clements! They had left their contact details in case of an emergency. It had been on a torn scrap of paper they'd stuck to the fridge door with one of those gimmicky gargoyle magnets. She remembered seeing it when they arrived. She turned her head sharply to look for it, but the refrigerator only showed its blank white face.

She continued to stare at the spot where it had been, gradually letting her gaze circle outwards like a searchlight. Finally she saw it, a small buff-coloured object, lodged underneath the fridge. She dropped to her hands and knees and perceived a veined wing-like thing tilted on its side. She reached for it, but her fingers could not fit in the narrow space. She got a bread knife from the drawer and managed to scoop the object free, but as it emerged she saw that it was not whole; all that was left was the bat-like wing and one bony shoulder.

Someone had shoved the thing under the fridge in an attempt to hide the fact they'd broken it. Or it might have been kicked under by mistake.

Marilyn thought hard and found herself picturing Scott clearing up the kitchen. He tended to be brisk and businesslike when tidying and now she saw him bending over to snatch a scrap of paper off the floor, then him screwing it up and throwing it in the bin without looking at it.

More dreams. More useless wild imaginings.

Marilyn stood staring at the dun-coloured resin wing as it nestled in her palm. A gargoyle was meant to protect against evil, what happened if it got broken?

And how many hours of our lives are fixed like this in uncertain and worried waiting? Tick tock tick. We should be better managers of our minds, Marilyn thought, then she placed her palm over her belly and felt almost palpably the hours and days of her child's life stretching off into the future. It seemed to march off confidently along a straight road and she saw that no matter what, it would always be moving away from her. As was proper. Yet she nonetheless palpably felt the loss.

She thought about her relationship with her mother again; her silliness, her clinginess, the fusses she made about Marilyn's ordinary childhood illnesses, the controlling scrutiny of first Marilyn's playmates, then her girlfriends and finally boys with their slipshod manners, their scruffy clothes, their pot smoking and guitars, their unkempt hair.

And then the nagging of Marilyn herself, why did she wear those ugly dungarees, those long dresses, she had beautiful legs and she should show them off! And her hair, there was just too much of it, get it cut, get it styled. You'll never meet Mr Right looking like that! And no bra? It's indecent. Poetry? Very nice dear, but it's only a hobby, unless you do greetings cards.

From upstairs she heard a sound, the creak of a bed as someone got up or perhaps just the noise of someone tossing violently in their sleep. She tiptoed up the stairs, listening for other clues as to the cause of the noise. She hoped it was only Aaron turning over, that she would not find him on the landing wanting to use the toilet, or wanting anything really.

The door to his room was closed, she listened for a moment, then as quietly as she could she turned the handle and peeped in. Somehow he had moved so that he lay diagonally across the bed, his arms outstretched on either side of him, one leg dangling off the mattress in mid air, but he was breathing peacefully; a slow almost silent inhalation then exhalation. She closed the door carefully, listened once more to be sure she hadn't disturbed him, then tiptoed downstairs again.

The sun was beginning to sink lower in the sky and the shadows were lengthening. Not much longer now and Scott would be back. She rallied with this thought. He would be back and hungry. She went to the kitchen and began with a sense of renewed purpose to assess what food was still there and what she could make for their supper. She put some Charlotte potatoes on to boil; with chives from the garden they'd make a decent salad.

There was flour in the cupboard too. It wasn't theirs, but the Clements wouldn't mind. She'd make quiche or a tart of some sort. Tomatoes in the greenhouse. A salsa then?

Marilyn threw herself into the work, caramelising onions and blanching spinach; the back door flung wide open as if she had at last taken possession of the house, as if she finally belonged.

# The Damage Done

'Recognise this?'

Detective Inspector Vivier held up a photograph of a white object. Florian glanced at it quickly then turned away and shook his head.

'Look at it!' he put the photograph on the table in front of Florian, who gave it the most cursory of glimpses.

'You're not paying much attention, are you? What's the matter, don't you like remembering?'

Florian stared hard at the inspector's face. He stared with hatred, absorbing the bleached pallor of the man's skin, the fine beads of sweat on his upper lip, the grim eyebrows, the lank black hair, the grey shadow on his lower face. The man needed a shave.

'Okay, you won't look at that, how about this?'

The detective pulled another glossy eight by ten from a folder and tossed it onto the table.

'Or this?' another picture was added. 'Or maybe this?'

Florian continued to watch the man's face, yet he could not help but get an impression of the photographs as they moved rapidly from the detective's hands to the table.

The human eye and mind are designed to follow the movements around them; hunting prey, avoiding predators, surviving. Florian got an impression of crime scene photos; a wasteland of yellowing vegetation, concrete, and also a human form; a woman dressed in white, with platinum blonde hair and unnaturally white skin. He continued to focus his gaze on the other man's face.

Something inside Florian kept making him want to hit the detective, fight his way out of the room and out of the building.

He knew it was hopeless, knew that while he was innocent of the crime they suspected him of, attacking the detective could send him away for a long time. Yet the impulse kept rippling through his body, flexing his muscles, sending out adrenaline, setting his heart racing.

He felt like prey; like a cornered animal, a rat or wild dog. Only humans can create this strange situation of imprisonment and power, forcing him to submit and behave in a civilised manner no matter how much instinct drove him to react in the opposite way.

'Look at them, man,' the detective insisted, leaning closer so that Florian could smell a combination of coffee and peppermints on the man's breath.

Florian shook his head slowly, blinked and moved his gaze to a distant spot at the back of the room.

'Alright, fine,' the detective said and he switched off the microphone and violently pushed back his chair as he stood up. The woman assistant who had been sitting silently beside him also stood. Without another word they left the room and Florian was alone. Through a glass panel in the door Florian could see a younger policeman had been left on guard outside the room.

Florian knew they had done this so he could look at the photos in private. But he didn't want to look, he didn't want to know anything about this crime.

He turned his chair so that he was facing away from the table. He sat this way for perhaps five minutes. He sensed he was being watched. He knew they would leave him alone in this room for a long time and that he would eventually look at the pictures, and that therefore he may as well look at them sooner rather than later.

He turned his chair around again and cast his eyes over the pictures. The photos showed a young woman lying near some waste ground. She seemed to be somehow suspended over a drainage ditch. She wore a white dress and her legs were slim and tanned. Her hair fell down concealing her face. The picture didn't look real – the girl was too graceful, too clean. A policewoman in a wig had posed for these. All part of set up to trick him. But why?

He closed his eyes. Covered his eyes with his hand. Suzette. That was why. She'd been a *flic's* whore. His property. Marked as surely as if her face had been scored with a knife, her perfection overwritten with a jagged scar.

He opened his eyes and this time his gaze lit upon a different sort of picture. This showed a white cardigan that had been arranged on a sheet of creased brown paper as if it were a present that had just been unwrapped. He picked up the glossy print and stared at it. There was something familiar about the cardigan, yet he couldn't quite figure out what.

Then he remembered. It was the cardigan he and Suzette had found the other night, the one they had replaced after they had a change of heart about keeping it.

He remembered finding it discarded on the shrubs outside a café. Pictured himself kissing Suzette. He'd had a few drinks so much of what he remembered either had a dreamy, slow-motion quality or it existed only as a series of single images or memories of sensations or tastes. The events of the morning after had more clarity. They'd made love again, eaten and had coffee, then on leaving Suzette's flat together they'd put the cardigan back where they'd found it. His memories were bathed in glory. Him and Suzette. Suzette and him, staring at one another. The gaze that passed between them steady and unblinking. Since that night he'd had that uncontainable, irrepressible feeling of boundless good fortune and luck.

Florian did not remember anything illegal he had done. He had not for example left Suzette's in the early hours as he might have done a few years ago to snoop around the rest of the building in search of something to steal. He'd had no drugs on him. There was nothing during that night and the morning that followed that was anything other than honest and legal, nothing which burdened him in the cold light of day with shame. Indeed the business of returning the lost garment had felt like a turning point, an act of shared goodness, a celebration of him and Suzette getting together.

There was no one-way mirror in the interview room they'd put him in. He looked up to the corners of the ceiling where he was sure he'd find a security camera looking down on him. There it was in the right hand corner, the little wall mounted device, a boxy silver rectangle with a single black eye. He turned the photo of the cardigan around to show it to the camera and nodded his head slowly. The lens made a faint quick whirring sound as the focus was changed by an unseen operator.

He gathered all the ugly pictures on the table into a single stack with the image of the cardigan on the top, then leaned back in his chair, folded his arms and waited for them to return.

# The Huntress

Marilyn had prepared the food in a frenzy of displaced energy. She knew that this was what she was doing even as she fussed with the food and all the alien cooking utensils in this French kitchen.

Aaron appeared without warning in the doorway. His face had the creased look of someone who has woken in the middle of the night and after a visit to the john will trudge back to bed, easily resuming sleep and perhaps even picking up the trail of interrupted dreams to continue on with the unravelling of their baffling mysteries.

Did Aaron dream? And if he did, what did he dream about?

Marilyn had covered the kitchen table with the food, bowls of salad covered with plastic wrap, the just-baked onion tart and a quiche with cheese and tomato and slivers of ham, an aubergine dip, basil and tomato salad, new potatoes that had been boiled with chopped mint leaves.

Aaron saw the food and went automatically towards it as though hypnotised. He pulled out a chair, sat down and lifted up his fork.

No words were said.

Marilyn sliced a portion of the onion tart and put it on his plate; he broke off a piece with his fork and ate with the sort of bug-eyed chomping wordlessness of children at a birthday party. He did not fuss as he normally would, shaking his head, pushing the plate away or clamping his mouth tight.

Marilyn continued to spoon more food on to his plate. She had a sense that he was not even aware of her, that for him the food was mysteriously delivered by unseen servants – as had been the case with Psyche when she dwelt in Cupid's golden palace.

He ate at a decelerating pace, until at last he put down his fork wearily and reached for the empty glass which she had set beside his plate.

He would want chocolate milk and luckily there was still half a carton of it left. Marilyn took his empty glass and set it on the counter to fill it, then before giving it to Aaron she shook two sleeping pills on to her palm.

He took the pills, throwing them expertly to the back of his throat, before taking the glass of milk from her. He drank noisily until it was all gone. He still had that slightly sleepy-eyed look about him as he pushed back his chair and began to trudge once more in the direction of the stairs.

She followed him up and at the top said, 'Go pee-pee now Aaron,' even though he was already turning in the direction of the bathroom. He left the door open and did not lift the seat, but otherwise Marilyn was grateful that he was being calm and acquiescent.

It was dark by the time Marilyn came downstairs again. She again lifted the phone to check it was working. She did not switch on the table lamp, but with the curtains open, there was enough light from the street for her to manoeuvre her way around the grey humped shapes of the furniture and over to the window.

She gazed up the road in the direction of the town centre and willed the familiar form of Scott to materialise in the distance. He had a distinctive walk, Marilyn thought, he kept his shoulders squared and level, his back straight. His long legs moved in regular strides as his feet rolled easily over whatever surface was underfoot. He possessed a grace that defied his height. Other tall men she knew seemed to stoop or slouch or swagger. It was as if their centres of gravity eluded them; their limbs were as alien to them as they had been at sixteen or seventeen when they suddenly accelerated upwards with awkward, gangly legs and long puppy feet and wrists which shot out of their shirt cuffs, knobbly and naked.

Even as the stocky little policeman had led him to his car, Scott moved with grace, and betrayed little sign of anger or apprehension. He walked tall.

It was all a terrible mistake.

She told herself that over and over.

Some day they would laugh about it.

Then, whenever the subject of France came up while they were in company, she and Scott would quickly find one another's eyes, and say with exaggerated warning, 'Don't talk to us about France!' before launching into their long and deliberately comical tale of this current nightmare.

All of that lay in the future. It was just up the road and would begin as soon as she saw his blond head and broad shoulders in the distance moving inexorably towards her.

But he did not appear.

She must have spent an hour going between the window, the hallway and the kitchen, not quite pacing, not quite like a person with an obsessive compulsive disorder, though she got a glimpse into the restless, anxious compulsiveness of the disorder's relentless uneasy thrall.

The phone began to ring at one point. Two quick rings, then silence. Marilyn had only got halfway across the kitchen before the phone stopped again, but despite this she continued towards it. She stared at it, willing it to ring again, then picked it up and said, 'Hello?' Even as she said the word she knew it was hopeless, the connection was lost and her word encountered no answering human presence, only a machine. Yet still she repeated the word. Once, twice, three times. And listened, all her senses attuned to something, anything.

She replaced the receiver and stood for a time gazing at the telephone. The only source of illumination came from the kitchen with its functional but harsh fluorescent strip lighting. Upstairs she was aware (as she and Scott were always, always aware) of Aaron's sleeping presence.

It must be this way with a child too, she thought, even after you have laid the sleeping baby in its crib, your mind cradles the image of it as you move about the house. And there was so much that could befall a baby after it was born; for instance, a cot death – that sudden inexplicable exit from life. Or the infant could be stolen, bundled off by strangers in the rare second when your back was turned, and then forever after you would pray that whoever did it were only childless people driven by desperation – people who took your child in order to love him or her.

What was it then, the crux of this desire to parent, given its attendant fears? It was certainly about love; the wish to take the empty space between a man and woman and make a third new being who was the sum of their parts. Or not the sum, but a selective borrowing from each; Scott's blondness warmed by her own red hair to make a coppery yellow, her blue eyes and his brown making a hybrid green.

Inevitably Marilyn's mind returned to the poem she had struggled with so long. It was no longer merely an unsatisfactory fragment of verse but the key to understanding something about, not only herself, but her mother and also parents in general.

All children, as they grow, discover that their parents have feet of clay; they coltishly shrug off the concerns and rules and controls and silly worries, unwittingly torturing them with their young recklessness. Understanding only comes when they in their turn become parents.

Just as now she was worried sick about Scott and invented a hundred terrible explanations for his long absence, so a parent extemporises on the thousand ways they might lose their child. And her mother had seen one of these unfolding before her eyes when her beloved only daughter went pitching forward into the green algae-rich soup of the pond.

It should have proved to her mother that bad luck and danger could be overcome, but instead it confirmed the constant threat.

She automatically reached for the receiver again, but then as if catching herself; she merely laid her hand upon it. She had been about to ring her mother. Her mother whom she'd quarrelled with at about the same time she'd begun seeing Scott. It was years since they'd spoken to one another. Too long.

Both of them waiting stubbornly for the right apology phrased in the right blame-taking way, at the right time. Which, were Marilyn able to pick up the phone and dial the number, she would still be unable to produce. Instead she would sob and say, 'Mom, I don't know what to do, I don't know what to do, help me, Mom...'

And her mother might just hang up. Or even if she listened to Marilyn's garbled tale, she could not really help as she was the most impractical of women, incapable of even changing a light bulb, terrified of computers, rendered into a state of childlike awe and obedience by anyone in a position of power over her – doctors, nurses, politicians, policemen, bank managers, insurance salesmen, teachers, the clergy, tax inspectors. She was, Marilyn knew, a silly woman, the typical product of her generation.

Marilyn had fought to rid herself of these same traits, to be her own woman, relishing a vision of herself armed with an electric drill, a domestic paintbrush, a plumber's kit, dependent on no one but herself. It was this thought that now galvanised Marilyn into action.

Aaron was asleep and with the help of the pills she had given him, he would sleep for the rest of the night. She tried Scott's cell phone again, but when it went straight to message, she guessed that it was dead. He'd had it plugged into the car charger as they were setting off that morning, but they had gone nowhere. And he'd been waving it around at the guy in the other car. Then he'd used it to ring the police.

She had no choice it seemed, but to go out to find him. She went through to the kitchen, put on her jacket, picked up her bag, then she tore a blank page from her notebook and scribbled a note for Scott.

'Time now nine-thirty. Aaron fine. Gone to look for you. Wait here. Marilyn. X.'

She propped the paper against the kettle, then turned to look at her notebook again. She opened it to the poem about her mother. She still had the pen in her hand and suddenly in a swift flurry of inspiration she wrote four new lines, which seemed for the moment at least, to sum up and allow an escape from the troublesome poem.

She would cross them out again tomorrow, of that she had no doubt, but at that moment it had been important to write them down, to say in words that she recognised the source of her mother's exaggeration, even while she chided her for it. Chided herself too, for buying into it.

She recapped the pen and put it, as was her habit, diagonally across the open page.

In the hallway she retrieved the house key from its hiding place and before unlocking the door she stood at the bottom of the stairs straining to hear any sound from upstairs that might suggest that Aaron was not asleep.

Silence.

She opened the door, then put it on the latch.

The air outside was wonderfully fresh and still carried some of the day's heat. The street lamps sent pools of warm yellow light onto the darkened streets. Across the road she could make out the evening's diners and drinkers inside La Coquille Bleue. All of them seemed to be settled into little groups, all were with friends or family, only she was alone. She remembered the poster she used to have of Hopper's 'Nighthawks' where an American diner is populated by four individuals, three men and a lone woman, each trapped within a private reverie. In that painting there was loneliness. Here was companionship. An easy companionship which excluded her.

Marilyn focused her eyes on the figures inside, searching (though she knew it was unlikely) for Scott. She comforted herself with the relief and joy she would feel at finding him. First she would throw herself into his arms, kiss him and say his name, then she would probably punch him on the shoulder. Not that she had hit anyone since grade school and even then it was no doubt pretty feeble and half-hearted.

Once she had passed La Coquille Bleue she quickened her pace. She was confident that she knew the route into the centre of town, even though Scott usually drove. There was a tree-lined avenue, then a right turn and a beautiful *maison bourgeoise* with its ornate white stonework and tall shuttered windows appeared on the left. Then there was the *Ecole* and the ugly apartment block, then another right turn down a road with houses on one side and a high stone wall on the other. After another turn, they reached the main square where the old men played *boule* under the shade of the cedar trees. At the far end overlooking the patch of green was the Hotel de Ville and next to it, the police station.

She could picture the route in her mind, but at night and on foot everything looked different. She had considered taking the car, but couldn't find the keys.

She set off down the long avenue exactly as they did when in the car, and took a right fork then continued down the nondescript street as before, but there was no sign of the beautiful house she had expected to see rising up suddenly beyond its long manicured lawns.

Confused and a little frightened, she comforted herself with the knowledge that distance contracted as one sped along comfortably in a vehicle. Roads and hills shrank.

Marilyn continued on along the road in the expectation of finding familiar landmarks. She tried by some mathematical process – whereby she figured speeds of somewhere between thirty and forty miles per hour against her own much slower walking speed – to measure the length of time it would take her to reach the place where the white mansion stood. But she did not wear a watch; was always dependent on other timepieces – her computer's clock, Scott, the read-out on her electronic radio alarm, or any of those external devices on town halls, in railway stations, in shops and cafés. Time, or rather reports of its progress were usually everywhere you looked, but not now.

In her worried state, she had only the false internal measure of distorted guesswork. This was a compass that she knew was easily set out of kilter. Good time – with its first kisses and birthdays and great sex and seamless, perfect performances of poetry and enthusiastic acceptance letters – always seemed to end all too quickly, while bad time – with its root canal work, its car breakdowns and queues and exams and banishment to bed without supper – stretched out into an infinity of aching, lazily moving seconds.

She therefore followed this one long road for twenty minutes before concluding that it wasn't the one they usually took.

She turned around and walked back the way she had come and after ten minutes came to a fork in the road. Here then, is where I went wrong, she thought. She gazed down the length of this new street and noted how similar it was to the one she had just walked down. Her mistake had been understandable and she swore there was something distinctive about the line of pollarded trees which she recognised.

She walked more briskly now as this road was more or less straight, but even in the darkness she saw that there was no sign of the tall ornate gates that guarded the big house and interrupted the regularity of the smaller houses' neat front gardens and modest fences.

She stopped walking abruptly and gazed around her. Why, she thought, why must Europeans build their streets in such a maze? What was wrong with the good old grid system with its blocks and easy north and south, east and west, and numerical avenues and streets? She knew the answer, knew that these villages and towns developed organically and gradually, following the contours of the land with its rivers and valleys and existing pathways and buildings.

This is just so stupid, she thought, so, so stupid, like something dreamed up by the surrealists, by Magritte or de Chirico. Everything that had happened from the moment they stepped out of the house that morning might have been the enactment of a convoluted Hitchcock plot whereby mistaken identity and concealed knowledge baffled protagonist and audience alike.

Everything unravels. It is all done to drive me mad, as in the film *Gaslight*, as in *Les Diaboliques*.

Marilyn allowed herself these excesses. The old habits of imagination, well-stirred and qualified by a liberal arts education. The gift of a mind that can find fire-breathing dragons and effervescent cherubs in cloud formations, but can also put the hairy sharp-toothed bogeyman under the bed and knows the precise measure of his grasping hands' strength and clamminess, and what it symbolises in Freudian terms.

Marilyn interpreted the world through its likeness to a Coen brothers' film, to a poem by W.H. Auden or Sharon Olds, to Greek myths and film noir classics; danger and pleasure and pain were all subjects. But now she wished only to remove herself from these tangled night streets and find Scott.

A door opened two houses away and a woman in a white nylon tab apron emerged carrying a watering can. Marilyn watched as the woman began to move around the small front garden tending the many flower-filled pots and tubs arranged there.

'Excusez moi! Excusez moi, Madame!' Marilyn called and hurried towards her.

The woman looked up in surprise, blinking in Marilyn's direction.

'*Ou est le Hotel de Ville si vous plait?*'

As she drew closer Marilyn saw that the woman was older than she had at first thought, though her body was as trim and straight as a much younger woman's. Marilyn repeated her question looking earnestly at the old woman's face, half of which was alive and mobile, while the other drooped down as if it had melted, and its eye had a deadness about it.

The woman said something in a drowned distorted French which Marilyn could not understand.

Marilyn mimed a body language of being lost, looking up the street, then down the street, shaking her head and raising her palms towards heaven.

The woman watched her uncomprehending, as if she were tired by the endless japery of Marcel Marceau and Jacques Tati. They did not amuse her, she was too old for humour and she had thirsty plants to water.

'*Si vous plait, si vous plait,*' Marilyn tried again, sensing she was losing the woman's attention. Then she pointed down the road in the direction she had been going. '*Hotel de Ville?*'

Slowly the woman's one good eye seemed to widen as if at last she understood, then aping Marilyn she pointed down the road and nodded.

'*Merci Madame! Merci beaucoup! Bon nuit!*' This last called out cheerfully as Marilyn broke into a trot heading confidently on down the road.

# The Lamb

At 8.45 they'd led Scott down a narrow corridor to the phone. He had begun by dialing Marilyn back at the house, but by the time it had rung twice, he'd changed his mind. One phone call only, so it had to count. There was the Canadian embassy in Paris, or alternatively, a lawyer friend in Toronto who might be able to advise him, even at long distance, but who might easily take everything Scott said as an elaborate joke, because that is what they'd done for a long time now, since High School in fact – mount elaborate hoaxes on one another. Scott could ring his father of course, but his parents would panic and flap and get the wrong end of the stick and would thus cause more confusion. If he rang Marilyn she could contact the embassy, get a good lawyer's number and, if need be, ring his parents.

He dialled the house again. It was engaged.

The young policeman looked at him sternly.

'Engaged,' Scott said. He understood what had happened back at the house, that his hesitant first call had brought Marilyn to the phone and that while it had stopped ringing she had probably still picked up.

'Try later,' the policeman said, taking Scott's elbow and guiding him back down the hallway to a holding cell.

'When?'

'Ten minutes.'

Scott nodded. Sat on the edge of the thin mattress that covered a metal shelf as the cell door was swung shut and locked.

Ten minutes. But they'd taken his watch from him. Also his keys, wallet, loose change, cell phone and belt.

In his wallet there was a photo-booth snapshot of Marilyn. He would have liked to look at it at that moment – to remember her grace and comfort and honesty. Her milky skin, her clear eyes, the red Pre-Raphaelite hair which in public slightly embarrassed him for its wild hippy connotations, but which in private, he adored.

He was such a damn hypocrite, he thought. So excessively hypocritical about so many things you would almost think he had two personalities locked together in one body – a Dr Jekyll and a Mr Hyde each unaware of the other's existence. Or aware only vaguely of strange half-remembered dreams, as when he recalled the murderous night in Aaron's nursery. As in the memories of his words and actions of a couple of days ago – his meeting with the English girl, his mood which had been unreasonable, gruff and sarcastic. Because?

Because? Now he hardly knew why he had acted that way. He hadn't been drunk, merely uninhibited enough to say things he would never have said were he completely sober and, he realised, were he not in a foreign country, a stranger talking to another stranger. And, damn it, she had been coming on to him, was throwing herself at him. She had followed him for God's sake! But the come-on was hardly a well-polished performance, beneath the make-up and blonde hair and bold words he had sensed vulnerability and sweetness, a fragility which he had been attracted to. That was why he had been so aggressive, it was to drive her off, swat her away, make her decide he was a nasty piece of work, an arrogant jerk who would screw her over.

He thought about her carefully, focusing his attention on the character of the young woman. She was beautiful. She was dressed in such a way that one could not fail to notice her, not because it was provocative or overly sexy but because it was girlish, almost virginal, the summery look of a girl from the nineteen-fifties.

If she had acted so oddly towards him (following him all the way from the house for example) she was capable of acting in a similarly provocative way towards other men. British and American women (and therefore also Canadians who got carried along in their wake) had reputations in Europe for being easy, for being sexually available. Or so he understood, though perhaps his data was outdated and inaccurate. He saw how the murdered woman might easily have gone like a lamb to the slaughter. Driven not by desire or lust, but sheer aching loneliness.

That was it. He saw it suddenly – she had, despite the bold front, been painfully lonely. Lonely and lost.

A perfect victim.

Half an hour later Scott was taken to the phone again. He rang and rang, but no one answered.

# On the Road to Calvary

'None of these men did it,' Sabine said. She was half sitting, half leaning on a desk, her arms folded over her chest, one ankle hooked around her lower leg.

Vivier looked up and met her eyes.

'You could be right.'

'I know I'm right.'

'No. You don't know that. You're talking about instinct.'

'So what's your instinct, Inspector? Or do you have none? Is it only women who go by intuition?'

'Don't let's get into that.'

'Into what?'

'Gender. Sexual politics. Don't muddy the waters, Sabine.'

'Then be honest, sir.'

Vivier sighed. 'The black kid was terrified, which might suggest guilt, but I don't buy it. He saw someone lose a cardigan, he tried to give it back, failed and put it in clear sight where it might be reclaimed. It was only chance that someone saw him.'

'And that someone jumped to ridiculous conclusions because he was black,' Sabine added.

'That idiotic woman.'

'And Florian Lebrun?'

'*Voyoux*. Hoodlum, small fry. We need to bring in the girl he says he was with. Confirm the story about the cardigan. Let's hope she's not overcome by modesty. Or married.'

'I know who she is, sir.'

'You do?'

'Waitress in the Café Rouge. She had an affair with Bertrand Severin.'

Vivier stared at Sabine in astonishment, but said nothing.

'It's true, everyone knew about it. Well, except you.'

'Sounds like that waitress has a taste for bad boys,' Vivier said, shaking his head at the irony of it.

'What do you mean?'

'Severin's being investigated. That's between me and you, strictly off the record.'

'For?'

'You name it – accepting bribes and favours. Turning a blind eye. I never liked the man, never trusted him, but we could never pin anything on him.'

Sabine nodded, then said, 'And the Canadian?'

'Arrogant. Angry. He's lying about something – but not this.'

'And he's only been in the country six days.'

'So that rules him out as our serial killer.'

'If it's a serial killer.'

Both fell silent, then Sabine spoke. 'And we still don't have her name.'

Vivier moved over to the board where they'd pinned up the photos of the victims and gazed at the picture of Lucy Swann that had been taken at the morgue. Apart from her skin colour and the bruise on her neck she might have been sleeping.

'Someone will miss her,' he said, 'we'll know soon enough.'

Sabine moved to his side and looked at the picture.

'Everyone we meet,' she said, 'those we touch or talk to, then immediately forget. People who see us, when we hardly notice them. None of it matters does it, until…'

'Until it does matter.'

Sabine sighed, 'Sorry, I'm tired, I was trying to say…'

'I knew what you meant and yes, to be honest I don't think any of these men are the one.'

'But?'

'But they tell a story, don't they? A story about her, about who she was and where she went. So at least…'

'At least what?'

Vivier looked at a photo of Lucy taken at the crime scene, was shocked once more at the way she was suspended like a discarded marionette over the filthy drainage ditch.

'So at least we know she didn't fall out of a clear blue sky. She had her road to Calvary and somewhere along that road…'

Vivier and Sabine continued to stand side by side in front of the pin board. There was an understanding between them. It was unspoken. It was to do with work, with a perfectly matched intelligence, a reluctance to jump to easy conclusions. To enter instead the labyrinth of the crime, all the while painstakingly following procedure.

But there was something else too, something physical, but not quite tangible. It was the other's nearness, mere inches away. Vivier shifted his weight from one foot to the other and in doing so his hand brushed the back of Sabine's hand, and she, forgetting where she was, let her fingers ripple smoothly against his.

He withdrew his hand quickly, brought it up to his mouth and coughed uncomfortably.

Sabine folded her arms over her chest again.

'I…' Vivier began, but whatever he had been about to say was interrupted by the telephone suddenly erupting into life.

# Field of Play

Marilyn continued to walk in the direction the old woman had indicated. She no longer expected to see the familiar landmarks along the way, but confidently assumed that this road ran parallel to the one they usually took in the car. She believed herself to be equipped with a fairly accurate internal sense of direction, though Scott often argued with her about this. He fell just short of repeating the cliché (or was it a proven scientific fact) that women couldn't read maps. The street she was walking along was all residential, and it narrowed halfway along, and the houses grew smaller and more cramped. Yet their shutters were freshly painted, the gardens well tended, and the window ledges were graced by boxes of trailing plants with abundant flowers; nasturtium, lobelia and clematis. In some of the houses the blinds had not been drawn and Marilyn glimpsed families sitting around tables, while TV sets sent out flickering multicoloured light, sometimes illuminating a man pouring himself a tumbler of wine from an outsized plastic bottle, or a woman hunched over a sink or children moving about in some strangely jerky rapid game. There was the scent of honeysuckle in the air, then onions, then the rinsed-earth scent of just-watered plants, then fish, then meat, then onions, petrol, garlic.

Two or three times cars passed, going down the street, with as few coming back up it. A boy on a bicycle whizzed by, he was pedalling furiously, his body raised off the seat, the front wheel wobbling slightly, his face rapt, in a storm of determination as if he were dreaming of the finish line at the Tour de France.

Marilyn thought guiltily of Aaron locked in the house, and yet she was glad to be out here on the street, taking action. Aaron would be okay. Scott would be okay, it was all some dumb error, a case of mistaken identity. Something to do with the hire car probably, all easily explained once the full picture emerged.

A little way ahead Marilyn saw a break in the line of houses on the right-hand side of the road. There was a long low wooden fence and beyond it open ground and a few trees. As she drew closer she heard the sounds of loud and excited voices, the rise and fall of laughter, the clunk and ringing sounds of metal moving against metal.

Set back from the pavement by ten or so yards was a children's playground, but as with such spaces everywhere, nightfall had driven away the younger children for whom it was intended and replaced them with a tribe of older kids; young teenagers who lolled against the slides and swings smoking illicit cigarettes, or raced BMX bikes, or used the play equipment's sturdy structures to practise feats of gymnastic skill; standing on the swing seats, then leaping off at the high point or hanging upside down from the cross bar.

There were about fifteen kids in there that she could see, mostly boys, but three or four girls too. Marilyn slowed her pace, then stopped to watch them. In the distance under the cover of the trees she saw that there was yet another boy and girl walking together, heads tipped slightly towards each other suggesting intimacy.

None of them noticed her watching them, so she was able to judge their level of menace. Why is youth always thought to be malevolent, she wondered, why do we bestow upon this in-between age group such levels of mistrust – why do we forget so easily that we were once thirteen, fourteen, fifteen, sixteen, seventeen – with our harmless gangs and cliques, our ripped jeans, our black eyeliner, wild hair, loud voices, our raging hormones, and countless insecurities deftly hidden by insolent stares. Not every kid in a tracksuit or with jeans hanging halfway down his ass to reveal designer underwear was a stoner, a mugger, a rapist. And besides, the nature of the playground's location, the proximity of those neat little homes, the smallness of the town, its quaint European charms, its resistance to the taint of urban blight and alienation, all spelled innocence.

Confidently Marilyn stepped over the low fence and began to walk directly towards the nearest group of teenagers. A few of them now noticed her, one boy nudged another in warning and something was quickly hidden behind a back.

*'Excusez moi, ou est le Hotel de Ville?'* Marilyn called, as soon as she was within earshot.

'Huh?' one of the boys said. He was the one with his hand behind his back.

Marilyn repeated her question, aware of the obviousness of her bad accent.

'Huh? Wha?' the boy said, his expression was playful, exaggerated. Then in a perfect imitation of a line from a rap song, he said, 'Waasup?' and shrugging his shoulders he shook out his hands in that distinctive way the gangsta rappers from Compton or Watts in L.A. did.

One of the girls giggled.

Marilyn had a sudden intimation of threat, she had misjudged the situation; she began to turn back the way she had come.

*'Vincent!'* A girl's voice cut through the crisp night air, it was schoolmarmish, scolding, then it changed, became pleasant, reasonable. *'Madame? Madame!'*

Marilyn turned. One of the girls had stepped forward from the group. She was exquisitely beautiful, with shining dark hair in tumbling corkscrew curls framing her fine-boned face. She might have been thirteen or seventeen, it was hard to tell, but she was confident, her gaze suggesting maturity and concern. The concern was for Marilyn and spoke of a sisterly understanding of the world.

'Are you lost?' she said in carefully modulated English.

'You speak English?' Marilyn asked.

Proudly the girl nodded, then lifted her hand to indicate a small pinch of air between her thumb and forefinger.

'The Hotel de Ville? Near the police headquarters? I need to get there,' Marilyn said.

The girl nodded, then pointed in the direction of the trees beyond the play equipment. As Marilyn looked towards the place indicated she saw that the young boy and girl who had been standing apart were now moving forward to rejoin the main group, alerted somehow by the quietness and stillness that Marilyn's presence had caused.

'Oh!' Marilyn said, uncertainly. She could see nothing beyond the black shapes of the trees, no lights, only indistinct greyness.

This was difficult. She had asked the way and they had answered, but to set off into that unknown darkness seemed folly. She shook her head, aware of the audience that now surrounded her.

Several of them nodded emphatically 'yes' and pointed into the furthest reaches of the park as the girl had done.

Marilyn shook her head. 'Non, non. Too dark. Is there another way?'

Again several enthusiastically jabbed hands and fingers pointed at the black void.

'Ah!' the pretty girl said at last. 'You are scared? No worry. It is okay. We'll walk with you.'

'Hey, Vincent!' she called, and when he stepped forward she spoke in rapid French to him and another girl. Then she set off towards the trees beckoning Marilyn forward with a broad circling gesture of her arm. Vincent and the other girl also set off, falling into step beside them and turning their faces towards Marilyn, smiling pleasantly, nodding in friendly encouragement and inviting her to trust them.

Two girls and a single boy.

Marilyn would not have followed three teenage boys into the darkest corner of the woods. Two boys and a girl might have tipped the balance slightly. But two girls and a lone boy decided her. She threw up her hands, shook her head as if shaking off her own silliness and mistrust then hurried forward to catch up with them. The two girls had already linked arms with one another and as Marilyn drew level her arm was linked too.

Oh, how long it had been since Marilyn had walked companionably arm-in-arm with another female? Not since the age of ten or eleven when some boys had pointed at her and her best friend and called them lesbians. She hadn't quite understood what it meant, but there was something ugly about the way it was said and her friend had instantly pulled her arm away. End of.

The boy called Vincent trailed along on the outer edge of the group with a slightly self-conscious swagger. Then without warning or reason, he suddenly took a running leap and ripped a longish branch from one of the trees. He then proceeded to rip off all the smaller stems and the abundant leaves until he had produced a four-foot-long switch which he used to swipe at the long grass, occasionally beheading stalky, high-growing weeds.

'Tsk,' the beautiful girl at Marilyn's side said. 'Stop the killing, Vincent, *mon amour!*'

Vincent scowled, but complying, flung the branch away. It whistled faintly as it spun through the air before it landed soundlessly in the distant undergrowth.

Soon Marilyn saw the trees thinning out and beyond them high aluminium fencing with industrial-looking buildings behind. They veered to the right-hand side of the downward-sloping sward where an open gate led to a narrow lane. Halfway along the lane was a single street lamp that cast a yellow pool of dim light.

# A Jealous Ghost

Suzette paced the room. She had cried fitfully for hours it seemed and now she was all cried out. There were two versions of truth that she had to consider, one was that Florian was a murderer, the other was that Bertrand Severin was back. What had said to her once, long ago? *If I can't have you, no one will.* Had his words frightened her then? Vaguely she seemed to remember they hadn't, she had taken them as an expression of his passion for her. Meaningless. *Like I'd do anything for you.* Or *you are the world for me.* Eventually she'd taken it for nothing but extravagant bullshit.

She'd never promised him anything and while he was still married she had presumed that she was free to pursue other lovers. Not that she had. Then he had left. Just at the point when the scales were beginning to fall from her eyes and she had begun to grow frightened of him.

Florian wasn't a killer. He lived a little beyond the law, but a killer? Yet how well did she know him? These truths sat uncomfortably side by side, each depended upon her judgement of the characters of two men. If she had been wrong about Severin she could also be wrong about Florian. A statue symbolising justice came to mind, a female figure holding a balance in one hand, a sword in the other, but her eyes were blindfolded. Suzette never understood that, to know the truth one must see everything.

Florian was innocent.

She was going mad. He was innocent. He'd been set up.

Nothing was real. There was nothing outside this room. Nothing.

She picked up a handful of money and jammed it into the

pocket of her jeans, then made her way over to the bar. Nothing was more real than the bar. The night air was refreshing, cool on her burning red-rimmed eyes. They would know she'd been crying. Not that it mattered.

She turned a corner and there it was. A few customers sat outside, inside she could see the familiar figures behind the bar. Then her eye caught sight of him. He was sitting with his back to the window, hunched over a table, shoulders bristling with angry muscle, the thick neck bullish, like the man. Severin.

She stopped walking, moved sideways to a doorway, stared and stared. It was him. It couldn't be him. It could. It was. It explained everything. Where else would he go to collect his prize, his possession? *If I can't have you, no one will.*

She turned back the way she had come, walked briskly, hugging the walls and shop fronts, shrinking from what she imagined was the searchlight of his gaze.

# Into the Shadows

'Here,' said the girl and she let go of Marilyn's arm.

Marilyn looked down the lane hoping to see an immediate sign of either the *boule* green or the Hotel de Ville or the police headquarters, but the lane sloped away downhill and at its end seemed to drop out of sight completely. Marilyn guessed there must be steps there.

She hesitated.

'Down there, turn…' the girl sought the English word, but failing to find it reverted to French and a hand gesture. 'OK?'

Marilyn wavered, she was on the brink of moving off and yet she wanted to be certain of her direction. Of her safety also, as she did not like the look of the narrow lane.

But the three teenagers were already losing interest and turning away. Vincent had thrown his arm around the prettiest girl's neck and was steering her off.

'*Au revoir,*' the girl called happily, turning her head and smiling, confident of her kindness.

Marilyn began down the lane, after a few steps she turned back to take a last look at the three young people, but they had already gone, vanishing quickly into the clotted shadows under the trees.

She walked briskly. On either side of the path there were high walls, to her left was one built from dirty grey breezeblocks, while the one to her right was brick and looked much older. Moss gathered on the outer edges of the path, as well as brambles and nettles and tall orchid-like flowers that must have been weeds of some sort. Above the breeze-block wall there loomed an ugly 1960s' steel and panel construction building with boarded-up windows. It might have been a small factory or office or school, but it seemed to have deteriorated rapidly, even in the dim light Marilyn could make out large shadowy stains streaking the building's side. She could not see much over the brick wall on the other side as it was taller and whatever buildings were behind it must have been some distance away.

It seemed unnaturally quiet where she was, her own footfalls barely made a noise, and she could hear the sounds of her clothing rubbing and rustling with her every movement. She was aware too of her breathing which she realised sounded a little strained and noisy as if she were exerting herself by running on a treadmill or up too many flights of stairs. There again the moment became like one in a film; a lone woman walking at night down a badly lit alleyway; the soundtrack would emphasise her breathing, it would alert the audience to her vulnerability. A more clichéd film would add a resonating heartbeat.

Stop thinking like this, she commanded herself, stop it.

By now part of her wanted to break into a run, but resisting this impulse, she walked more briskly until she came to the top of the steps. She looked back once; the lane was empty behind her, as she knew it would be. The steep steps leading down were also empty. They were dimly lit, but in the distance, partly obscured by a filigree of leaves and branches, was another streetlamp, promising a broader, more populated avenue.

She descended the steps quickly and cautiously. She had moved away from the first streetlamp whose light had been localised and meagre so she couldn't see where she was going and the steps were uneven. Far off she heard a dog barking, suddenly and furiously.

Ten more paces and she was out of the alleyway onto the street. The road she found herself on was narrow and quiet. A number of vans and lorries, all of them with black and saffron-coloured liveries that bore the same inscrutable geometric logo, were parked in front of the concrete industrial building. Like wasps crawling over an abandoned picnic table.

There were no residential buildings that she could see. To the right, bounded on both sides by trees, the road disappeared in a sharp, uphill curve which she figured must lead back in the direction she had come. But the girl had instructed her to turn right. Marilyn pictured the girl smiling; so pleased with herself and so earnest, saying *'droit'* and indicating with her slim elegant hand a right-hand turn. To the left the road swept away downhill towards a more brightly illuminated area where there must be more houses and perhaps shops and bars.

A number of cars passed, a van, one motorbike.

Marilyn moved to the edge of the pavement considering her choices. She should go right following the girl's directions. She had no reason to doubt the girl and yet it just didn't seem to make sense.

Some people had difficulty with left and right, even people with high intelligence who are able to deal with the most complicated of facts, theories, debates, science. A lecturer who had taught her years ago could effortlessly quote entire poems, everything from Spenser's *The Faerie Queen* to Eliot to Seamus Heaney and Billy Collins; his knowledge was frightening, encyclopedic, and yet he mixed up left and right. He drew attention to his muddle-headedness, even telling the class how that morning he was late because he had lost his car keys, had searched high and low, then eventually found them in his microwave oven. So there was a chance, a very small chance, that the girl had made a mistake.

As Marilyn pondered her dilemma, (looking from left to right and slowly coming to the conclusion that she should go left, then at the first sign of a shop or someone on foot, she would ask for directions again) she noticed that directly opposite was another lane which, except for the interruption of the road, seemed to lead on from the lane she had emerged from. Inside the entrance to the second alleyway was an old fashioned street lamp with a curled neck like a shepherd's crook. It gave the scene an aspect of enchantment. Marilyn crossed the road and looked down this new lane. It was much shorter than the other, with another set of steps. She could see how in the young girl's mind the two lanes separated by a narrow road merged into one. You might be so used to taking this route, focusing on your destination, moving on automatic pilot that you would no longer think about or notice the road dividing it, and would forget to mention it to a stranger.

Less than twenty yards down the second lane was another crook-necked street lamp the same as the first, though its light seemed whiter and brighter, the hedges and shrubs beneath it were as green and glossy as if it were daylight.

She had hesitated long enough, she decided, and without another thought, Marilyn set off down the second alleyway. She was aware once more of the different effect this place had on sound, bordered as it was on two sides by high walls. Her breathing once more seemed amplified, and she heard, almost against her will, her barely perceptible footsteps and the swish of her clothes.

She remembered one of the lines she'd added to her poem, just before she left the house, 'But I am only paper, mother.' Paper mother – no comma and the meaning changed.

She stepped on something that snapped loudly underfoot.

Damn it, she would remember this, take this orchestra of sound and emotion and light and shade and remake it anew on a later date. Make it a poem.

She was only ten yards from the end of the lane with its stark, almost dazzling blaze of white light when a man suddenly appeared, as if from nowhere.

He had obviously been walking along the road which the lane led onto and had turned quickly and confidently up the alley. A tall, thin man (she had no doubt it was a man) dressed in a short black jacket such as a workman would wear.

Marilyn gasped. An audible sharp intake of breath speaking clearly of her fright, which caused the man to become as suddenly aware of her as she had been of him. The light was now behind him, but she saw recognition register in him, something in the forward slouch of his shoulders changed, stiffened, his head tilted upwards. She could not see his face, but knew instinctively that he saw her clearly and had all the advantage in that.

Self-consciously looking beyond him to the end of the lane, Marilyn continued to walk briskly forward, just as he continued towards her.

To pass a stranger, even a stranger in a narrow lane at night, all one had to do, all one was meant to do was to act as if they did not exist. How many thousands of individuals do we pass day by day, our paths like threads, twisting and turning, moving one step to the left or right to negotiate those in our path and hardly ever (unlike cars) colliding. Barely seeing or recognising one another. Deliberately keeping one's gaze away, avoiding eye contact.

The lane was narrow, but there was easily enough room for Marilyn and the man to slip past one another.

She walked on. Not looking, not looking. Or rather only looking towards the distant space that was her destination; the end of the lane beyond the blaze of light. Everything else was absorbed only through her peripheral vision. The figure of a man dressed in a black jacket. A jacket at first glance, like a squarely cut workman's coat, broad-shouldered, thigh-length, then she noticed that it wasn't black, but navy blue, double-breasted, stylishly tailored.

The main thing was not to look at his face. To look in a man's face; to meet his eyes was to suggest engagement, it was an invitation. The woman must set her face so that no emotions were betrayed. Do not smile. Do not show fear. The face must be a detached stoical mask. Even if she is certain she is being scrutinised, gazed at boldly.

All of this, the flood of thought in the seconds between seeing the man and plunging on forward down the lane which is bounded on both sides by high walls and is well lit.

Eyes fixed on the distance, two legs scissoring sharply, her breathing once again becoming rapid and shallow.

All of it happening so fast.

Three of her strides and two of his (he is faster, his legs longer) and she should be past him.

There is a sort of rush of wind, not wind but the velocity of two objects going in opposite directions, each pressing, pushing, agitating the air.

Or not wind but the rustle of his clothes, her clothes. Or her breath, loud suddenly, magnified by effort, by fear.

Or his breath. His heavy breath. Asthmatic. Laboured breath. The lungs pulling hard in preparation for action. His ribs opening like wings.

A rush then, of something, a near object in a narrow space, an object far larger than her. Her eyes off somewhere, but noticing that the coat is a pea jacket. Yes, that is the name for this sort of garment.

And then she is knocked sideways.

The sickening body-jarring thud of his shoulder striking hers. The massive force of it – a shock. She staggers – she was mid-stride, half off-balance anyway and so her left ankle bends, her left shoulder hits the wall with as much force as her right received when the man barged into her. The same force, but this one sharper, against a solid object: a crack, the wind knocked out of her with a word half-formed on her tongue. The word an exclamation, oh!

What was she trying to say? Ow? Or ouch? But it's not really one of those silly words, it's just a sound.

Her knees buckle and she goes down, her body twisting and folding, arms raised to catch at something, anything to stop herself. Her left hip strikes the stone path, bearing all of her weight, carrying all the velocity of her movement, all the suck of gravity, and her head rolls back and hits the wall. The explosion of pain is familiar, there is a sharp, cracking, brittle quality to it.

Automatically, she scrambles to right herself, to get back on her feet and continue on down the lane to the destination she has been so focused on. But she is a twist of awkward, boneless weight, stars sparkling before her eyes as if to prove that those cartoons in her childhood were not merely imaginative in their visual tropes and clichés.

She scrambles inelegantly, the brick wall offers no purchase and she feels heavy and weak.

For a second or two she has forgotten the man, forgotten how this happened. Or perhaps she assumed, (as much as a thought process as complicated as assuming: assessing, analyzing, guessing, assimilating knowledge of past, present, future and strategising can be said to happen in such circumstances) that he, like a machine, a steam engine, a rolling rock, a falling boulder, a charging bear, a stampeding horse has continued on his way barely noticing the small obstacle now sprawling in his wake.

Failing to right herself, she half-twists around, pushes herself forward so she's on her hands and knees, like a dog. She is self-consciously aware of this humiliating pose, of how stupid she must look. Then she draws one leg up, so her foot is now flat on the ground, and her pose is like that of a runner on the block and her head is beginning to clear.

She sees a disembodied foot out of the corner of her eye. A foot in a white trainer with a trim consisting of several narrow stripes in navy. A leg too, unsurprisingly. Dark denim trousers, the dye thick and rich, midnight blue, brand new, unwashed as yet.

She begins to push, to heave herself upright and when she is halfway there (when she no longer needs help) a hand is wrapped around her upper arm, another around her elbow and she is carried upward a little faster and more violently than she might have expected. She sways giddily, lurches forward towards him.

'Oop la!' he says in a sing songy way.

Such kindness.

'Oh!' she says. 'Oh.' The poet with only one vowel sound in her vocabulary to mark this moment.

He is still holding her arm with both hands.

'Oh,' she says again and registers the signals of pain coming from various parts of her body; her ankle, her hip, both shoulders, her head.

'Oh.'

He is bending towards her, leaning in, adopting an attitude of concern.

She senses something wet and warm on her forehead, a trickle, a tickle of movement across the skin above her eye. She reaches up with her free hand to touch the place. Her hand which is trembling now and thus clumsy, jerks tentatively at the place where she feels the wet seep. The pads of her fingers touch something warm and sticky. She tastes iron on her tongue. Or perhaps she smells it, smells blood and fear and shock.

Her hand fidgets away from her head, and she holds it in front of her face so that she might see the blood-dipped fingertips.

He is standing too close.

He lets go of her elbow, takes hold of her upraised wrist and lowers it from her sight.

'Non, non, non, non,' he instructs her in a breathy whisper.

She looks at him now. His face looming over hers, too near, almost out of focus. A long face, the light striking one side of it, deep eye sockets. His breath hot and moist on her face, mint toothpaste that almost smells cold. Also perfume smells, a sharp grapefruity cologne. Flecks of dry skin in his eyebrows.

'Non, non, non,' he shakes his head, clucks his tongue against the roof of his mouth.

Slowly he lets go of her wrist (though his other hand still encircles her upper arm, the grip, firm, unrelenting) and brings his hand up to her head.

'Non, non, non, non.' He draws his fingers over her face, brushing her hair away, first from the wound, then in a more general way, lifting a single stray hair and replacing it. All the time staring intently as if he is inspecting her. As if he were a doctor, or more disturbingly, a hairdresser or perhaps a sculptor making her anew, improving her to his standards. Then he began stroking her hair, smoothing it in place, leaning in closer, closer.

She did not like the repetitive pressure of his fingers on her head, the side of her face. She suddenly realised it was not comfort, it was nothing to do with her injury, with tending the wound, it was just what he wanted to do.

She was recovering by degrees, absorbing more fully what had happened, what was happening, what might happen.

And all the time he was stroking, stroking her hair.

His 'non, non, non' had mutated into rhythmic murmuring, 'hmm, mm, mm.'

Enough, she thought and jerked her head away from the relentless stroking. 'I'm…' she managed to say, but the movement of her head had been too sudden, too fierce, and she lurched unsteadily, giddy, her head swimming in a galaxy of stars again.

'Sit,' he said in English, his voice becoming more assertive suddenly, as he forced her down, pulling on one arm, pushing down on her shoulder until she was in a squatting position with her back against the wall.

'No, I don't want to sit. I need…'

'Anglais?' he had squatted as he forced her down, so that he was now resting on his haunches. Both of his hands remained in place, the one gripping her arm, the other pushing her shoulder back and down.

'Just let me…' She began the frantic scrambling with her legs again. Useless with him holding her in place, his greater height and strength all giving him the advantage.

'Non!' he said sternly and in one quick movement he had pushed her down sideways, so that she was lying on the path against the wall. His knee and lower leg were pressed across her thighs, his left arm was pinning her right arm down and with the same hand he held her other wrist. She struggled in earnest now, grunting a low guttural, 'No.'

With his free hand he pointed at her face, a warning. His nails, she saw, were bitten and ragged, the skin around the fleshy pads raw and blood-spotted.

'Non!' he growled.

She was almost completely mute. When does the screaming begin? When?

First comes appeasement.

'Sorry,' she said, then blinked slowly, swallowed. Mouth dry, heart thumping. 'Sorry.'

This seems to please him, he begins to brush stray hairs from her face again.

She looks at him, then looks away, looks at him again

His eyes move over her face, from her mouth to her eyes, to her neck to her forehead.

She tries to tune him out. To tune herself out. To remove herself mentally from this place. But there is no place she can send herself to. No past, no future. Only this.

He strokes her hair, her hair, her hair. The same place obsessively, so that it almost hurts.

Stop it, a voice locked inside her head says, stop it, stop it!

'Please,' she says in a whisper.

He strokes her face, then brings his hand down so that it is lightly resting on her throat, the thumb under her jaw, the heel of his hand on her Adam's apple, his fingers curling towards the back of her neck. She has a very little neck, like … who was it?

Was it Anne Boleyn or Lady Jane Gray who mentioned this fact helpfully to her executioner? Marilyn knows this because of the man she was seeing before she began dating Scott; he had playfully measured her neck with his hands and mentioned the murdered queen, then, ever the braggart, had quoted a poem he had written on the subject.

This was different. She felt the threat of this stranger's hand, even though his touch was gentle. To scream now would cause the hand to tighten.

She thought of the baby.

If she died now, then so would the baby.

Tears sprang to her eyes. Her mouth distorted, she whimpered, not meaning to.

The hand around her throat, the fingers and thumb moving slightly were either attempting something like a caress, or they were testing her neck, measuring the job in hand (literally) or else it was she herself who was being tested in order to discover the measure of her willingness to submit.

The tears spilled from her eyes, burned as if they were caustic, were made of some unknown chemical compound that might act as a primitive animal defence against attack, a bee sting, a snake bite, the hot stink of a skunk, the black, veil-like release of squid ink in water.

He was making those 'mm, mm, mm' sounds again, breathing deeply as if immensely satisfied by this pleasurable moment.

It was ridiculous to find herself lying down on a public path with this man holding her down, pinning her arms and legs as he casually played his fingers over her neck, while she did not scream or fight, but merely succumbed to his power.

She blinked and tried to focus beyond him; the street lamp seen through tear-blurred vision gave off long rays of light like a pale yellow star. Above it the mesh of leaves and branches revealed glimpses of an indigo sky and a waning moon.

417

What did he want?

If she knew she could provide it, pretend it.

Sex? Was that it?

Power?

Love? .

She could only acquiesce. Should she make those same mewling 'mm, mm' noises he was making, so that he would think they were in accord; that she chose to lie here on this filthy ground, that this was something she wanted?

She saw now that he must have barrelled into her deliberately, knocking her sideways into the wall with tremendous force, and understood that her confusion in the first minutes after (because it seemed as if what had happened was accidental and he was helping her) had stopped her from fighting, running, screaming.

But then she had been shocked, shaken, probably concussed and unable to think straight.

He took his hand from her throat at last.

Good, she had been wise to just allow it, to neither struggle nor pretend desire.

But now he was unbuttoning her dress. Or trying to rather, as one-handed, the row of tiny seed buttons was almost impossible to undo. He was painstaking however.

When he had managed to unbutton three, he stopped and smiled at her. A stupid dreamy lunatic grin.

Marilyn attempted a responding smile, but her mouth (she could feel the various small muscles and tendons quiver and twitch with the effort) only drew itself down at the corners in a hideous grimace.

He loosened his grip on her wrist and relaxed the pressure on her other arm, then as if he were adjusting a shop mannequin he jerked both her arms above her head and somehow gathered both her wrists in one hand and held them there. He shifted position so that one knee was holding her wrists in place while his other knee was on her thighs. His groin was thus aimed at her face The back of her left hand was pressed hard into the stone path. Marilyn could feel several small sharp objects, stones or pieces of broken glass, digging painfully into her skin, but he wasn't really hurting her. Not since the initial body blow anyway.

She was doing the right thing then. No noise, no taut bucking or desperate wriggling to escape, no pretence of any pleasure.

He probably hated women. Hated them and also feared them, except as now when he had all the power.

He was not hurting her now.

He was smiling. She had pleased him. Perhaps he had noticed the tears and they had made him smile.

No, he was not hurting her.

His knee and lower leg were pressed, bony and hard across her thighs, the weight of his body was concentrated there and also into her crushed, crossed wrists above her head.

He tried another button. This one a few inches down from her breastbone. The stupid row of stupid little buttons – details she had loved about this dress – thirty or more tiny pearl-coloured buttons that nestled tight in their minute button holes. When dressing or undressing she only ever undid the top four before she lifted the loose-fitting dress easily on or off her head.

He fiddled and tugged at this stubborn button, pressing down hard with his fingers at one point in order to free it.

She could say, 'let me', but what French she had once possessed had flown and scattered, as if her mind had expunged all superfluous knowledge in order to concentrate on only this – this pitiless moment in hell.

No, he wasn't hurting her. He had pinioned her. Her hands and legs were trapped. She would be bruised, badly bruised, but she would heal.

Except he was hurting her by making her an accomplice to her own rape. This was the sort of hurt which would lodge itself inside her marrow. Tears, broken bones, puncture wounds might heal, but this silence, this giving in, giving it up, giving it away would hurt forever.

This button, every button, would take a lifetime to undo. He was onto the fifth or sixth now. The sun would rise before he was done. Her fingers were growing numb and cold, the circulation cut off by his weight. Her legs too, jammed flat out with his kneeling weight across her thighs so that it was impossible to do anything other than wiggle her ankles.

The painstaking work on the damn buttons. She wished he would hurry, hurry. Get on with it. Undo the buttons quickly. Rape her more efficiently so they could be done with it.

Her thoughts now became perverse. The question of why, having so violently hurt her at first, he would then so slowly and delicately, without ripping her dress, attempt to undo the buttons seemed absurd. Perhaps he did not want to rape her at all, perhaps his thing was buttons!

She almost laughed, though it came out a painful half sob, half grunt.

He looked at her face suspiciously, enquiringly, as if he had only just remembered she was there. As if she were a dog that suddenly answered her master back.

'Sorry,' she whispered, surprised to hear how her voice had acquired a dry rasping croak.

He frowned, his face growing dark. Marilyn looked away quickly and as she did, he suddenly tore at the dress, ripped it hard and violently so that she felt the fabric burn at her shoulder and underarm.

She cried out in fear and pain. But even then it wasn't a scream, not the deliberate alarm call of distress, only a response.

But it was enough. Something had changed.

He was still for a moment, breathing more heavily than before. She knew he was staring at her, considering what he might do.

She began to tremble uncontrollably, to spasmodically twitch and jerk as if she were in the throes of an epileptic fit. She wanted to say something – to find some words that could reach him, make him see her. But she was shuddering, her teeth chattering, every nerve quivering. I should tell him about the baby, she thought.

She saw the shadow of something fly across the field of yellow light just beyond his head, then she saw no more.

# Pastoral

Vincent and Katherine had stayed in the playground long after the others had gone – some sloping off to the café with the pinball machine and the one-armed bandit – others to go home because they had to or even wanted to. Vincent had rolled a spliff (he'd cadged a bit of Moroccan from his brother Dennis) which he shared with Katherine as they sat on the slowly moving roundabout. The night turned around them, the thin sliver of moon rotated on its axis, the warm wind caressed their skin.

Summer nights, the sort that seem endless, this one giddy, but in the sweetest possible way. Giddy with the spinning of the ride and their heads arched upward to share a whirling vision of the sky, and the richly perfumed scent of the hashish, sucked at, then held in the lungs and breathed out leaving that light-headed, skin-tingling dreamy aimlessness in its wake. And there was another source of new sensation too; Vincent had taken a long toke on the spliff and offered Katherine his mouth, sealing his lips over hers and breathing the smoke into her mouth. Not a kiss, but a prelude to it, an excuse.

Their first time alone together and they'd had to wait so long for everyone else to go. Some of the boys stubbornly nagging Vincent to join them at the café, too stupid to see that he had better things to do right then. And Katherine's best friend, Juliette, hovering by her side, reminding her of the recent murder, telling her to take care, to not walk home alone. Vincent saying, 'It's cool, chill, she's with me.'

Then Katherine had lain back on the wooden floor of the ride and Vincent had pushed it hard to set it spinning, then leapt on board and lain down beside her so that their heads lolled together and their feet (his especially) dangled off the edge of the roundabout.

They had talked about the moon and the stars. Stupid nonsense talk about aliens, werewolves, vampires. Meteors that, hurtling through space, might hit the earth, wipe out the human race just like the one that had destroyed the dinosaurs.

'What about the animals?' Katherine has said.

'All kaput,' Vincent said.

'God, really all of them?'

'Yep. Oh, except maybe cockroaches.'

'Yuk.'

'Oh, and me and you.'

'Yeah?'

'Yeah. This place,' he waved his hand airily. 'This is the one place where anyone can survive.'

'Oh, yeah? How come?'

'You don't believe me?' He raised himself on one elbow in order to look at her face.

'Yeah, I do,' she said slowly. 'When's it going to happen?'

Vincent made a show of looking at his wrist as if there was a watch there. 'Five minutes?'

'Oh. No time to get my cat then?'

'No, but there's time for this,' he whispered and lowered his face to hers to kiss her quickly on the mouth.

'What if we don't survive?' she said and boldly put her hand on his neck, pulling him to her for her first (last) real kiss.

The roundabout slowed down, its faint creaking and rumbling stopped. The silence was punctuated by the high-pitched calls of bats. An owl hooted. Katherine and Vincent's mouths made wet noises. They wrapped their arms around each other, intertwined their legs. He did not try to touch her breasts or wriggle his hands inside her clothing (though those thoughts occurred to him) but just kissed her and was kissed.

Scraps of thin pale cloud drifted across the moon. He breathed in the apple-fresh scent of her hair. Opened his eyes once or twice to find hers shut, her lashes thick and dark, her eyebrows raised slightly in what must be pleasure. Then a new sound could be faintly heard. It was distant, but getting closer and louder.

The sound of someone running, of footsteps falling hard and rapidly and the loud, laboured breathing of someone or something exerting itself. The noise coming fast along the worn, hard earth that made a rough path from the lower gate, up through the trees towards the play area and the roundabout.

Vincent heard it first. He lifted his head.

'Hey,' Katherine said, blinking with surprise.

'Shh … listen.'

They stayed where they were, prone, but with heads lifted as they strained their ears and eyes to seek out the source of the noise in the darkness.

Then they saw it, a fleeting shadow amongst the solid vertical blacks of the tree trunks. It lurched from side to side, growing larger, noisier, more defined, more distinctly human as it cleared the trees and emerged into the weak yellow light. A tall figure running with the loping, almost stumbling wildness of exhaustion, or panic.

He was not heading for them but running in a diagonal direction that cut past the swings just fifteen feet away. He did not see the two figures lying side by side on the running board of the stationary roundabout. Or showed no sign of having seen them anyway.

Just beyond the swings he stopped momentarily. Bent over, hands on knees, his breathing wheezy, like an old leaky bellows, recovering himself. His face in profile, glimmering white with a sheen of greasy-looking sweat, mouth hanging open, a dewdrop of snot glinting under his long nose catching the light.

Then he arched his back, heaving himself erect once more,

pinched his nostrils, then cast off the droplets of moisture from his fingers with a sharp flick of his hand. Wiped the same hand on his trousers, then with the other hand drew his coat sleeve over his face, over his forehead and damp hair. Catching his breath, straightening his jacket, the waistband of his jeans, inhaling deeply through his nose, then out through his mouth, lips pursed as if he might be whistling. Then with a quick look from side to side, he walked towards the open gate, passed through it and sauntered off down the street at an easy pace.

Katherine and Vincent watched his retreating back.

'Creepy,' Katherine said and involuntarily shivered.

Vincent gathered her in closer to his body, rubbed her arm rapidly to make her warmer, 'You cold?' he asked.

'No, I'm okay,' she said, 'it was just him.'

'Bruno?'

'Yeah, he gives me the creeps. He followed me and Juliette all the way home one night last summer. We kept telling him to get lost, but he wouldn't listen. Ugh, he's too old to be hanging around the park with us.'

'Too ugly, too.'

'Just too weird.' Katherine shivered again.

'Don't worry about him, you're with me now,' Vincent said and squeezed her, drawing his shoulders up in a happy, comforting shrug.

Katherine grinned. He kissed the tip of her nose.

'What time is it?'

She freed her arm and looked at her watch, tilting it so that the dim light illuminated the face.

'Ten thirty-seven. Shit! Better go soon.'

'Five minutes,' he said, then kissed her as if to plead his case. 'Five minutes? Then I'll walk you home?'

She nodded, then craned her neck to look in the direction Bruno had gone. Through the trees by the fence she thought she saw a movement, a shadowy black shape that might be him returning, but as she looked more closely she saw it was only the effects of a sudden gust of wind. Wind as warm as breath, gently lifting the tree's broad leaves, then setting them down again.

# Part Five

# AFTER

*Our world has no more events, no more history, no more structure. It is full of signs signifying nothing.*
Charles Penwarden, Artscribe International,
March/April 1989

*When these early people became conscious of their mortality, they created some sort of counter-narrative that enabled them to come to terms with it.*
Karen Armstrong, A Short History of Myth.

Part Five

# AFTER

# The Angel's Share

Scott was led out of the interview room and back down the green-tinged corridor to the reception area. The beautiful woman detective was waiting there. She nodded enigmatically at him, her face betraying little. She was holding a clear plastic sack which seemed to contain certain familiar objects which he at first didn't quite recognise as his own; the charcoal-grey canvas belt with the pewter-coloured buckle that doubled as a bottle opener, the car keys, his wallet and cell phone, the loose change; Euros and Canadian loonies, dimes and nickels. His navy jacket, his watch.

He looked from the bag to the woman's face. It was like a mask, the dark hair in sleek curtains neatly drawn back, the skin pale – though it wasn't as pale as Marilyn's – it was only the mahogany hair that made it seem so. And she had circles under her eyes, shadows where the skin was thin enough to show the veins and arteries, the hollow eye sockets in her skull.

'What's going on?' he asked in English, knowing she could understand the language better than she'd at first let on.

'You're free to go.'

'To go?'

He should have felt relief, but there was nothing inside him. He took the bag from her and saw, lying uppermost, an alien object, a playing card, creased and torn at one corner; the ace of hearts.

'This isn't mine,' he said and at last she showed some emotion, frowning and shaking her head as she read the label attached to the bag.

'These are your belongings.'

'Not this,' Scott said and he pulled out the playing card and laid it face up on the reception desk.

She glanced at it, then shrugged. 'A small mistake. Now, as I said, you're free to go.'

He felt his anger rising.

'Free to go? Free to go! What the ff…' He held the last word back, a habit he'd acquired in formal situations. At work, with his parents, his brother, with Marilyn too, who thought the word ugly and cheap, the sign of a limited vocabulary and lack of imagination.

He took a step closer to the policewoman. She did not flinch.

'You are free to go,' she said again. Then in a gentler pleading tone, added, 'Your wife will be waiting for you.'

He felt his body sag. Marilyn. He was tired.

He sat on one of the benches and threaded the belt into the waistband of his trousers, shrugged on his jacket. He found that he was shaking his head as he did it. Shaking his head in disbelief and breathing noisily through his nose. He put his watch on, distributed his wallet, phone and loose change to various pockets in his trousers and jacket, just as he would in the morning before leaving for work. But he did it self-consciously now, as if he were somehow putting on a disguise.

He stood up, patting his pockets and adjusting the collar of his jacket, while searching his mind for something he should do or say.

The woman was still standing near the reception desk with an elbow resting lightly on it. In her hand was the playing card, which she turned from its face to its back by twirling it in her fingertips, all the while staring at it fixedly.

He turned away, pushed open the exit door and walked slowly across the small parking area out front. He quickened his pace, his long legs taking enormous strides, then like an unlikely bird, a swan or heron, once he had picked up enough speed he spontaneously exploded into a run. And when he reached the house he (surprisingly as there should have been other things on his mind) congratulated himself on his undiminished capacity to sprint over a longish distance without tiring.

The front door had been left on the latch and lights were on in the living room and the kitchen. Quietly he pushed open the first door and took a few paces forward so that he could see over the back of the couch. He expected to find her there asleep, but she wasn't there. He tried the kitchen and she wasn't there either. For once she'd actually gone up to bed instead of waiting up for him. For once she'd been sensible.

He got a glass from the cabinet and opened the bottle of whisky Marilyn had bought in the duty-free as she did every year. A gift for the Clements. Oh well. He poured out a measure and added equal parts of water from the tap. He sipped it slowly, aware of its curative warmth.

He did not sit down – he had spent far too long sitting on hard seats – but leaned against the counter, trying to absorb and dispel all that happened that day and in the days before.

Surveying the room, he noticed that Marilyn had left her notebook lying open near the window by the sink. That was unlike her, she tended to always have it to hand, along with a pen. He'd take it up with him when he went to bed, put it where she usually kept it on the bedside table. He pictured himself doing this, saw in the dimly lit room of his imagination, her hair tumbling over the pillow, bleached of its vivid colour in the dark.

If she woke he'd touch her sleep-warm cheek, tell her how much he loved her, needed her. Ask her, did she know how much he loved her? Did he tell her that enough?

He sensed that he had been punished for his indiscretion with the young woman who'd followed him. There had been no need for him to act the way he had, it would have been easy enough to be kind to her while also explaining in no uncertain terms that he was married and loved his wife. But then he had also been ashamed because of Aaron. His whole life had been blighted in one way or another by Aaron. And he had been attracted to the blonde girl, flattered and confused by the whole situation.

Now he had been punished.

Punished too, for whatever terrible thing it was he had done or tried to do or dreamed of doing, once long ago, to his pathetically vulnerable sibling.

He had enough education and training in psychology to recognise the symptoms and causes and difficulties in his own psyche, yet seeing them, knowing them intimately, did not bring about a cure. His guilt was eternal, because he was the lucky one; the firstborn son who escaped the curse that befell the second child.

He poured another shot of whisky into his glass, didn't add water this time, wanted to feel its burning golden sting. He shouldn't have opened the Scotch. Single malt, aged for twenty years in oak casks. The good stuff.

He'd pretend the liquid had evaporated.

'Mar,' he'd plead when she scolded him, 'it was only the angel's share.' She'd demand to know what that meant and he'd explain that it was the term used to describe the reduction in volume that occurred when whisky was aged.

She'd like that; the idea that something as prosaic as the manufacture of hard liquor could create such a poetic term to describe a merely physical side effect of the process. He smiled, imagining her smile.

He knew he should eat something, but worried it would lay heavily on his stomach. Just whisky. A little whisky to help him sleep.

He left the bottle on the counter, put the glass in the sink and ran cold water into it. He switched off the light, then did the same in the living room. He checked the front door meaning to lock it and discovered that the key was nowhere to be found. This meant that, theoretically, Aaron could go AWOL again, but Scott was too tired now to do anything about it except silently pray that Aaron had learnt his lesson and lightning doesn't strike in the same place twice. Then, wearily, gratefully, he crept quietly up the stairs.

The door to Aaron's room was closed. Usually it was left open a few inches or so, because at certain times Aaron would not open doors for himself – though he was quite capable of doing it – but would stand behind them rocking either from side to side or to and fro. On a couple of occasions, he had done this so violently that his head hammered a slow hollow rhythm on the wooden panel and a yellow-purple bruise spread across his forehead like a stigmata to show his suffering.

Scott opened the door a crack and saw, reflected in the dressing table mirror, the humped shape of Aaron under the white cloud of the duvet. His breathing was heavy and slow with deepest sleep. Faintly, Scott detected the acrid aroma of warm urine.

This, Scott thought, would be the last time. No more trips to France for Aaron. No more trips anywhere – not with him and Marilyn babysitting anyway. There were respite homes for people like him and after a day or two Aaron would get used to it. In this way their parents might also be eased toward the idea of permanent residential care for their youngest child – their lost boy, their borrowed angel.

There it was, that word again, angel. How his mother could conceive of Aaron as an angel of any sort was beyond him, but this is what she said, filtering reality, he supposed, through the Victorian sentimentality of the novels she read; *Anne of Green Gables* and Dickens and Willa Cather and *Little Women* and *Gone With the Wind*. Her favourite films were *Inn of the Seventh Happiness*, *A Tree Grows in Brooklyn* and the one about the little deaf-mute girl, Helen Keller. She cried with all the predictability

433

convention demanded of a woman of her age and generation. Especially when the children were saved and the dedicated teacher at last reached the lonely, silent, dark world the little girl existed in.

But no one had succeeded in reaching Aaron so far and he was not condemned by some rare syndrome or inherited disease to die young. He was healthy and robust, would before long add the muscle, strength and bulk of true manhood to his willowy frame and then what might happen?

Scott crossed the hall to the bathroom. The frosted glass there showed a limpid pinky grey light pressed against it, the sun edging upwards from the eastern horizon, illuminating the distant clouds before it peeped into view.

He splashed cold water on his face avoiding his reflection in the mirror, knowing too well how he would look – exhausted, in need of a shave, guilty.

He dried his hands, picked up Marilyn's notebook from the top of the laundry basket and crossed to their bedroom where the door was (in a reverse of the usual state of affairs) half open. At the threshold he saw at once that the bed was empty, the covers as flat and smooth as becalmed sea. But not believing his eyes, he flicked the light switch on.

Where had she gone? He had felt her presence here, seen her in his mind's eye minutes ago when he rehearsed laying her notebook on the bedside table. He stepped quickly forward and put the book in place as if that act would reset the real events that were happening into the assumed pattern. He looked around the room. The curtains hadn't been drawn and the windows were all shut – nothing but the very worst winter weather or storms made Marilyn and he sleep without a healthy dose of fresh air.

There was a third room upstairs – the Clements' bedroom which, over the years, out of respect for their privacy, Scott and

Marilyn always locked on arrival, placing the key out of sight on the top of the door frame.

That's where she was! Of course, it made sense, she would sleep in the master bedroom, because it was at the front of the house, because the extension phone was there.

He tried the door handle, turning it down then pushing with his shoulder. Locked. He drummed the pads of his fingers on the wood, called softly, 'Mar? Mar! It's me.' Then rattled the handle to indicate his intent.

He tried a second time, increasing the volume of his voice, the weight and speed of his knock, the rattling of the handle.

He dropped to his haunches, put his eye to the keyhole and saw, outlined in tendrils of out of focus dust, the far wall of the room softly lit by weak pinkish light. No key in the lock.

Because.

Because Marilyn…

He tried to finish the end of that thought, even as he heaved himself upright again and stretching, groped with his fingertips along the dusty lintel. He found the key and flying in the face of logic, unlocked and opened the door. The Clements had a beautiful antique bed, carved and painted white, an elaborate armoire, a full length cheval glass, everything one would expect in a sophisticated and well-to-do French couple's home. But it was overlaid with chaos; an untidy pile of *Le Mondes* on the bed, along with mail, box files, a plastic laundry basket filled with clothes and a guitar. Coats were heaped on a low upholstered chair, glossy magazines and paperbacks were stacked in three clumsy towers under the window, a laptop computer sat incongruously on a dressing table surrounded by a silver-backed hand mirror and matching hairbrush. Before leaving for their holiday they had collected all of the detritus of their lives and stored it haphazardly in the one room they knew their visitors never used.

Yet at that moment the room looked ransacked.

He fled, leaving the door open, the key still in the lock. He returned to Aaron's room, creeping in on silent feet, circling the bed and studying the form on the bed, Aaron's face slack on the pillow. No point waking him. No answers there, only another problem to be dealt with, Aaron wanting food, wanting the toilet, not wanting to be washed or shaved. And he'd pissed himself. Closer, the smell was stronger.

Scott ran downstairs again. Flicking on every light in the house, he looked in the living room, the dining room, the kitchen, the cupboard under the stairs. Went out the front door where the hire car was still parked, peered inside its windows hopefully, hopelessly, for why would Marilyn be there?

Then back through the house, searching his memory for rooms he had forgotten existed, secret rooms that led from one to another in a maze, as in certain dreams he'd sometimes had, and wasn't it said that in such dreams the house symbolised the mother?

Into the kitchen again, taking the key for the back door from its hook on the whatnot, fumbling to unlock it, then out to the garden. Night evaporating. Pale grey light, the grass sprinkled with dew, the greenhouse ghostly at the end of the garden. He might find Marilyn inside it, writing, making detailed notes about the delicate white hairs on a heart-shaped leaf, or the wiry tendrils a pea plant wraps around sticks, string, walls, other plants, itself. It would be no surprise to find her there amongst the tomatoes and chillies and cucumbers, sitting cross-legged on a square of cardboard on the floor, her eyes closed so that she could listen more acutely to every sound. The birdsong, the constant distant thrum or roar of something like a river, or traffic, the imperceptible creak of a root growing under the soil, the furious buzz of a drugged bumble bee blundering in the boudoir of a magnificent red poppy.

He studied the greenhouse carefully from where he'd paused near the house; the lawn seemed like a green sea he would struggle to pass. The window at the top had been opened to control the temperature, and the uppermost leaves of a huge tomato plant spilled out of it giving the impression that the plant had forced open the window in a bid to escape.

Deep down he knew Marilyn wouldn't be there and that was why he lingered, postponing the moment when he ran out of places to search for her.

She had once said, and he had laughed, that it hurt her to write. Her expression told him she was in earnest.

'Your hand?' he said, stupidly.

'No.' Then she wouldn't say more, because he had laughed and she took the comment about her hand as sarcasm.

He swayed for a moment on the edge of the path, then stepped onto the grass and crossed to the greenhouse where he peered in through its open door. She wasn't there. Of course she wasn't there.

She had left him, as he'd always known she would. Because he didn't deserve her, because his heart was ice.

# The Love Parade

Gerhardt Miller, feeling virtuous, left his lover in bed in order to walk the dog. How he had found himself in love with Henri, a provincial French schoolmaster, the owner of a toffee-coloured daschund called Proust, was still beyond him. They had met at the Love Parade in Berlin in 2004. Three years of this strange, wonderful, forbidden enchantment, always feeling that he should leave France, return to his birthplace of Cologne and the pretence of heterosexuality. Lonely, unsuccessful heterosexuality. He was a good-looking man. He knew that. Women fell for him. He dated, but nothing stuck.

Proust wriggled his rump with joy as he saw Gerhardt open the drawer where the dog lead was kept, and when Gerhardt bent to attach the lead to the collar he leapt up to lick his face, coating his cheek with fishy smelling slime.

Still holding the lead, with Proust eagerly following, claws clicking over the tiled floor, Gerhardt rinsed his face and dried it with paper towels. They went out through the back door, leaving it unlocked so that he would have no need for keys. Proust strained at the leash and Gerhardt released the catch that let the rein spool out to its full length, so that the dog trotted smartly along, long nose like the tip of an arrow, twenty paces ahead of him. Gerhardt had given up allowing the dog off the lead. Shouting 'Proust! Proust!' was embarrassing – even more so as the dog showed absolutely no sign that this was his name or that he even knew the handsome man with the black hair, five o'clock shadow and baggy green combat pants.

It was just getting light, must have been the first glimmer that woke him, either that or another of his bad dreams, those dreams where he was falling. The recurring nightmares he suffered since he was a child that had got worse after he watched the live coverage of the twin towers on 9/11, and even worse after he'd begun his relationship with Henri. Gerhardt knew why; guilt, fear, shame.

But he was in a buoyant mood as he walked down the tree-lined street, and he remained so even after Proust deposited a large glistening turd on the pavement. He had a plastic bag in his pocket and did not mind the ritual of picking up after the dog, did not mind apart from the warmth of it in his hands through the plastic. There was a bin beside a house nearby and Gerhardt quickly lifted the lid and threw the bag in.

He headed for the short cut, an upward-sloping lane with a few steps that led straight into the park. Usually he'd go through the park and out by its main entrance to the bakery for fresh bread then home again.

He was a good distance away from the turning into the lane when he saw Proust disappear. There was nothing unusual in that, but what was strange was the sudden tug on the leash as the dog pulled harder and the cord rubbed against the brick wall. Taken off guard before he knew it the plastic device that held the lead jumped out of his hand and skittered away along the pavement.

'Proust!' he yelled, then raced to try to catch the flailing lead and its clattering handle, which flew out of sight before he was even six feet away.

'*Ficken!*' he hissed and stopped running. He ran a hand through his hair, shook his head in frustration then continued on towards the lane. It sloped gently up, then there were four concrete steps. Proust was standing at the top of these steps and barked as soon as he saw Gerhardt.

'Good boy,' Gerhardt called and the dog gave another sharp yap. The dog did not wag his tail, but stood squarely on all four legs. The end of the lead with its rectangular box lay on the first step and the nylon cord was curled and draped elaborately over all of the steps, spelling out the journey of circles the dog must have made.

'Good boy,' Gerhardt said again and quickly stooped down to recapture the lead before the dog took off again. He pressed the button that caused the line to rewind, so that the dog would not be able to run out of sight again as easily. He had often thought that Proust could run into the road given such freedom.

'He knows not to do that,' Henri had said, laughing at Gerhardt's utter ignorance when it came to animals.

Gerhardt had never been allowed pets as a child. His mother thought them dirty, his father, a quiet and profoundly good Lutheran pastor in a conservative town near the Swiss border, claimed to be allergic. Henri, on the other hand had grown up on a smallholding with dogs and geese and ducks and goats and cats.

The dog barked again. There was definitely something different about the sound and the way the animal was standing there waiting for him. Gerhardt wondered if the dog wasn't finally going to go for him with his sharp little piranha teeth.

'Good boy. Good boy,' he said soothingly as he drew near and bent to stroke the dog's bony silky head, its long back. He felt around the collar to check that the metal clasp was still attached. He always worried about losing the dog, about it becoming hurt in some way. Henri would not forgive him.

Then he saw her. He should have seen her straight away but he had been so focused on the dog that somehow he missed her. Or perhaps he had seen her but something in his mind had refused to transform the tangle of red hair, the pale battered flesh, the torn dress into a human form. He'd seen her in the corner of his vision down there by the side of the path, weeds growing up behind her, camouflaging her.

And it was only just getting light.

The dog gave another sharp yap, as if they were having a conversation and the animal was winning the point. 'See?' it seemed to be saying. 'See, I told you, but you wouldn't listen.'

She was lying so still. He could not bear to look at her.

Gerhardt moved back and down, pulling the lead hard. On the next step he stumbled a little but righted himself. He turned and hurried back to the street, the dog now running a little ahead of him again, straining at the short leash so that its breathing was rasping and laboured.

Once he was on the street, Gerhardt stopped and clapped one hand over his mouth – a theatrical gesture that was entirely natural and unplanned. He hadn't brought his phone with him, just enough cash for the bread. He felt he should stay where he was, stop other people from going up the path, but how could he inform the authorities if he did that? There was no one else about on the street and on his way he'd seen hardly a soul. He could run home and call from there. Or find a payphone? Or go to the police station itself, which was not very far?

Proust was skittish, running around his legs, tugging at the lead, first one way then another. He couldn't concentrate while the dog was doing that so on impulse he scooped him into his arms and was rewarded by a warning growl, an indignant wriggle and a nipped finger. Roughly he half dropped, half threw the animal down. Another yelp – piqued this time, but the dog stood squarely on all four legs, trembling, but not hurt. Thank God.

He remembered there was a payphone less than ten minutes walk away, on the crossroads outside a closed-down garage. He hurried there, his mind racing, his stomach hollow. He found that his fingers were trembling badly as he fumbled with the coins, the receiver. He dialed the emergency number and kept worrying that his small change would run out before he had said all he had to say. In his agitation he had forgotten that such calls are free.

He was precise with the details he gave of the road, the lane, the position of the body, but when asked for his name he told them it didn't matter; they said it did. He said his name was Jansson. They said they must have his full name. He might have said 'Moomintroll Jansson,' as that is where his imagination had flitted in this abrupt construction of a lie, but he remembered another name in the nick of time. 'Mats Janssen,' he said, inflecting it with the seesaw sound of a Scandinavian, knowing of course, that his accent would never pass as a Frenchman's.

He had been reading Tove Jansson's children's books that summer, persuaded to do so by his older sister, Anna, for their brew of innocence and darkness she'd said, though he'd been unconvinced.

He spelled out the name. 'M-A-T-S J-A-N-S-S-O-N' and promised to go and stand by the entrance to the lane until the police and ambulance came. That done, he walked quickly away from the phone kiosk, leaving a pile of coins on the ledge there, silver coins like those abandoned by Judas.

When he got home, Henri was still asleep. He closed the back door quietly, undid Proust's lead and returned it to its drawer, slipped his feet out of his sandals and put coffee on the stove, then sat on the edge of the settee frowning darkly. Proust retreated to his basket, turning in a circle many times before finally settling down with a sigh and closing his eyes to sleep.

# To See a Whale

It seemed that he had only just put his head on the pillow when the phone rang. He flung his arm out, blindly groping for the light switch, knocking over the glass of milk he had meant to drink before he went to sleep. The phone continued to ring as he wrenched himself upright and, blinking at the darkness, he found the lamp, turned it on, then lifted the receiver.

'Vivier,' he croaked, his voice heavy with sleep.

It was her voice on the other end of the line. 'Sir?'

'Yes.'

He swung his legs out from under the warm bed covers and surveyed the damage created by the falling glass. On the floor by his bed, lying open as he'd left it, was an expensive monograph on Albrecht Durer. Milk sat on the surface of the glossy page in a large opaque pool. The picture illustrated was a superb silverpoint drawing of a man's head and shoulders. Above the folds of his cloth cap was the man's name, Caspar Sturm. Behind him there was a lightly sketched shoreline and turreted buildings and an empty cloudless sky. It was like a photograph in its composition. One could imagine these two men, artist and artisan, standing facing one another as Durer made the drawing, the mild fresh air between them somehow palpable in the drawing.

The spilled milk was like a film of mist occluding the past. Vivier had been reading the book the night before, gazing at this drawing from 1520, then turning back several pages to read the text. Durer had gone to the swamps of Zeeland because he had heard of a great whale beached there, but it was gone before he had a chance to see it. However the swamps were malarial and

Durer contracted a fever, after which he never quite recovered. Eight years later he was dead.

'Another body has been found,' Sabine said. Given the time of day, the words were not unexpected.

Vivier lifted the book and turned it on its side so that the liquid ran off it onto the varnished floorboards, then he set it open on the bed beside him.

'How much do we know? When did this come in?' he said, and pulled a wad of tissues from the pack he kept in a drawer, dabbing them gently over the page, knowing even as he did so that the book was ruined.

'A member of the public rang emergency services at six minutes past six. Reported a dead woman on the lane between the park and rue Cordier.'

He stopped dabbing the page.

'I'm on my way. Get another car around to the park side of the lane too. How soon can you get there?'

'Five minutes, I'm in my car, sir.'

'Alright…'

Sabine was about to hang up when he added, 'Listen. No sirens. Got that?'

'Yes sir.'

# Hotel Rooms

On the seventh day, Elise, the chambermaid at the Hotel Eden in Belle Plage, had been about to gleefully miss room six from her routine again due to the 'Do not disturb' sign on the door. On previous days she had chosen to take a fifteen-minute ciggie break on the roof of the hotel among the sheets and towels on the washing line, instead of cleaning the room. She was meant to tell her boss, Teri if she missed a room so that she could make the time up doing something else – chopping onions in the kitchen or cleaning the toilet in the bar. Yeah, like hell! And no one had caught her skiving up on the roof yet, and she had developed a sort of proprietorial relationship with it – it was her space, no one else's. Teri grew herbs and tomatoes up there and she often took one of the small cherry-red fruits and popped it whole into her mouth. Mine.

Outside room six she hesitated, thinking things over, judging the chances of overdoing her disregard, of getting caught. Seven days was a full week and there might be a new guest due. She stared at the door gauging probability, thinking longingly of her sojourn beneath the blue sky, the cigarette long overdue. She thought about the spoilt bastards inside the room with their bad French and lousy tips, their filth and wet towels and stained sheets. She had come to hate the clientele, because she hated her work. Her only comfort was getting one over on them, on Teri, on the world.

She gazed at the door, the cardboard sign, *Ne pas déranger.* Her gaze dropped to the floor. Movement. A thin grey trail of movement. Ants. A single file of them, busily streaming into the room. She leaned over, studying them more carefully. A column of them going in, another coming out. An army of brainless, thoughtless workers. This was not good.

She knocked on the door, then unlocked it with her master key and peered in. Still occupied, she knew that at a glance. Perfume and lotions on the table in front of the glass. A hair brush, dryer and straighteners. A pretty cotton dressing gown had been thrown limply over the bed. A suitcase on the folding stand and inside the wardrobe several dresses and other items had been carefully hung up. No men's clothes to be seen. An English newspaper in the bin under the table along with a couple of grubby cotton wool balls. She followed the line of ants with her eye. Under the door, along the wall, up the side of the chest of drawers. Tramp, tramp, tramp. Over the top and into a pretty ceramic bowl. To the over-ripe fruit there.

'Hello?' she called, knowing that there was no one there. The bathroom door was open and she could see it was unoccupied. She picked up one of the perfume bottles, read the label and sniffed it. Issey Miyake. Slightly grapefruity and peppery. She dabbed a little on each wrist and behind her ears. Nice.

She looked at the clothes in the cupboard. Very nice clothes. Nothing worn or scruffy. British size 10. Elise was bigger than that, a 44, which would be a 16?

She opened the drawer in the bedside table nearest her: nothing. Then walked around to the other side. Nothing but a piece of silver foil from inside a cigarette packet. She sat on the bed thoughtfully and brought her wrist to her nose to sniff the perfume again. Her eyes were drawn to the suitcase.

All hotel guests are much the same aren't they, she thought, there are things that they never leave in full view, but put in places that are pretty obvious and unlocked. Those zippered pockets inside suitcases, somewhere to put the passport, the loose change from their own country, pound coins or Danish kroner. Elise often took a portion of the coins; just enough to add to her nest egg at home, never enough to be noticed. But as she gazed at this suitcase, she grew increasingly troubled. In a nearby town a young unidentified woman had been murdered. Had this been her room? Were these her things?

Elise locked the door again leaving the 'Do not disturb' sign in place, abandoning her cleaning trolley in the corridor and went down by the back stairs, down, down into the underbelly of the hotel, through its furnace room and laundry and into the kitchen where Teri was smacking the side of a pig with salt as if it were Elise's bare arse.

'Hey!' she said to get his attention. The radio was on, the volume loud enough to drown out her voice. She turned it off and he looked up, angry that someone had dared to touch his radio just as it was playing one of his favourite songs.

Her face told him straightway that something was up. Elise was one of the toughest women he'd ever known – her hard life showed in her gun-metal eyes. She stole things from the hotel – he'd seen her do it – eggs, coffee, bread rolls, sachets of sugar, vegetables, slices of meat, toilet paper. She probably stole from the guests too, though no serious loss had ever been reported. He knew she hid up on the roof, smoking when she should have been working, but with all these things she knew her limit, never took more than could be missed and he paid her less than he should because of what she helped herself to. And reduced her share of the tips. Because of her low pay she felt entitled to cream that little extra. Reparations, she might have called it. They were caught in a dance of cheating and deceit, the pair of them, and could not escape.

But her expression now was something new.

Salt on his hands, gritty between his fingers, he wiped them on his apron.

'What?' he said.

'That woman in the news? The dead one? Unidentified? Room six seems like…'

'What?'

'…like someone left it, left their stuff, never came back…'

# The World, as Learned from Pictures

The night before, and after those first lingering kisses in the playground and walking home arm in arm they had arranged to meet early the next day. In the same park. Very early. At first light or thereabouts. Neither knew what time the sun rose, so they were vague about the time, but not about what they said they would do. His older brother was the captain of a pleasure boat that picked up passengers on the river jetty every two hours and sailed out to sea, around the coast, then back again.

They would get out at the furthest point and spend the day there. Far away from their friends in the town, far from any chores their parents might want them to do. Almost like running away. But not really. His brother lived with an older woman in the town.

'He's cool,' Vincent said.

'You're lucky,' Katherine said.

'Tomorrow.'

'Tomorrow.'

He'd put on a red football shirt first, 'Beckham' written across his shoulder blades. Then he changed his mind, pulled it off and slipped a plain white t-shirt over his head, then grey combat baggies. Changed his mind again and left the house wearing faded jeans with a t-shirt that some kids at school had screen-printed with MC Solaar's photo and the words *Le bien, le mal*. Little plastic baggie of dope in his jeans pocket. Rizlas. Plastic lighter. Tobacco. Money – some. Not much, but just enough. Sunglasses. Tried them on, then discarded them envisioning awkwardness when kissing. Key to the door.

Vincent got to the park first. The streets on the way there had been quiet. The sky, vapour white. He looked around for her. No sign yet. That was cool.

He sat on a swing and rocked himself to and fro until he realised he looked like a kid. Jumped off and ambled over to the roundabout, pushed it into motion without climbing aboard. Paced up and down, around, then went and sat on one of the benches where the mothers always congregated as their children swarmed and squabbled over the play equipment.

There was not a glimmer of doubt in his mind about Katherine showing up. She would. He knew it.

He thought about rolling a spliff. A one skinner. Patted his pocket to check that his contraband was still there.

Sensed someone coming through the entrance to the park. Her. Didn't look up immediately. Stupid grin spreading over his face. Composed himself. Looked up. Not her. Shit! So not her. A man. A *flic*. And just behind him his *flic*-mobile and another *flic* standing by it looking up and down the street. As Vincent watched, the guy outside the park seemed to see him, he hissed some words and the other *flic* turned to see what he wanted.

Vincent pulled the baggy from his pocket and dropped it through the slats of the bench onto the gravel below. He registered its presence there, a square of plastic not much bigger than a postage stamp illustrated with a jolly emerald-green marijuana leaf.

He looked up to see the *flic* on the street pointing at him, the other turning his head in the direction indicated.

Vincent stood up as the policeman started towards him. Going to face danger, leaving danger behind under the bench.

'What are you doing here?'

An elaborate shrug.

'How long you been here?'

'Ten minutes.'

'Name?'

Vincent gave his name.

While this was going on he could see the other *flic* getting some of that special tape the *flics* used for crime scenes and wrapping it around the gate posts, across the entrance.

'So what are you doing here?'

'Meeting my friend.'

'Friend's name?'

He said Katherine's name and as he did she appeared, walking rapidly towards the park and the *flic* who was blocking the way in.

'That's her now.' Instinct made Vincent start off towards her. His upper arm was firmly gripped by a strong hand and he was yanked back.

Katherine must have seen this as he heard her give a little scream.

'Did I say you could go?'

'No, sorry, sir.'

'That's better.'

She was standing with the other *flic*, talking rapidly, gesticulating with her hands; she gestured palms up, fingers splayed, stabbing the air, then dropped one arm limply to her side while with her right arm she pointed at Vincent. She did this in rotation a few times, then gave up and folded her arms in that way that girls do when they are done with something. When they are fed up and belligerent and won't speak or move or listen anymore.

'You got here ten minutes ago?'

'More like fifteen minutes now.'

'What did you do?'

'Huh?' He played for time, thinking about the dope under the bench, thinking about what his parents would say, thinking about being arrested, sent away, his life.

'So you left your house, walked here?'

450

He nodded.

'Then what?'

'I dunno … I just like…' he wondered about saying he'd sat on the swings, but this man, this *flic*, this burly grunt would laugh at him. 'I looked around for Katherine, then I walked around there and sat on the bench.'

'Where did you walk?'

'Just from there,' he pointed to the swings, 'to there, to the bench.'

'See anyone else? Anyone see you?'

'No.'

'Why did you come here?'

'I said, to meet Katherine.'

Saying her name again to this *flic*, standing there being interrogated while she watched, something suddenly welled up in him and he felt himself on the edge of tears.

'I've done nothing,' he wailed, 'let me go.'

The *flic* softened suddenly, his voice was gentle. 'It's alright son. No need to get upset. Come on, we're done.' He guided him back to the entrance and lifted the tape for him to go under. Vincent went meekly to Katherine and stood by her side.

'Park's closed,' the *flic* said gruffly. The boy struggling not to weep, furiously rubbing his eyes, his mouth contorted. The girl, all concern and indignation, put her hand on the boy's back.

'Why?' she said.

'Go on, run along now.'

'I want to know why!' She was fierce. Fierce and beautiful and so young.

'Can't say. Go on, scoot.'

The boy was ready to go, he murmured something to her and grabbing her hand turned to move away. He began to walk, tried pulling her with him. She pulled him back.

'Something's happened, hasn't it?' she said. 'Something bad.'

'Nothing to do with you.'

'Last night. Something happened…'

'Now listen, kid, if you don't scram…'

'We were here,' she said, her eyes wide and glittering with mingled realisation and fear. 'We were here last night. We saw Bruno…' Again she lifted one arm and pointed. She had played the leading role in a Greek tragedy that Vincent had seen a while ago and in it she had stood like this, back erect, head held high and one arm raised, the index finger pointing, accusing. It was when he first noticed her.

'And…' she said, remembering the foreign woman, remembering everything, putting it all together now, seeing a picture she hadn't seen before. '…and before that…' She lowered her arm. She had been pointing to the place where Bruno had emerged last night — it was also the place they had directed the woman to.

'Oh, Vincent,' she said to the boy and gave a little cry.

At this the boy also seemed to remember something.

Both of them began speaking at once.

'Hold it! One at a time,' the *flic* said. 'You.' He nodded at the girl.

She took a breath, then began to speak.

'We were here last night with everyone and this woman came into the park. She was lost. She didn't speak French. Or not much. I can speak a little English. She wanted to know the way to the police station. She, ah, she was frightened to go through the trees there. So we walked with her, showed her the lane. She was nice. She had red hair. She thanked us.' Here the girl faltered again. Another little cry escaped from her lips, a sharp sweet sound in the crystal air. 'Did something happen to her?'

'Just tell us what you remember. Okay?'

She nodded her head vigorously, 'Yes, yes. I'll try. We left her by the top of the lane, we said goodbye. Came back here. The others drifted off, then there was just the two of us. We sat on the roundabout and talked. We lay down to look at the stars. We kissed and then...'

The *flic* raised an eyebrow. Waited.

'We kissed and then we heard this sound. At first we didn't know what it was, an animal crashing through the undergrowth or, or something. Then we could see someone, running out from the trees, breathing heavily, panting. Then he came closer, into the light so we could see him. He didn't see us. He stopped to catch his breath, just there, near the swings. Bruno. Then he walked on and when he was out of hearing I said, "Ugh, Bruno" or something like that. I said, "He's a creep." And then we went home. Vincent walked me to my door and we arranged to meet here this morning.'

The *flic* looked at the boy. 'Is that true? Is that how you remember it?'

He nodded solemnly.

'Either of you over eighteen?'

Both shook their heads.

'Alright. We'll want statements. Have to be at the station with your parents. Okay?'

The girl nodded. The boy said, 'Are we in trouble?'

'No, son. Not unless your parents didn't know what you were up to last night.' He winked and gave a lopsided grin. 'No law against kissing.'

Katherine scowled at him. Her attention was on the red-haired woman.

How could he smile? How dare he smile? That poor woman, they had sent her down the alleyway in the middle of the night. They had waved cheerfully. They – she had felt the glow of being kind and helpful. Of being an adult.

At school they were studying the 1789 Revolution, their teacher liked to talk at length about the miseries and deprivations of the people and the unabashed luxuries of the court. He spoke of causation, of retribution, but one of the books she had seen was illustrated with images of Marie Antoinette, of her before, and then the rough drawing of her in a tumbrel being taken to her execution. Poor woman. In the first picture she was a plump-cheeked and exotic caged bird, a cockatiel or dove; in the second a hastily scribbled, wind-battered crow with a sulky down-turned mouth.

'You would have been peasants,' the teacher said with relish. 'Have no doubt about it. You would have known starvation, disease and unremitting hard work. Your brothers and sisters would have died early, your parents and your children too. Think of that. Think of an ache in your belly when you have had only a mouthful of bread for days. What joy you would have felt to see Madame Guillotine do her work! Hmm?'

A severed head, held aloft by the hair, the neck a spew of tangled vein and sinew, dripping blood. Cheers from the gathered crowd.

She could not help the sympathy she felt for the executed aristocrats.

Now she had inadvertently sent an innocent woman to a terrible fate. She had bundled her into a tumbrel and sent her on her way with a smile and a wave.

One of the policemen took her and Vincent to one of the benches and asked for their parents' phone numbers, then he had gone back to the car to ring them.

No one had said they couldn't talk to each other, but she and Vincent sat in silence.

They watched as people arrived at the entrance to the park and were turned away. Mothers with young children, some in strollers, some walking. As they retreated the children stared longingly at the swings and roundabouts, while the mothers looked hard at her and Vincent, curious as to what those two young people had done, what crime they had committed.

It was not long before she saw a familiar car draw up behind the police vehicle. A pine-green Nissan Almera, her mother at the wheel in her white nurse's uniform. Then, minutes later, a sleek black car joined it.

'It's my dad,' Vincent said.

Their respective parents stood awkwardly and impatiently listening to the policeman for a few minutes. Katherine could see the restlessness in her mother's movements; she was hugging herself and shaking her head, then craning her neck to see her daughter.

The red-haired woman had been only a little younger than her mother. Had been. Past tense. Why would the policeman not tell her what had happened? His refusal was telling in itself. To close the park like that. There was something here. Unseen, but very close.

She glanced over at the trees that hid the lane. People came into the park by that route all the time. They came with their dogs and their children. Others used it as a short cut on the way to work. But no one had come that way this morning so Katherine guessed that somewhere, at the end of the path, there were more policemen with more lengths of plastic tape. And between these two places? Her and Vincent and empty swings and motionless roundabouts and looming trees and silent grass. And death.

Beside her Vincent was sitting with his elbows on his knees and his head in his hands. Tentatively she rested her hand on his thigh. She thought he might respond by holding her hand, but he didn't, he only sat there in his posture of defeat.

'Vincent?' she whispered.

He shook his head, keeping it hidden in his hands.

There was a movement by the entrance, three figures advancing towards them, the policeman, her mother and Vincent's father.

Now it begins. Now it is real, Katherine thought when she saw her mother's expression of mingled fear and relief. She is thinking that it could have been me. Her mother's lower lip is trembling, her brow is furrowed. 'My baby,' she will wail. Then she will squeeze me so tightly that I can hardly breathe. But I will carry this always, this burden, this innocence lost, this shadow of the girl I was once was.

# A Flower Closing

'The cold gets into your bones.' This was an English phrase he'd copied from a novel into a hardcover exercise book. It came to mind now as he found he was shivering. He wasn't sure if it was delayed shock or the onset of flu, but not being a qualified doctor he refrained from diagnosing himself.

So cold. So very cold.

Even though the day had been warm and the evening balmy, throughout the night, sitting on that wooden bench in the windowless room thinking of bad things, he had grown colder and colder.

When they released him, he had walked briskly back to his hotel. Afraid to run. Only guilty men run and he was innocent.

In his room, which suddenly looked different to him; more alien, dirtier, suspect, he put a sweater on over his tracksuit, but felt no warmer. He got into bed fully clothed and wrapped the duvet tightly around himself, but still he felt a chill. It rippled over his skin under his clothes, so that he felt naked.

After they had eaten from the tree of knowledge they knew that they were naked – a cold wind might have had the same effect. Whose God was this, looking down on Joseph with his icy blue eyes? The God of the white man, the missionary, the God who had baptised him Joseph.

Between science and God he hung suspended, waiting for the transit of the moon. Once more he wanted to reverse the clock and undo all that had happened to him, but also to rush forward, away from here to a future when this was a distant memory.

He looked at his hand, the words he had written there as an aid to memory were gone, but he saw them in his mind's eye still;

glottis, epiglottis, larynx. Lowering his hand onto the quilt he turned his head away.

His own hand seemed the symbol of that which suddenly disgusted him. Mankind.

Mankind who created civilisation. Civilisation that begat science that begat medicine that begat diamonds that begat property that begat war that begat rape that begat slavery that begat bombs.

Mankind. That entity which he had meant to dedicate his life to healing, whose pain he had wanted to ease. Mankind who was destroying the world with his greed and mindless cruelty and prejudice.

His eye, roving hopelessly, settled on the wild flowers he had picked the other day. Daisies, pink tinged on the outside and just beginning to unlock their petals to welcome the light.

Plants and insects had been the first subjects of his interest as a child. His grandfather had given him an old magnifying glass, an unused desk diary from 1956 and an old box of 'MEPHISTO' copying pencils. His first drawings had been childish approximations of trees and flowers and animals, but soon the business of classification (not that he would have called it that then) led his drawings to become more precise, more detailed. Then once he began High School and learned more and more about different animal species and their specialisations he was smitten, and being smitten, he was an enthusiastic pupil, guided very happily and very easily into the sciences. Everyone assumed he would study to become a doctor – this being the pinnacle of all ambition for a gifted boy like Joseph.

Joseph considered himself critically; clever, academic, enthusiastic, yes he was all those things and had exam certificates and teachers' reports to prove it. But he was also unworldly and gullible and easily hurt.

He stared at one daisy in particular; it was wilting, lolling over the edge of the small glass in a soft exhausted way. He had read a story in English class about a beautiful blonde-haired, blue-eyed girl who had plucked the petals from a daisy to discover if the boy she liked returned her feelings. She had intoned certain words as she did this, 'He loves me, he loves me not, he loves me,' until she came to the last petal which told her that the boy did not love her. She ran away from the small village and went to the city where she fell prey to rogues and Lotharios. Only at the end of the terrible tale did the author disclose that in her eagerness with the flower the girl had inadvertently pulled out two petals at a time so the flower's prediction had not been right – the boy did love her, but she would never know and her life was ruined.

He had felt frustrated by the story – a made-up thing, a lie and to what purpose?

Traditional English children's books were always illustrated with pinch-nosed, blue-eyed blondes whose mean little mouths were painted red and permanently wore an expression of consternation. Rather like the young woman he'd spoken to that night, the one who had dropped her cardigan then disappeared when he'd tried to catch up with her.

She'd been murdered, but he could not somehow reconcile that fact with what his senses had told him of that night. She had been there walking ahead of him, he could see her and hear the hollow clip clop of her heels on the pavement, then she was gone. Gone somehow – what was that phrase? – in the blink of an eye. As if a secret door existed in the universe. He tried to think how such a door would work. Imagined it as mirrored; it would reflect the world around it, showing pavements, houses, trees, cornfields, yawning blue skies, then as one passed into it, it would flip open, revolving vertically on its axis, swallow the person up and flip shut. Seeing this at a distance all one might detect would be a brief flash of light as the mirror spun. There, then gone. Unscientific. Illogical.

As illogical as the idea that he was a killer.

His mission in life was to save lives, not to snatch them away.

He plucked the wilted daisy from the glass and laid it upon his palm, considered it for some time, then closing it in his fist he crushed it. He ran his hand under the tap letting the green sap and bruised petals and yellow pollen escape down the plughole.

He would not do it. He would not choose medicine. He was a free man in the free world. He would be a botanist, a zoologist – like that killer of God, Darwin.

# Prayers

To know, but not to remember, this must be a kindness. A membrane had grown over the events of that terrible night, keeping them from her.

The Canadian woman seemed surprised by it all. As surprised as a child on Christmas morning. Her expression in her hospital bed was one of wonder. A type of stupefied wide-eyed wonder.

She was a writer of some sort. A poet, but not famous, but then all the famous ones were dead, weren't they?

The bruises on her face were terrible, though the marks on her neck were hardly visible anymore. Her lower lip was still badly swollen; the delicate skin there stretched thin, was glossy and violent pinkish red. Her left arm and wrist were in a cast, as was her right lower leg. There had been bruising to the genital area, but no trace of semen. A handful of leaves and grasses (all plucked from the immediate vicinity) had been pushed into the woman's vagina, nettles, feverfew and daisies. She was approximately three months pregnant. The baby had survived, its tiny heart, loud and clear on the ultrasound. A miracle.

The victim was sitting in her hospital bed, a white blanket covering her. Marilyn, that was her name, Sabine must remember it. 'Victim' denotes and defines the person only by what has been done to them not who they were and are. Marilyn held a black hard-backed, faux leather notebook on her lap as she spoke; occasionally she fiddled with the black elastic strap that held it shut or ran a finger down the smooth edge of its clean pages.

Sabine sensed that this notebook (which from its appearance was brand new and had yet to be used) was a source of strength for the woman. Like a rosary, she worked it with her fingers.

Sabine had her own notebook – the one issued from the central storeroom in which she should record dates, times, places and the words of victims, witnesses and suspects.

So far all she had written was Marilyn's full name and the day's date.

'So tell me what do you remember; the last thing before the attack.'

The woman looked steadily at Sabine as if the answer was there in her brown eyes.

'Anything you remember. It's a starting point we need, that's all.'

'I was…' she began.

'Yes.'

'…writing something. About…'

'About?'

Marilyn sighed, 'Oh, just a poem. About…' She stopped speaking. Sabine could see the glancing light of memory strike her. Her eyes widened, rolled heavenward, then she laughed. It was not a bitter laugh, but gentle and genuinely amused. 'That's all I can remember … that and the baby. They said the baby's okay. That's right isn't it? They told me I was out walking at night, in a park. Was Scott with me?'

'You were alone.'

'Was I? Golly, I wonder why.'

'We think you were looking for your husband, Scott.'

'Oh… he doesn't know about the baby, you know. I hadn't told him. I should tell him shouldn't I?' Marilyn smiled beatifically. Had she always been like this, so otherworldly, so calm? Sabine wondered.

'Well, look, you need your rest. But let us know if you remember anything at all, even if it seems silly or irrelevant. Yes?'

Sabine waited. She had never met a victim of violence who took it as lightly as this. She wondered at the woman's sanity, at the effects of the blow to the head, the squeezing of the neck at the carotid artery, shutting off the oxygen supply. But the doctors had said there was no lasting physical damage and she had scored negative on all the tests which indicated serious trauma to the brain.

The woman stopped laughing and shook her head gently from side to side. 'I'm sorry,' she said. 'It just seems silly now as you say. The poem, the baby, the poem. It had seemed so important then.'

'We will be the judges of what is important.'

'Well, this wasn't really. It was just a poem. I've been working on it forever. It's just it was the last thing I remember, but that's meaningless because I've been worrying away at the damn thing every day since we got here. But it's ironic, which is why I laughed, because it's about nearly dying...' She paused, then added, 'I'm sorry.'

Sabine wanted to say we know who he is, we have a suspect, we will find him, he will be punished. Sabine's own yearning for justice was acute, honed on years of policework, sharpened on those cases where the culprit was never found. 'The man who did this...' she began, then casting her gaze about she happened to look up and saw Marilyn's husband's face behind the glass panel in the door. When she met his eyes she saw the vivid hatred still burning in them.

'Well,' said Sabine, standing up and gathering her belongings. 'Perhaps if you remember anything else you could write it down.' Her gaze dropped meaningfully to the black notebook.

But the woman had now also seen Scott in the doorway and she put the notebook to one side and shifted her position in the bed to raise herself up as much as she could.

He opened the door and swept into the room before Sabine had taken more than one step towards it. He did not look at her again, focusing all his attention on the woman in the bed whose green eyes, Sabine saw as she glanced back, were brimming with tears of happiness.

# House of Cards

Florian can hardly bear to say what it is he has come to say. Suzette looks at him, waiting for his words. He doesn't look at her face.

'What's wrong? What's wrong? Tell me what's wrong.'

He shakes his head, looking as if he might cry. Then in that way that men are more capable of than women he lets out an angry growl.

'Florian.' She reaches for his shoulder, but resists touching him. She cannot read him, does not know what is wrong, what he wants, what she can do, or should do. She knows what she wants to do, what her impulse is, what her body wants. And that is to throw both her arms around him and hold him. Hold him, smell him, taste him, hear him, breathe in his breath, touch the back of his neck, his cheek with its rough pinpricks of hair – he needs to shave. All this is perhaps written on her face, concern, alarm and fear.

Which is why he cannot quite bring himself to look at her. The longer he takes to say what it is he has to say the more likely he is to weaken. So he blurts the words out.

'I'm leaving.'

'Florian?'

'OK? I can't stay. I'm sorry. I love you. Can't stay.'

Staccato phrases. He's giving her a list of facts. It's a matter of simple mathematics. He might have told her this over the phone. Or avoided it entirely, said nothing, just disappeared, but he needed to see her. Not because that was the right thing to do when you dumped someone, but because he had to see her.

Perhaps he imagined that this last meeting with her could somehow be stored away and kept. Kept forever or kept until he no longer needed it? Or kept until it was worn thin and ragged. Ghost-like and vague.

'I'm sorry. I have to because…'

There he was with that list again

'I'm coming with you.'

'What?'

'I'm coming with you.'

'You can't.'

'Why not?'

'Because, your job, your apartment …'

'My lousy waitressing job! My two and a bit rooms?'

'You told me you loved it here, close to the sea, the estuary, the salt marsh…'

'So? There're other places near the sea. It doesn't have to be this town, this few square metres on the coast. I want to be with you.'

His mathematical projections haven't figured in that equation. He's dumbstruck by its simplicity, its unfathomable beauty. Zero plus zero plus zero is a pointless exercise. While he absorbs this he is worryingly quiet.

Suzette reformulates her own calculations, not that she had much time to prepare. His zero plus zero plus zero was a sum she could only add herself to and perhaps she isn't wanted after all.

'Unless,' she says.

'Unless what?' he repeats.

She gives, then takes away. All his life this has happened to him. What impossible clause will she now add?

'Unless what?' he repeats.

'Unless you don't want me.'

Now they are packing their bags. Now he is buying a car. A battered old car that leaks oil and leaks water and has in the depths of its engine a knocking sound like the arrhythmic heart of a dying man. For three hundred Euros what did he expect?

Suzette puts the last week's rent in an envelope along with her keys and posts it through her landlord's door. Florian kisses his mother and tells her not to worry. He promises to ring.

They drive south. They have a small tent. Some money. Suzette's duvet in a bin bag. Clothes in suitcases. A plastic carrier bag with soap, shampoo, razors, deodorant, toothpaste, brushes, nail cutters, tweezers. A radio that eats batteries, a couple of torches, hers and a large one that's spattered with paint and oil, his. Along the way they will add to their belongings; a camping stove, a saucepan, knives, a tin opener and a cheap corkscrew that breaks the first time they use it. They hug the coast, here, dotted helpfully about, are the municipal campsites France is so famed for. Subsidised by the government, simple in their arrangements, but egalitarian in principle. One family may park up in their motor home, plug themselves into the electricity supply and spend their evenings watching T.V. while others put up their tent, spread a blanket on the ground, make a simple meal and in the dimming light watch only one another's faces. Or the stars.

They move through the country, the days pass. Soon it will be September and the campsites will all close and the weather will change.

Suzette and Florian have no regrets, but the money is running out.

They drive into a small town, following the signs which direct travellers to the campsite. Here on the edge of town is a church and before the church a larger-than-life crucifix. The figure of Christ has been cast from metal and painted white, but there is a crack in the figure's left shin that is barely visible until it reaches the top of his foot where the metal has rusted copiously, pouring out a dark red stain that has all the violence and vivid horror of blood. Stigmata. Or an accident of physics.

Suzette crosses herself. Florian does not see the statue, his eyes are on the road, he's tired and hungry and wants to get there, now, soon;

not get lost which they have done more than once. Suzette crosses herself as she too does not want to get lost. As in lost in purgatory, for her sins are multiplying. Soon she will need to go to confession.

It's late when they arrive at the gates of the campsite. Once they are booked in, the caretaker of the site changes the sign to full. Suzette and Florian take this as a good omen. Someone is looking after them.

A group of men are playing boule on the green in the last of the light. Children's voices can be heard calling and echoing one another in some sing-song game. People cross and recross the campsite carrying rolls of toilet paper or towels and washbags, some are in dressing gowns, some in shorts and t-shirts. Others carry plastic bowls full of pots and pans to wash. One man has a large silver fish and an enamel plate and long thin-bladed knife; he holds them all in his folded arms, almost defensively.

Suzette and Florian put up their tent, eat bread and cheese and apricots, then climb into the tent pulling the duvet in after them as if it were a recalcitrant and overgrown child. Or a cloud.

There is a slight chill in the air the following morning. The towels they had hung on a hedge the night before are damper now than they were yesterday.

'Let's go for a walk,' Florian says.

Holding hands they leave the campsite and follow the signs to the beach. On a bulletin board near another church, Suzette sees a card that reads 'Housekeeper/gardener wanted. Non-residential. Couple preferred.'

'We could do that,' she says.

'Non-residential,' Florian says. 'No room at the Inn.'

'We could get somewhere.'

They walk on, deep in shared thoughts. Neither needs to voice what is worrying them. They have reached the edge of the known land; beyond there are dragons.

The paved road ends and there is a path that winds down to

the pebble beach. The tide is out and only a few souls are about so early. Walkers with dogs, one man up to his waist in the water with a triangular net, catching crevettes.

They walk under the cliffs, the rocks stirring and clacking beneath their feet. Florian stops and begins to search the stones as if he has lost something. Suzette does the same though she does not know what she is looking for.

'Ha!' he says and stoops to pick up one roundish bit of rock about the size of an egg.

'What is it?'

'A fossil. A sea anemone.'

'Really?'

She takes it from him, turns it over in her hand. It's the colour of slate, similar in shape to a doughnut peach, plump and round with an indentation at its centre, marked with white dots that run in clear lines that fan out like the petals of a flower.

While she studies it, Florian begins searching again. She cannot believe that he can possibly find another, as one is miracle enough, but soon he's found one more.

But two is enough. He straightens his back and looks up and around. They retrace their steps, walking slowly and thoughtfully, happy in the moment.

'Look at that house,' he says and points up.

She sees the house high on the hill above the beach, its face turned to meet the sun. It's a beautiful house, the ground floor is white stone with a redbrick trim at its corners and around the downstairs windows and the front door. The upper half is a steeply pitched roof with three dormer windows at the front and two more at each side and at both ends tall red chimneys. All of the windows are shuttered.

'It looks empty,' Suzette says.

'Yeah. What a waste.'

'But it's so beautiful.'

Later, having called about the housekeeping job and left a message, they dismantle the tent, pack everything in the car and drive back to the now deserted beach. They park a short distance away and, taking only a torch and a couple of useful tools, they make their way to the empty house. The only obstacles are a padlocked gate and a wire fence that is easily scaled. The gravel drive is overgrown with weeds.

'Why would anyone abandon such a house?'

'Someone grew old and died there. Maybe they had no one to leave it to. Or there's a dispute over the will.'

As the front door is sealed shut and visible from the road, they sneak around the back of the house which nestles against the hill and is shadowed by overgrown trees. Florian finds a window whose metal shutter has already been half-prised open. With a crowbar from the car he manages to bend it back so that he creates enough space to crawl through.

'Might have to smash the glass,' he says, but then with the merest tug he manages to open the window. 'Not even locked.'

While Suzette holds the torch he climbs through. She hears the soles of his shoes slap the tiled floor as he jumps down.

'Kitchen,' he says, then whistles in appraisal.

She follows, passing him the torch, then wriggling through and into his waiting arms.

'Wow!'

The room is still furnished; there is a table and chairs, a dresser with some crockery, pots on the stove. In the next room there is not so much, brighter squares of wallpaper where pictures once were, a few worn-looking cushions and a large and expensive looking Turkish rug that has been half rolled up as if someone suddenly changed their minds about the merits of taking it.

'Let's get our stuff,' Florian says and for the next hour they go to and from the car, Suzette passing stuff up to Florian as he sits on top of the fence either dropping things onto the weeds below or climbing down to deposit them more safely.

They unfurl the carpet, throw a blanket, then a sheet, then a duvet on it and their bed for the night is made. They put their camping stove on top of the big stove in the kitchen.

They make love and talk about the onset of winter, of their good luck. The next day they wake to changed weather, a cold wind from the north and gathering clouds that threaten rain.

They explore the rest of the house, the creaking wooden stairs, the pink bathroom, the three bedrooms, one of them equipped with a narrow single bed, another with a double bed frame but no mattress. Upstairs the smell is dry and dusty like chalk and wood dust and talcum powder mixed together.

They sneak away from the house by tracing a path through the trees and find that in one corner the fence ends giving easy access to the road. They walk up the steep hill then into the small town where they buy candles and bread and fresh pastries and vegetables.

On their way back it begins to rain and the sky grows strangely dark. Distant thunder rumbles as they race towards the house.

Suzette climbs nimbly through the window and as Florian is passing through the bag of food, someone not very far away, calls out, 'Hey! Hey you!'

Florian glances around to see a man standing by the fence and knows the man has seen him too. He scrambles through the window and lands badly, turning one ankle and smashing his knee on the stone floor.

The thunder is growing louder. Lightning flashes, illuminating the window he has climbed through but only the edges and cracks around all the other windows.

Florian imagines he hears the man's voice calling after him again, but what with the torrential rain and the gusting wind and the intermittent thunder he can't be sure.

Limping, he struggles to refasten the window, then together he and Suzette lift the scrubbed pine table on its side and put it over the window, then they push the enormous old fridge freezer against the table and stand in the darkness waiting.

Their ears are deceived when the noise of nature is partly blotted out, and comforted by the closeness of the dark cave of the house, their nearness, their shallow breathing, the faint creak of a floorboard when weight is shifted from one foot to another. Minutes pass. The storm moves away, retreating by degrees, the thunder is muted by distance, the flashes lose their magnesium-bright violence, the rain devolves into a more reasonable patter. No voice continues to call, no animal bays at their door. Nothing now can touch them. They are safe.

Tiptoeing, they go through to the room they have chosen as their haven. They light the candles, eat the bread and the tomatoes, drink the wine from odd glasses they have found.

A sudden noise like someone taking a sledgehammer to a huge stone breaks the silence. They each picture some violence done to their sanctuary, uniformed men with battering rams or one man with some ghastly machine, a farmer with a tractor.

Florian gets up and prowls around the house looking and listening. He goes upstairs and into the bedroom with the empty bed frame. The windows are shut and behind them are metal shutters. But one window, perhaps because it faces the sea and the unadulterated salt-kissed wind has latches and hasps that are so rusted that they bend and break easily. He pulls this window out. The rinsed cold air floods into the room, over his face, the skin of his neck, his hands and arms. Now there is only the metal shutter and he pushes this at one corner where the brick it is fastened to is already crumbling. It pops out and with a push it bends allowing him to see outside.

'Suzette!' he calls. He is as excited as if he has found treasure.

She answers with a faltering voice, then runs upstairs to join him.

'Look at this!' he says.

She goes to him and bends to peer down through the window and through the triangular space where the metal shutter has buckled away.

A cool mist falls on her face as she sees the sea directly down below her with only a narrow fringe of vegetation between the footing of the house and the blue-black agitation of the waves.

'You wanted to live by the sea, didn't you?' Florian says and touches the back of her neck. When she has tied her hair up, as she has now, he is always surprised by how perfect and slender her neck is. He can never resist touching it.

She responds by turning from the sea to him. They kiss, tasting salt on one another's lips.

'Come on, let's go to bed,' he says. 'No one is going to come and evict us at this time of night. By the morning we'll be gone.'

Holding hands they went back downstairs, both still wary of invasion and listening for sounds, but by now even the rain had stopped and outside the clouds had parted and dispersed leaving only veils and shreds that drifted across the waning moon.

They drifted towards sleep in one another's arms, Suzette hearing what he'd said earlier over and over in her mind, 'In the morning we'll be gone.' It reminded her of that bedtime prayer, 'If I should die before I wake…' And ever since she was a child she had often closed her eyes to sleep, half expecting death. You cross yourself in hope of salvation and ask for it before sleep just in case.

The abandoned house stood on chalky-white limestone cliffs. They gave the area its name, Cote d'albatre or the Alabaster Coast. But the coastline has been retreating at a rate of 20 centimetres a year. Cliffs like these are excellent sites for fossil hunters as what has been hidden for millennia is readily released as landslides, erosion and water seepage gnaw away at the land.

This was why the beautiful house with the grey slate mansard roof, the flint and brick walls, the gabled dormer windows, was empty.

Just as Florian predicted, by the morning they were gone.

# Acknowledgements

Many thanks to those friends who read first drafts of this book: Katy Train, Mark Matthews, Laurel Goss, Deryl Dix, Mark Robinson, Ann George, Tony Graham and Ceri Thomas.

Thanks are also due to Literature Wales and The Royal Literary Fund for their generous support.

Many thanks to Penny Thomas at Seren, and to Lizzie Clarke who very kindly posed for the cover image.

Extract from *The Interpretation of Cultures: Selected Essays* by Clifford Geertz (Basic Books, 1973) with kind permission of the copyright holders.

Extract from *A Short History of Myth* by Karen Armstrong, first published in Great Britain by Canongate Books Ltd, 14 High Street, Edinburgh, EH1 1TE.

# About the Author

Jo Mazelis is a writer of short stories, non-fiction and poetry. Her collection of stories, *Diving Girls*, was shortlisted for the Commonwealth Best First Book and Wales Book of the Year. Her stories and poetry have been broadcast on BBC Radio 4, published in anthologies and magazines, and translated into Danish. She worked in London as a graphic designer, photographer and illustrator for *City Limits*, *Women's Review*, *Spare Rib*, *Undercurrents* and *Everywoman*, before returning to her home town, Swansea, where she now lives and writes.